THE TRUE QUEEN

ALSO BY SARAH FINE

Of Metal and Wishes

Of Dreams and Rust

Of Shadows and Obsession, an e-short-story prequel to *Of Metal and Wishes*

The Impostor Queen

The Cursed Queen

THE TRUE QUEEN

Sarah Fine

Book Three of
the Impostor Queen series

MARGARET K. McELDERRY BOOKS
New York London Toronto Sydney New Delhi

MARGARET K. McELDERRY BOOKS
An imprint of Simon & Schuster Children's Publishing Division
1230 Avenue of the Americas, New York, New York 10020

Book design by Debra Sfetsios-Conover
The text for this book was set in Goudy Oldstyle Std.
Manufactured in the United States of America
First Edition
10 9 8 7 6 5 4 3 2 1
CIP data is available from the Library of Congress.
ISBN 978-1-4814-9060-3 (hardcover)
ISBN 978-1-4814-9062-7 (eBook)

FOR LYDIA—HERE'S TO THE EPIC
JOURNEY, ALL THE CHEESE WE CAN EAT,
AND ALL THE LAUGHTER WE CAN STAND

CHAPTER ONE

Ansa

On the first day of new spring, we march out through the gate of Vasterut and turn to the west, toward Kupari. My new wool cloak hangs in thick folds down to my calves, and I have a shining set of daggers strapped to my forearms and sheathed at my side. I think that I look fearsome and sure, the type of person who can sit on a throne without inspiring laughter.

Then I think the same thought again, because I didn't quite believe myself the first time, and when that doesn't carry me all the way, I remind myself that I have time to practice being queenly before we get there.

With that in mind, I keep my head high as I wave to the Vasterutians who have come out to cheer our departure. They seem elated, and why wouldn't they be? We were the barbarian invaders, the fearsome marauders, and now we leave their city as a tribe without a homeland. Through their patient scheming and alliances with the Korkeans and Ylpesians, they brought us low, but together we defeated the evil of Nisse and drove his son and heir, Jaspar, away—along with hundreds of rogue warriors. The Vasterutians treated Thyra and those of us who were loyal to her with respect after that, but it was always clear what they really wanted.

Our absence.

Thyra catches my eye and gives me a wry smile as the Vasterutians' shouts of joy rise to the heavens. "It's clear they are missing us already."

The humor in her voice, the morning sunbeams glinting gold in her hair, the easy affection on her face—all of it melts my tension. "Yes, I expect they'll enter a period of mourning now."

I look over my shoulder, up the hill to the walled tower fortress where I spent the last several months. Halina might be watching us from one of those windows. Like all the rest of her people, she is relieved and triumphant to see the Krigere finally clear out of her city, but I like to think she will also miss me and Thyra, just a little. *She* certainly enjoyed laughing at me, both before and after she knew I was a destined queen.

Behind me and Thyra, our warriors stride forward, their steps certain and strong. Thanks to our hosts, who in their eagerness to be rid of us were generous with the food and supplies we would need for our journey, Preben and Bertel and all those who traveled with us from the north have lost the hollowness in their cheeks. As we prepared for this march, they trained and rested in equal measure to regain their vigor.

Just outside the wall, our andeners have camped. The nights remain cold but the days are warmer now, and we agreed to move them out of Vasterutian homes so that the rightful owners could return, in exchange for help building this temporary city outside the city. Now there are tents sprawled across the grassy hills and spreading all the way to the dunes by the shore of the Torden. Our andeners have many skills and know how to fend for themselves as long as they are not being raided or attacked, and for now, we must leave them behind. It is safer this way.

Their cheers are of a different tone and tenor than those of the Vasterutians. In their shouts, I hear desperate pleas, searing hope, and delicate but growing faith. Not in me—in Thyra. She's their chieftain. I'm just her war counselor. We haven't explained the other things I am just yet—only our small band of senior warriors knows that—for fear it would be more confusing than reassuring. But as I pass close to Gry, Cyrill's widow, whose belly is swollen with the baby of one of Jaspar's traitorous warriors, her hands go white-knuckled over her children's upper arms, and she yanks them back. Thyra gives her a sharp look, but the widow's chin rises in defiance. A few others withdraw from the side of the road to avoid me, too, including Aksel's mother—and she stares hard at me and spits on the grass at her feet as our procession reaches her.

Something tells me she has long since realized that I am the one who killed her son. If I thought it would help, I would explain that he tried to kill me first in a warped effort to avenge his father, who died after challenging Thyra's chieftainship, but I already know it won't change a thing. To her I am a monster. An enemy.

I don't call Thyra's attention to Aksel's mother because I don't want to raise the memory for her. My murder of Aksel nearly tore us apart, and I will do anything to keep us from being separated again. When I glance at her, though, it is clear that Aksel's death is not on her mind. She's looking toward the boundaries of the camp and biting her lip. "Did you go over the plan to guard the camp with the watch group?" she calls over her shoulder.

"Twice, Chieftain," Bertel replies, shielding his eyes from the sun as he looks toward his own andener, a stout woman with skin as pale as his is dark. He jokes that together they are time itself, night and day made one. I believe that is his way of saying he loves her, and I can see it in his face when he catches sight of her. "Alfrida told me to assure you they have a plan. If there is a raid, the Vasterutians will offer them safe haven."

"Good," Thyra says. "And the signal?"

"Lantern flashes by night, red flags by day. The Vasterutian sentries will watch over both the camp and the road that leads to the forest."

Thyra's smile returns, but this time it's grim. "And they'll protect our families, because if they don't, they know we'll exact a price in blood."

Bertel tears his gaze from his mate and nods at Thyra. "For that we're thankful, Chieftain. It makes it possible to leave them."

"We'll send for them as soon as we can," I say, wishing my heart weren't skipping at the thought of what we'll have to do to ensure that future. "You'll be reunited before you know it."

"When that happens, a group of us would like to ride as escort and guard," Preben says, clapping a scarred and calloused hand over Bertel's thickly muscled shoulder. "We don't want the andeners and children to travel without protection."

"I will grant that request," Thyra replies, her eyes on the horizon now, where the distant black line of the Loputon stretches from the lakeshore as far south as can be seen.

Somewhere in that forest, our enemies hide. Jaspar and his seven hundred warriors, well-armed with stolen weapons and well-nourished from months of thieving food from the mouths of the Vasterutians. He has Elder Kauko at his side or in his possession, and the old man is full of magic and cunning. He also has over a hundred horses and a few hundred andeners who, with the right materials, can forge weapons, craft armor, and heal wounds. With so many people and animals, one would think that it is impossible to be secretive about one's whereabouts, but Kauko's magic made it possible. Vasterutian scouts lost the trail at the edge of the Loputon, when they encountered a blizzard so massive that it nearly took their lives.

Sig told me it was a sign that Kauko has only grown in power, most likely the effect of drinking a bowlful of my blood. The scarred fire wielder lurks on my other side, wearing a light cloak with the hood pulled up to shield the back of his neck from the morning sun, which is already making him sweat. He, too, has grown stronger over the past weeks. Now that the elder is gone, Sig seems calmer and slightly less unhinged. His Krigere has improved as well, so he has been able to tell us more about what we might face when we arrive in Kupari. But as the time of our departure neared, he became quieter and more withdrawn, disappearing for hours at a time without telling anyone where he was going. His furtiveness explains Thyra's frown whenever her blue-eyed gaze finds him.

We need him, though, and she knows it. Swords alone will not be enough in Kupari, and only Sig truly understands the place—and the magic that seems to ooze from the land, finding its way into the veins of its people. Sig is an expert wielder, though he suffers because he only has fire and no ice to balance it. As for me . . . I have both ice and fire, so much that I am supposedly infinitely powerful. Except instead of balancing each other, these two elements inside me seem to be at war, with my body as the contested territory, my skin as the battlefield. My fingers stroke the bloodred runes of the cuff of Astia, which is wrapped heavy and snug around my right wrist. It somehow acts as a peacemaker. I have not taken it off since the moment Sig put it on me.

I'm scared of what will happen if I do.

Our steps are rapid and certain as we snake our way along the road to the west, leaving our cheering andeners behind. After an hour of hiking, the laughter and jovial conversation fueled by the joy of being in the crisp open air fades to quiet murmurs and low rumbles of uneasiness. And by the time the black of the forest turns emerald green in the afternoon light, all I hear are footfalls on packed dirt, the occasional clink of iron bits and weapon blades, and the cries of the seagulls that dive and swirl above our heads. We tread a path wide enough for five or six warriors to stand shoulder to shoulder or three horses to pace, and in all that means we have perhaps fifty rows.

We are not an overwhelming force, but we're hoping we won't have to fight anyway. We're hoping my claim to the Valtia's throne will be enough. If the pretender who currently occupies the temple is willing to give it up, we'll have a new home for the four thousand andeners we had to leave outside the protection of the Vasterutian walls. But if that impostor queen tries to cling to her power, then we will have a battle on our hands.

It's not about me having my throne. Honestly, I'm not so sure I want it. It's about the Krigere having a homeland—something we lost in waves, first when the Kupari Valtia decimated our warriors and ships, then when Jaspar forced the rest of us to march south in an attempt to merge our tribe with Nisse's traitorous band. Now we are small in number, more vulnerable than we've ever been, but Thyra thinks we have an opportunity. She wants us to remake ourselves as an independent people, to live and thrive without raiding, without killing. I have come to believe in her vision of our future. I'm determined to make it reality and lay it as a gift at her feet. I glance over at her and barely resist the urge to kiss a drop of sweat from her temple. It is hard, sometimes, to be this close to her and not touch her. Even now, as we lead a procession of our only surviving warriors toward an uncertain fate, my fingers twitch for the feel of her body and my eyes stray to her.

As two warriors, we should not be paired. But I know what I want, what I've always wanted when it comes to her. I want my chieftain safe, happy, and victorious.

And I want to spend every single night of the rest of my life in her arms.

"The boundary of Kupari," Sig says, his accent thick. It curls around the words, softening their edges. "Just within the tree line."

Thyra squints. "I didn't think it extended so far south."

Sig nods. "Do you want to rest your head on Kupari soil tonight, *Valtia?*"

Every time I hear that word these days, my stomach drops. "That's up to the chieftain."

Thyra laughs quietly. "Once we cross into Kupari, we'll be in your domain." Then she leans toward me and whispers, "My queen."

Her breath sends a cascade of shivers across my chest and down my spine, drawing me taut as a bowstring. I let out a nervous laugh just to dispel some of my sudden unsteadiness. "How I wish I had a few subjects to hunt down some fresh meat and cook it over a roaring fire tonight. But I think I'll have to fend for myself."

"We'll have plenty of time before sunset, and it'll give us a chance to explore the edge of the forest." Her throat moves as she swallows. "I'm not sure I want to lead everyone in there before we've scouted."

"Jaspar and Kauko," Sig says. He is sweating in earnest as his eyes rake the boundary between meadow and forest.

Thyra grunts in agreement as he names the threat. "There are so many places to hide, and they have weeks of practice now."

The sun hangs at midsky over the trees by the time we reach the edge of the wood. Our warriors begin to make camp, breaking into groups of ten or twelve and straying along the edge of the forest to gather kindling and branches. We have rations that don't require cooking, but the warmth will be welcome when the chill hour of midnight comes. We are not moving with stealth—there is little point. And we are much more powerful than we look; Sig and I can burn the entire forest to the ground if we need to.

Once again, I rub my palm over the cuff. The hum of its ancient power, one only I can hear, seems to be growing louder as we near the land where we were both created. Up to this point, it is my ally, my shield. With it, I have been much steadier.

I want to believe that the cuff is strengthening me, but the closer we get to the edge of the Loputon, the shakier I feel.

"Are you all right?" Thyra asks quietly as I shed the rolled bundle of weapons, rations, and blanket that I've been carrying on my back. We're only fifty yards or so from the forest now, and setting up our own little camp with Sig, Preben, and Bertel. The latter two are helping the others manage our horses and Sig has wandered off, and so we are as alone as we've yet been today. Perhaps that's why she reaches over and touches the backs of my hands.

They're trembling. So much so that I cannot unbuckle the strap around my blanket. I drop the bundle and wipe my palms on my breeches. "It's nothing."

She gives me a look. "After all we've been through, you don't get to say that to me."

I run my hands through my short hair, and they come away damp with sweat. "I think perhaps I'm just nervous. We don't know what we're facing."

"That is almost always true these days."

"But there is so much at stake!"

"Also very true, at all times."

"I'm not sure of myself," I snap, turning away. "I'm so tired of not being sure."

"But you said the cuff—"

"It helps." For some reason, though, my whole body is thrumming with an energy I haven't felt before. "Maybe I'm just hungry and tired and nervous. Nothing a good night's sleep won't fix."

Thyra has gone still, and her blue eyes are locked with mine. "It's me, Ansa," she murmurs, and then she strokes my cheek. "I can tell something is happening to you."

I wince and hug myself as a burst of frigid wind ruffles our hair. I don't know if that was me or just the weather. It feels like it could have been either. I give her a pleading look.

"I knew this wouldn't be easy for you," she says. "This is the land of your birth. Our people ripped you away from all of this. Returning is not as simple as putting one foot in front of the other."

"You understand very well." I put a hand on my stomach. "Maybe that explains why I feel like the ground beneath me is about to shift right out from under my feet."

She chuckles. "Maybe we should keep your feet moving, then. Shall we gather wood?"

I raise my eyebrows. "I could keep you warm tonight, if you like."

She moves a little closer. "I'd like that very much. But I don't feel like sharing you with Preben and Bertel."

I laugh as we start to walk, and heaven, it feels so good. "Then I suppose we should scrape up some kindling."

When we reach the shade of the trees, she takes my hand, lacing her fingers with mine. "As we enter Kupari, I want you to remember what I said to you a few weeks ago."

We are weaving our way through dense brush, brambles scraping against the leather of our boots. "We've said many things to each other over the last few weeks." My tone is light, but my voice wavers.

"You know very well what I'm talking about. Maybe

the Kupari impostor will back down quickly, but maybe she won't. People in power tend to want to stay that way."

"But to the Kupari, we are the stuff of nightmares. It could work in our favor."

"Not if we want to make our home here." She pulls an errant twig from her hair. "We must try to keep the peace. What we do not want is what we faced in Vasterut."

Nisse and his rogue tribe may have conquered the Vasterutians on the surface, but beneath their skin, in the thick silence in the streets, there was mutiny brewing, seasoned with incredible determination. They never really surrendered and were only biding their time. "Agreed. But once they recognize me as the—the V-Valtia—"

Thyra smiles as I falter. "I look forward to the day you truly understand what you are. Then you will rule us all."

I shiver. That strange unsteadiness has set my heart galloping. "I d-don't want to. You will always be my chieftain."

"I will not always be anything, Ansa. Nothing lasts forever. And we don't know how things will change in this new land."

I stop, leaning against a tree because it feels solid and safe. "I don't deny that. But I will *always* be your wolf."

She puts her hand over mine and moves near enough to nudge my nose with hers. "I think I am the luckiest chieftain in the history of the world, then. Although"—she looks around—"we might be in Kupari now. Sig said the border was just inside the tree line. Maybe *you* are the ruler here."

When her lips touch mine, the smoldering heat inside

me jumps to full flame in an instant. I can feel her smiling against my mouth, and the taste of it is sweet on my tongue. Somewhere in the branches above us, a bird trills, and in this moment I cannot think of a more joyful sound. As if they can feel my soaring mood, an entire flock of winged creatures suddenly explodes into flight, screeching to the heavens. Thyra chuckles and cups my cheek. "We're unsettling the entire wild wood."

I laugh, but it seems to be true—I can hear the sudden rustling all around us, claws scrabbling in the underbrush, which waves and bounces as creatures flee. "Perhaps Kupari forest creatures are simply polite and want to offer us priv—"

A deafening crack silences that happy thought, and the ground beneath us drops. We land in a hard sprawl, Thyra's head colliding with my breastbone and knocking the breath out of me. Nausea and panic churn in my gut as the entire forest pitches, branches lashing and snapping and raining down like sharpened pikes. One slams down on Thyra's leg, and she cries out, a sound that echoes inside the chambers of my racing heart. I throw my arms around her and roll, shielding her with my body as the world falls apart.

CHAPTER TWO

Elli

The first day of new spring brings new fears—but so have the many days leading up to it, and so that doesn't make it special. It happens to be the birthday of my Saadella and heir, though, which makes it very special indeed. I will do everything within my meager power to keep my own cares from touching Lahja.

I rise early and dress myself. On ceremony days I allow my handmaiden, Helka, to assist, but most of the time I take pride in doing everything alone. It is not how things have traditionally been done, but I am not a traditional queen.

Technically, I am not the queen at all. But only me, Raimo, and Oskar are in on the secret.

I am in Lahja's chambers, enjoying a midmorning feast of sweet buns with jam and butter, laughing as she licks her sticky fingers, when Raimo pokes his grizzled head in. I know he's there before I see him, because Lahja jumps up and runs to him, jammy hands waving. "I want the dancing fire," she calls.

I rise from the cushions, grinning as Janeka, her handmaiden and older sister, hooks an arm around Lahja's middle just before she collides with the old man. "You must clean your hands," she clucks. "Remember who you are!"

Lahja frowns, her coppery curls bouncing around her face. "I never forget. I'm the Saadella, which means people must do as I want."

"Oh, darling," I murmur as I reach her. "It really means you must do what the people need." I kneel next to her and stroke my hand down her back. "But today?" I lean forward and kiss her freckled nose. "Today it definitely means we must all do as you want."

Still smiling, I look up at Raimo, but as soon as I see his expression, concern rides a cold trail up my back. "Are you ill?"

On his best day, Raimo is a stooped old man with a long scraggly beard, tufty hair around his ears, a spotty dome of bald head, stringy arms, and knobby hands that always clutch a walking stick—but he is nevertheless spry and hardy. Today, though, he blinks as if his eyes sting, and his mouth works as if he's swallowed a bite of tainted meat.

When Lahja peers up at him, though, his face splits into a wrinkled smile. "Not at all." He holds out his upturned palm, and a flame immediately appears, twirling and undulating in a shape that resembles a dancing child. My Saadella shrieks with joy and matches the movements of the flame, spinning in a circle while her skirt flaps around her ankles and knees.

She doesn't notice Raimo sweating and shaking, and that is a good thing. I step between them and scoop her into my arms. "You look so lovely when you dance! How would you like it if Kaisa came in and played you a tune on her kantele?"

"Oh! Yes! She must do that!" Lahja is a giggling ball of sweetness as I carry her deeper into her rooms.

I give Janeka a steady, commanding look as I hand the serious young woman her wriggling younger sister. "I will send for Kaisa. Will you entertain Lahja until then?"

She casts a glance toward the corridor, where Raimo leans against the stone wall, then nods and pulls a silly smile onto her face. For a moment, my heart twists—she reminds me of Mim, who would have done anything to keep me happy and warm and healthy during all the years she took care of me. I swallow back the sudden sorrow of missing her, the poignant memory of her beautiful face, as it looked when she stood right where Janeka stands now. So when she says, "Of course, my Valtia," I merely wave and turn away so she will not see the glaze of tears in my eyes.

"I will be back later to dance with you," I call over my shoulder to Lahja, my voice strained but brisk.

"You must do what I say today too!" Lahja replies.

"Yes, I must," I say, smiling once more. "Because today you are the queen!"

And with that I walk quickly to Raimo, the cares of the

world dropping onto my shoulders once again. "Tell me," I say as I take his arm and guide him into the hallway. As I do, I feel the tingle of ice and fire along my palms, and it does nothing to allay my fear—he's usually in complete control of his magic.

"I'm just a little off today," he says. "But given my age, I believe I have a right to be."

I chuckle. He's hundreds of years old and has cheated time like a street thief. "Like few others do." And as for those others . . . two are dead now, and one lurks in places unknown, probably planning his next attack.

Still holding Raimo by the arm, I walk slowly down the corridor. "Where is Kaisa? Shouldn't she be with you?"

"She's my new apprentice, not my nursemaid," he says, his mouth working again, his face drawn into a grimace.

I wave at a passing acolyte and tell the boy to fetch Kaisa from wherever she might be tucked away today. She's grown stronger and more confident in her magic, but she's a quiet, gentle soul who prefers to practice her skills when no one is watching—whether it be her ability to wield ice and fire or her gifts for playing chiming tunes on the kantele. Raimo acts like he resents having an apprentice, but he usually finds it hard not to smile when she's around.

We reach the magnificent domed chamber of our Temple on the Rock. "Oskar will be here soon," Raimo says.

"What?" It comes out of me as a kind of surprised yelp. My hand strays to my hair.

Raimo laughs. "Elli, you do realize Oskar has seen you

on the verge of death, yes? I can say with certainty that you look much better now. Besides, the boy is so utterly besotted that he will hardly care that your hair is in dire need of Helka's special brand of magic."

I give him a sour look. "That doesn't make me feel more confident."

"Do you really fear he will be disappointed by how you look? He's been in the outlands for two weeks, among bears and outlaws. Even on your worst day, you smell a lot better than either."

He's right. It's just that I see Oskar far more rarely than I would like, and therefore would prefer to look my best during those times. "You are full of compliments. Do you know if he brings news?"

"Not yet. He simply sent word that he was coming." Raimo glances down the massive steps of the temple and into the white plaza, which is still pockmarked and scarred from the battle that took place here two months ago. "But the news of a few days ago still troubles him. It troubles me, too, if I am honest."

My eyes stray to the copper inlay that winds through the walls of our grand temple. "Are they sure it is the last?"

"We've known the copper was running out. Mine after mine has turned up nothing. The Pimea mine was the last one giving up any ore at all. They will continue to dig and scrape, but they've found nothing for nearly a month, and now the snowmelt and ground water is running into the empty veins. The miners had to clear out."

"What does this mean for us?" My fingers run over the coppery thread that gilds my dress. For Kupari without magic, the copper we have steadily mined for the last few hundred years is our wealth, our leverage, our safety. Everyone knows it. But few know the other half of the truth—for those *with* magic, copper is the source, the beating heart, the origin of that power.

"We have ton upon ton of smelted bars in the catacombs," Raimo says. "Enough to give us time, I hope."

"And to make us a more tempting target, perhaps. For desperate Kupari and invaders alike."

He squeezes my hand, letting me feel the tremor in his fingers. "Which is why all of them must continue to believe you are the true Valtia."

I hold my head high, though the weight of my secrets threatens to crush me. It's not that I mind the responsibility—I will bear anything if it means my people can be safe and happy. It's the constant pretense, the constant fear of discovery. It's the fear that whenever Raimo or Oskar are elsewhere, I have no one who can even help me cast the illusion that I have any magic at all, let alone infinite amounts of it. "But Kauko, wherever he is, knows the truth. So does Sig."

There was a time when I thought Sig might become a friend, or at least an ally. But after what I did to him, and how I left him in the hands of the man who had already tortured him and sipped at his blood, I would not be surprised if he hates me more than Kauko does.

"But perhaps they are dealing with their own travails now. It's possible they didn't even survive after escaping the rubble." Raimo reads my skepticism and shrugs. "Yes, I don't believe it either. Sorry."

I gesture out over the plaza, toward the town square. "I'm finding it grimly amusing that Kauko and Sig are the least of our problems right now. Since we don't have the Valtia's magic to ensure the food supply, we've got to figure out how to store up for next winter, and that might be particularly difficult if the Soturi decide to invade."

"Strange rumors from Vasterut these days."

"We should have cultivated our relationship with the Vasterutians when we had the chance."

"We? Ha! We had no chance at all, thanks to the elders. They thought we'd be fine, an island unto ourselves."

And so they turned away any offer of alliance and rejected any pleas for help. Now we have no friends to come to our aid should the Soturi barbarians invade, and it seems almost certain they will. A month or two ago, when Oskar investigated fires along the western lakeshore, he found bands of fighters from Korkea, who were headed east through the Loputon toward Vasterut. And rumors from Vasterut itself indicate the Soturi force left there a few weeks ago. We just don't know where they are. And we're too isolated to find out.

"Perhaps instead of trying to train our own fighters, we should have offered the Korkeans and Ylpesians goods in exchange for protection," I say. "Maybe we should have tasked Oskar with that instead of sending him to build a militia of wielders."

Raimo scoffs. "Magic is still our best weapon for the war that stalks us. The Suurin will fight alongside the Astia to save the Kupari." He looks down at his tremulous hands. "I know the prophecy was right. I know I was right."

He sounds less certain than he ever has, perhaps because one of our Suurin has disappeared. But also—"You never told me what the prophecy said about the Valtia," I say quietly.

His watery eyes rise to the domed ceiling of the temple. "Because the stars are veiled when it comes to her fate."

"She's alive, though. And she's out there somewhere." Otherwise, surely Lahja would have inherited her magic. "I think she will save us all."

He grunts. "At this point, I think we have to conclude she is far from here, and perhaps we will never know what became of her."

"I will never conclude that." Because without her, I am only half of what I am supposed to be. I feel the emptiness inside. It gnaws on me in the darkness as I try to sleep.

Raimo sways on his feet, and I put my arm around him. "Maybe I should have a rest," he admits. "Something is not right with me today."

I wave over an acolyte, who bustles forward with his head bowed. "Take the elder to his chamber. Do not leave until he is safely in his bed."

Raimo grumbles something about being treated like a child but leans gratefully on the unusually peaked-looking acolyte as they begin to walk away. I remain standing in the center of the domed chamber, turning slowly in place, remembering how we fought to wrest this temple from the elders, how we fooled everyone into believing I had a right to it. And yet, I would give it up in an instant if *she* were to walk up the steps of the white plaza, carrying the magic I was raised to believe would be mine someday.

The *clip-clop* of horse hooves draws my eyes downward, and my breath catches as I recognize the broad shoulders of the rider. "Oskar," I whisper, and it takes all my restraint to keep from flying down the steps to reach him. Instead, I turn and walk to my chambers with my heart hammering. Helka rises from her embroidery as I enter. "The Ice Suurin has arrived," I tell her. "I will meet with him in here. Please arrange for a meal to be served on my balcony."

She glances at my hair. "May I . . . ?"

Oskar and I are secretive about our relationship. It is a thing we like to keep for ourselves, tucked into this room, away from all our fears and responsibilities. But my handmaiden knows all. It is written in her tender smile as she reaches for me.

I nod, grateful. "Do what you can, Helka."

Within a minute she has me looking less haphazard, and then she's off to do my bidding. I pace my room in an effort to dispel my nervous energy.

"Elli."

I whirl around at the sound of his voice. And this time, I do run to him, my arms outstretched. His face is smudged with the dust of the road, and long strands of his dark hair have escaped the tie, but to me he is perfect. He gives me a tired smile as I approach.

As soon as my hands find his skin, I know something is wrong. His cheeks are covered in icy sweat, and he's shaking. "Oskar—"

He puts his hands out, reaching, and together we help him get to a chair, which he sinks into. "It was a long ride," he says.

I step back from him, eyeing him from head to toe. "Your hands are trembling." I look out the window, to where the blue water of the Motherlake glints under the sun. "You shouldn't be this cold."

I move to stand between his knees and lay my palms on his cheeks again. He sighs as I draw some of the frigid magic from his body, and leans so his forehead rests on my chest. I wrap my arms around his head and hold him there, letting my power pull on his. He gives it up willingly, as he always does these days. I am his haven and relief. "Tell me what's going on."

"I don't know." His voice is muffled, but I feel the chill of his breath even through the fabric of my dress. "I'm just off today."

I frown. "Off," I murmur.

"Yes. I've felt a little shaky since I woke up. Dizzy, even. And I . . . I had to walk some of the way because I was afraid of freezing my horse."

Something barbed is turning in my chest. A fear I don't want to rise to the surface. "Raimo is off today too."

Oskar leans back so he can look up at my face. "Have you checked with any of the apprentices or acolytes?"

"Some of them did seem a little more pale than usual. Why?"

"Because Veikko and Aira felt strange this morning too." His hands close around my upper arms. "Are *you* all right?"

I treasure the concern in his gray eyes. "I am as I always am, Oskar."

He smiles. "My Elli."

"Yours," I whisper, leaning down to kiss his cold lips. I inhale his icy breath and savor the frosty sweetness of his mouth. He groans and tilts his chin up, sliding his arms around my waist to pull me closer. I am worried and churning, but being this close to him blankets my thoughts with pristine snowfall, making everything silent and beautiful. My hands rake through his hair as a fire in me burns that has nothing to do with magic at all.

Oskar gasps and his fingers claw at my back. "What—"

That is all he has a chance to say before our world splinters.

CHAPTER THREE

Ansa

The shaking doesn't stop. I have no idea how much time passes before it occurs to me that it might *never* stop. But as soon as the thought enters my mind, I know I have to get Thyra out from under this legion of wooden spears that waves and cracks over our heads. With the ground rolling like waves beneath my feet, I lurch onto my hands and knees over her, and then shove myself up as I clutch her hand. She's right there with me, her eyes round and her face white as foam on the Torden, but when I shout that we have to run, she goes in exactly the right direction.

We stumble and stagger and bounce off swaying tree trunks. When I hear a whistling sound above my head I throw my hand out, sending a blast of wind upward and blowing the toppled pine away as if it were a twig. My fingers sting with magic, and Thyra digs her fingernails into the back of my hand, maybe fighting the pain of it.

She doesn't let go, though, not until I feel the tremors of terrible magic inside me and tear my hand from hers. Still, she stays close, as we trip over branches and blunder through brambles while the earth roars its ferocious displeasure. I nearly sob with relief when waning daylight comes into view between the trees, and we cover the last hundred yards with speed born of desperation and terror. I can hear the horses screaming. I can tell from the grimace on Thyra's face that she can as well, and that we're both thinking of our warriors, the few hundred left out of the thousands we had this time last year, and all of them could have been swallowed under a mountain of dirt by now for all we know. She might be the chieftain of an extinct people.

When we burst into the open, though, tripping over our own faltering feet, our warriors are alive, if not well. And as we stagger toward where they are clustered around the panicking horses, the earth shudders once more and goes quiet, leaving my ears ringing with the contrast.

I fall to my knees, still feeling the shaking inside my bones. Sweat drips from the tip of my nose and runs down my arms and spine. Sickness curdles inside me and I retch onto the stiff grass.

"Chieftain," shouts Bertel.

I raise my head to see the white-bearded warrior pull Thyra from the ground. Her slender fingers clutch his tunic as he steadies her, but she's already twisting in his grip.

When she sees me, she shoves Bertel away. "I'm fine. Help Ansa."

When he moves near, I hold up a trembling hand. With ice and fire spiraling along the bones of my arm, I flinch away from his touch. "D-don't," I stammer. "Give me space."

He backs off as a deadly heat warps the air around me, stinging my skin. I lower my head and breathe, remember the one useful lesson the evil elder taught me—I will never be steady inside if I don't breathe.

"Any wounded?" asks Thyra.

"No, except one of the horses. Broken leg."

"Shame. But I'm thankful that is the extent of it. I've never felt anything like that in all my life, except . . ." She sighs.

She's thinking of the witch-made storm on the Torden, I know it. The one that killed her father and nearly all our best and strongest. "I didn't do this," I say in a low voice.

"Ansa, look at me."

I raise my head at the authoritative voice of my chieftain to find her giving me a hard look.

"I *know*," she says.

"I . . . don't think it was quite as bad out here," Bertel says, caution in his deep voice. "We could see the ground moving and the entire forest pitching, but out here it was more of a rumble. We could stay on our feet."

We all look toward the forest. I can see damage there. Large swaths of trees leaning, as if all of them snapped at once, but the woods are so dense that many of them had nowhere to fall. To the northwest, I see a curl of black smoke, but it is dozens of miles away. The air feels heavy, laced with uncertainty. My magic burns inside, and I am still breathing, breathing, breathing as I slowly sit back.

Just inside the trees, something moves. A few warriors shout a warning, and I glance over to see a few draw their hunting bows. But as soon as I see the flash of white blond in the light, I shout, "It's Sig!"

He walks as if he's had far too much mead, and the air around him bends with heat. His lanky form is loose as he approaches. He is wearing pants and boots and nothing else.

"Ansa," Thyra says, her voice low. "He doesn't look good."

I wipe my face against my sleeve and squint at him. "He looks like I feel." My voice cracks. My mouth is so dry. I wonder if the hot breeze I'm now feeling against my cheeks is coming from him or from me.

"Ansa," Sig calls, his voice shredded.

I rise, waving off Thyra's assistance. Focusing on each step, I walk toward Sig. He has scrapes and cuts along his bare arms and the side of his scarred face, and sweat pours from his body.

"Ansa," he says, this time more quietly, and the uncertainty in his voice strikes a jangling chord inside me.

Two steps nearer, and I realize his eyes are glowing. "Sig."

His head tilts back as he looks up at the sky. His chest is heaving. His hands rise from his sides. I yelp as two enormous balls of flame sprout from his palms. The sound that explodes from his throat is agony and rage and horror all in one. It stabs into my ears, making them pop with pressure. Instantly, my magic rises to protect me, but my eyes clamp shut immediately against the wave of heat.

I open them again as I hear crackling.

And then a scream. "The woods!"

They are on fire. Smoke blocks out the sun.

Sig has collapsed in a circle of blackened grass, his skin steaming. I lunge toward him, drawing on my ice magic and wishing for a cool wind to keep his brain from cooking inside his skull, assuming it's not too late. As a searing wind spirals around us, it carries the panicked voices of our warriors to me once more, and I turn to see the flames creeping toward them as they frantically pull their clothes and tents from the ground.

No. Begging the ice inside me to take over, I act on instinct, throwing my arms out and harnessing the air around me. Icy flakes of snow melt on my brow. Crystalline shards of white creep along the grass like an army of ants.

"Ansa, stop," Thyra calls.

I flinch and cough as I inhale a lungful of smoke. As if reacting to the fiery pain inside my body, the ice pushes outward again, and now everyone is shouting and screaming. A body plows into mine, breaking my focus on the ice and the cold. I catch a whiff of Thyra's warm scent, and terror cuts through me. "Get off!"

"Calm down," she shouts. "You're about to freeze us all where we stand!" Her whole body is shaking and her teeth chatter.

"Get off me," I yell, bucking beneath her. Doesn't she remember I've killed this way before? Even the cuff of Astia on my wrist can't fully harness this magic—but it is the only thing protecting her from me now.

Her warm, steady hands slide under my tunic. I hold so still, scared to exhale, scared to move lest I harm her. She lies across me, curled around me, and my heart rattles in its cage as she kisses my cheek. "Don't," I whisper.

"I'm going to let go of you now."

"It cannot be soon enough."

She releases me, and I can breathe again. As I rise, I look over at Sig, who is slowly sitting up. Behind him, the still-smoking forest is glittered with frost, no flames to be seen.

His eyes meet mine, and in them I see the grim realization. Together, we might have killed every person within a mile. That we didn't seems more a result of luck than anything else. He winces as he clumsily gets up. His trembling fingers run along the slick skin of his arms, and he looks down at his palms as if trying to read a message there.

"What just happened?" I ask him.

"I don't know," he mumbles. "Something is . . . I can't . . . I have to . . ." The muscles of his arms and back go tense, and for a moment I think he's going to be sick, but then he starts to run toward the woods.

"Sig," I shout, starting to jog after him. "Wait!"

"Let him go, Ansa," Thyra snaps. Her fingers close around my arm and she points to the ground, where a line of fiery footsteps marks his path. His pale form disappears back into the trees again a few seconds later, leaving me with my hands outstretched.

Thyra stomps out a few wisps of flame. "He's out of control."

I glance at the melting ice that stretches across the space between me and the Krigere warriors, who remain huddled some distance away, shuffling uneasily through the tall meadow grass. "And me?"

"You have the cuff," she says briskly.

Our eyes meet. We both know it isn't enough. "You tackled me to get it to stop."

"I did what was necessary."

"You understand I could have killed you?"

Her gaze is so steady. "Our warriors were about to be consumed with fire and ice. I preferred not to leave another two hundred widows in Vasterut." Her jaw clenches when she sees mutiny in my expression. "Ansa, I told you. Warriors before chieftain. Before me."

I flatten my palm over the deep hum I still feel in the copper cuff. "Something is wrong," I murmur. "Sig was trying to tell me as much." I search the tree line for him, but as white as his skin is, he's still hidden well by darkness.

"When the earth shakes, everything is wrong," Thyra says. "There may be other temblors. We have to be ready."

I laugh. "Ready? How do you propose we ready ourselves for the moment the earth turns to water beneath our feet?"

"We stay out of the trees for the night, for one. We'll march through tomorrow, quick as we can." She nods toward the warriors. "Let's go build our fire. I'll get a few of the others to gather kindling."

I turn toward our warriors, who look jittery and worried, especially when they glance my way. "No."

"What?"

"I'll sleep by myself tonight." I point to a clump of bushes a few hundred yards to the south.

"Don't be stupid."

My fists clench around magic trying to burst from my palms. "I don't know why, but I'm not right today. Sig wasn't either. And both of us are dangerous. I'm guessing that's why he ran—he didn't want to hurt any of us."

"He's never struck me as the selfless type. But there seems to be no question that he's dangerous and out of control, and we're better off without an unstable warrior."

I bite the inside of my cheek. "Sig has seemed saner in recent weeks than I've ever known him to be."

"But now we're almost back in Kupari, the place where he was scarred and burned by the impostor queen and her helpers. Who knows what it's doing to his mind?"

A warm breeze ruffles my hair, matching the unsteady flutter of fire inside me. "And who knows what it's doing to me? I'm just as dangerous as he is, if not more so—cuff or no cuff."

Anger flashes across Thyra's face, and she strides forward. She takes my face in her hands before I can escape, and then her lips are on mine, just for a moment, hard and cool. She doesn't seem to care that the others could see us if they cared to look. She doesn't even glance in their direction. When she releases me, her brows are low and her mouth is tight. "I won't order you to sleep next to me tonight." She takes a few steps back. "But you know where to find me if you get chilled."

She pivots and walks toward the hillock where Bertel and Preben have seated themselves, keeping a watchful eye on the forest. I am aching to follow her, but instead I head in the other direction. I need to put distance between us in case I lose control again. Turning my focus outward, toward managing the basic needs of my body, I snap twigs off the bush and gather more wood from the outer edges of the forest, careful not to stray too close to the dripping, charred mess. The smell of smoke fills my nose and turns my stomach.

My first footsteps into the land of my birth were met with its efforts to tear itself to shreds. I know it was an unhappy coincidence, but I can't help but feel like I'm not wanted there, like something deep inside the earth feels my presence and is howling. It preys on all my fears—perhaps Kauko was wrong. Perhaps I was never meant to rule here. Perhaps I shouldn't be here at all.

I sink into a squat in front of the little pile of wood nestled into a hollow I carved into the dirt. As soon as I wish for flame, it springs to life, and I hold my breath in an effort to avoid setting the entire meadow on fire. I stare at the results of my magic and wonder if I should do what Sig did—run far and fast, before I kill someone accidentally. I had thought I'd moved past it, but today has raised my fears and doubts like swells in an early winter storm.

A gust of breeze carries the sound of laughter to me. Now that the darkness has fallen, all I can see of my fellow Krigere is the glow of their fires a few hundred yards away, but I can hear their voices if I strain. I hear worry. But I also hear hope.

Two hundred of them marched away from their andeners and children this morning, only because of that hope—for a new homeland for our people, a safe place to rest our heads and raise our young ones. Our kind have been decimated. Our entire way of life has changed. All we have left now is this plea to heaven that there is a future for us in Kupari.

And I seem to be the key to securing it, if it is to be had at all.

"I can't run," I whisper. I can't go anywhere until I've done everything I can for them. I promised Thyra, and she needs this from me.

I tuck my trembling hands into my armpits, holding everything still. I have to rest. I have to sleep. In the morning, surely this shaky uncertainty will have passed, and I will be right again.

I cannot bear to think of what will happen if I'm not.

CHAPTER FOUR

Elli

Oskar's arms clamp around me and we're falling as a roar fills my ears. I scream and cling to him, my hands finding the skin of his throat. His body shudders as chunks of the ceiling pummel his back. Rage and horror flood my lungs as I hear him gasp with pain.

I will not let this happen.

With Oskar braced above me, I pull on his magic with all my strength, directing it outward. Panic bites at my focus, shredding its edges, but I fight to control the ice as it pours through me with the chaotic force of an avalanche. My head snaps back as I feel it burst from me as a blizzard. I fight to channel its fury and have the fleeting thought that Oskar has grown more powerful—and his magic has grown sharper, an edge that kills with precision as well as strength.

It's fighting to wrest itself from my grip as the floor beneath us cracks and buckles. Oskar curses and holds me so tightly that I cannot breathe. Spots float beneath my closed eyelids, bursts of white and yellow on black black black. . . .

"Elli, please!" Oskar's voice rings with need and pain.

I claw my way toward the sound of it, swimming up through a frigid ocean of icebergs and frozen slush that fills my ears and mouth. The magic shivers, vibrations that roll along my bones. When I finally reach the surface, I arch and cough. My eyes blink open. Oskar is above me, his face framed with white. His body shakes like he's having a fit. His teeth are gritted. "Please," he gasps. "Stop."

My eyes focus on our surroundings. We're surrounded by ice, pristine and smooth. I am crushed beneath his weight and do not feel cold at all. But Oskar's face is ashen, and pain is etched into the line of his clenched jaw.

He is freezing to death.

Terror jars my heart, sending it into a gallop. I wriggle to free my hands, but it's not easy—Oskar weighs twice as much as I do and his full weight is on me as ice presses to his back. His scent makes me ache even now, wood smoke and earth and pine. He is past talking; even his eyes are mute with pain. He has no fire inside him to warm his skin, no heat to keep his blood from freezing. The certainty of his agony pulses into my muscles, and I wrench my left hand free. My scars shine silver in the gleam of sunlight on ice as I press my hand against our icy coffin.

I don't know if this will work, and if it doesn't, my love

is going to die on top of me, possibly killing me slowly with his weight. I close my eyes again, but this time it is a different kind of pull, like taking a giant breath. This time, I don't try to shove the magic out around me—this time I inhale it, sucking it into the vast empty space inside me. The three remaining fingers of my hand dig into the frigid walls, feeling it give way to my power, oblivious to the cold. It's made from magic, and I am immune to it.

"Oskar, I need you," I say, my voice barely a wheeze. "Can you push up, maybe get to your knees?"

My clothes are soaked with the melt, but my skin merely tingles. It doesn't even raise goose bumps. But Oskar's breath fogs as his muscles tense, as he tries to do as I've asked. I whisper encouragement in his ear as I continue to siphon the deadly magic into my body and hold it there, keeping him safe. His skin is gray, and a terrible moan escapes his mouth as he arches his back.

The ice falls away and reveals the truth of what has happened.

There is sky above me, nothing but blue and white and brilliant sun. I whimper as I turn my head and see the piles of rubble around us, which might have pulverized our bones had the ice not shielded us.

"Elli, my hand," mumbles Oskar.

"What's wrong?" I glance around, realizing one of his arms is still pinned beneath me. He was cradling me as the temple crumbled, and beneath my spine I feel his hand. I sit, and he groans and draws his arm up, supporting it with his other hand.

His right hand is white and bloodless, and when he sees it, he pitches to the side as if he is about to be sick. I grab his shoulders, trying to hold him steady as his body heaves, my ears ringing with shock and fear and disbelief. From somewhere in the rubble, or maybe beyond it, I hear voices crying out. I hold Oskar's head against my chest and call, "Who's there?"

No one seems to hear us.

"What happened?" Oskar asks.

"I think it was an earthquake," I say. "I've read about them. The bones of the earth shift and move, and it tosses and tears its skin. They . . ." They happen in foreign lands, far from here. "There is no history of earthquakes in Kupari."

"Now there is," he says weakly, pulling his head from my breast to look around. His right hand is hidden in the folds of his tunic now. His face is pale as marble. But his gaze is sharpening with both alarm and determination as he turns to me. "You saved us."

"We saved us, Oskar. I would have been crushed without your magic." I lay my warm palm on his cold cheek. "And your body."

He gives me a weary smile. "I told you I was your shield."

Tears prick my eyes as I brush my lips over his, feeling the lingering trickle of his magic on my tongue. But then I draw away as I hear another cry, and suddenly I remember—"Lahja!"

I am on my feet and pulling Oskar to his, my heart a fist pounding on a wall. Without thinking, I lay my hand against Oskar's throat and pull, and he does not resist. His winter magic bursts from my palms in a vicious wind that blasts rocks out of our way. My teeth grit and my eyes narrow. My Saadella needs me. I can feel her near and I will not surrender her.

She is alive. Even the collapse of the world could not take her from me.

Like a mother wolf surrounded by coyotes, I stalk forward, tearing through a wall of rubble as if it were parchment. It is nothing before my love. Oskar leans on me, close and endless in his power, and we move together until I have cleared a path all the way to the great chamber.

The massive copper dome is still above us, though the floor is littered with debris, and before me lie more collapsed walls, but I can see that the wing of the Saadella, which is nearer to the front of the temple, is still standing. "Lahja," I shout.

"We are here," Kaisa calls. "She is whole." Her voice is high and shaky, but loud enough to echo.

"Raimo," I murmur, looking around. He had said he was going to his chamber, which is in the catacombs, the maze of caverns beneath the temple. "Oh, stars."

"Here he is," Oskar says.

Raimo stands in the entrance to the catacombs at the back of the great chamber, his tufty hair dripping, his scrawny body shivering, his face covered in stone dust, his gaze sharp as ever. "The Saadella?"

"Alive," Kaisa says as she limps out of Lahja's chamber.

My Saadella is clinging to her, skinny arms around her neck, her little face buried in the folds of Kaisa's robe. "But her sister is trapped and needs help."

"I'll do it," Raimo says, his voice hoarse and cracking.

"I can help," Oskar says, but as he steps forward, he sways, and I catch his arm as he slowly sinks to his knees. "Or maybe I can't."

"You stay where you are," I say firmly. "Rest for a minute."

He bows his head so I can't see his expression, and I gently stroke his messy hair before turning back toward Kaisa. She is rubbing Lahja's back, and I rush forward to meet her at the edge of the chamber. When my hands touch Lahja's skin, she whimpers and turns, trying to crawl into my arms, and the apprentice releases her to my care. I clutch her trembling body to mine and whisper tender reassurances in her ear as tears slip from my eyes. If I lost her, I'm not sure I would survive it.

I rock her as I walk to the open front of the grand chamber, which faces out on the white plaza and the city beyond the walls of the temple. What I see lances at my heart. Plumes of smoke rise over Kupari, and a few of its tallest buildings have collapsed, leaving nothing but jutting timber and loose piles of rock. The plaza itself is fissured, with slabs of marble upended to reveal bare earth underneath. What had remained of the towering Valtia statues after our battle for the temple is now two shattered stumps of crystal and stone. My city lies in ruins, and my people are hurting, and to protect them, I must rely on the magic of others.

I turn my back to it, focusing within for the moment, because without the souls in this temple, I am lost. "Kaisa," I call out, "are you hurt?"

Kaisa rubs stone dust from her short blond hair. There is a smear of dirt across her cheek that covers the mole there. She laughs, a rustling, labored sound. "I'm not hurt. Just . . ." Her hand shakes as it falls to her side.

Like Oskar and Raimo, something is not right with her. But when she sees me watching her with concern, she shakes her head. "I am completely at your service, Valtia. Tell me what you need from me."

"I need you to take her," I say, kissing Lahja's tear-damp cheek. Her grip on me tightens, and I press my lips to her ear. "You are safe, my darling," I whisper. "And I must make sure everyone else is safe too. This will be your responsibility one day, but on this day, it is mine. Can you understand? It's what we were made for."

Well. I'm not sure what I was made for, but I know it wasn't to sit around and let others face their fate alone. Perhaps because she is truly meant to be Valtia one day, Lahja nods her agreement. She senses that the Kupari are ours to protect and nurture, and she understands that our own comfort is less important. She allows Kaisa to take her once more.

"Is her chamber safe?" I ask.

"It is." Kaisa turns as Raimo slowly walks out with Janeka leaning on his arm, making sure Lahja is looking at me instead of her sister. The girl has scrapes and bruises on her face but otherwise seems unhurt.

"Please get her cleaned up before she comes to attend the Saadella," I tell Raimo. Lahja will be scared if she sees Janeka bleeding like that.

Raimo nods. "Afterward I'm going to the library." His tone tells me all I need to know—he is as surprised by this earthquake as the rest of us.

"Only a few columns in Lahja's chamber collapsed," Kaisa says. "Janeka was on the balcony clearing the tea when the ground began to shake. She caught the worse of it."

"Stay with Lahja and do not leave her side," I instruct. "You know your priority."

She nods solemnly, and when I catch her eye, the flames there tell me she will protect the Saadella with her life.

With my princess as safe as our current predicament allows, I turn back to Oskar. He still sits on the floor of the grand chamber, his long legs stretched over the gold infinity symbol of the Valtia, his right hand still tucked into his tunic.

"Let me see it," I say.

"No."

"*Oskar*."

He raises his head. "I am not your concern." I can tell he is working to keep his voice steady. I can also tell he is scared.

I drop to my knees. "You have no right to say that to me, and you know it." I gesture impatiently at his hidden hand.

He sighs and slowly draws it from its hiding place. He breathes slowly, his nostrils flaring, as it dangles limp in front of him. His fingers are still white, like the hand of a corpse, and his skin only becomes alive at his wrist. "It's not good."

Gently, as if handling the most delicate porcelain, I lift my palm to hold its weight. It's not cold, not frozen. It's just . . . dead. "What happened?"

He opens his eyes but looks away from me. "It froze."

"But you've been wielding ice magic for many years. You—" As he squeezes his eyes shut, I realize. . . . "I did this?"

"No."

"Yes. I did." I did something wrong. I pulled too hard or too quickly or in the wrong way. "Oskar." That is all I can say. Tears swallow the rest of my words.

"It was us together," he says quietly, staring at the back of the chamber, at swirls of copper that have torn loose from the walls and glint dully in the rays of the sinking sun. "I felt it happening. My hand was caught beneath your body, and it just . . ."

I cover my mouth to stifle the sob. "We can see what Raimo can do. He can heal you."

"Perhaps," Oskar says, sounding bleak.

"I want you to rest now. Will you do that?"

It is a testament to his exhaustion that he does not argue. "Will you be with Raimo?"

I nod. "Regain your strength. Will you do that for me?"

"There will be other people in this temple who need help."

"I understand. You must rest so you can assist. But right now . . ."

"Go see Raimo. I'll be all right." He holds his arm pressed to his middle as he rises from the floor.

I stroke his sleeve as he steps out of my reach. "I will come find you soon."

He nods as he walks away. I watch him for a moment, my throat tight, and then march toward the library. My steps are hardened by fear for the people I love. I find Raimo sitting on the floor of the library, surrounded by scrolls. They've all fallen from their shelves, most of which are overturned or collapsed. The old man has cleared himself a space and reads by the light of a ball of fire that floats a few feet from his shoulder. Every few seconds, it sputters and throws off sparks. When they land on his shoulder, he brushes them away with an unsteady hand.

"We'll need to meet with the council," he says without looking up. "The city will need help from the temple to recover."

I groan inwardly. The last thing I want to do right now is meet with our esteemed town leaders, the richest merchants of Kupari who always seem to be seeking ways to get richer. They resent my refusal to use the Valtia's magic to solve every problem, as well as my demand that we arm ourselves against the barbarians.

This earthquake is unlikely to make them more cooperative.

"I will summon them here tonight." Because it is my burden, and there is no one else to bear it.

I bite my lip as I glance down at the scroll he's reading. It's a star chart, not a text. "Has anything like this ever happened before?"

"It is completely without precedent." He offers a wry smile. "But so are you. So is our lost Valtia who has none of your balance."

"Are we responsible for this?"

His smile fades. "I don't think so. I think this was caused by something else."

"Do the stars give you answers?"

"Ha. They only reveal more questions." He curses and tosses the scroll aside before grabbing another. "But I have long wondered what would happen if the Kupari people pulled all the copper from the ground."

His words wind around my chest, making it hard to breathe. "You think we've destabilized the land itself."

"It's possible these wounds are entirely self-inflicted. I must do more digging before I'm sure, but I've been expecting something like this. The elders were hoarding copper, thinking that would save them. Instead, they've pushed us to the edge of a cliff."

I think back to what Raimo told me about what might happen when the last copper was mined. "You told me the fire and ice magic might just disappear—or turn on its wielders. . . ." I look down at his shaking hands. "And it looks like the latter. Every magic wielder felt it before it hit. You, Oskar . . . all of you said you felt off today. And then the ground began to shake."

He holds his trembling fingers in front of his face. "Oskar felt it too, you say?"

I nod. "Worse than you did, I think."

"Of course he did. Much more power. Far less balance," Raimo mutters, then curses again. "Elli, I might have been right about the copper but wrong about the war."

"I would be grateful if you were. You think the Soturi will leave us alone?"

He shakes his head. "I think we're more vulnerable than ever, and if they still desire our riches, now would be the best time to attack." He chuckles, but it is pure desolation. "I mean that it might be the least of our worries now."

"How can invading barbarians be the least of our worries?"

When he looks up at me, my stomach knots. I have never seen the old man look scared until this moment. He searches my face, then smiles. "I shouldn't have said that. I've barely begun to explore what could be happening and how it might be remedied. Go summon the council and let me do some research, and we will speak later tonight."

When I don't move, he shoos me away. "Go busy yourself being the queen! Take Oskar with you."

I swallow back the sick feeling I have when I picture his hand. "I can't. He is injured. He needs your healing touch."

Raimo sighs as he lowers his unsteady hands to the scrolls piled on his lap. "I will attend to him shortly."

"He needs you now, I think."

"Elli, at present I'm not sure I could do much for him. Or, more accurately, I'm afraid I might damage him further."

I stare down at his twitching fingers. "Gather your strength then," I say firmly. "Then you and I will attend him together, and you will tell me what to do. I can amplify your magic—these tremors do not affect me." And I feel desperately guilty—if it weren't for me, Oskar's hand would be fine.

Raimo's bushy eyebrows rise. "Now, there's an idea."

"When I next see you, I would like to hear answers. I need to know why this is happening now. And I would like to know what I can do."

I leave him with the weight of that responsibility and stride back toward the domed chamber, breathing steadily and counting each step. If I think too hard about what I am facing, I will fall to my knees and weep. If I give all these threats to our existence even one chance to grip me, they will pull me down into its watery pit and drown me. So I steel myself against the doubt, the worry, the future. I take one step, and another, and another, and do not let myself think beyond it.

I am one girl. I am an impostor. My city is rubble. My people are hurting. And the Soturi are coming for us. The gnawing ache of what is missing—my Valtia, the real one, the half of me I have never met but crave with every heartbeat—coils inside me, hidden and hurtful. But she is not here, and I am all the Kupari have. Somehow, I must be enough.

CHAPTER FIVE

Ansa

When I wake, I am beneath Thyra's blanket. Her lean arms are wrapped around me, and she is molded to my back. I can feel her warm breath on the nape of my neck. The sun is sparkling off dewdrops in the meadow and lighting the edges of the blackened forest, and the air is clear, no longer hazy with smoke.

"Are you awake?" murmurs Thyra.

"I am now." I lay my palm over hers where it rests over my heart.

"Last night, when you came to me, you didn't answer when I spoke to you," she says as I turn to face her.

Our noses touch as I reply, "I think I was walking in my sleep."

"Your body knows what it needs even when your mind is stubborn, then."

I let out a quiet laugh. "I suppose it does. I didn't hurt you?"

"The opposite." Her fingers push my coppery hair away from my brow. "Are you ready for today?"

My gaze strays over her shoulder, back to the forest. "I don't know. I still feel unsteady inside. Like a dam about to burst."

She touches the cuff of Astia. "Doesn't this make it better?"

"I'd hate to think of what I'd be like if I didn't have it."

"So . . ."

"I'll be fine." Even if it takes every ounce of restraint I possess. I will not lose control again—the future of the Krigere is depending on it. "Shall we go?"

She smiles. "As you wish, my queen."

I spend a few luxurious moments kissing her, and then we get up and help the others break camp. They are quiet, grim and focused. As warriors, they are not about to voice fear aloud, but I can smell it on them—and on my own skin. My attention keeps straying to the forest like a rabbit to bait in a snare.

By the time the sun tears itself loose from the horizon, we are leading our skittish mounts into the Loputon Forest. I leave the narrow, barely there footpath for a few moments to do my business behind a broad tree, and as I return, I catch Preben's eyes as he and Bertel move up to walk next to Thyra. The cold distrust in his gray gaze chills me, mixing with the icy magic inside me and wrenching a shiver down my spine. This is the way he looked at Sig, and now Sig is gone.

It reminds me of how all of us were calling magic "witchcraft" only weeks ago. It reminds me of what we have done to suspected witches among us. I remember, so long ago, when I was still a raid prize, only just brought into camp. The man in blue was a prisoner too, and warriors had staked him to the ground. His screams made me clap my hands over my ears. Then I couldn't see him anymore, because all the Krigere gathered around, stones in their hands. His shrieks didn't last long after that.

Afterward, I asked the warrior who had stolen me what the man had done. I still recall how the Krigere language rolled in my mouth like stones in a tumbler. My captor gave me a funny look, and I thought at the time it was because he was shocked that a child—a prize of war, no less—was bold enough to speak to him, or maybe that I had mastered his language so quickly.

"The man is a witch," he said to me. "From Kupari." Then he spat on the ground at my feet. "Remember that."

Now I know his look, his disdain, his warning. . . . It is because he knew—I was Kupari as well.

My memories roam the inside of my skull as we pick our way along through thigh-high brambles and brush. It is slow work, and the already tense mood only gets worse as the daylight disappears behind the forest's shield of leaves and branches. My own temper grows thin and taut, stretched like a hide on a rack. With every step, I am deeper into this land, but it feels like it's about to fall out from under my feet. My heart beats wary and wild, unwilling to carry a solid rhythm to calm my nerves. And the cuff on my wrist hums, a vibration that travels along my bones and into my skull, where it grows into a blinding headache. The strange urge to tear the cuff off my wrist nearly overtakes me on several occasions, but each time, I clench my fist on the reins of the piebald mare I'm leading. She whinnies her displeasure, or perhaps her fear, but I'm too lost in my own suffering to tend to her.

On three separate occasions, the ground rumbles beneath our feet. Nothing like the first temblor, but enough to make us stop and hold our breath as the trees sway over our heads, branches clacking in warning while our horses scream. The shaking ends quickly each time, though, and we press on, our pace a little quicker.

We stop for noonmeal long after our stomachs complain. It is dark even though the sun must be directly overhead, streaming over the forest canopy. In the depths of the woods, almost none of it reaches us, save for a thin golden beam here and there along the surface of the rotting leaves at our feet. We do not light fires; I think after watching Sig make the forest explode into flame, none of us are tempted.

I squat next to Thyra, who is sharing a log with Preben and Bertel. "Sig said it would take a day to clear the forest and reach the outlands of Kupari. We must be close."

"Assuming he was telling the truth," mutters Bertel.

I squint, trying to read his expression. "You think he wasn't?"

"It would have been a great way to lead us into a trap,"

Preben says. "We're all so desperate for a new, safe haven that we followed him here—"

"Are you questioning Thyra's leadership?" I ask.

"It's a fair question," Thyra says quietly. "Sig left us the moment we reached the border. He could have run to tell the impostor where we are, and the exact number of our forces. Or he could have fled to find Jaspar and Kauko, wherever they are. We only know he didn't stay with us."

I stand up again as the fire inside me flares. "You saw him. You all saw him. He was scared. It was not the look of a schemer."

Thyra's eyes lock with mine, and I know she's recalling what I told her about how Sig got me away from Kauko—by using the elder's own thirst for power against him. It was indeed a clever scheme. "That was different," I say. "And it should tell you how much he hated Kauko. Why would he run to him now?"

"Seeking revenge," Preben says. "Or maybe his mind is so warped that he returns to the one who abused him. We see this in prisoners and raid prizes all the time."

I turn away from him, unable to dismiss the implication as unintentional. "I am going to fill my waterskin at the stream." It comes out of me flat and cold, my breath huffing in a white cloud in front of me.

Part of me hopes that Thyra will follow, but the rest of me is glad when she doesn't. I kneel by the burbling stream, and a thin skin of ice crackles over its surface the moment I wet my fingertips. I bow my head and breathe, willing away the unsteadiness.

"She wants to think the very best of you."

My head jerks up and I look over my shoulder to find Bertel leaning against a tree. All I see of him is the snowy glow of his beard and the whites of his eyes, so deep is the shadow around him. It occurs to me that I won't know whether he's holding a weapon unless he moves, a strange thought to have of one who is supposed to be your brother, your people. "And you—what do you think, Bertel?"

"I am trying to decide."

I shift on the balls of my feet, unwilling to turn my back to him. "And Preben?"

"The same. All of us wonder."

"Whether I am stable, you mean. Because you cannot question my loyalty."

"That is true. Nor can we question the chieftain's loyalty to *you*."

"Ah. And that's what bothers you."

An impatient sigh bursts from his mouth. "Loyalty is a gift. But sometimes it is a blindfold, too."

"Are you really questioning her wisdom?"

I see his eyes narrow and know it is a silly question. Of course he questions her wisdom. Though she's the chieftain, tested in combat, daughter of the greatest warrior the Krigere have ever bred, she is eighteen years old—and Bertel has more than twice that number, as do most of the surviving warriors. The others have even more than that. "Bertel, her cleverness saved your life."

"Cleverness is not the same thing as wisdom."

"What do you call her decision to seek a land where we can make a permanent home?"

"I will not speak ill of my chieftain," he says, holding up his hands.

"You already have," I snap.

"No. And I will say no more, except to ask you . . . to beg you, even . . . to look inside yourself. We all saw you in the fight circle the night Thyra battled Nisse's warriors. We all saw the mad look in your eyes, the way you would have killed all of *us* to save *her*. And we saw it again last night as you sent winter gales swirling through the air and thick ice crawling along the ground like poison."

"I *was* trying to save you!"

He leans forward, his gaze on me enviably steady. "We *know*. In the end, we are not sure how much your good intentions matter in the face of the power that hides beneath your skin. We wonder which is the wielder and which is the weapon."

"Are you saying you think I should leave? You do realize I may be the key to gaining us territory within the borders of Kupari, don't you?"

"Kupari has no army. It is possible we could carve defendable territory on our own."

A fierce, sharp kind of rage is growing inside me, like a blade of ice. "Kupari is *mine*," I growl.

He rocks back, and so do I, surprised at the animal sound of my own voice. The tremors are back too, sending ripples of heat and cold through my bloodstream. I close my eyes and concentrate on taking a slow breath. "What I meant is that they have magic wielders too, and you know that is a power that no Krigere should face alone."

"But it seems our ally could kill us just as easily."

My stomach is frozen and heavy inside me. "I'm not an ally. I'm your sister. I'm as Krigere as you are."

"I don't deny it. But you are also something else. And you can't deny *that*."

"So again I ask—what do you want from me?"

"I—and so many others—only want to live, and to have a place to keep my family safe. I don't care what I have to do to achieve that. I suppose what we want is for you to search your soul, and to be a true, loyal Krigere. If you are unstable in battle, you put the lives of your fellow warriors in danger. Then you are as much an enemy as the enemy herself."

Which is why the Krigere banish any warrior who cannot control his or her mind and mood. It always made sense to me until I thought about what it would be like to be deprived of the tribe—how can one be stable at all when everything you know and love is stripped away? "You cannot be asking me to banish myself, Bertel. What would Thyra say if she heard you?"

"And this is why I am speaking to you in confidence. Because I care about my chieftain."

"Care is what you do for a child. Respect is what you give a chieftain."

"There are many kinds of respect."

I groan. "I am in no mood for philosophy." My head feels

like it is being ground between two stones. "I will always do what I think is right, Bertel. For Krigere, and for Thyra. I value both more than I value myself."

"That is all we can ask of you." He regards me for a moment, nods to himself, and walks away.

We follow one narrow path and then another, and by the time the beams of sunlight wither and disappear, leaving us in darkness, we realize we are lost.

Actually, I have to be told, because I am in too much pain to realize anything past that. The cuff feels like an enemy now, humming constantly, a sound I feel but can't hear no matter how I strain. Nothing inside me is still, not the magic, not my thoughts, not even my eyes in my head. I think I might be going mad.

Thyra seems to know that I am not well, but she is quiet about it. She guides me to a fallen log and tells me to sit, then presses a waterskin to my lips. She casts impatient torch-lit glances over her shoulder at the others, and I know it is because they see her tending to me and wonder what it means. "We're going to bed down here for the night," she says. "We need better light to find our way out of this forest."

"I miss Halina," I say, because it is the loudest of my racing thoughts. "She would know which way to go."

"Indeed she would. But we must find our own way. Tomorrow." She takes my face in her hands. "Ansa, you're getting worse. I don't know what to do for you."

"This land is making me sick."

She stares at the ground. "Or maybe the land itself is sick. I wish it could hold steady for us."

"What if this is happening because of me, though? Maybe this broken magic inside me is the sickness," I whisper.

"Stop it." She pulls my head against her stomach, wrapping her arms around me to hold me there. "You are still our best hope and defense in Kupari. You hold the only legitimate claim to the land, and our people need you. You'll see. Tomorrow we will emerge from this forest, and then you'll feel different. This darkness would drive anyone mad."

I glance at the torch in her hand, and it flares. She holds it a little further away from her body but closes her eyes as she feels the warmth on her face. I watch the play of shadow and light across her cheeks and brow, dazzled and dazed until I hear one of our warriors shout, "Fire!"

Thyra turns at the sound of his terror, and my eyes go wide as I catch a whiff of thick smoke. Goose bumps rise on my arms. My cuff hums. I swear it sounds like whistling.

"Preben," Thyra calls, "go—"

The fireball lands in the middle of our camp, blinding me with brightness and heat, stealing my breath. Thyra and I end up on the ground behind the log, but we are not in darkness now. The trees rain fire upon us, making the chaos easy to see. Warriors scramble like prey animals to get away from the flames, to shield themselves from the heat.

The ice rises in me like a reflex, pouring outward. I raise my hands, directing it above our heads instead of toward my people. Thyra is shouting even as shards of ice begin to fall on us. "Is that you?"

"No!" Because they disappear into rain and steam as they fall. My magic holds it back. "It has to be another wielder!"

"Sig?"

"That's ice," I yell. "He can't do that." I catch her eye. "It has to be Kauko." My head throbs as I swivel it, trying to spot the source of the attack. "Or an army of Kupari wielders." Maybe Sig betrayed us after all?

An orange glimmer draws my attention back to Thyra. She has drawn a dagger, and there is a deadly look in her eyes.

"What are you doing?"

She squats next to me as I try to shield our warriors from the death that falls from the sky, knives of ice and the killing kiss of fire. "I'll find Kauko, or whoever is attacking us. They won't see me coming."

I would grab her arm, but I'm afraid I'd freeze the blood in her veins. My magic is making my whole body shake, dangerous and unsteady inside me. The pressure against my rib cage is building, as if it wants to burst free and lay waste to the entire forest. The only thing I can do is keep it aimed upward, where it naturally fights whatever descends on us. "Thyra, please. It isn't safe."

She laughs. "And this *is*? Stay here and keep the worst of it off our warriors."

"No, I'll come with you! You can't fight the enemy alone!" I start to rise, but she aims the blade right at my face.

There is no laughter in her eyes now. Only ferocity. "If you abandon them, I will banish you."

"Please," I say, my voice cracking. "I'm your wolf."

"Yes, you're my wolf to command. And I command you to protect our warriors. Disobey me and you are my wolf no longer." Her eyes are bright, maybe with tears. "I'll keep my word, Ansa. I told you how it had to be."

I can tell by her expression, by the steady hand that holds her weapon, that she'll do it. She won't relent. It only makes me love her more. "We'll be a lost tribe without you."

"I can kill one fat old man, magic or no."

"And if there's more than one enemy?"

"I'll kill whoever I find. Stealth is a weapon all its own. They think they've pinned us down, but they're wrong." She draws her shoulders up to her ears as another fireball whistles down through the trees, and as another falls on us, her eyes follow the path. She smiles.

My throat is so tight that I cannot breathe. "Come back."

She lowers her blade and extends her fingers but does not touch me, probably knowing that right now such a thing is deadly. The ice and fire spiral along my arms and into the air. "I will sleep by your side tonight."

She turns toward the source of the fireballs and lopes into the darkness of the wood.

CHAPTER SIX

Elli

I clutch the edge of the table as I feel the earth tremble yet again. It's happened a few times this morning, and every time, from all around me, I hear people crying out with fear. My own response is to be silent, and to brace for the world to fall apart again, but these are smaller tremors and end much more quickly than the first time.

Across from me, Topias, the leader of the town council, is white with anxiety as he clutches his long brown beard, as if it were a rope that could pull him to safety. Truly, it's a comical picture, but I have no laughter left inside me.

When the ground is still once more, I lean forward to draw his attention. "You were saying?"

He lets out a stuttery little hiss. "I was saying that the people need to hear from the temple, Valtia. They want their queen to tell them how she will keep them safe."

"I have fire and ice," I say. "I do not control the earth."

He glances around at his fellow council members. "We are threatened by more than the shaking ground, Valtia. I thought you knew."

"We will continue to prepare for any incursion by Soturi forces—"

"That's not what we're talking about at all." Agata, the dressmaker, steps forward. "Don't you feel it?" she asks, peering at my face. "All the other wielders seem to. An unsteadiness. A loss of control."

Heat blooms across my skin and I hope I am not blushing. "My priests and acolytes at the temple felt it as well. That something was off with them. But I . . ." I offer as serene a smile as I can muster. "Perhaps it is the balance of my magic that protects me from this feeling."

"There have been accidents," Topias says. Now he is stroking his beard as if it were a nervous pet. The council medallion of heavy copper shines dully on his chest, and it is a reminder that we may have done this to ourselves. "Wielders have . . . done damage."

"Please be specific," I say. "Let us be straight with each other."

Agata puts her hands on the table, and I gaze down upon her spindly fingers and the glittering rings that decorate them. "An ice wielder killed the child she was minding this morning. Froze him in her arms."

I put my hand over my mouth and swallow back a wave of sick. "How horrible."

"It was the youngest son of Yrian, the blacksmith. The wielder—her name is Ivette—she claims she did not know she was a wielder until that moment, but no one believes her."

I bite back a comment about how I could not blame her if she were hiding her ability. Until several weeks ago, wielders either escaped to the outlands—or were taken to the temple to serve. No one had much of a choice. Very few wielders have revealed themselves to their fellow citizens, who cannot always suppress their fear and suspicion. To them, wielders belong in the temple, unseen, toiling in the service of their people. "Is she safe?"

"Is *she* safe?" Agata folds her arms over her bosom. "What about the boy she killed?"

"That is a tragedy, but I cannot raise him from the dead. It sounds like a tragic accident—and I'd like to make sure there is only the one victim."

"Then control your wielders!" The words burst from Topias in a spray of spittle, and he uses his velvet sleeve to wipe it from his lips. "Appear in the town square and tell them to reveal themselves! Invite them to the temple or figure out some other way to bring them to heel!"

"I can appear before the people, but I will not ask frightened wielders to step forward in the midst of a potential mob," I say, taking care to keep my voice steady. "That is not the way to quell anyone's fears. Magic will spring forth to protect the wielder—the last thing we need is our people attacking each other. It wouldn't go well for anyone."

"Is that a threat?" Topias asks quietly.

I stand. "I would never threaten the people I rule and care for. Those with magic and those without. I love you all equally, and I will not participate in your proposal to single out wielders for suspicion."

"They are dangerous!"

I lock gazes with Agata. "So are you." I step away from my chair. "I am returning to the temple now. I will send guards to bring Ivette to the temple. And I would ask each of you to remember the greater good over your own fears and prejudices. We all must work together to rebuild and to defend this city." I turn in place, taking in the fissured stone walls of the council chamber, the spills of rock in the corners, the crack in the ceiling, and then all the council members themselves, bedecked in dust-streaked robes and gowns that were possibly pulled from the rubble of their fine houses. "Wielders are critical to our protection. Attacking them will only divide our society at a time when we should be most united. See how we have worked together these past weeks? This is how it always should have been."

"The elders and the Valtia used to take care of everything!" says one man who stands near the doorway, looking ready to run if the ground shakes again. "Now we must do more than we ever have."

I tilt my head. "Thank the stars for that. We were sorely deprived of your gifts until now. Think of what we could have accomplished had you been required to use them sooner."

He looks at me as if he cannot tell if I am sincere or mocking him. In truth, it's both.

"I will appear in the square tonight," I continue. "I will reassure our people and offer safe haven to wielders who are unsure of their magic, for it is clear that the unsteadiness in the ground and in the magic are linked."

"Are you saying that magic is causing our land to tear itself apart?" Agata asks.

"Not at all." My patience is wearing thin, but I keep a smile on my face as I glide toward the door, where my guards await, ready to carry me on my paarit back to the temple. "I am saying that the unsteadiness in both is connected, and we at the temple are searching the texts to uncover a remedy."

I have already thought of one: I can only hope, if the cause of the temblors is indeed that the copper has been drained from the land, that there is a simple way to offer it back to the earth, but I do not say this to them. Right now it would cause them to panic—I'd be telling them to throw their wealth into a deep hole, something they will not right now be willing to do. I first have to be sure—and then I have to find a palatable way of feeding it to them. "For today, though, let us focus on keeping peace. The townsfolk will be looking to you for an example. Please be your best selves."

I walk quickly to my paarit. My guards, disciplined as always, wait until I sit on my chair. Then they raise me into the air. As I float several feet above the road, dipping and tilting as my guards carefully avoid the tears in the ground at their feet, I watch smoke curling into the air, several columns between the temple and the city wall. I don't know how people in the outlands fared—I can only hope that none of the old mines collapsed, as that is where so many find shelter.

I wave to our citizens, who cry out to me and lift their arms, beseeching. I do not call out to them, because I think it is best to hold my words until tonight, when I address all our people. Rumors spread like sickness in times like this, and one careless promise could be fatal.

When we reach the white plaza, I have the guards let me down and walk the rest of the way. It's pointless for them to carry me when I can walk perfectly well—the only reason I ride in the paarit is to reassure the citizens that not that much has changed, even though so very much has changed.

Raimo and Oskar are in my chamber when I stride in, and I feel the magic swirling in the air as I cross the room to my ice wielder. He sits on a chair at the table, his dead white hand resting on its surface. I look away from it as guilt snaps its jaws closed over my heart. "There are wielders out in the city who are losing control," I say as I lay my hand on Oskar's shoulder, needing to feel his cool and solid presence.

Raimo, who has been standing by the fireplace, turns. "And I bet the town council is howling about it."

"An ice wielder killed a child this morning."

Oskar flinches. "Her own child?"

"No, but one in her care. I am having her brought here."

"She'll be lucky if she makes it in one piece," says Raimo. "People will need someone to blame for this catastrophe." He nods at me. "You will be lucky if they do not blame you."

"I am appearing in the square tonight. They need to hear my voice."

Oskar puts his arm around my waist. "It doesn't sound safe, Elli. If they riot . . ."

"They'll riot if their queen abandons them in their time of dire need," I say firmly. I look down at him. "Oskar. I know how to do this. I was raised to do this."

"You were raised to wield magic that never came to you," he says, his gray eyes fierce. "And without it you are vulnerable. I'll go with you tonight."

"As will I," says Raimo. "But first we need to see what we can do with Oskar's hand."

As he moves toward the table, he leans heavily on his walking stick, and his gnarled hands grip it tightly, the veins sticking out blue beneath spotted, papery skin. I tuck my arm under his and help him the rest of the way. "How are you feeling?"

"Like I've swallowed two dozen snakes."

I blink at him. "That sounds rather awful."

"The magic is unstable, Elli. And I think it's only going to get worse."

I find myself staring at Oskar's face, and his look does nothing to reassure me. "Are you feeling this way as well?"

He clears his throat. "The truth?"

"Oskar."

"Worse." He turns to gaze out the window, where the Motherlake undulates beneath the hazy sky. "Elli, I don't know how long I can hold on to it."

I bite my lip, because I feel like crying but I know I can't. It won't help anything. "What if I try to siphon some of the magic?"

"That might help."

And so I do, laying my palms on his cheeks and bowing my head over him as I pull his icy suffering into my own body, where it dances a gusty snowfall through my thoughts. My forehead touches his, and he sighs. "I could stay like this forever," he whispers.

"Me too."

"But we have other things to do," Raimo says. "Elli, that's enough. Let's see if we can work on his hand."

Reluctantly, I let go of Oskar, though I can still feel his cold power inside me. "Tell me what to do."

"You have to strike a perfect balance of the two extremes," says Raimo, moving in behind me. "And you have to direct it to just the right place."

I look down at Oskar's hand. It is bloodless and unmoving. "Does it hurt?" I ask him.

"Not right now."

"Will it hurt?" I ask Raimo.

He shrugs. "Would it be any worse than it is now?"

"Nothing is worse than this," says Oskar. "Please, Elli. For me."

I could never deny him. I hold out my palms over his hand as Raimo lays his own tremulous palms around my neck. Instantly, I feel the unsteadiness, the shocks of hot and cold. This is why Raimo doesn't want to heal him directly.

But as the two magics combine inside me, they settle and meld. I lean over Oskar's hand and focus on the gray veins beneath his skin. A living thing needs blood to quench its thirst, to feed it and cleanse it. Blood is the answer.

Oskar gasps and then clenches his teeth to hold in a moan. "Don't stop," he says, his lips barely moving. He is sweating now, glistening beads that freeze on his temples and forehead.

"Focus, Elli," Raimo snaps.

"Valtia!" a voice cries out from down the hall.

Oskar snatches his hand away with a stifled cry of pain.

"Did I hurt you?" I ask as he turns away. My fingers are dripping ice and fire, and I ball them into fists.

Oskar doesn't answer my question—he has gotten to his feet and is standing between me and the doorway. "Come any closer and I'll freeze you where you stand."

"Try," says a shaky, familiar voice.

I step from behind Oskar to see Sig leaning against the door frame, looking like he's been trampled by a herd of wild horses. His white-blond hair is standing on end, and his face is covered in scratches and scars. Ugly, weeping blisters trail across his forearms and bare chest, which shines with sweat that evaporates in steamy clouds as he walks forward.

Raimo hobbles over to stand on my other side. "Where have you been?"

Sig's brown eyes slide over the three of us. "Here and there. What you should be more interested in is who I've been with. I'll tell you if you fix me."

"Fix you," Raimo says.

Sig nods. He holds up his hands, palms lousy with more blisters and charred spots. His face twitches as he looks at them, either with pain or disgust. "I was gone from Kupari, but when I crossed the border . . ."

"Yesterday?" asks Oskar.

"Yes. Something started to happen with me." He glares at Raimo. "I need you to fix me. I feel as if I'm about to burn from the inside out."

"It's happening to all of us," says Oskar. "Every wielder in the land feels it."

"Not like this," says Sig, though he gives Oskar an appraising look. His gaze lands on Oskar's white hand. "But maybe like that."

"We think it's the copper," says Raimo. "The last of it was pulled from the earth a few weeks ago. And now the land is rebelling. I'm still searching for the way to calm it."

"Work fast," says Sig, "because you may have other problems."

"The Soturi?"

A small smile plays across Sig's scarred face. "Yes and no. This is where things get interesting. This is where I can help."

"Stop playing games," Oskar snaps. "Tell us what you know."

Sig's eyes meet mine. "The Valtia. I know who she is. I know where she is. And I can take you to her."

CHAPTER SEVEN

Ansa

I have no idea how long I've been holding my hands to the sky, letting the vast magic inside me shield us from the hell that pounds on us from above, but I ache to my very bones. Bertel and Preben have gathered the warriors and horses around me to ensure each is protected. The middle ring tends the animals, keeping them calm with blankets around their heads, their ears muffled against the sound of splintering wood and wailing wind, against the crackle of ice and fire. The outer ring has weapons drawn.

The inner ring does too. But they face me. I know this not because I see it, but because I feel it. I am a warrior too, and I know when a sword hangs over my head. If I lose control, one of them will drive a blade through my heart, and I will let it happen. There are moments when I believe that it would be a relief.

The cuff around my wrist does not hum right now. I believe it has what it wants at the moment—enough power to freeze the world solid and to burn it down, all at once. It spreads that magic like a shield over us, and with my watering eyes, I watch it battle the enemy for me.

Eventually, my arms begin to shake. My body begins to give out. My thoughts are ground like meal on a stone. Only instinct and duty keep me upright. I will remain here until magic of one kind or another devours me where I stand.

"Ansa," shouts Bertel. "It's stopped."

I open my eyes. He and Preben are poised on either side of me, but Preben's eyes are on the canopy as my magic flies upward and outward, meeting no resistance. I realize I can see the sky, stars smeared with smoke.

Night has fallen.

I let my arms drop to my sides as I inhale, calling the power back into my body. The cuff sends vibrations up my arm, as if in protest. But I push it aside—I have only one thought. "Has Thyra come back?" I crane my neck, trying to peer through the crowd around me, but I can't see past the horses.

Preben shakes his head. "And we should move camp. We're bait here."

"We can't move," I say. "We don't even know where we are or which direction to go, and she won't know how to find us."

"She's well able to track, and we're not exactly stealthy," says Bertel.

"I'm her war counselor," I say. "And I say we stay until she returns."

"Might be never," says Preben, wiping sweat from his weather-beaten brow.

Bertel looks down at the weapon in his hand, a short sword he has carried for years. "Maybe we should send a group after her."

"And how would they know where to go?" Preben asks. "She's one warrior, quicker than all of us, and unlikely to have left much of a trail." He shakes his head. "Better to let her find us than to send more warriors blundering off into the darkness."

As much as I hate what he's saying, I cannot disagree. Instead, I am opening my mouth to suggest that I go after her alone when my words are sliced away from me.

By an arrow. It punches into my arm in an explosion of searing agony, and as I stare down at it protruding from my shoulder, the shouts of the others engulf me. There is a strange, echoing detachment as I watch my fingers, dripping fire, close around the shaft of the enemy arrow. The pain is so intense that I cannot tell if it is magic or mortal; all I know is that it burns me. When I tear it from my body, my blood sprinkles my tunic, black and wet. There is chaos around me again, stomping horse hooves and scattering warriors seeking shelter from the arrows that now rain down.

But me, I am still and dazed, staring down at the arrow in my hand. I hold it close to my eyes. I do not recognize the markings on the shaft. It is not of Krigere make. Nor of

Vasterutian. Hatred boils inside me. It must be Kupari. The fraud-queen must have learned of our presence here, and now she is trying to crush us.

"Are you insane? Get to cover," shouts Bertel. He holds me under his arm like a bundle of blankets as he hauls me toward a thick cluster of trees behind which several other warriors have taken shelter. One, a stout woman named Tomine who bears kill marks along both arms and has silver hair she keeps cropped close to her head, has an arrowhead embedded deep in her thigh. She has broken off the shaft and is poised against a tangle of roots with her daggers drawn. Her face shines with sweat under moonlight when she looks to us for orders. I have the impulse to lean down and kiss her for wordlessly reminding me who we are.

"We're surrounded," Bertel says as he tears off a strip from his tunic and uses it to bind my bleeding arm. "They used the magic as cover so they could get into position, and we obligingly kept still and let it happen." His disgust bleeds through every word.

I am ashamed I didn't consider that. "It's not Jaspar, though." I hand him the arrow.

He glances at the markings on the shaft before handing the arrow to Greger, who is hunched next to Tomine but has his bow in his hand. "Send this back to them with a kiss," Bertel says to him.

"Would if I could figure out where they are," Greger says with a grunt, shoving the arrow into his quiver. "We've got it from all directions. This is bad."

Bertel touches my shoulder, but cautiously, like he might poke a snake to see whether it's dead or merely napping in the sun. "Can you do anything?"

The laugh comes out of me unbidden. He sounds as if he hates the idea. "I don't know." My hands tingle with magic, but my muscles ache with exhaustion. It's me who is tired, not the magic, and one look at Tomine, bleeding but ready to defend herself and the rest of us if necessary, tells me what to do about it. "Wait. Yes. Tell everyone to get down."

Bertel shouts the order and the call echoes in the wood as warriors pass it around, as we always do when scattered. The sound of Krigere battle calls stirs inside me. This is like a raid. And we will prevail as we always do. I breathe and breathe as I climb the cluster of roots, bringing myself into the open. But as I do, I summon the magic inside me and let the cuff devour it, growing it in the womb of those red runes carved into its surface. *Wind*, I think. A gale that no fiend could stand against.

I bring my hands up, fists clenched, my arms shaking, the wound in my left shoulder screaming. When I spread my fingers, the roar of my power makes my ears pop. I stand in silence as the earth moves around me, as the air is torn from my lungs. When my arms fall to my sides again, the sky is laid out above us, no longer obscured in any way by branches.

"You can see north," Bertel shouts, pointing to the winter star. "Make for it and stay close!"

Before I can think or object, our warriors are moving,

the ones at the front sending arrows flying ahead to cut down any enemies between them and the north, where Kupari lies.

"No," I bark as he drags me forward. "The arrows are of Kupari make! They could be waiting!"

"Would you rather us flee deeper into this hellish forest?" He has not slowed, and now the ground is shaking with the impact of boots and hooves. A less disciplined group would have been shredded by the last many hours, but our warriors do not fray. They carry the wounded who cannot walk, but thankfully there seem to be only one or two of those. Most are on their feet—even Tomine, who limps along just in front of me.

I am struggling to keep up. I try to steady myself, but the ground won't support my feet. Either my body is giving out, or—

"Another quake—" Greger gets those final two words out before he is crushed by a falling tree. It smashes to the ground not ten feet in front of me, sending Tomine falling backward onto me and Bertel. The touch of the ground to my back makes my spine feel like it's shattering piece by piece. I arch to get away from it but can't go far because a heavy body squirms on top of me.

Writhes, more like. Tomine's skin steams and smokes.

She rolls off me as the earth bucks and roars. I catch a glimpse of Bertel's horrified eyes and see fire in their depths. I cannot find the steadiness to rise, though. My entire being vibrates with the ground. Others seem able to keep moving, but I can't. The stench of smoke laces the air, and my stomach twists. "Fire," is the cry on the air.

It's not Tomine—she is being dragged away by Preben and Bertel, but she is not aflame. The forest is, though—our path to the north is now blocked by fire. "It wasn't me," I mutter, trying to get my eyes to focus, trying to get my feet beneath me. The ground settles abruptly, and I am finally able to rise.

"To the east, then," shouts Bertel, still supporting Tomine. I can see it all clearly now because the fire to the north is so bright and vicious. It rolls toward us at an unhurried but sure pace, confident of our destruction. Bertel throws me a rage-filled glare. "Try not to kill us before we find our chieftain again," he roars.

"I didn't do this!" I don't even know if he hears me. The fire is too loud, our horses are too loud, our warriors are too loud. *The east*, they all cry. *Hurry*.

I didn't create this fire. But someone did. Someone who does not want us to flee north.

"I'll find you again," I yell, but no one heeds me. They are one body, and I am not part of them right now. I can't be.

Because I know where Thyra is. She must be there, behind that curtain of fire. She must be. That is where the wielder is, or the army of them, and she would have found them by now. I turn toward the fire and hold out my hand, and the cuff channels a blast of icy wind that cuts through the flames. With my eyes narrowed against the stinging smoke, I run forward, hunched over. I am unsteady again, whether from the quake or the jittery, churning magic lodged inside me.

I scurry through the gap in the flames, keeping low, and dive into the pit left by a felled tree as soon as I am on the other side. Between me and the rest of the Krigere stretches a wall of fire, but it is moving away from me and toward them. It is too organized, too focused to be natural. Hidden in my hole, I peer into the night on this side. My windy blast to stop the arrows toppled several trees, but there are no bodies here, no fallen enemies, only churned earth. After a moment, I crawl upward and examine a patch of thick mud, where I find a set of boot prints, headed to the north.

After passing a few more minutes in silence, I decide to go hunting. Somewhere in this wood, there is a powerful magic wielder, maybe more than one. And my chieftain is also here, stalking this enemy. I make my way slowly, not because there is no urgency, but because I can't manage more than that. It's been hours since I last ate or rested, and in that time I have called upon my body time and time again, and I was already weak from the shakiness that has descended on me ever since we reached Kupari.

I try to shove the fear that this place hates me out of my head. Kupari is mine, or it is supposed to be. Surely I will find a home for all of us here.

Directly in front of me, there is a burst of fire, followed by another. My heart jolts. My hands curl into fists. I weave through the trees, most of which are upright now, saved from the devastating reach of my magic. The only light is the fire, but my skin is cooled by a cold wind. It blows from the north, the same direction as the flames, and I creep toward them—there's a clearing up there, and I have a feeling this is where I will find the enemy wielder, or wielders. It doesn't matter.

I'm going to kill them all.

I wish I could move faster. Usually I am swift and quiet in a wood. I know how to hunt prey. But ice and fire swirl angrily inside me, and my muscles tremble. Both betray me, forcing me to slow in order to avoid staggering right into the open. As I near the clearing where the magic plays in bursts of frozen cloud and balls of fire, I imagine what I might find.

And yet, somehow, I am still surprised.

Thyra is pinned down near the center of the clearing, behind a wall of dirt formed from east to west as the earth tore at its own flesh. She has her shoulders hiked up around her ears as her head swivels toward the north, the east, the west. The magic seems to come from everywhere, and she is pale and slender and so fragile as her skin is lit by the fire that rains down around her. She is shouting, but I can't make out the words.

The other side of the clearing—to the north—is concealed by the black wall of earth. So I peer toward the east, where fire flies out from the trees in a jagged burst of light. And in that moment, I find Sig, pale arms waving, his white-blond hair almost glowing as he flings fire at my chieftain. But as he does, ice bursts from the other side, to the west, and I turn to see a dark figure there, one arm held out, fingers spread.

In the moment Sig's fire explodes from the trees, the ice wielder is revealed by its light—tall, clad in furs, massive shoulders, a mess of dark hair and cold magic.

"Thyra," I call. She cowers as the ice and fire collide over her head. She doesn't hear me. Nor does she turn to Sig or the ice wielder, who may be his enemy or his friend. I don't care. My chieftain is in terrible danger. Rage smolders in my chest as I start to move forward, almost to the edge of the trees.

It gives me the perfect view of Thyra climbing from her shield of earth. Her movements are fast and sure, and I know her so well that I realize she's been waiting for this moment. She flings herself over the edge of the ground and runs forward, out of my sight as I stumble out from beneath the canopy of leaves. In front of me is the wall of dirt, and I must climb it to follow her. I stumble as my foot catches on a rock, and when I raise my head again I see an explosion over the other half of the clearing. Thyra screams.

The sound of it sends me running. I hold out my hands and send blasts of magic outward, not sure whether it's ice or fire but hoping it finds Sig and the ice wielder. I will consider why he might have betrayed us to the impostor queen later, but now I only want him dead for endangering Thyra. The magic thunders as I reach the earthen barrier and dig my toes in, grasping for rocks and clumps of grass as I climb. Panic pushes me upward. Why did Thyra leave the protection of this wall? What in heaven is she doing? Was she trying to flee?

My fingers close over a thick covering of grass and I pull myself over the edge and onto the tilted ground on the other side of the wall, then roll down a steep slope formed by the chaos of earth.

The magic has gone quiet. Only the moon lights the clearing. But when I see what it reveals, I am running and running and running, praying with each step that my eyes are telling me a terrible lie.

CHAPTER EIGHT

Elli

Sitting in Lahja's chambers because my own have been destroyed, I let Helka put the gold paint on my face, but not the white. If I wear the white paint, I won't be able to speak, because it would crack. The people are not used to hearing the voice of their queen, because she was always silent behind her mask. Yet another trick of the elders to silence and cage the Valtia. But those days are over, and today I wear only the gold around my eyes and the red on my lips. Helka seems to be of two minds about this. She insists on powdering my face to make it look paler, but then she smiles and says, "You look like she did. Beautiful."

Sofia, she means. I wonder what my Valtia would have thought about what I am doing. I think she would have approved.

Helka's fingers close over my shoulders as the earth begins to shake again. From the bedroom, I hear Lahja cry, and I am forced to blink away tears because I cannot go to her now. I cover Helka's hands with my own as I close my eyes and beg the stars for the quake to stop. Fortunately, like the others earlier today, this one is not so terrible. It's more of a reminder that our land is unhappy, sick, falling apart. It can't hold us up forever now that we've bled it near to death. Raimo has spent the afternoon and evening seeking answers from his texts, and tonight after my public appearance we will talk about what he has found.

When the shaking stops and I am ready, wearing the heavy dress and the copper-agate crown, I call for Lahja. I need to see that she is all right—she is staying in this place tonight with a cadre of guards instead of going with me to the square. After I let her kiss my hand, I stride down the hall and sit on my ceremonial paarit in the dusty chamber where the clammy, unsteady apprentices have used the afternoon to clear away debris. Raimo stands next to the bearers. He is my magic, though no one else knows it. He is clad in an elder's robe, the hood pulled over his face, so I can't see his expression. I frown when I see his hands tremble, though. He is still not well.

I am worried for more than his welfare—his unsteadiness reminds me of the plight of all the wielders. Oskar and Sig left hours ago to gather them and head to the Loputon. Sig insisted that the true Valtia was there, and that she needed help. She has no balance, and Raimo said this would make her more vulnerable and dangerous than even Sig and Oskar. Sig said she might be an ally if approached the right way, but that she is in the company of Soturi, to whom her loyalty is absolute—apparently they call themselves the Krigere, a brutal, ugly word in my opinion. He said they hope to make Kupari their new home.

I am not sure how I feel about that, having these barbarians on our land. Sig said they are not all bad, and that in fact some of them are quite good, but I'm not sure I trust him. After all, these are the people who stole our queen when she was still a little girl.

When Sig told us her name, both Oskar and I knew exactly who she was, and that is why Oskar insisted upon going with Sig to find her. Oskar could barely believe it—his cousin, Ansa, thought to be dead all these years. Now we know she was taken in the raid that killed her parents, and stars only know what they did to her after that. Somehow, though, they secured her allegiance. He said she is noble and brave—and in love with the Krigere chieftain, whom I also remember. Chieftain Thyra, the young woman who stood on the steps of the platform the night Sig burned Mim to ash. I remember being drawn to her, somber eyes set into such a fine-boned, serious face. She seemed more human and civilized than the rest. But she is still Soturi, and still a warrior, and still the enemy until I am convinced otherwise.

Sig said there is another threat too, because the tribe is split, and the rogue element has joined forces with Kauko.

None of this is good news, but if we have the Valtia on our side, we can destroy any enemy who attacks.

My mind is a maelstrom of calculation as I am lifted from the ground. One challenge at a time. When Sig and Oskar return with my Valtia, I know she will feel the bond with me and with Lahja. She will remember who she is, and she will know she must protect the Kupari over all others. Tonight, though, it's still up to me, and the enemy is our own fear.

I sit up straight and still when I am carried into the torch-lit plaza. My stomach tightens as I see the flames dancing over spills of shattered rock, as I feel the paarit wobble while my bearers try to carry me smoothly over crumbling stone stairs. As we walk between the broken gates to the city, people line the road. They are pinched and frightened, and their eyes fix on me with such fierce hope that it holds me up and lifts my chin. The weight of the crown on my head reminds me that it is my responsibility to lead them through this terrible time. And I will.

I raise my arms, and Raimo knows his cue. He brightens the torches in the square—they flare as I am carried into the center of the space. Normally I'd be on the platform, but it has been destroyed by the quakes. Still, I am held up by my bearers, so all can see me.

"People of Kupari," I say loudly as a hushed silence falls across the vast square. The townsfolk are shoulder to shoulder, crowded in, leaning forward. "Once again our strength is being tested. And once again we are going to prove to the stars and the land that we can endure the trial."

I stand. Raimo makes the torches flare again, but then they gutter and nearly go out. I glance to the side and see him leaning heavily on his stick. Fear is ice in my belly, and I feel it ripple through the souls in the square, drawing a few whimpers and cries.

"This morning a wielder killed a babe," shouts a gray-bearded man who stands near my paarit. "She claims she couldn't control it and blamed the quake. Are you also affected?"

"No," I say quickly. "My magic is as it always has been."

"Prove it," shouts a woman on my other side.

"No." This time my voice is hard. "I will use the magic as I always do—to protect all of you. I will not use it to prove myself to a people who should know better."

Inside, I tremble. But I know how to be confident when I am cowering inside. I look over my people with love.

I find terror looking back at me.

"The wielders of the temple will continue to help with rescue and rebuilding," I tell all of them.

"What if we don't want their help?" cries a young man who has a scythe propped on his shoulder. It's not harvest season—I can only think he has brought it as a weapon.

Grumbles of agreement roll like a wave through the square. "Wielders are dangerous! They belong in the temple!"

"Wielders are citizens," I say, my voice ringing over the complaints. "They have the same freedom anyone else has."

"Not if they kill our children," comes a hoarse shout. It comes from Yrian, who is standing on a pile of rocks near the start of the Lantinen road. "My son is dead because of this woman!" He points a thick finger at a doorway to his right, and a limp form is dragged through it while others press out of the way.

"I asked for the wielder to be brought to the temple." I don't say it loudly, but my eyes find Topias, who does not meet my gaze. I look at Agata next, and she stares boldly at me until the torch nearest her grows huge and bright. She flinches, and Raimo lets out a grunt of satisfaction.

"Her crime is too great to go without punishment," Yrian roars, and the men who have Ivette shake her, then toss her to the ground in the space that has cleared in front of my paarit.

While the people around her back away or jeer, Ivette lifts her head to look at me. "My Valtia," she says. Her face is bruised and her lip is split. "I am so sorry."

"Punish her," comes a shout from the crowd. Others clap and cheer. "She killed a baby!"

"I didn't mean to," she shrieks. "I would have protected him with my life!"

"Liar," shouts Yrian. "You used your magic to end that life!"

"Wielders can't be trusted," a woman shouts. "None of them!"

The crowd encircles Ivette, and she covers her head as the first stone hits her.

"Enough," I say, raising my arms. A gust of murderously icy wind blows over the square, and my people collectively cringe away from me—and the terrified ice wielder at my feet. Raimo's knuckles are white as they clutch his stick, and I know it is taking all his power and control to wield the magic he usually uses so effortlessly.

If we don't get out of this square soon, several very bad things could happen.

"Guards," I say, sharp and sure. "Take the ice wielder to the temple." I glare at Agata when she opens her mouth to protest. "If we are divided as a people we *will* fall," I shout to the crowd. "You may meet as citizens and discuss whether you would like the benefit of magic as you try to protect yourselves from the Soturi. But rest assured—if you turn on your own neighbors, if you deny them justice, then you will be weakened."

"We demand justice," calls Yrian. "You deny it to us, Valtia!"

"No—the temple will pay for the life of your son in bars of copper, and you have my grief alongside your own, because I know there are not enough riches in our stores or all the world to dry your tears."

Yrian gives me a searching look. I know he wants to believe—like everyone in Kupari, he has been taught to have faith in the goodness and power of his queen, and I am relying on that now. Others are clearly awaiting his response, because there is silence in the square again except for Ivette's terrified sobs.

After a long, tense moment, Yrian nods. Raimo's shoulders sag, and I realize he was ready to clear a path for us to leave the square by force if he had to. My guards rush forward and haul Ivette from the ground. One of them hoists her into his arms because she seems unable to walk.

"I will wait to hear if you will accept the help of the temple in rebuilding," I say. "Council, I will meet with you in the morning. We have things to discuss." I let the last word come out of me in a hiss, a selfish indulgence that doesn't completely quell my anger at them. Instead of working with me, they are letting old prejudices drive their actions. I want to shake each and every one of them.

"Remember that we are one people," I shout across the square. "Remember that, or we will fall, and my magic will never be enough to protect you. It requires your loyalty to survive."

My words seem to strike many of them right in the heart. I see many nods, but many heads remain still, bearing eyes that gaze upon me with a new kind of chill. I feel every icy stare as I am carried from the square.

I have won the life of Ivette. I have forged a very temporary peace.

But I am afraid I am losing my people in the process.

When we arrive back at the temple, I call on Kaisa to take care of Ivette. The woman is insensible with fear, and she has no idea how to control her power. Raimo tells Kaisa to mix up a sleeping draught to calm her down, because she nearly freezes the blood of the guard who carried her from the square in her reluctance to let him go.

"I didn't know," she says, sobbing. "I didn't know it would happen."

Her magic is not the only thing preying on her mind—

today she ended the life of a child. My throat is tight with sorrow as I watch Kaisa lead her to the apprentice quarters, which remain standing even after the quake, being on the east side of the temple like the quarters of the Saadella. My Valtia chambers are impassable, and that wing has been abandoned.

Raimo sees me looking with longing toward my sanctuary. "The entire temple will collapse if we have another bad quake, and it's only a matter of time." He hobbles in the direction of the library, and I walk by his side.

"Do you have any answers for me?" I ask.

He gives me a sidelong glance. "I'm still seeking them."

There is something in his voice. Hesitation. "But you did find something."

"I am one old man. One mind. And I am staggeringly stupid in the face of all the secrets of this land and the magic it nurtures."

We have reached the library, where I see that the scrolls have been neatly stacked on a table in the center of the room. A star chart is laid out on the only remaining flat surface. I recognize it. "That's the prophecy. The one that predicts how the Suurin will join the Astia and save Kupari when all hope is lost."

Raimo stands over the chart. He's so stooped that a few wisps of his scraggly beard brush its surface. "I'm not sure about anything yet."

"But you have some idea, and you think you're right." I stand close, watching the twitchy movement of his fingers over the parchment.

"Elli, you must prepare yourself for what's coming."

"You've been saying that since we first met, and truly, that's all I've been doing! I'm not sure there's anything I can't face at this point. Haven't I proved that?"

His hand crumples the parchment in one violent movement, and he tosses the ruined prophecy to the floor. "I have never understood why the stars are so cruel to those who are so young. Why can't they come for those like me who have earned their ire?"

"Does it predict my death? Because I am ready for that. I have been ready since I was chosen. You know that."

He turns to me. "No, it does not predict your death. Which doesn't mean you won't die, only that it hasn't been foretold by the stars."

I am ashamed of the loosening of my muscles at that news. "And Lahja?" Because if she dies, I will die too. We are linked so tightly, my heart and spirit to hers, whether I have magic to give her or not. That little girl is mine.

"No. The Saadella is not even a part of this. For all I know, the magic will pass to her and the line will continue—if the land continues to exist. But, Elli, that's the problem. I can't see past what is happening now. *No* prophecy exists that tells of a time that is far in the future, though we used to have predictions that spanned for years. The elders must have realized it—I've read every chart, every prophecy, and all have come to pass. They knew what they were doing. And there is nothing past this season. Past now."

I feel as if my bones have turned soft, and hold the table for support. "You can't be predicting that this is the end of Kupari. Why wouldn't you have mentioned this before now?"

"Because there is hope! In war, and in the winning of it, there is hope. And I foresaw a battle, one fought by the Suurin and the Astia against a terrible force."

"A force."

His mouth twists. "I assumed a human force. An army."

"And now you think it's this. The land falling apart."

"It could be both, for all I know."

"The Suurin and I will face it, then. Sig has returned to us. That has to be a good sign, doesn't it?"

"You're a child," he says quietly. "You are just a child. So is Oskar. So is Sig."

"All of us are children compared to you." I try to lighten my voice and earn a smile, because the way he looks right now is terrifying me.

What I receive instead is the shine of tears in his eyes, and that is the most frightening thing of all. "Now you will tell me everything," I say. "Enough with evasion. If I am to face it, take off my blindfold and let me *see*."

"Knowing changes nothing. It only adds to your burden."

"And it should be my choice!" Now I am the one who is shaky.

"Elli, you know the truth already." His eyes meet mine, and it feels as if the ground has dropped from under me.

"Oskar, you mean."

"Sig, too."

"You believe they will not survive the battle." Yes, I knew this. Yes, I have known for some time. And yes, I have refused to think about it too much, because the thought of losing Oskar makes me want to curl in on myself around the gash in my heart and the loss of a future I have built in my dreams. Where there used to be nothing but darkness, there is now an empire of hope.

It looks like this: If we found the Valtia, and if she could rule . . . what would stop Oskar and me from being together? With me to siphon his magic and keep him well, what would stop us from having a life?

I bow my head as a tear rolls down my cheek. "You could be wrong."

"I could be."

"Tell me how you think it happens."

"I don't know yet."

"Are you lying again?"

With an impatient sigh, he crosses the room and stoops to pick up the discarded parchment. "You want to try to make sense of this?" he says. "Go ahead." He tosses it onto the table. "I can take no more tonight."

"That's too bad," I say, my voice turning hard. "I need you to help me decide what to do. Do you think the quakes are happening because the copper has been drained from the earth?"

"I think it very likely."

"Then I want us to put it back. We can melt it and let it flow back into the veins of the earth."

"Elli, there is nothing in that prophecy about—"

"I don't care!" I flinch at the shrill sound of my own voice and close my eyes. After a slow, careful breath, I continue. "In the catacombs, under the sections that have collapsed, lies a huge portion of the copper we have pulled from the land. We could use that. We can also gather it from the townspeople—"

"Ha! It doesn't take a prophecy to know that you'll have a full-scale revolt on your hands if you try. You may even if you don't."

A rare kind of rage has sparked in my chest, searing me with its heat. "So what shall we do? You think I should just toss Sig and Oskar into a hole instead? Are their lives so cheap?"

Raimo is very still. "I never said their lives were cheap. But this problem? It comes with a very steep cost."

"Forgive me if I'd rather offer it all my wealth instead of casually discarding the lives of the Suurin!" I am pacing now, because otherwise I think I might burst into flames on the spot. My skin feels flushed, feverish. "Besides, if the Soturi attack us, I cannot hold them back on my own! I need Oskar and Sig if we want to have any hope of protecting our people."

I hold up my hands, one whole, one scarred, both shaking with frustration. Over the last few months I have grown resigned to my utter lack of magic, and it does not ache the way it used to. But now that grief is on me full force—without other wielders, I am nothing. I am ordinary and weak and powerless.

"You're right, of course," Raimo admits. "And if Sig is correct, there's a large force of Soturi out there, aligned with Kauko. If that's true, then they will surely come for us, because the elder thirsts for the throne of Kupari even more than he thirsts for the blood of wielders. He'll use anyone and any trick to regain it." Raimo leans on his stick. "The war could be just that. An actual war."

"And the land? Could giving it back its riches pacify it?"

He looks into my eyes. "There is nothing in any prophecy that suggests otherwise, but there is nothing to support the idea, either."

I glance at the copper lacing the walls, the ends of the scrolls, the knobs of the doors, the thread in my dress, the heavy crown on my head. I reach up and pull out the pins that hold it in place, then lift it from my hair. "The land is hungry," I say. "And in our greed, we've starved it. We must feed it again."

Raimo watches me lay the crown atop the crumpled parchment. "This will make you a most unpopular queen."

"Better to be the unpopular queen of a living people than to rule over a dead realm."

Raimo's brow furrows and he tilts his head. "You . . ." He chuckles weakly. "The Astia with a will of iron, as foretold by the stars. Right again. Always right. It's a curse, I suppose." He is still cackling as he shuffles from the room.

I can't follow. My eyes have filled with tears again.

Those words should make me feel better. Proud and ready to face the future. But instead, all I feel is dread.

CHAPTER NINE

Ansa

My racing footsteps carry me across a clearing glittering with ice and scarred by fire. It is a battlefield of magic, and it has claimed its prize. On the air, there's a familiar scent, one that fills my mouth with sour bile. I swallow it back and run to the figure lying on a patch of blackened grass. I am heedless to any danger, but none stalks me. The night only carries one sound.

Thyra is gasping for breath.

I fall to my knees as soon as I reach her, but I don't know where to touch her. Her left side is burned, blistered, and charred, half her hair gone, half her face as well. Her other side is white with frost, though some of it has begun to melt. One eye is swollen shut with burns, the other is open and frozen and blind.

A sob escapes my mouth.

"Ansa," she whispers when she hears, a ragged, barely there sound.

"I'm here." I touch her chest, over her armor.

"Hold me?"

"Anything." I lie down next to her, my face soaked with tears. I gently stroke the cold skin of her right cheek. A million thoughts are trying to crowd into my skull, but there's no room. There's only her.

"Thought I could catch . . ." Her lips are stiff, mangling her words.

"I'm sure you would have. And we will, as soon as you're better."

"Blind," she whispers, and I hear the fear in her voice.

"I'll be your eyes."

Her breath rattles. "Can't move." Her dagger lies melted by her scorched right hand.

"I'll be your arms and legs."

"Ansa." It's a plea, and I feel it close like a fist around my heart.

"I'm always that. And always yours." I swipe my cheek against my shoulder to dry the tears, then press it to hers. "I'll keep you warm too."

"Don't let me go."

"I could never. Even if you asked me to."

Her open blue eye stares at the sky, though I know she sees nothing. "You must lead them now."

"No, you'll do that. You're the chieftain."

"Please, Ansa. Promise."

"I'll carry you," I tell her, sorrow nearly strangling me. "I'll heft you on my back. I'm strong enough. And I'll feed you. I'll hold you at night. I'll be your voice. I'll—"

"Promise."

"Please don't make me." Because if I do . . .

"Ansa," she says, her voice merely a rasp. "Do this for me. And then I can go with peace in my heart."

"I won't let you go, though. You're going to stay with me, and we're going to live through this together. And then we'll make our new home, and I'm going to sleep next to you every night. We're going to love each other until we're old, and I don't care that we're both warriors, because I'll kill anyone who objects. You're mine. You've always been mine, and I'm yours. That's how it is." I touch my forehead to hers. "And you have to be here for that to happen."

"Wish I could," Thyra says. "Because you . . . always made me . . . feel alive."

It takes her way too long to say those words, and they seem to steal all her air. The sound of her last battle with her own body slices the selfishness right out of me. "All right, I promise," I say. "If I must carve a border with my bare hands, if I have to kill every single Kupari, if I have to offer my own life in exchange—I will make a new home for our warriors. They will sleep safe with their families and raise their babies to dominate this earth. Blood and victory, always."

Her mouth twitches, and I think she is trying to smile. "Blood and victory, my sister. My love."

My love. Words I have craved for so long. And they are the last she ever says. Thyra's spirit slips free of her destroyed body as I kiss her lips. I swear I feel it brush past me in its fierce flight to the eternal battlefield, to join her father and sister and Sander and all our valiant warriors who died before her.

Leaving me looking down at her body. Her *body*.

I stare at Thyra, the anchor of my future. The chain that binds our hearts has been torn away, taking a bloody chunk of me with it.

In the empty, desolate space left behind burns an icy fire that roars through my veins and muscles, seeking freedom. The magic. I hate it. I hate where it has brought us. I hate what it is and what I am and she is gone and there is *nothing* left. Dimly, a promise echoes in my bleeding mind, but then it flies the way of her spirit and is gone.

When the pain is more than I can bear, I throw my head back and scream it to the heavens, past caring who or what I destroy, including myself. As if it shares my grief, the earth shudders and then explodes with fury.

I welcome it as it swallows me whole, offering the relief of quiet, black death.

When the pain comes back, I know mercy is not mine to have in this life. We were always taught neither to expect it nor offer it, but I was still desperate enough to welcome it when it kissed my cheek. And desperate enough to cry, as I do now, when I realize I was foolish to think I could hold on to that mercy of death, to think it would stay at my side.

Like Thyra.

The memory of her charred and frozen face flickers in my mind before it goes dark again, extinguished by hurt. It's all I'm made of now.

"I think she's waking."

I go still at the sound of a female voice nearby. I *recognize* it. While the thick fog of confusion still swirls in my skull, my ears collect the clank of iron, the snuffling of horses, the low rumble of conversation. I work to open my eyes, but they are crusted over. When I try to reach up to scrape the remnants of my grief and sorrow away, I find I cannot.

My wrists are shackled.

A warm, wet cloth is pressed over my eyes. "This will help," says an accented male voice. Another I recognize, one that sends a cold drop of horror down my throat and into my belly.

Kauko. I try to say it, but my throat is so tender and swollen, my lips so cracked and dry, that I am mute. The cloth slides across my cheeks, and my eyes open to the view of the leafy canopy above me, slits of sunlight peeking through. The elder leans over me, his thick lips pulled into a gentle smile. "The earth tried to swallow you, but Jaspar reached you just in time."

I glance down at myself. I am wearing an overlarge tunic and loose breeches. My feet are encased in warm stockings. But my ankles and wrists are chained to the cot on which I'm lying, at the base of a towering oak. A sweep of my eyes around me reveals a sprawling camp. Carina, whose voice I heard earlier, is poking at the contents of a stew pot over a fire.

I have been found by the rebel warriors. And that means . . .

"It's for your own safety, Ansa," Jaspar says as I start to struggle against the restraints. The traitor moves to Kauko's side, and I take in the face I used to think was one of the more handsome I'd ever beheld. Now his cheeks are hollower than they were several weeks ago. But he still looks strong. And dangerous. Hatred for him burns inside me, the flames of my magic awakening from their slumber.

"You," I try to say. *You wanted her dead. And now she is.*

His brow furrows. "Don't do this to yourself again," he pleads.

Kauko leans close. "So many burns. I have healed you many times already."

Thyra is dead. I don't care if I'm reduced to ash on the wind.

His hands float over my body, palms down, and another hard shock rolls through me. He is wearing the cuff of Astia. Fear and rage singe my lungs, and I gasp with the agony.

"More of the sleeping draught," Jaspar yells to Carina, his voice rising with urgency.

I wish for fire. I wish for the world to burn.

Frigid magic flows hard from Kauko's hands as pain devours me. Without the cuff, the magic inside me is not controllable. But worse than that, I'm so weak that I can't even raise my head. It's not just the chains that hold me to this cot. It feels as if I'm held here by a thick blanket of sand, heavy and impossible to fight. I've never felt this powerless.

My eyes meet those of the elder. "You are safe," he says.

"Liar!" It bursts from me like the screech of a crow. Sparks fly from my mouth. I'm going to kill them all. I don't care if I die too. I want to be dead. I want this pain to end.

Thyra's gone. She's gone, gone, gone, and without her I am no longer a wolf—I am a storm, and I must rage and then fall apart. There is no reason to go on.

Promise, Thyra whispers in my mind. *You promised.*

"No," I say with a moan as Carina comes over with a wineskin. Jaspar takes it from her, his fingers straying over hers in an overfond way, and presses it to my parched lips.

"Ansa, I know you're confused and hurt, but you must believe me—you're safe, and among Krigere." Jaspar strokes my jaw and tries to coax my mouth open, but I grit my teeth and turn my face away. My skin crackles with hurt as my magic bursts through in blisters and the bite of frost. Kauko is muttering to himself as he holds his hands over my body, probably trying to counteract the curse inside me, which is uncontrollable because *he has stolen what is mine*.

Everything that is mine has been stolen. A harsh scream is all I have left to offer the world. But as my mouth opens, Jaspar moves like a snake and pours the pungent liquid from the wineskin right down my throat. I cough and choke on it, then swallow reflexively, unable to stop my body from trying to keep breathing and living. I writhe, but it is a feeble effort. I spit at Jaspar, but it only results in a dribble of saliva down my cheek that he gently wipes away. His eyes are full of pity and concern, and I want to melt his skin right off his face.

"Get back," says Kauko before he continues muttering. "Her magic is still so strong."

Jaspar steps away from me, the wineskin dangling from his fist. "We won't abandon you, Ansa. You're not alone. I'm going to keep saying it until you believe me."

Dizziness steals over me, and I close my eyes against the feeling that I'm falling down a deep hole.

"She will rest now," I hear Kauko say. "Much safer."

I imagine a spear of ice piercing his heart, and I feel the cold inside me start to rise up before it is swallowed by a wave of heavy warmth. I don't know if it's coming from him or me, but I'm drowning in it, too tired to swim. My tense muscles go loose. Darkness pours into my burning thoughts, extinguishing the flames. I try to hold on to my understanding of where I am—an enemy camp, tied up and helpless, my one ally on the wrist of a man who once drank my blood, my one love dead and gone, but nothing makes sense, and I am having trouble summoning anything but numbness.

Finally, I surrender, and sleep claims its victory.

CHAPTER TEN

Elli

"What you are suggesting is nothing short of madness!" Topias paces in front of the wooden table that my attendants carried from the damaged temple this morning. His soft leather boots squish through the muddy grass just outside the menagerie fence, where we have erected a canopy to shade us from the sun. After last night's quake, it seems too dangerous to have the city's leaders gather under a roof that could collapse on us all.

Right now, though, I cannot help the wicked wish that a clump of broken brick would hit this stubborn, shortsighted man right on the top of his velvet-covered head. "Think about this, please," I say, looking from him to Agata to the rest of the assembled council, who all wear identical looks of horror. "We were informed that our last copper mine had been emptied out only a few weeks ago, and suddenly our entire peninsula, which has lain still as a corpse for centuries, is crumbling into the Motherlake. How can this be a coincidence?"

"Our written history does not extend so far, and the land was here long before we made it our home," says Agata, sounding as if she is lecturing a child.

I press down my anger. "Although that is true, we must agree—when you hollow out a mound of earth, it is more prone to collapse. We have emptied the veins of Kupari. Why are we pretending that has nothing to do with its illness?"

"That is a theory and nothing more. You have no proof."

I stand, unable to sit quietly anymore. The council goes still, perhaps afraid I will strike them with my magic. If only they knew.

I'm so glad they don't.

I tuck my hands into the silk folds of my skirt to show I mean no harm. "We must do something," I tell them. "How can we look our citizens in the eye if we sit back and do nothing while they lose everything, including their lives? If Kupari falls under my rule, it will not be because I did not try to save it."

"But your proposal will destroy us too! You ask us to pour our wealth into a grave. How will we survive without our copper? We'll be peasants—starving peasants at that."

I look out on the Motherlake, easily visible from this lakeside plateau that was long ago built for the temple's gardens and menagerie. "The soil is rich. We can save enough copper to trade with Ylpeys for seed if we need to. We can—"

Agata snorts. "And that's it? What will the people do when they have no coins to purchase things they need?"

"They can trade with each other! Is having coin more important than breathing?"

"You make it sound so certain that sacrificing all our wealth is the answer. But you've already admitted you don't actually know." Topias snatches his cap from his head and runs his hand over the few strands of hair that were hiding underneath. "I for one cannot support this."

"Nor can I," says Agata. "You've already sheltered a known murderer. And now you want to demand people give you all their hard-earned wealth so you can toss it into a hole. I cannot stand by you any longer, Valtia. I am sorry."

She doesn't look sorry. A few others do, but it doesn't stop them from murmuring their agreement with her betrayal.

"So you all feel this way. You are against me now?" I wish I could slow the frantic beating of my heart as my thoughts whirl with words. I need to figure out which ones will win them back, because if they speak against me, it will only enflame people's doubts. They're already scared enough as their homes collapse and rumors about imminent Soturi invasion persist. I was hailed as a hero for driving the elders and priests from the temple, but now I know they wonder if things should have remained as they had been. If the council speaks against me, that could be the final weight that collapses my roof.

"What if . . ." I secure Agata's skeptical gaze. "What if the temple sets an example? Our stores are buried in rock, but with help, we could unearth it. What if we were to use that as an offering to the land? Surely, if I am right, it will at least lessen the intensity of the quakes. If that happens, you will know the missing copper was the problem. And if it doesn't end the quakes, then we can ask the people for more. The temple will assume the risk and sacrifice. I will toss my own crown into the ground if that will make it happy."

Topias slides his cap back on and straightens his copper council medal. He exchanges glances with Agata, and she shrugs. "We do not control the temple coffers—only the city treasury," he says. "If you wish to toss away your copper, we cannot stop you."

"But don't expect us to pay for your fancy dresses once you are a pauper," Agata says.

I walk slowly toward her, enjoying that I am a little taller than she is. "All the Valtias before me died protecting the Kupari people. I would happily do the same, and perhaps someday I will. You think I am worried about what I'll be wearing when that happens?"

Agata has the good grace to look away from me, her cheeks a dusky pink. But she doesn't take back what she said.

I turn and look upon the other council members. Many of them have not changed their clothes since the last time I saw them. "Very well," I say. "We must dig up the temple's copper and sacrifice it to the earth. I pray to the stars that it is enough."

Topias bows his head. "We all do, my Valtia."

Of course they do. It would mean they wouldn't have to sacrifice anything themselves.

"I am grateful for your support," I say, unable to completely rinse the acid from my tone. "Please gather a group of strong citizens who might be willing to help unblock the caved-in passages inside the catacombs so that we may bring the copper to the surface and melt it."

Agata folds her arms over her chest. "The copper is already buried and we're still having quakes, but you think digging it up and burying it again is the way to fix things?" She snorts.

Some of the others have wide eyes at the sound of her disrespect. "I can offer two of my stone crews," says Livius, a tall man who is known for constructing some of the finest houses within the city wall. "That's twenty men."

"They're needed to clear debris from the roads," Agata says.

Livius stares her down. "And they will return to that task once they do the Valtia's bidding."

"I'm grateful for your loyalty, Livius," I say.

He nods at me but does not return my smile. "I just hope you're right about this."

"I am." *Oh, stars. If I'm not, what will happen?* I smile serenely, though I am anything but. "You'll see."

"How long will this take?" asks Topias.

"My men can give an assessment once they take a look at the collapsed tunnels. But they work pretty fast."

"Good," Topias replies. "Because there are rumors of Soturi in the Loputon. It's all over the city this morning."

My stomach drops. "If they've crossed the border, they will feel the quakes just as surely as we do. Perhaps it will slow any advance."

"Perhaps," says Topias. "It would be the only good thing about the tremors. More wielders have lost control of their magic, Valtia. I didn't want to bring it up, but . . ."

I am opening my mouth to assure him the temple will take them in, but that is when Kaisa comes running along the menagerie fence, her cheeks red with exertion. "Valtia, I've been sent for you. There's news."

"What is it?" says Agata.

I blink at her. "It is *temple* business." Does she suddenly think she rules this place? "Please excuse me," I say to the council. "We can meet again tomorrow, but I believe we are all aware of the plan for now." I try not to run as I follow Kaisa away from the ears of the council. But as soon as we are out of hearing distance, I grasp the sleeve of her robe and pull her to a halt. "Do we have word from Oskar and Sig? Do they have the Valtia? Are they here?"

Kaisa grimaces. "They are in the woods south of the city," she says. "They've sent word."

My stomach drops. "Why didn't they come themselves?"

"I'm not sure they can," she says softly.

That strips away any remaining restraint I had. I lift my

skirts and run for the rear entrance of the temple, where cracks radiate outward from the arch along the stone wall. I leap over fallen stones and sneeze as I inhale the dust, but I don't slow until I reach the domed chamber. There waits a familiar figure, tall and thin. It's Veikko, an ice wielder and a friend of Oskar's. He looks pale as he stands next to Raimo, towering over the older man. I hold out my hands as I approach, and Veikko drops to his knees and kisses my knuckles before rising once more. "I bring word from the Suurin," he says.

I glance at Raimo, trying to get a hint at whether he knows what I am about to hear. He is staring at a point a few inches in front of my feet. I swallow back fear and return my attention to Veikko. "Tell me."

"They're alive."

I put my hand on my stomach. "You have to do better than that."

He gives me a pained look. "Something happened in the Loputon last night. Just before the most recent quake. A group of us were traveling south after Oskar rode past our camp and let us know where he was going. Our mounts were tired—we couldn't follow at their pace. And many were shocked to see that Sig—"

"He was taken by Kauko, but he returned with knowledge of the Soturi."

Veikko nods slowly. "Oskar did say that he and Sig were hopeful some kind of peace could be negotiated."

That was the story we agreed Oskar would share. To tell

everyone they were going in search of the true Valtia would only cause fear and possibly panic—because in that case, who am I? Even the cave-dwelling wielders believe I am the true queen. Until we have a good replacement, I must fill the spot.

"And did they say whether they succeeded?" My voice is sharp. Desperate. If Veikko is not bringing word that they found her, where is she?

Veikko shook his head. "We found Oskar and Sig just inside the forest after the quake. Thus far they haven't been able to tell us what happened to them. But—" Veikko winces.

"They're injured," Raimo says in a hollow voice. "And it's bad, isn't it?"

"Yes," Veikko says. "We carried them to the camp where Maarika could take care of them. But we didn't think it safe to bring them into the city in such a vulnerable state." Now he looks angry. "We've heard stories of citizens throwing rocks at wielders. Threatening them with scythes. If not for my love for Oskar, I wouldn't be here myself." He pulls his cloak more tightly around him.

"I'm grateful for that love," I say. "And I know Oskar is too."

"Can you help him?" Veikko asks. "I know you have before."

But that was just when Oskar needed me to siphon his excess magic, not when he was actually hurt. I give Raimo a desperate look. Our first attempt to heal Oskar's dead hand didn't work, but I can't abandon him now. I could never abandon him. "Of course I'll help him."

Raimo looks conflicted. I lean forward and look him in the eye. "We need the Suurin," I remind him quietly.

"I know," he mutters. "The timing couldn't be worse, though. If anyone hears that the Valtia is leaving the city when the people are in such desperate need . . ."

"They won't know," I tell him. "We'll go help them, and then we'll return, and in the meantime Kaisa and Helka and the others will help preserve the illusion of my presence in the temple."

"What of the Saadella?"

I close my eyes. I hate leaving her unprotected, but taking her with me into the outlands—putting her even closer to the Soturi if they truly are in the Loputon—seems even riskier. And she is our future. "Her guards are loyal to her and will protect her with their lives, and besides, I do not think the people would hurt the Saadella. She is sacred."

"Nothing is sacred these days," says Raimo. "Look at how they treat *you*."

But I am not the Valtia. I'd say it aloud if Veikko weren't standing next to me. "They're scared. I don't blame them. This is a problem magic can't fix."

"I'm not sure," Raimo mutters.

"What?"

He leans heavily on his staff. "I'm still searching the texts. I found Kauko's private library—it was revealed last night when the wall in his old chamber collapsed."

My heart leaps. "So there might be a magical solution?" If we do find the Valtia, she could be the key to healing our land. She's the key to everything.

Raimo doesn't look as hopeful or happy as I feel. But he merely shakes his head. "One thing at a time. Let's go see what we can do for the Suurin—and perhaps get them to tell us what's happened."

Energized with possibility, I pace while my attendants quickly and quietly prepare three fresh horses. I am given an old priest's robes while Raimo instructs Kaisa and the other temple dwellers on what to do in our absence. We don't plan to be gone long. With any luck, we'll have Sig and Oskar back on their feet quickly and will return to the temple together. They can easily defend themselves if they are well.

As soon as the sun sets, we sneak out a side entrance of the temple and then follow Veikko through narrow, rain-rutted streets. Some of them are blocked with collapsed buildings, but no one is better at sneaking in and out of the city than Veikko—except Sig, of course. We lead our horses through a breach in the city wall and ride into the wood, and the moon is still high when I inhale the scent of smoke and know we're nearing a camp. We pass several uprooted trees, torn from the ground by the shaking and twisting of the earth. Veikko explains that the cave dwellers are in this small forest now, seeking shelter under trees. A cavern collapse could kill so many, but it seems the wielders in the outlands have fared slightly better than the city dwellers, because they don't sleep within stone walls, under stout timbers and slate shingles.

Finally, when my nerves can take no more, we sight the distant glow of campfires. I grip my horse's mane and urge it on.

As we reach the edge of camp, I take in the pinched faces. All of them look shaken and tired. It reminds me of the toll the unsteadiness in the land has taken. We dismount and Veikko leads us through the tangle of people around the central fire. The closer we get, the more familiar faces I see, and when I see Maarika, her face shining with sweat and her eyes haunted, a lump forms in my throat. She opens her arms and I walk into them.

"How is he?" I ask. "Where are they?"

She jerks her head toward a lean-to on the other side of the fire. "I've done my best for them, but . . ." She lets out a choked sound.

I feel like I'm going to be sick, but I focus on being steady and calm as I peel myself away from her. "Take us to them."

Veikko goes to stand by some of the other young wielders, including Aira, a fire wielder who used to be in love with Oskar. For all I know she still might be, but she has let any enmity between us die in the fire of common purpose, and has been a good ally for Oskar as he recruits wielders to defend Kupari. I nod my respect to her as we rush past, and she does the same.

I brace myself as Maarika pulls aside the blanket that serves as the lean-to's entryway, but it still doesn't prepare me for what awaits inside. Raimo curses as he sees our Suurin, our sword and shield in the great prophesied battle. They lie side by side, nearly touching.

"It was the only way to keep Sig cool and Oskar warm. Otherwise I think they would both be dead," says Freya, Oskar's younger sister. She rises from her position at Oskar's side, where she was mopping his frostbitten brow. I enfold her slender body in a hug. It is hard to let go. I feel like I need someone to hold me up.

Oskar and Sig look as if they both walk the tightrope that spans life and death. Burns, from fire, from ice, cover their faces and exposed skin.

"Are they asleep?" I ask. Both lie so still.

"No," Oskar whispers, his eyes opening just a crack. "Elli."

Tears start in my eyes as I sink down at his side. "I'm here, my love. I'm right here." I touch his chest, the least damaged part of him.

Sig's brown eyes also open, and they look me and Oskar over before falling shut again. He doesn't say a word.

"We need to know what happened," says Raimo. He looks at Freya and Maarika. "We must have privacy."

Oskar's family looks aggrieved, but they obey when he nods. "It's important," he says in a strained whisper.

Once they are gone, Raimo and I lean close, because it seems to hurt the Suurin to speak.

"We tried to reach the Valtia," Sig says. "But . . ."

"There are Soturi in the woods." Oskar sounds so tired.

His eyes are closed again. It hurts me to look at his face. Half his beard has been burned away.

"We knew that," says Raimo. "Isn't the Valtia with them?"

"Two groups," says Sig. "It was chaos. And then Kauko and some of his protectors ran through a clearing."

Oskar sighs. "We thought we could destroy him. But he has gotten *much* stronger." He moans as Raimo examines an oozing wound on his thigh.

"Because he drank the blood of the Valtia," says Raimo, sounding disgusted.

Sig nods, then grimaces, then lets out a shudder as it pulls at the blisters on his face. "We almost got him."

"Did he do this to you?" I ask, my voice breaking over my hatred for the elder.

"No," says Oskar. "We have a new enemy."

I blink down at them in horror. "The Valtia?"

"She is unbelievably powerful," Sig says raspily. "And unbelievably out of control. We were lucky to escape the forest alive. Only the earthquake stopped her from killing us."

"Why?" It bursts from me, one agonized note. "Why would she hurt you like this?"

Sig opens his eyes, and all I see there is desolation. "Because, thanks to Kauko, she probably thinks we killed the one person in the world she loves. And I know her. Now she will not stop until we are dead too."

CHAPTER ELEVEN

Ansa

The Torden will be the death of me. I swallow its murky depths before coughing them up once more.

"Ansa, this is for your own good!"

I buck, turning my face away from the liquid sloshing out of the wineskin Jaspar tries to press to my lips. But I can't go far—I am weak as a nestling and chained to a cot. Warm broth trickles down my cheek and along my neck; I can smell it now, salty and rich. Hunger burbles inside me.

"I'm going to keep at it until you've downed at least half of this," he says in an exasperated voice. "Kauko says he can heal your skin, but he can't keep you from wasting away. That's my job."

"Let me die," I croak. Tears sting my eyes. "Thyra . . ."

I don't mean to say her name aloud, but it bleeds from me all the same.

Jaspar's jaw clenches. "I know, Ansa. I know."

I glare at him. "You hated her." It's such a broken whisper that I'm surprised he seems to understand.

"We had our differences. But—" He bows his head abruptly, and when he raises it, I am shocked to see the shine of emotion in his eyes. "She was my cousin, and she did not deserve to die like that."

"You saw her?"

He nods. "We were camped on the very northern edge of the great forest, and we saw the fires in the woods. Kauko said it was magical. He was worried that the Kupari wielders were coming for us. Then we realized—they were attacking someone else."

I close my eyes in complete weariness as I recall the hours I spent protecting our warriors from the magical onslaught. "Thyra thought it might be Kauko who attacked us."

"We would never have attacked you! My hope since fleeing Vasterut was to reclaim a homeland for our tribes, and to reach out to Thyra again." He sniffles. "I realized she was right all along."

"How stupid do you think I am?"

He lets out a grim chuckle. "Fine, Ansa. Have it your way. But we didn't attack your camp. You know we'd rather stand with you than against you. I could have had my warriors lay siege to the tower in Vasterut. Even with the fighters from the other city-states, we would have had a long and terrible battle if I'd ordered it. But instead we left the city, and surrendered my father for you to decide his fate."

"He's dead," I snap. "And he perished knowing you had abandoned him."

There is something unreadable in his eyes, something deep and broken. "Did Thyra kill him?"

"No. I did."

His lips twitch upward at the corners. "That was my next guess."

"So now you can have your revenge."

His pained smile disappears. "Krigere against Krigere is wrong, Ansa. Believe whatever you want of me, except that I would turn against my own brothers and sisters. I know that the last time we were together, we fought. But please remember that I wanted you on my side. I care for you. I always have. You must believe *that*."

"I believe you want power, and nothing matters more to you."

He touches my chin, and I open my eyes to see him leaning over me, his shaggy blond hair framing his face. "Yes, I want power, Ansa. Power to protect my tribe, and power to enable them to raise their young as rulers. Our numbers are dwindling. I've lost good warriors and andeners to sickness and starvation. We have no haven but Kupari." He sighs. "It seemed possible. Kauko said they have no fighting force of their own, and no allies that will come to their aid like Vasterut did. The only thing standing in our way was this impostor without magic, and a few powerful wielders. We had no idea they would be so aggressive."

Neither did Thyra. "So they came to the forest to keep us from setting foot in their land." And Sig was with them. It is so hard to accept, but how else could they have known exactly where we were?

"They rained hell on you, judging from the damage."

"Our warriors?" Suddenly I remember—they fled, on my orders. "Where are they?"

"No idea. I took only a few scouts with me to find out what was going on. We had almost reached you when two things happened at once—fire and ice billowed through the wood, forcing us to take cover. And then another quake struck. When both went quiet, we found the clearing, and you and Thyra in it, half concealed by torn-up earth."

"Her body," I whisper.

"We buried it, Ansa. With her daggers on her chest." He holds his palm out, showing me a bandaged cut. "I bled over her grave. I know you would have if you could." He strokes my cheek. "I thought I was going to lose you," he says, his voice cracking. "I carried you back here. When you are strong enough, we can go in search of your lost warriors. I know it will take time for you to trust me again, but when you do, we can unite our tribes and take Kupari for ourselves."

My throat is tight as I say, "I promised her I would lead them. Make a home for them." I wince. "In Kupari." My supposed homeland and domain—and the source of all this agony.

"We're not in Kupari right now," Jaspar says. "The ground is so unstable there that we camped outside its borders. Kauko here says that it's the impostor queen and her followers—they've upset the balance of magic. Kauko himself was feeling the effects—it was making him sick."

As if summoned by the mention of his name, the old man appears at Jaspar's side. He's no longer completely bald—he has a helmet of dark hair over his round head. It makes him look younger, though I'm not sure how old he actually is. His skin is smooth and holds a healthy glow at odds with the gaunt looks of the Krigere warriors who cautiously pass my cot and gather around the fire where Carina sits. How has he fared so well? "My magic," he says, wiggling his fingers over my body. "I nearly lost control."

"He and his priests nearly set the camp ablaze," Jaspar says. "But once we crossed the border out of Kupari again, all of them were fine."

Kauko must discern the look on my face, because he says, "You felt it too. The sickness in your magic."

I cannot deny it. "As soon as we reached the Kupari border." I glare at the cuff on Kauko's thick wrist. "And *that* was the only thing keeping me well."

He touches the cuff. "I needed it to heal you, my Valtia. Without it I might have killed you."

"It's true," Jaspar says. "He tried. It hurt both of you."

I still hurt. Every part of me aches and itches. "Give it back, then."

"When you are well and able to wield your magic, it will

be yours, my Valtia. Until then, I use it to defend the camp and heal all wounds."

He thinks I have forgotten how greedy he is, apparently. But right now there is nothing I can do—I'm too weak to move and held here by bonds of iron. If I tried to use magic to melt them, I would burn my own hands off. "I'll need it before I go back to Kupari. I'll be dangerous without it."

They both nod. "The impostor is destroying the land," says Kauko, frowning. "It rebels against her rule. Or perhaps she has found a way to cause the tremors—to stop us."

I look up at these two men. They've both earned agonizing death several times over, and I dearly wish I could offer it to them now. I don't want to believe a word they say, but something about this explanation makes sense. If this fraud does not have magic, she wouldn't be affected the way true magic wielders are. Has she found a way to hold me back and defend her throne?

Was Sig her ally all along?

The memory of him and the other one, the big ice wielder, flashes in my mind. Sig had told me that the impostor queen had a powerful ice wielder at her side. Did the impostor send the two of them to destroy us? Was it her wielders who attacked our camp? She could not have landed a more devastating blow to our people.

Or maybe these two men are lying to me, just as they have in the past. Maybe they are using me, just as they have so many times before. But they are also offering me something—a target for my vengeance. "Jaspar, I'll drink the broth."

He grins and carefully holds the wineskin while Kauko slides his arm under my head to lift it. He is gentle and sure in his movements, as if he is accustomed to caring for people. "You must drink it all," he says. "You will run dry if you don't." His breath is terrible. I'd obey him just to escape it.

Also, he's right—I feel like a fallen leaf crisped by the sun. I drink slowly, and finally the old man takes the skin from Jaspar. "She will need solid food by tomorrow. Meat."

"I'll have Carina and Rask go hunting." Jaspar pats his belly and gives me an apologetic look. "We've mostly been living off the edible plants this forest has to offer—it's a good thing it's so vast, for there are nearly two thousand of us with warriors and andeners combined. If Kauko hadn't been with us, we all would have starved by now! But he was able to send a signal that drew many of his fellow exiled priests and apprentices back to his side, and they have kept us protected and fed."

He pats the elder's back and walks away, leaving me chained and helpless and staring up at the man who drank my blood. "I would kill you if I were strong enough," I blurt out.

I didn't mean to say that, and again he seems to read my chagrined expression, because he laughs. "Warrior Valtia," he says, his tone one of approval. "You and I will reclaim Kupari from the impostor. My brothers in magic will help."

I stare up at him, a war raging in my chest. This man is evil. And he is a liar. But he knows magic, and he knows Kupari. He knows this impostor who sits on the throne. I know none of those things. I don't even know where our loyal warriors are—they might not even know Thyra is gone. They might have perished in the fire *I* created in my storm of grief. I am blind, and Kauko has eyes. He also, apparently, has allies who can help. And I will need that help if I am to avenge my love.

Despite all that, I crave his destruction. But . . . it is almost as if I can hear Thyra whispering in my ear. *Control yourself*, she says. *For once*. The memory of her rueful smile makes me grimace to keep from crying. Kauko clucks his concern and swipes a warm cloth across my face.

"You are the strongest Valtia who has ever lived," he says quietly. "You have the power to punish the ones who destroyed her. I can help you. We want the same thing."

I think this might be the first truth he has spoken. Our eyes meet. "I want to be the one who kills the impostor," I say slowly.

He smiles. "You cannot kill her with magic. It has no power over her."

"I can kill her with a dagger just as easily."

"Yes," he says. "We must cut through her wielders first."

"They're the ones who killed Thyra."

"Yes. Sig. You were saying his name as you started to awake."

"He betrayed us."

"Because that is what he is. Remember he betrayed me first. After I had saved his life." The old man's softish face has taken on a hard look. "He and I will meet again."

For some reason, I am relieved to hear that he wants to be the one to kill Sig. I still can't believe what the fire wielder has done, and I want him dead, but . . . I remember what he taught me, how he and I were friends once. Or, at least, I had thought so. "Who was his ally?" I ask. "The dark ice wielder."

"I do not know his name. But he and Sig are a pair. They are Suurin. Together they are nearly as powerful as the Valtia." Kauko looks as if he has swallowed something bitter. "I do not know why they serve one so unworthy."

"Who is this impostor?" I ask. "How does she have that much control over them if she has no magic?"

Kauko sinks down and settles himself next to my cot. "It is my fault. I nurtured this snake, and I should not be surprised it bit us." He points to my calf, where my red flame mark rests beneath the covering of my stocking. "Your mark emerged the moment of the old Valtia's death. Her name was Kaarin. She served well for many years, and we served her. She was succeeded by Sofia, another loyal and tireless queen. She gave her life protecting Kupari from Krigere."

For a moment I can't breathe. Sofia. The witch on the lake. She was the one I nearly touched. She was the one who killed all my people—and saved me. "And her magic is inside me now."

"We thought it would pass to Elli. That is the impostor's name. She has a mark as well, and we were so sure we had the right girl. Now I know how wrong we were."

"What did you do when you realized she wasn't the rightful heir to the magic?"

He looks anguished. "We tried to explain to her that we

had been wrong! But she wouldn't accept it. She said the throne was hers. When we refused to let her rule, she stole away to the outlands to recruit an army of wielders from the criminals who live there. Sig was among those she enticed, probably with promises of wealth and power. When they stormed the temple, we fought hard to protect it—and the young Saadella who is still captive there."

My heart squeezes suddenly. "The Saadella."

His eyes glint. "She will receive the magic when you die. In many ways, she is your daughter."

Daughter. I look away. I cannot imagine it, yet as he says the words, I know he has spoken another truth. Unbidden, a part of my heart that I did not know existed steps into the sunlight and takes its first breath. "What is her name?" I ask quietly.

"Lahja," he says. "She has hair exactly your color. Eyes exactly your color. A mark exactly the shape of yours—only hers is on her back. It hurts that I cannot protect her now."

"Will they hurt her?"

"If the impostor decides Lahja is a threat to her claim on the throne, she might have done so already. And if that is the case, the magic will die with you. This cannot happen."

"And if I die now?"

"The magic will enter her. But she is just a little girl, with no priests to train her."

I think back to all the times this magic has hurt me. Burned me, frozen my skin, left me with scars. And I picture this tiny girl, a younger version of myself, suffering and screaming in pain. I suck in a deep breath, and for the first time since Thyra's death, there's a moment when I am grateful to still be alive.

"You look like a woman who lives for more than herself again." Kauko pats my arm.

"You think we can regain the temple?" I ask. "What of the people of Kupari?"

"When you show them you are the true Valtia, they will rejoice," Kauko says. "With priests by your side and magic at your fingertips, it will be easy to show that you belong on the throne. Though we may have to fight for the temple, the people will not stand in your way. They crave a queen who will take care of them."

"But I . . . I have to take care of the Krigere first."

Kauko bobs his head, sounding excited now. "Yes, you must. I understand this is your responsibility. Which is why I will help manage the temple. I did it for years."

"But the Saadella is mine." It comes out of me without thought or calculation. It is just a fact.

Kauko chuckles and holds up his hands. "I would expect nothing less. But perhaps you will agree she is safer in the temple than in the wilderness, assuming the temple still stands."

If it does, I will take it apart brick by brick just to get to her. "She will be wherever I am."

His hands fall to his lap. "I am your ally."

My hatred of him doesn't allow any room for trust. Sig told me Kauko drained the blood of the Valtias past, and that matches what the elder has done to me. But I also know the impostor queen is my enemy, and I have no hope of getting to her if I don't have help. I am weak—and I could wander lost in the woods for months without even knowing how to find Kupari, let alone make it to the temple. "Tell me what you want of me."

"I want you to heal. Then we will march on the city and save the land from the impostor. You can avenge your chieftain. You can save your Saadella. You can make a new home for your people. I can help you make all these things happen."

"And in exchange?"

His expression goes soft and sad. "I am an old man. Older than I look. I merely want a safe haven for my priests now. I want the Temple on the Rock for my own. I want to see Kupari prosper as it did before the impostor attacked and destroyed my home."

I care little for buildings. Before Vasterut I had never even seen shelters so huge—they felt like caves. Or cages. I prefer sleeping under stars. "Very well. You can have your temple."

Kauko bows. "Allies."

I stare at the top of his dark brown head. Thyra made me promise to take care of our people. This is what she would want, if it keeps our warriors safe and alive. And it is what *I* want, if it means avenging her death. "All right. Allies."

CHAPTER TWELVE

Elli

My hands shake as I hold them over Sig's sweat-streaked chest. I avoid his gaze, because the last time I looked into his eyes, I saw how frightened he was. He is probably remembering the last time I was this close, and how I turned his own fiery magic against him. "I won't hurt you, Sig. We're on the same side."

A dry, nervous chuckle escapes him. "Ah, words. I learned long ago not to trust them."

Oskar reaches out an unsteady hand and touches Sig's shoulder. His other, the one that is white and still and dead, remains tucked against his side. "She has more control than she did when you were with us last."

Sig looks over at his opposite, his enemy and, I suspect, the only person in the world that he actually loves. "Easy for you to say. She's never roasted you from the inside out."

"I never deserved it like you did," Oskar growls.

Sig grins, though it looks more like a grimace. "You're just as boring as I remember."

"I saved your life in those woods."

"And I saved yours."

"Yes, yes, we're all happy to be back together," says Raimo, who is sweating even though the only fire in the lean-to—apart from Sig himself—is a single candle held by Freya, who we allowed back in to assist. But she is a fire wielder as well, and is giving off waves of heat. "Child, calm down or I'll send you outside."

Sig raises his head. "I always knew you were more like me than your older brother," he says to her.

Freya throws her shoulders back. "Quit trying to put this off, you big coward. Shut your mouth and let them heal you."

He laughs now, more than a chuckle. "I missed you too."

I stare at his face, his scarred cheeks. Freya and Oskar are as close to family as Sig has, and though he has done terrible things to them, somehow they have welcomed him back. I have too, because I think Oskar needs him. As bad as both of them look, I think they'd already be dead without each other. "I'm going to channel Raimo's magic now."

Raimo and I talked about how to perfect this process as we rode through the woods. Last time, he was trying to control it while he used me like a funnel. But the unsteadiness of the land has infected his magic, and I must be more than a simple tunnel through which the fire and ice flows. I have to learn how to heal as if the magic were mine alone. So Raimo lectured me on how it's done, and now he mutters reminders.

"Stay focused on one place—don't let your eyes or mind wander."

I stare at the blistered patch of skin just below Sig's right collarbone.

"Don't overdo it, or you'll go too deep. You'll damage what's beneath the surface."

"Stars," mutters Sig. "Maybe I'm better off—" He gasps as the magic pours from the old man, through my body, and then from my hands. I do exactly as Raimo instructed, narrowing my gaze to a tiny patch of skin, making it my whole world. My hands tingle, pins and needles, tiny sparks of ice and fire combining in a way that defies nature. This is the heart of magic—we understand ice and fire, but when their source is magical, their power goes beyond heat and cold, snow and flame. They become something vast and indescribable, inhuman . . . divine. Suddenly, the responsibility of bearing this gift from the stars weighs heavy on me. I know I'm meant to do something with it, but right now I will use it to heal this Suurin, because we need him to save us.

I am not aware of time. I am only aware of the skin beneath my hands. I try not to think about whether it belongs to Oskar or Sig. As Suurin, they are equally important. As men, only one has my heart. Right now, though, I am not a woman—I am the Astia, and I will magnify and direct the magic of a powerful old wielder as it does its work on their bodies.

"Elli, that's enough," Raimo says. It's the catch in his

voice that causes my fingers to curl into fists, which ceases the flow of power from my palms.

"What?"

"You look like you're about to fall over."

I look down at my hands and try to steady them, but it's impossible. "I . . ."

"You did well," says Oskar. He looks so much better. I can still see the faint flush of frost on his cheeks and brow, the harsh crust of it in patches on his arms and chest, but he is no longer a ruined mess, and neither is Sig, though the fire wielder bears scars from other run-ins with fire—probably from that night in the temple when I kept him from getting his revenge on Kauko at the expense of Lahja's life.

"Not bad," says Sig, running his hand over his scarred jaw. "I may yet find love." He snorts.

"Now that every word isn't agony, you need to tell us what happened," says Raimo. "How on earth did you end up killing . . . who did you kill, exactly?"

"That's just it," Oskar says. "I don't think we killed anyone."

My heart skips a beat. "So Ansa only thinks her love is dead? This is much better news than I—"

"No, Elli—I saw the woman fall, and I saw Ansa run to her."

"He's saying *we* didn't kill her," says Sig.

I look back and forth between them, and Raimo does the same. Then, at the same time, we both say, "Kauko."

And Oskar and Sig say, "Yes."

Raimo tugs at his beard, his fingers tangling in the scraggly strands. "Explain."

"We spotted the elder as we approached the place where Sig thought the Valtia would be," Oskar says. "There was fire raining from the sky. When we got close enough, we saw who was attacking—it was Kauko. But as we got closer, the young warrior came charging up from a hollow."

"If I know Thyra, she was stalking him," says Sig. "That one never made an impulsive move in all her life." He winces and turns away. "She didn't deserve to die that way."

Oskar looks grim. "She chased him into a clearing, dodging the magic he hurled behind him. We ran along either side, and we tried to counteract what he was throwing. We protected her." His broad shoulders sag. "Until she charged unexpectedly."

"And here is where the elder's cunning comes through in the extreme." Sig's lips have a harsh and bitter twist to them. "He brought his hands together and hit her on either side—with fire on the left, and ice on the right. So it looked—"

"Like the two of you were the culprits," says Raimo. And then he curses.

Oskar nods. "Ansa ran out of the trees a moment later. She saw us. I know she did."

"She definitely recognized *me*," says Sig. "She probably thinks I betrayed her."

"Why didn't you try to explain?" I say. "Kauko was her known enemy, based on what you've told us."

"We might have," says Sig. "I think I could have done it. But she . . ."

"She sort of . . ." Oskar tries to continue. His fingers flare and his eyes go round.

"Exploded," says Sig. "We saw her begin to glow. We started to run. And thank the stars we did, because if we hadn't . . ."

"Well, you saw us," Oskar says lamely. "If Aira and the others hadn't found us, we would still be lying in those woods, food for the foxes."

"And what of Kauko?" Raimo's voice could slice the toughest meat.

"No idea," says Oskar. "He might have been killed in her . . . whatever she did. The quake hit soon after. It was chaos."

"Do we know what happened to Ansa?" I ask. "Did she actually make it out of that clearing? Did she survive the explosion she created?"

"I think we'll find out soon enough," Oskar says, looking hollow. "If she comes after us, we have our answer."

"Wrong," says Raimo. "If Ansa had died, Lahja would have received her magic. She was herself before we left, just a normal little girl. Ansa is alive."

Sig grunts and sits up. "Then I'm going to enjoy a cup of ale while I still can." He shakily crawls through the flap of the lean-to.

"I'd better help him," says Freya, sounding exasperated. "Otherwise he'll probably pick a fight and lose control of his magic again."

Oskar and Raimo murmur their thanks while I fight a wave of dizziness that passes over me. A moment later the two of them are lowering me to the mat Oskar had been occupying.

"I'm fine," I say, though I sound awfully breathless.

Raimo is pale and shaky too, but he looks happy. "You completely balanced that magic. It would have killed them otherwise—I still feel off."

"So do I," said Oskar. "I think this is our new everyday." He says it lightly, then frowns as he sees me and Raimo exchange glances. "What have I not been told?"

"I think Elli can fill you in," Raimo says. "I need some ale and bread or I'm going to expire."

Oskar lets him go, though now he looks worried. He lies on his side next to me and I turn so we are face-to-face. He smiles. "Stars, every time I look at you, I feel like I've run a mile. My heart races."

I put my hand on his bare chest, right over his heart, and feel the tickle of his ice magic. Outside, I can hear laughter and a few snatches of song. The sounds are livelier with Sig and Raimo out there—it tells people the most powerful of our protectors are alive and mostly well. I glance down at Oskar's still, white hand, but he tips my chin up. "Don't worry about that, all right?"

I touch that hand with my own scarred fingers. "How can I not worry about you?"

He kisses my forehead, his half beard rough against my skin. "Sometimes I think I am two men," he says. "Two different people. One is the Ice Suurin. And you shouldn't worry about *him*." He presses his forehead to mine and speaks into the warmth between us. "But the other is just me, just Oskar, and he is very grateful that you care."

"I know exactly what you mean. Do you ever wish we could just be Oskar and Elli, not the Suurin and the Astia?"

He chuckles. "All the time, my love. Every single day."

I scoot closer to him, and he puts his arm around me, holding me against his body, which is cool but not frigid. "Tell me what it would be like."

"If we were just Oskar and Elli, I would ask you to be my wife."

I pull back a little, my eyes wide, and he gives me a sheepish look and clears his throat before adding, "I would ask *very* nicely."

I laugh. "And what would we do after I said yes?"

Now we're both giggling. "I know you had a very sheltered upbringing, but I'd like to believe you already know the answer to that."

My cheeks blaze with that knowledge, and on impulse I kiss the soft skin of his throat. "I'll keep you in suspense."

"Well. If you don't, we can figure it out together." He brushes his lips over mine. "I could build us a warm cottage by the lake. In the winter it would rattle with the wind, but we'd have a blazing fire."

"I would cook the rabbits and deer you brought home. I'd learn to fish and make bread."

"Mother and Freya would visit us in the summer, and our children would play on the dunes. Their laughter and shrieks would reach us all the way up the hill."

My throat tightens a bit. Oskar's family used to visit Maarika's brother at his farm near the shore—until his family was killed by Soturi, and his daughter, Ansa, with whom Oskar used to play on the dunes, was kidnapped. She lost so much. And now, if Sig is correct, she's lost the person she loved. I cannot imagine the pain she's in right now.

But it makes me hold Oskar tighter. "It sounds like a dream," I murmur.

"We could make it real," Oskar says fiercely, his hand rising to cup the nape of my neck. "We will get through all of this, and then we will make it real."

"I want that. More than anything. But—"

"No," he whispers. "Not now. Not tonight."

"All right." I sniffle and swipe a tear from my cheek. "We'll make it real."

I spread my fingers across his chest, and he sighs and lets his magic trickle between us through the places our skin meets. It spirals up my arms and encircles my heart. I was raised believing that I could not love or be loved by one person, because my duty was to the people. I still believe in that duty, with all my being. But I love Oskar, and I know he loves me, and in this moment it seems wretchedly unfair that the life that would make both of us happy is so far out of our reach.

"Sleep next to me tonight, like we used to," he says against my ear.

I nod and snuggle in. There is nothing in my life that has ever left me more content. The world outside the lean-to still exists, but it fades as the minutes pass. The ground shudders but doesn't erupt, and though Oskar groans a little, as if it hurts him, he settles as I pull excess magic from his bones. As we drift in that peaceful place, dreaming of a shared future that both of us will fight for, I push away memories of Raimo's desolate look and vague predictions. He admitted he wasn't sure what would happen. The future is a blank parchment, and perhaps Oskar and I can write our own destiny on its creamy surface. Maybe we can earn that.

I am in the midst of that happy dream, watching Oskar stride from the forest, smiling in the sunshine and lifting a brace of rabbits as he returns home for the night, when I am awakened by a scream. Oskar and I bolt upright at the same time, him emanating a deadly cold.

"Elli," someone calls.

My brow furrows as I scramble up. "Kaisa?" She shouldn't be here. I left her at the temple to make sure . . .

"My Valtia, you must come!" Kaisa is out of breath. I push my way out of the lean-to with Oskar at my back. The apprentice slides clumsily off a horse. "I'm so sorry."

"Just tell me what's happened," I say. My heart is beating so fast.

Kaisa drops to her knees. "We couldn't stop them. We tried, but—" She holds out her shaking hands.

"Where is Lahja?" It comes out of me as a wail, raw and instinctual.

"They took her, my Valtia," she says, crying now. "They stormed the temple and carried her away. The blacksmith and the others who wanted to see Ivette stoned. They've taken the Saadella away." She raises her head. "And they said they won't give her back until you meet their demands."

CHAPTER THIRTEEN

Ansa

Carina unlocks my shackles to allow me to relieve myself. She seems wary as ever around me, but she lets me lean against her as she escorts me back to my resting place. "I'm not going to let you shackle me again," I tell her.

She shrugs. "I'm not going to try. Jaspar said to let you be."

Begrudging gratitude stirs inside me. "Wise of him."

She holds my arm as I sink onto the cot. "He's a good chieftain, Ansa. I know you've had your differences, but you should know that all of us look to him for our orders. We're his wolves, and will be until we die."

I rest my elbows on my knees. "Do your andeners feel the same? He and his father forced many of ours to pair with warriors who already had mates."

"They only wanted to ensure the survival of our tribe."

"By crushing the spirits and wills of some of its members? By making it clear that their lives aren't as valuable as a warrior's?"

She grunts. "You sound like Thyra. She said such things to me, when I was guarding her in the tower."

The sound of her name is like a knife sliding between my ribs. "Thank you for the compliment. If I can show even a sliver of her wisdom, then I am happy." I bow my head. She's gone. I will never hear her voice again. I press my hands over my face.

"I'll leave you alone." Carina's footsteps are silent, but I know she's gone, and I'm glad.

When I am certain that I'm not about to start sobbing in a camp full of hardened warriors, I let my hands fall from my face. I am surrounded by the bustle of morning. We're not leaving here today—Jaspar said we will have another day of rest. But warrior-andener pairs are preparing to hunt and scavenge, and many are sharpening or repairing weapons or armor. We have no new supplies, so everyone must preserve what they have. The hours will be devoted to survival—and preparation. But no one expects me to do a thing. No one talks to me. They do toss me mistrustful glances, though. Probably they remember the night in the fight circle, when Nisse nearly defeated Thyra with scheming—and I killed nine of them in my magic-fueled rage.

I look down at my hands. For the last several days I've felt so shaky, as if the fire and ice inside me were about to explode into a storm I had no hope of leashing. But today I feel only the barest tingle of it. I am mostly aware of the ache and itch of my injuries. Perhaps it is our distance from Kupari . . . ?

Through the trees, I see a flash of fire, the kind I know is not natural. It's like a small sun, one that flies amid the branches—until it is caught. I stand up, squinting, and see several black-robed men milling about just beyond the area where a group of andeners is straightening shafts and sharpening stones to create new arrows. Slowly, making sure my steps are steady, I make my way toward the robed men. There are perhaps a dozen of them, and I know they must be the exiled priests who survived the impostor queen's attack on the temple. Their robes are tattered and patched, and all of them have short hair and beards. Their ages vary—as I near, I see that a few of them are closer to my age, while some are closer to Preben's and Bertel's.

Kauko has his back to me, but as I reach the edge of their clearing, he turns as if he feels my presence. "Valtia," he says, bowing his head low.

The word has a dramatic effect on these priests—they all stop and turn to me, then fall to their knees. "Valtia," they all say.

"Tell them to rise," Kauko suggests. "Say *nousevat.*"

I clear my throat and repeat the foreign word. It feels strange on my tongue, and yet oddly familiar.

Kauko smiles. "My Krigere is much better than theirs, but they are learning."

Some of them mimic his smile as they rise to their feet, and Kauko holds his arms out as if presenting them to me. "We are but a sad echo of what we were, but we are at your service, Valtia. These men have devoted their lives to serving this magic."

"No women?" I ask, frowning.

Kauko's cheeks redden. "Well. We have found that men are more suited to priesthood. But remember that the forever-magic runs through your veins. Always a woman's veins."

"What do you mean, more suited?" This makes no sense to me at all. "Not a single woman has ever had the inclination to be a priest?"

Kauko waves his hands. "Surely you would like to see what they can do? These will be the wielders at your side as we face the rebels. We will be the front line, and the warriors will come behind us."

My lip curls. "I suppose."

Some of the priests' smiles falter as they read my skeptical look, and for their sakes I nod. If I am to lead them, I'd like them to trust me, even if I don't trust them.

Kauko has them show me their prowess. Some of them can make objects move, and others can conjure ice or fire from the air, while others pull it from the fire at the center of the clearing or the water from a nearby stream. They can make it take different forms too, such as arrows of ice or ropes of flame. As I watch them, I feel the urge to try, but the magic inside me doesn't answer the call, for some reason. I wince as I look down at my hands and feel the pain in the crook of my arm. When I poke at it with my fingers, I feel a bandage beneath the sleeve of my tunic, and a wound beneath the softness. My brow furrows as I think back. "Kauko, didn't you heal me?"

He stops in the middle of controlling a massive ball of flame that is making the others, mostly the ones who wield fire, sweat rivers. It disappears instantly. "What? Yes. I healed all your wounds."

"What about this one?" I lift my sleeve, and then start to peel the bandage away.

Kauko rushes toward me, clucking his tongue. "Oh, that—"

"You bled me." I stare at the wound on my pale skin. My fist clenches.

"Valtia, please understand."

"Oh, I understand." I take a step back, wondering if I can find a weapon and stab him before the priests realize what I'm doing.

"No!" Kauko's smooth brow is crinkled with his distress. "No, this was different. The magic was so out of control when you were found that it was killing you. Without balance, it is so dangerous."

I point to the cuff of Astia on his wrist. "Which is why I need that!"

He shakes his head. "It wasn't near enough! I had to drain some of it away before you weren't strong enough to contain it!"

"Did you drink it?"

He blinks at me, as if it is a rude question.

"Did you drink it?" I shout.

"Blood is life, and magic, and power. Your blood is precious—the foundation of everything we serve. Do you really expect me to pour such a treasure into the dirt when it can be used to strengthen those who would die to protect your rule?" His voice is so quiet, the words spoken in his odd, trilling accent. But I feel the rebuke.

And it does not please me.

I lean forward. "I won't kill you for it this time," I murmur, speaking in his ear. "But my blood is not your nourishment."

He kneels before me and grasps my hands, his eyes on the rotting leaves at my feet. "My Valtia. It will be as you say."

His moist skin makes me shudder, and I pull my fingers away. "It had better be."

The others are watching me with wide, terrified eyes. I'm trying to decide what to do about that when I hear a quiet laugh behind me. "Oh, you've got them quaking already," says Jaspar.

I round on him. "Kauko has been making a snack of my blood."

Jaspar's smile dies. "*What?*"

Kauko jumps to his feet, surprisingly agile. "And I explained to our Valtia that it was strictly for her benefit. I would not do anything to weaken her now."

Jaspar's shoulders are tense as he looks back and forth

between us. "He told me that if you die, your magic will go to the Saadella, who is controlled by the impostor. It would not be wise for him to do anything but try to keep you alive, Ansa. That, at least, you can rely on, even if nothing else."

At least he understands how far we are from trust. "I can't even feel my magic inside me now. How much did he take?"

We look at Kauko, who is back to holding his hands up as his priests shift warily behind him. "Only a pint or so. Little more. Enough to stabilize the magic. Remember I am a physician! Have I not brought you back from the brink of death many times already?"

Yes, but only because it benefited him. It's already clear to me that this Saadella—this princess who will inherit my magic when I die—must be kept away from him. If he controls her, he has every reason to kill me.

I tilt my head. "I want the cuff of Astia back."

Kauko nods. "Yes. When we reenter Kupari, you must have it. But for now . . ." He smiles at it, then pulls his sleeve over it. "While you recover, and while I am the primary defender of this camp, I will ask that you allow me to keep it safe for you."

Jaspar touches my arm. "It makes sense, Ansa. You're panting after walking across the camp, and if the wielders who killed Thyra come back, we have to have protection from them."

I think back to how I was forced to shield our warriors for all those hours under siege. Even the thought makes me want to collapse on the ground. "Fine. But only until we reach Kupari."

Jaspar's hand slides to my back. "There. Now will you come and let me give you some stew? Your strength won't return without good nourishment."

I step away from his touch. Something about it makes me want to cry again. "Let's go."

I wave to the priests, and they all bow as I walk away. Jaspar seems to think it's extremely funny. "I've always thought you were special, Ansa, but this?"

"The Kupari are so bizarre," I say. "Are they all like that?"

"I've never been there. You and Kauko and his priests are the only Kupari I've met."

If I had a knife, I would draw it. "So now I am Kupari."

"Aren't you?"

I stop dead. "Really, Jaspar?"

"Why does that bother you?"

"How can you ask me that?" I ask in a choked voice.

"I mean no insult by it. You're also Krigere, Ansa. I didn't mean to take that away from you."

"Good," I whisper, turning my face away. "How do you expect things to work in Kupari, Jaspar? I won't help you deal with the people there as you and your father dealt with the Vasterutians."

"Well, that didn't exactly end well for us, and I'm not stupid. We can install the priests in their pretty little temple since that's what they want. They can deal with the people while we make sure we get what we need. I want our warriors' pockets bursting with Kupari copper. That's it."

"And you plan to be chieftain of these rich warriors."

"Of course. Who else? You?"

"No." Because . . . I cannot see a future beyond this battle, this vengeance.

The line of his shoulders loosens. "I want you close, though, Ansa."

I backtrack as he takes a step into my space. "I can't be close to anyone right now. I am an open wound."

"I could be part of the healing."

"How would Carina feel about that?"

He lets out a sudden chuckle. "She'd just have to share."

Our eyes meet. "No." There might have been a time when I felt conflicted about being with Jaspar, but that time is past. With Thyra gone, I know I am meant to be alone. There is no one else for me, and my future is darkness. "But as long as our interests are aligned, we will be allies."

He holds his arm out. We've reached a fire near my cot, and there are reed mats laid out to protect us from the damp. "Now, for that stew—"

A shout from back in the clearing wheels us around—just before an arrow hums through the air and embeds itself in a tree right next to my face. Jaspar tackles me to the ground, and the camp explodes into a cacophony of war cries and a rain of arrows. But I am staring up at the first one, which is still vibrating from its impact with the wood. Jaspar follows the line of my gaze and his eyes go wide. "It appears your lost tribe has found its way home to us," he says in my ear as he shields me with his body. His right hand slides down his side to draw a dagger. "And it looks like they're determined to kill us all."

CHAPTER FOURTEEN

Elli

We don't bother to disguise our reentry into the city—the gates are open, hanging crooked from a part of the wall that has crumbled away, and the guards seem to expect our arrival. They watch me as I ride through, flanked by Oskar and Sig, tailed by Raimo and Kaisa. I can tell that all of my wielders are trying to project confidence and strength, just as I am. But I can also tell they are unsettled, fighting the pull to turn inward.

The bloodless land seems to be calling to them—maybe warning them.

I don't feel it, nor do most of the people in this city. We only see the wounds—the collapsed buildings, the crumbled walls, the crack that runs jagged like a lightning strike from the gateway up the main road, toward the temple at the tip of the peninsula. It's not a wide fault—perhaps only one to two feet wide in most places, deep enough that you wouldn't want to fall in—but it makes it look like the city is about to break in two and fall away from its center.

We steer our mounts up the road. The courtyards are full of grumbling, anxious people, some of them with bandages on their heads and limbs. We pass several people carrying buckets of water, and one little square in which maids are ladling soup into bowls for hungry children and grizzled-looking old men and women. I am happy to see the people taking care of each other, but they turn cold gazes upon me as I wave and smile. One man spits on the ground as I pass, but then he yelps as a nearby fire lashes out at his backside with its flames.

"Sig," I whisper sharply. "You're not helping."

His lip curls. "I didn't hurt him permanently."

"The people are already suspicious of wielders," Oskar says from my other side.

"I could give them something to be scared about."

I close my eyes and ask the stars for patience. "They're already terrified, Sig. Many of them have lost their homes. They've just made it through a terrible winter. They're hungry and thirsty. They're scared to death that the Soturi are coming. You're drawing on a well that's running dry. And there's only hatred at the bottom."

Behind me, Raimo chuckles and mutters to himself. Then he says, "Where is the Saadella exactly?"

"They said they were taking her to the council hall," says

Kaisa. "Part of it is still standing." Her face is tearstained, and her robes are torn. She and the others fought—even Helka and Janeka, who have no magic at all, tried to keep the mob from getting to Lahja. Apparently, Janeka was hit in the head during the struggle and injured badly. As for Kaisa, she fought with her magic and her body. She muttered to me earlier that she tried to give her life, but they wouldn't kill her. They told her to deliver the news to me instead.

"Did they say what they wanted?" I ask. We were in such a mad dash to get here that I didn't bother to inquire before.

"The council announced your belief that copper was the reason the earth shakes, and told of your desire to throw the temple stores into the ground. People were outraged. They stormed the temple to confront you, but not finding you there, they decided to take the Saadella. But some of them remain, trying to dig out the copper from the catacombs. They want to distribute it among the people."

My face flushes hot with anger. "So they merely pretended to help, and then they betrayed me. How lovely."

"They don't sound that scared," said Sig. "If they were, they wouldn't have challenged you like this."

"What do you want to do, Elli?" Oskar asks.

"I need Lahja back," I murmur. "I can't think of anything else while she's in danger."

"If she dies, the magic will truly be lost," says Raimo. "Besides, we're not sure the copper is actually—"

"It will work," I snap. "We're giving the land back what we stole."

Raimo sighs. "It might not be enough."

I give Oskar a worried look, but he is turned toward Raimo. "What do you mean?" he asks. "What else would the land want?"

"We can talk more of it once the Saadella is back in our hands," says Raimo, his voice a little too light.

Sig shifts on his saddle and curses. "Hopefully that will be soon. I feel so . . ."

"I feel it too." Oskar lifts his calloused palms from the reins and peers down at them. "I'm not sure how well I can control it."

"We can make a big entrance," says Sig. "Shock them into giving her up."

"We have to be careful," I say as the council hall comes into view. Up ahead is a huge crowd of people. The morning sunlight glints and sparkles off newly forged blades and sharpened scythes. We armed the people to defend themselves against an invasion—all blacksmiths in the city worked night and day for weeks—but now it seems they might use them to attack us, the very people who would protect them. "We don't want to hurt any of them—and we especially don't want to put Lahja at more risk. I will go in alone."

"No," Oskar barks.

"You can stay near, but they need to see that I mean no harm."

"Forget *meaning* no harm," he says. "You can't *do* any—"

I touch his sleeve, the one that hides his terribly injured

hand, then look over my shoulder at Kaisa, who doesn't know I'm not the true Valtia. "I can do anything I need to do, but my people are mine to protect. I refuse to try to intimidate them with my magic."

She gives me a grateful, hopeful smile I don't really deserve.

"Raimo," Oskar growls. "Talk some sense into our Valtia, please."

I laugh. "Am I a stubborn child now? Or am I the queen?" The edge in my voice seems to keep all of them silent. We reach the edge of the crowd, and I dismount. People back away from our little group of wielders, and I walk toward the badly damaged council hall through the space they create. Topias has been told of my approach, clearly, for he stands just outside the entrance, which is blocked by shattered stones that have fallen from the outer walls.

"Valtia," he says. "We came to talk to you at the temple last night but discovered you had fled the city."

"I did not flee," I reply. "I went to heal my Suurin, who had been injured in a battle with rogue priests in the Loputon." I gesture to Oskar and Sig, who loom on either side of me. "You see that they are strong again."

Topias cringes back. "You bring your strongest wielders. Do you need them to protect you?"

I tilt my head. "Do you need to kidnap a little girl to get your way?"

He sputters, and I hold up my hand. "Let's not continue to ask silly questions. I want my Saadella. She is my daughter in magic and our future queen, and she is no pawn. If you have issues with me, take them up with *me*."

"We had to have your ear," Topias says, looking around at the crowd.

"You have to listen," shouts a woman in the crowd.

"You can't just serve yourself and your wielders," cries another.

"The Valtia is supposed to protect us," roars a man, a sailor by the look of his weather-beaten skin and washed out eyes. "All we've had during your rule is hunger and death!"

Topias seems emboldened by this support. "Your plan to destroy the city's wealth when we need it most was quite unpopular. As many of your decisions have been. We demand a change in return for the Saadella."

"I must see her," I say. "We can talk after I know she's safe."

Topias casts a nervous glance at the four wielders pressed in around me, shielding my back from the churning mob behind us. "You will come alone."

My heart is racing. If my bluff is called, what will I do? I smile at him. "If you like. I am more than enough."

The blustery council leader swallows hard, and this pleases me. "This way, then."

I turn to Raimo and Sig, Oskar and Kaisa. "I'll be back soon."

Oskar looks like he wants to shake me, but instead he gives me a jerky nod.

I follow Topias around the side of the building, to a tunnel that has withstood the wrath of the earth thus far. I barely pay attention to where I am going—my mind is whirling with all the things I must do, and my heart is craving my Saadella. We reach an enclosed courtyard with walls covered in budding vines. In the center, what used to be a fountain has crumbled. On the far side is a canopy made of rough burlap skewered on wooden poles, and beneath it sits a knot of perhaps a dozen people or so. Some of them rise when they see me coming, and then I hear the one voice I need shriek, "Valtia!"

I open my arms to receive her, but a brown-haired woman grabs her and holds her back.

"Let me go, Mama," Lahja screams.

My stomach tightens. They've brought her parents to be with her, people who tried to escape the city rather than give her to the temple. I let my arms fall to my sides. "Lahja, it's all right. I see you, and I'm glad you're safe."

"Where did you go?" she asks, still squirming in her mother's arms, her coppery curls loose and bouncing. They've dressed her in a simple peasant's gown and put little leather slippers on her feet.

"I was needed outside the city."

"With the outlaw wielders?" Agata steps from behind Lahja and her mother. The woman has her hair wrapped in a cloth and a plain dress on instead of her usual richly embroidered garb. "Do you care about them more than you do about the people?"

"You are all my people," I say, forcing patience into my tone. "And there are no outlaw wielders. There are only citizens who defend Kupari using their gifts, whatever those might be. . . ." I glare icily at her. "And those who don't."

Agata purses her lips. "Does that include you?"

"I won't dignify impertinent questions."

"How about this one—will you use your magic to defend the city and rebuild it?"

I blink at her. "You may rely on it."

She gestures up at the crumbling edifice of the council hall. "Then why not start right here, right now? You can mend our hall and make it safe to meet there once more."

"You kidnap my Saadella and draw me here to test me?"

She gives me a look of wide-eyed innocence. "Valtia, I only ask for a small thing that will restore the confidence of your people. Why do you deny us even the smallest display of your magic?"

"Because my magic is meant for great things," I say. "Not as a tool for pettiness."

She drops her veil of guilelessness and looks around her at the council members and other prominent citizens gathered beneath the canopy. "Didn't I tell you?"

"It's as you said," Lahja's father, a tall man with a weak chin, says.

Agata nods, looking satisfied. "I told them you wouldn't show us your magic. I knew you wouldn't."

I clench my fists—my palms are slick with sweat. "Because I was brought up knowing that a queen does not have to justify her decisions as long as she always focuses on protecting and nurturing her people."

"A *real* queen, yes," says Lahja's mother. She clutches my Saadella tightly. "I thought I had offered my baby to a real queen."

I hold out my arms to Lahja, and she kicks and struggles to reach me. "And that is what I am. Lahja knows this. She feels the bond."

"She's a child," barks her father. "She sees a pretty lady in a fancy dress. Nothing more."

The citizens spread out in the courtyard, surrounding me. Agata waves her hand, and one man pushes a wooden door open—it reveals the street outside, just up the road from where I left my wielders. The townspeople see the opening and push inside, flooding the tiny courtyard as I try to backtrack. Sig and Oskar are nowhere to be seen, and they might not even realize what's happening. Fear trickles down my back. Lahja's father and another man, who I realize is Yrian the bereaved blacksmith, take hold of my arms. They are not gentle.

"The Valtia won't show us her magic," Agata shouts. "Would you all like to know what that means?" She turns and points to me, hatred burning in her eyes. "It means our supposed queen is an impostor. She has no magic at all."

CHAPTER FIFTEEN

Ansa

Jaspar rolls off me and together we belly-crawl for the cover of a fallen tree. Arrows whisper through the air and thump into wood and dirt. Most seem to be falling short of our position. I cautiously lift my head, trying to figure out how to stop this fight, and witness Kauko raise his arms and send a massive blast of ice into the darkness of the trees just outside his clearing. One of his priests lies dead at his feet, and several more are huddled against trees with arrows protruding from shoulders and thighs and backs.

"They're aiming for the wielders," I say, and then I'm up and running, knowing it's up to me to stop this before Kauko kills what is left of Thyra's tribe. "Stop!"

I am breathless by the time I reach Kauko's side, but I keep pushing forward, heedless of the few arrows that slice through the air around me. "It's Ansa," I shout. "Cease your fire!"

"Cease fire," shouts Preben. The silver-bearded warrior emerges from behind a tree, bow in hand. A moment later, a few dozen others come into view. They run to two of our older warriors who lie in the open—frozen solid by Kauko's counterattack.

Bertel rises from the hollow, his bow on his back but a dagger in his hand. His brown skin shines with sweat even as his breath fogs from his mouth in the frigid air.

I turn to Kauko and try to wave him off, but the elder smirks. "That is coming from you, Valtia. Not me."

"And whose fault is that?" I glare at his wrist.

He looks unapologetic. "The magic truly is infinite," he says quietly. "You have no idea how powerful you are."

I face Bertel again, as the elder seems preoccupied with my power and not our current predicament. I'm facing nearly fifty of our grizzled old warriors who are looking at me as if I'm a traitor.

"Where is Thyra?" Bertel asks, leaning to look behind me. "She went after this old sorcerer here, and he looks soft and healthy as ever—with you at his side."

The mention of her name, spoken outside the confines of my own head, brings on a fresh wave of hurt. I put my hand out to steady myself against the nearest tree. "Thyra is . . ."

Bertel's face sags when he hears the grief in my voice—and then his jaw clenches. "Did this—" He has started to pull his bow from his back when Jaspar appears at my side.

"Elder Kauko is not guilty of killing Thyra!"

"So she really is dead," Preben says. "Our chieftain is dead."

Shoulders slump and a few of the warriors cover their eyes or mouths, trying to contain their shock and horror. Jaspar puts his arm around me, and I realize I was sinking to the ground, my grief too heavy to bear.

"What happened?" asks Bertel. "We were under attack for hours." He sweeps his arm toward the clearing where the wielders were practicing their arts just before the ambush. More of the priests have emerged from behind trees. Together with some of Jaspar's warriors, they are tending to the wounded and casting suspicious glances at our motley old group of fighters.

Jaspar explains what happened, how he and his scouts observed the attack and came upon me and Thyra. He looks to me for the rest, and his hands are warm and firm on my body, holding me upright, as I explain. "It was Sig. And another Kupari wielder."

"I knew it," snaps Preben. "That one was unstable from the start. Thyra was right."

Bertel gives me a hard look, and I hear his thoughts as if he'd spoke them aloud—*and you were wrong*.

"He was even more unstable once we reached the Kupari border," Bertel says as he hangs his bow from its quiver once more. "And so were you, Ansa."

"All wielders suffered," says Kauko. "That is why we

withdrew to prepare and gain strength." He gestures at his beleaguered priests. "The impostor queen incites the land itself. She has violated all that is right."

"We're going to take her throne from her," I tell our warriors. "After I kill her, and after we punish the ones who killed our chieftain with the most painful deaths we can devise, we're going to set things back on the right path—and take a new homeland for the Krigere." I glance behind me at Jaspar's camp, hating the next words that come out of my mouth. "With all our warriors united, there will be no stopping us."

"Thyra would not want our tribe united with one that mistreats our andeners," Bertel says. I know he is thinking of his own mate as he levels a piercing look on Jaspar.

"Circumstances have changed," says Jaspar. "And I am not my father."

It's true. Because I think he might be worse. But there is no way around the reality of now: I need him until my mission is completed. After that, perhaps I'll slit his throat as he sleeps. "Thyra would have wanted our tribe to survive." I swallow the lump in my throat. I cannot tell them the rest. How she begged me as she died. How she looked at the end.

"We will help," says Kauko.

"But you just said that when you cross into Kupari, your magic becomes unstable, just as the land is unstable." Preben moves forward and stands shoulder to shoulder with Bertel. "Ansa, you nearly killed us before."

"I can help her," Kauko assures. "I am old in the ways of

magic. The ones who suffer most are the ones without balance between the ice and the fire. My priests have balance."

"Does she?" asks Preben, waving his hand at me.

"No," says Kauko. "But I know how to keep her magic harnessed."

By bleeding me. My cheeks burn, and I feel the flames kindling inside me. "I am under control," I say, stepping away from Jaspar. "And I am the reason all of you will have a new land to call your home."

"One that quakes beneath our feet?" asks Bertel.

"The stars foretold the most powerful Valtia to ever live," Kauko says, putting his large hand on my shoulder and squeezing, perhaps to keep me from jerking away. "The land suffers from her absence. When her magic is back within the borders, it will settle."

"You're sure?" Preben looks wary, as do most of the old men and women standing among the trees.

"Kupari has never been a restive land," Kauko explains. "Not until our Valtia was *stolen* from us. What other reason would there be for the earth to protest?"

Jaspar beckons the warriors closer. "There must be no more aggression between us! Bring all of your tribe to our fires," he says. "You can think on all of this for the evening. But in the morning, we march. We need every sword and bow to honor and avenge Chieftain Thyra. I hope we can be unified, but if not, you may go on your way and choose a new chieftain to guide you."

There is no good reason for Bertel and Preben to deny

our warriors warm fires and hot food, so they do as Jaspar says. I am focused inward as the sky darkens. I swear I feel a distant tremor in the earth, but perhaps it is in my imagination. It takes several minutes for me to feel even remotely settled again, but most leave me alone as they go about their tasks for the evening. I squat near the base of a tree and stare at nothing, just listening to the dull roar of blood through my veins.

"Another quake," Kauko says as he hands me a steaming bowl. "Do you feel it?"

"Yes," I whisper. I am shamefully glad I am not within the borders of the land right now. "I don't think it's going to stop when I'm back in Kupari. It didn't before."

"Kupari is dying from the absence of your magic. It craves the power." The flames from the nearby fire are drawing beads of sweat to his bearded face.

I rise to my feet with my bowl. "I suppose we'll see. At least I'll have the cuff."

He chuckles. "Of course."

I walk away from him—there is something eerie and unearthly about the elder, and I don't want to spend an extra second in his presence. Instead, I go in search of Bertel and Preben.

I find them in a huddle with some of our other warriors, deep in conversation. Bertel spots me coming and their talk falls silent. They make no room for me at the fire and keep their backs turned. It feels as if my ribs have closed tight around my lungs.

I have no tribe, not anymore. Thyra was the only reason they tolerated me.

I look down at my bowl of soup, clear broth with mushrooms and a few green bits floating on top. I need this sustenance to regain my strength, but my stomach is churning. My feet carry me backward until my rear hits a tree, and then I slide down until my knees are tucked under my chin. I stare at my reflection in the bowl, a dim, ugly face reflecting the shadows of the fire.

"You can join us," Bertel says, taking a seat next to me, holding his own bowl.

"I know when I'm not wanted."

He sighs. "You are something we don't understand, Ansa. A Krigere is—"

"I am Krigere." I grit my teeth. "I have fought and bled for this tribe. I will die for it too."

"Thyra was right about Sig," he says slowly, securing my gaze. "I think she was probably right about you, too. She valued your loyalty."

I don't know whether I want him to stop talking, or to never stop. Hearing her name is both salve and saber. "She told me to protect all of you," I say. "She made me promise. As she"—I swipe my sleeve across my face—"as she died."

He looks toward the sprawl of camp, where wielders are gathered near the biggest fire now that Kauko has healed their wounds. Jaspar's warriors watched with fascination—if he can do that for them in the fight to come, they believe they'll be unstoppable. "And we're sure the elder is innocent?"

"I didn't see him when she was hit with the magic. I only saw Sig and another. A dark ice wielder."

"But you don't trust Kauko."

"He can be trusted to seek power, and to be faithful to his own interests."

"Ah. And you?"

I look away. "I can be trusted to follow Thyra's orders until her vision for our tribe is made real." And to avenge her death with fire and ice and agony.

He is staring at the side of my face. "And once that happens?"

I take a sip of my broth, and it is hot and salty, like blood. "Once that happens, my fight will be over."

"Your fight."

"You heard me. You'll have your wish, Bertel. No one has anything to fear from me."

He doesn't challenge or question me. He merely sits next to me as I gaze into the fire and drink my soup and imagine the moment when I fulfill my promise and can leave this life for the eternal battlefield. I'll find Thyra there. She'll know I was faithful to the very end.

I cannot wait for that moment to come.

CHAPTER SIXTEEN

Elli

They all press in, jaws set, hands hard, and somehow, of all the voices raised in the courtyard, the only one I'm aware of is Lahja's. She screams as her mother pulls her back and lets the crowd at me, and the sound is a noose around my heart. I call her name, but her father and Yrian squeeze my arms so tight that it steals my volume. I struggle and crane my neck while they drag me toward an iron well post in the center of the courtyard. Yrian holds my wrists and Topias hands Lahja's father a rope.

"We'd banish you to the outlands if we thought that would stop you, but you've done more for the criminals there than the citizens here!" yells Agata.

I try to think of the right words. I usually have the right words! But as my heels drag in the dirt and Lahja's father ties my wrists to the post, all those words abandon me.

The space is churning with people now, but Yrian shouts to give me some space. At first I'm grateful, but then I see Agata hand Yrian a broken stone, one that has fallen from the archway of the council hall. Others see this and begin to scrounge for stones of their own.

They're going to kill me. Right now. Right here.

Yrian raises his stone. "This false queen stole justice from me. Now I will avenge my son!"

I see in his eyes that he has no hesitation, no qualms, only the grief of losing his baby boy. I wonder if that pain is good—perhaps it means he will strike hard and this will end quickly. I close my eyes.

The crowd cheers, shouting that this is what I deserve for posing as the Valtia, that I have ruined Kupari, that I am responsible for all their bad luck. I sweat, awaiting the moment the stones will start to shatter me.

Yrian grunts. I bow my head. Screams fill the courtyard as several people plow into me, blown by a thunderous, icy wind that I feel like the kiss of a star.

"Get away from her," roars Oskar.

"He can't take all of us at once," Agata shrieks.

I am being crushed. Trampled. Around me, wind swirls, but it is clear that Oskar is trying not to hurt anyone—he knows it would only spark greater hatred toward wielders. I suck in a breath as I am knocked to the ground. Someone yanks me up by the hair, and I am held against a hard chest.

"Get her into the hall," Yrian says, cutting my bonds and

shoving me toward Topias. "We'll deal with the wielders."

"Elli!" It's Oskar, surrounded and fighting. His left hand is pinned to his side, useless. His gray eyes are desperate with fear—and hurt. He jerks his arm up to block a large rock someone has aimed at his head. In this close proximity, he's either going to lose control or lash out just to survive. And with all the trouble wielders have had harnessing their magic lately, this situation could be deadly for so many—including Lahja, who is still screaming nearby.

Her cries tear at me, uncovering my rage. I need a wielder. One wielder. That is all I need to put a stop to this. I fling my arm out, but Oskar is several feet away, still fighting to get to me while people try to smash him with stones. He is barely fending them off, and the air is getting colder by the second. The frost licks at my fingertips. It feels as if I am a hair's breadth away from wrapping my fingers around that power and using it as my own. . . .

Topias starts to drag me toward the arched entrance to the council hall, but then he cries out and releases me. "Please, no!"

His eyes are on the shirtless man who has forced his way between us.

Sig has snaked his way through the mob—his eyes are wild and his face is dripping with sweat. "I'm trusting you," he shouts.

He reaches for me. I tangle my fingers with his and dive into his arms before someone else can tear me away. "Wield it," he says against my ear. "I can't right now."

The inferno of his magic blasts across my palm and up my arm, and I shove my scarred, three-fingered hand into the air. My teeth are gritted as I try to control the massive power. Flames sprout from my fingers and rise as orange serpents, hissing and sparking. Sig's eyes go wide as he holds me close.

"Your eyes," he says in a choked voice, but I don't need him to tell me.

I know they are glowing. I'm glad. I'm elated, in fact, as people gasp and stagger back from the heat with terror on their faces. "Let the ice wielder go or I will burn you," I say, and my voice is monstrous with the magic inside me. Sig holds me tight, bracing against anyone who tries to separate us. He is trembling as I magnify the heat and flames. His head is bowed against my hair.

Oskar lunges for us as soon as the mob gives him a chance, sending a hard burst of wind to push them away. His good hand finds my bare wrist, and suddenly I am the Valtia, both ice and fire at my command. I wiggle my remaining fingers, and ice and fire entwine like lovers, a swirl of snow and spark. I search the faces and find Agata, who is crouched with Lahja and her mother against the wall.

"I don't want to hurt you, my citizens, but if you do not yield, I will. Clear a path to the street. Now."

Warily, they do, revealing Raimo and Kaisa just outside, holding the rest of the crowd at bay. But their hands are shaking badly. And so are Sig and Oskar. If they falter, the mob will be on us. I can read that future in Yrian's glittering dark eyes. He holds another stone at the ready.

I stare him down, allowing some of the magic to dip and undulate just over his head. A promise. He hunches his shoulders and scowls.

"My wielders and I are going to return to the temple now. In spite of your attack on me, I leave you in peace. But I will not abandon you, even though you have abandoned me," I say. Authority rings in every word.

This, I think. *This is what it would have been like*.

That is not what I should focus on now. "Give me the Saadella."

Her mother only holds her tighter, and it pricks at my heart. I need my Lahja, but her mother is the one who bore her and loved her before I ever knew she existed. To have a Saadella for a daughter is to have a shredded heart. "Bring her," I say to her mother. "She is mine, but you may accompany her."

The woman is white with fear of me, but she rises and comes slowly toward us.

"We're going to walk to the temple," I say quietly to Sig and Oskar as they stand on either side of me. We stride toward the street.

Raimo and Kaisa step aside as we emerge. "We'll watch your back," says the old man. "But for star's sake, hurry."

We're surrounded by round-eyed townsfolk, who watch my spectacular display of magic with a mixture of awe and mistrust. Both my Suurin are quaking now, unsteady on their feet.

"Don't feel right," Sig whispers.

"Me neither," mutters Oskar.

I glance behind me to see Lahja's mother carrying her, and Raimo and Kaisa falling in behind. We are a ragged procession in a hostile crowd, but right now, no one dares threaten us.

That is good, because I am dangerous. More power than I've ever felt or controlled is coursing through me, spiraling high into the air. The clouds have parted to escape it. The air has turned sticky and electric. I am affecting the weather. I feel as if I could pull the sun from the sky and harness the moon.

Oskar groans. "I—I don't know. . . ."

Sig stumbles over his own feet and nearly loses his grip on me.

"Am I taking too much?" I ask. "Draining you?"

He shakes his head, and drops of his sweat hit my sleeve. "No, it's—"

The crack is deafening. We're tossed to the ground like grains of sand on a windy dune. All around me, people yell and scramble and screech. Sig and Oskar struggle to rise from the churning earth. I call for my Saadella, but my world is a swirl of dust and grit, of falling rocks and rumbling earth, and she is gone.

"The plaza," Oskar shouts, his voice hoarse. "The rocks—"

We'll be safe there, out from under the looming buildings nearest the temple grounds. I shove up to my feet. The townsfolk have forgotten all about us as they scurry back into the square or down to the shore to escape the danger of collapsing buildings. I stagger up the road toward the broken gates of the white plaza. It's so close, but it takes minutes to get there instead of seconds.

Minutes during which the land seems determined to rid itself of all of us, as a dog might shake drops from its fur. Dust billows around me, filling my mouth and eyes with grit. It feels as if, at any moment, the ground might simply give way beneath my feet.

The only reason I know when I reach the plaza is that the stones go from dirty gray to white. I try to run for the temple but Oskar tackles me, and we fall. I cling to him, wondering if these are our final moments, wondering if that was the battle we were to fight, and if Raimo foresaw no future because this is the day it all ends.

The slabs of marble tilt suddenly, and we roll down a steep slope where once the world was flat. Oskar lands on me, squeezing the air right out of me. Spots bloom beneath my closed eyelids. His magic simmers against my skin. I don't know where anyone else is—I'm only aware of Oskar trying and failing to shield me as we crash down. He is wheezing, struggling for breath. And I can do nothing for him because our world is falling apart.

But then it finally falls still. My hand finds his cheek, which is frigid and stiff. I siphon the magic, but he still fights to breathe. I raise my head—we are on one side of the plaza, and white slabs jut up like broken teeth from the gates to the temple.

"Oskar?"

"I'll be all right." He sounds so weary, and his face is once again a battleground of frostbite. "See how the others fared."

Reeling, I rise to my feet. Kaisa and Raimo are huddled closer to the gate, both ashen. Sig is on the other side of the plaza. And between us is a crevasse. Heat emanates from it as I climb the white slabs and survey what used to be the pristine, grand entrance to the Temple on the Rock.

Now it is occupied by a crack in the ground wider than the main road and deep enough to see the blood of the earth glowing in a thin orange river at the bottom. My eyes follow its path out through the gates and through the city until dust obscures it. I turn and trace it all the way toward the steps leading to our temple. It stops right at the base of them.

I have never thought of the earth as a being. But at this moment, I swear, I feel its threat. Another quake will widen this fissure, and the temple will be swallowed.

Behind me, Oskar moans. I scramble down the slabs and go back to him. Unsteadily, he sits up. One hand is red and blistered with cold, while the other is white and dead as ever.

"Is it bad?" Kaisa calls.

I glance over to see her helping Raimo to his feet. The old medicine man is pale and shaky, but his eyes are sharp. He says something to Kaisa, who nods. "Raimo says you must attend to Sig."

Of course. If Oskar is bad, Sig will be worse. "Go to him, Elli," Oskar says when I hesitate. "He needs you more than I do right now."

I run toward the steps of the temple, because that's the only place the fissure is narrow enough to cross. I feel its deadly heat as I climb a few steps and end up on the other side, then jog unsteadily to Sig, who is crumpled in a raw patch of dirt where the slab has been torn away completely. My stomach turns as I see him, his skin an oozing mess.

"Don't touch me," he whispers through cracked lips. "Unless it is to stab me in the heart and end this pain."

"We'll heal you," I tell him. My eyes are stinging. This is so cruel. He's dying before my eyes. I motion frantically for Raimo to join me, and Kaisa leads him toward the steps.

"The Saadella," he says.

"I can only hope she survived." My throat constricts even thinking of her. She's not here in the plaza with us. She's somewhere out in the city, beyond my reach for the moment. I pray her parents have kept her safe. "We have to find her. I'll send people. . . ." For now, there is no one to send.

"We're all going to die," Sig says, so quiet I barely catch it.

"We won't," I snap. "I'm going to fix this."

He laughs, and it's wet and tortured.

I look back to the temple. Kaisa limps over with Raimo. Her short blond hair is standing on end, and as she nears I can read the despair in her bloodshot eyes. There are a few red patches on her face, but no other marks of the magic inside her—but only because she does not have nearly as much as Sig or Oskar. I imagine all the wielders in the land are hurt. Raimo looks like he can't even stand on his own, but it seems as if the balance in his magic saved him from its worst effects.

"My Valtia," Kaisa says when she reaches me.

I offer a sad smile. "We can drop that pretext now. You may call me Elli."

She shakes her head. "I . . . I've known for some time that you did not have the same kind of magic as the previous Valtia. But you are still a true queen."

Tears sting my eyes. I don't feel like a queen. I feel exhausted and terrified and hungry for someone else to take over, to lead, to tuck me into a warm bed and tell me everything will be all right when I wake.

There is no one to do that now, though. All the wielders in the land will have been injured, each according to his or her power, and the more of it, the more they will suffer. Oskar and Sig barely survived this quake.

Even if I can summon the strength and balance I need to channel Raimo's magic and heal them—without killing the old man himself—another tremor will probably end them. Determination is the iron in my spine, holding me upright under the weight of all the sorrow and death that threatens my land. "Then I will be the queen you need," I say to Kaisa as I put my arm around Raimo and lower him to the ground next to Sig. I look up at the young apprentice. "Find the healthiest wielders we have left, and have them begin a search for Lahja. We must find her."

After Kaisa runs toward the temple, Raimo mutters, "I know what you're thinking, and it might not work."

I take his face in my hands and wait for him to look at me. "We can't wait any longer. We have to stop these quakes."

He nods weakly. "I know."

"What are you going to do?" Sig asks.

"I'm going to demand that our strongest men come to me," I say. "I'm going to have them carry the temple stores of copper here to the plaza." I point to the crack in the earth.

It is an open, hungry mouth. I know it is.

"They will work all night. And in the morning, we're going to give the land back what we stole."

CHAPTER SEVENTEEN

Ansa

After a sleep spent chasing Thyra through the dark woods, never quite able to catch or protect her, I rise before the sun touches our camp and wash in a stream. I can feel the fire and ice awakening inside me, and I'm glad. With the cuff of Astia, I'll have some hope of controlling it, and I crave the moment when I stand before the impostor and do to her what Sig and the other wielder did to my Thyra. The fraud-queen will feel the ice and the fire as she dies, and I'll feel the freedom that comes when a future meets its horizon.

Kauko is guarded by his priests as I approach, and they rise, pushing their hoods away from their faces. "I'm here for my cuff."

Kauko sits up from his nest of blankets near the cold fire

when he hears my voice. "You are very reliable, my Valtia."

I stick out my hand. "We're going to have a problem if you aren't."

He gives me a gentle smile. "I am on your side. Remember that we want the same thing. Death to the impostor, vengeance for what happened to Chieftain Thyra, safety and prosperity for our people. I am not your enemy, and I never have been."

"Stop talking and give me what's mine!"

He isn't the slightest bit cowed by the harshness in my tone, or the fact that sparks leap from my mouth as I speak. His priests put their hands up, prepared to wield their various powers, but Kauko jumps to his feet with that startling agility of his. "She's right!" He removes the cuff from his wrist and hands it to me, still smiling. "This cuff will help our Valtia as she reclaims our land and her throne."

I don't want the throne. I don't care about it at all. But I take the cuff and snap it shut around my wrist. Instantly, its heavy, warm weight relaxes my tense muscles and calms the brewing storm inside. I smile. This was how I felt as I aimed at Nisse's jugular. I could finally control the power that is mine to wield, and with the cuff, I will be able to see Thyra's vision through. "Thank you."

I turn and march away as the camp awakens and packs. Our wounded have all been healed by Kauko, and they smile at him as they go about their work. They are willing to accept magic when it is used to serve them, I suppose.

Jaspar finds me and invites me to march with his inner

circle. Carina stands near him, her braid of thick hair coiled at the base of her skull to keep it out of the way. I wonder if they are simply entertaining each other, or if she wishes she could be his mate. Or maybe she simply wants to be near the seat of power. She is clearly his wolf, and Jaspar relies on her to carry his orders throughout camp. Her gaze slides warily in my direction from time to time, but she's not antagonistic. She never has been, not really. She simply knows who she serves and what her role is, and I think I envy her that.

I serve a dead chieftain, and my role is to be hated and feared and mistrusted, apparently. I absorb the watchful stares of so many warriors as we pass their lines and start the march. They don't dare whisper about me now because their chieftain, Jaspar, is at my side, but I know that tonight as they gather around their fires, they will.

I hang at the rear of Jaspar's group, keeping an eye out for Bertel, Preben, and the remaining warriors who were loyal to Thyra. Some of them seem glad to be back with the larger group, but others, including Preben and Bertel, seem more reluctant and suspicious. Thyra truly did win them over, and their loyalty is a heavy thing, not easily shifted or swayed. For Thyra, I owe them my all. But because of her, I am having trouble thinking past my need for the blood of those who stole her from us.

In all, we are a thousand tense warriors marching a narrow path through the damp morning forest, winding north. The priests hike along near the front, keeping close to their elder. His steps are steady and graceful in his tattered robes, and he looks eager to return to his homeland.

It's my homeland too, but as we reach a part of the forest where the trees are bare and blackened, I feel the unsteadiness return. The feeling stirs deep in my bones, but I decide to ignore it. This will be different. I know to expect tremors, but I have experienced wielders to guide me. No surprises this time, and much less fear.

Jaspar leads us on a curving path that for a while has the sun directly behind us, and it hits me that he has circumvented the meadow where Thyra died. "We're almost to the border, I believe," he announces, looking to Kauko for confirmation.

The older man nods. "Those of us with magic inside us have felt it coming." He gives me a curious look, and I nod, running my hand over the warm red runes of my cuff. The priests are unsmiling and seem tense, but they don't appear to be suffering.

Jaspar smiles as Carina joins us from running an order to the rear of the line. He wants them to catch up so we aren't as stretched out once we clear the forest. "I see our destination up ahead," he shouts. "We will not aggress toward the citizens of these outlands. This is not a raid. We march to the city and its temple to unseat a false ruler. Stay focused on that objective."

Kauko bows his gratitude. "You will be seen as a liberating force. They will be scared of you at first—so many terrible stories, understand. But once they realize you bring with you the true Valtia, ah!" He grins and claps his hands. "You will have the people on your side!"

My heart thrums in my chest. What will they want from me? Jaspar once told me the Valtia provides for all the needs of her people, but I haven't the faintest idea how to do that. I also don't have the will or energy. I only have the will to finish my mission.

After that, there will be a new Valtia, and she will be raised Krigere.

We reach the edge of the trees, the place where the great forest ends abruptly, and are greeted by a vast, hilly expanse of grassland dotted by craggy hills. Seagulls spiral overhead, reminding us that the Torden surrounds this place on three sides.

"My first raid was on a sheep farm on the eastern side of this peninsula," says Preben, sounding wistful. "It's strange to come at it this way, up from the south—and on foot."

Bertel lets out a grim chuckle. "At least we're still on our feet, old man."

I look back at our rows of graybeards and silver braids, men and women who have lived two or three of my lifetimes and still manage to carry their weapons and supplies on their backs without complaint. "You are the strongest of us," I murmur.

Jaspar looks beyond them to his straight-backed, much younger warriors. Their andeners and children are staying at the forest edge until we determine it is safe for them to cross into their new homeland. "May all of mine live to see their silver years."

"They will," I say. But I won't. With every step I take, I am brought closer to Thyra, though, and that is why I march.

"I think this land is quite pretty," Carina says, surveying a little valley with a pond dotted with lilies and rushes. Little birds with humming wings flit by us.

"I'd try to hit one of them with an arrow, but I don't think it'd have much meat," comments one warrior. Others laugh. The sunny day and absence of death have put them in a good mood.

Even I smile as the warmth kisses my brow. It is nice to be beyond the reach of the trees, the stench of suffering that hangs in the Loputon. I am happy that I will never return there again. It is the place where Thyra's body rests, but her spirit is my goal. Nothing here matters to me anymore.

We don't see a single living soul as we march north throughout the morning, but we see plenty of evidence of the recent quakes. Felled trees, long fissures exposing red dirt, empty lake beds where the water was drained into the ground through a tear in its skin. We follow the road for a time, until we reach a wide crevasse that traverses the land east to west. It takes us quite a time to climb through that and reach the other side—and we are forced to leave our mounts behind with a few who will try to find a way around it. But Jaspar says we will be all right without them, because Kauko assures him there is no army here, no fighting force of any kind, and certainly no horse warriors—but he also tells him there are plenty of mounts to be stolen in the city once we get there.

I'm glad. I don't want to sit and wait any longer. I am ready for the end game.

Once we begin the march again, I let the buzz of conversation wash over me. The priests could talk privately among themselves too, as none of us speak Kupari, but they stay silent, maybe because they know it will arouse suspicion if they are babbling words the warriors cannot understand. Or maybe because they feel an echo of what I feel—an unsteady vibration in my body, one strong enough to make my breaths unsteady, one powerful enough that I must focus to keep all the power inside me under control. I concentrate on the cuff and let it do its work, but the further we move into the territory of the impostor, the more I sweat and shiver, and the more it hums.

After several hours of steady quick-marching, we reach another large wood. "North woods," Kauko tells us. "Past this is the city of Kupari."

"We'll stop for our meal here, then, and be to the gates of the place before sundown," Jaspar says. His warriors pass the message along the line, and relieved smiles stretch across weary, dust-coated faces.

"I'll be back in a moment," I say, motioning to the woods. I might be the Valtia, but I still have to do my business like anyone else.

"I'll go with you," says Carina, giving Jaspar a look. He nods and touches her arm as she strides by.

I roll my eyes but don't protest. If I wanted to run, Carina couldn't stop me. We set off walking toward a scattering of boulders among the trees that will offer nice privacy. Carina clears her throat. "Jaspar is glad to have you back with us," she says.

"Because he believes I can help him get what he wants."

"He has always wanted you in his tribe, Ansa. You know that."

"And you?" I look over at her. She's everything a warrior should be. Lean and strong and brave. I can't hate her. "What do you want?"

"I want things the way they were," she says. "I want to raid and plunder. But I can't have that, so I'll take what I can get."

I think about that. "What if it's not enough?"

She shrugs. "I think sometimes getting through this life is about making what you have enough to sustain you."

"I always thought it was about fighting until you had enough, not accepting less."

"That warrior doesn't survive very long."

"So true," I whisper.

We use the privacy of the boulders and begin to make our way back to the others. "Look—frost berries," Carina says, jogging up the length of the boulders. Her bow and quiver rattle against her back as she runs. She gathers the little purple berries in her palms with a look of delight on her face. "Now this feels like a place that could be home."

She pockets several handfuls, making an absent comment about how Jaspar likes them too, and I wait. She offers me some, but nothing tastes good and I'm not tempted.

When she's plucked the bushes bare, we head around the biggest boulder.

And come face to face with two Kupari women. They wear rough gowns and their hair is dark, almost black. The younger one is skinny with sharp cheekbones, and the older one . . .

Her gray eyes go round when she sees my face. "Ansa?"

I gasp at the sound of my name on her tongue, and the shape of her face and nose and eyes . . . and suddenly I am staring at my father's empty gray eyes, and I can't breathe.

Carina draws a dagger, and the younger girl grabs the older one's arm and yanks, wrenching the woman out of her shock.

They run toward two horses that are tethered to a branch perhaps twenty yards away. They move like rabbits, swift and scared, and all I can do is stare as the woman's voice echoes in my head.

"Come on, we have to stop them," barks Carina, but I don't move, and the women are already on their horses.

Carina draws her bow.

The older woman, her dark hair flying around her face, reels her horse around. Her face is wild with fear and surprise. She says something to the young one in that trilling Kupari language and says my name again.

"They know me," I say in a choked voice.

"All the more reason not to let them escape this wood," Carina growls, nocking an arrow.

I stumble forward. "No, you can't—"

She takes aim. I stretch out my palm as she lets fly, and something inside me erupts. It escapes me like thunder, a brutal, swirling wind that surrounds Carina, ice glittering brightly within the maelstrom. She lets out one harsh scream before going silent. I fall to my knees, my fingers burning with cold, and raise my head to find that the two women are gone. They escaped.

But Carina . . . I crawl to her as the ground rumbles, and as I reach her I realize it is not another quake—it is perhaps fifty warriors answering their sister warrior's terrified cry.

They find me kneeling next to her. I look down at her face. Ice melts in shards all around her, and she bleeds from cut after cut after cut. Her fingers tremble as she reaches for her throat, where at least three icy splinters have pierced her flesh like arrows. As they slip out of her warm skin, blood flows readily from the wounds they leave behind.

Jaspar reaches us first and lets out a wretched groan. "Get Kauko. Now!"

Two warriors take off running as he turns his green eyes on me. "How could you do this?" he asks as he drops to his knees and pulls her into his lap, cradling her as she gurgles. "She did nothing to you!"

What am I to say? I killed her because I was protecting two Kupari?

One of those Kupari knew me? And she had my father's eyes?

I look down at my hands. "I didn't mean to. I wasn't trying to kill her."

"Look at her," he roars, rocking her as her eyes go blank. A little pile of berries has fallen from the pouch in her trousers. He crushes them with his knees as he tends to her, and their purple juice mixes with her blood.

Kauko jogs into our midst, his brow furrowed.

"Fix her," Jaspar shouts. "Make her whole again!"

Kauko kneels and touches her throat. "I cannot," he says sadly. "She is already gone."

"Bring her back." Jaspar's voice breaks. "She was alive only seconds ago."

Kauko shakes his head. "When the spirit is gone, life is gone. There is no bringing it back."

Jaspar throws his head back and lets out a jagged noise of grief while warriors gather around us. When the sound dies, he bows his head. I sit numbly, knowing I can't fix this, not able to feel anything beyond the confusion of the past few moments.

"Ansa, you've betrayed me," Jaspar finally says in a low voice. He gives Kauko a sharp look and a quick nod.

The hard hands of the priests wrap around my arms and pull me from the ground. As my magic rises to defend its vessel, Kauko moves in front of me, his palms out. Quick as a snake, he pulls the cuff from my wrist and puts it back on his. Rage boils in my chest. I don't care if I burn with him—I'm going to watch his flesh melt.

"Bertel, Preben," Jaspar shouts. And then the two old warriors are on me too, their expressions conflicted but their hands certain and hard, and I clench my fists because I promised Thyra. I promised her. She would never forgive me if I killed any member of our tribe, but especially these two, who have been loyal to her since the day she bested their comrade Edvin in the fight circle. When I find her on the eternal battlefield, she'll turn her back on me if I so much as blister them. I hold my breath and arch and kick as they secure my hands behind my back, as ropes wind around my body, but I don't lash out.

"Leave one arm exposed," orders Kauko. He turns to one of his priests. "The cup. Bring it here."

"No," I scream. "Don't you dare!"

He is walking toward me with a knife. And Jaspar is still on the ground, cradling Carina against his body. He shakes his head when I call his name. "I believe you when you say you didn't mean it," he says to me. "But that means you are unstable—and that means you are a danger. We still need your magic, though. We must have it to defeat the impostor's wielders. This is for the good of the tribe, Ansa." He is looking at Preben and Bertel as he speaks.

Kauko gives me an apologetic smile as I snarl and spit at him. I stare at his jugular and he coughs, perhaps feeling the cold. He says something in Kupari to the priests surrounding me, and then I feel the bite of their magic every place their hands touch me. I can't think past it.

Until I feel the slice of the knife, right through my sleeve. Kauko tears away the fabric and puts his mouth right on the wound, sucking hard. He comes up with a grin that shows bloody teeth. Preben and Bertel turn away, faces twisted with disgust, but they don't stop him.

No one stops him. They all watch as he deepens the cut—drawing the blade from my elbow to my wrist, a line of fire almost to the bone. He has his priests angle my arm just so.

I shudder and struggle as I hear my blood dripping into the cup. I fight with all I have inside, but the pain makes it impossible to control the magic, as does the fear of hurting Bertel and Preben. Tears streak down my face as cold descends on me along with a heavy fatigue.

Kauko strokes my hair. "You see," he calls to Jaspar, who is blurry now. "She will rest." He looks down at me. "Your magic is a gift, my Valtia. And I will use it well."

CHAPTER EIGHTEEN

Elli

By midnight I have Livius and his promised stone crews, though they are a few men short, as two did not survive the most recent quake. All the men are dusty and glassy-eyed from the destruction in town. One man has lost his entire family, but unlike the mob in the square, he is loyal to the Valtia, or at least believes I might have the power to set things right.

The others just seem exhausted and wary, and when I tell them of my plan, they are incredulous. "Don't we need the copper?" one of them asks. "My brother's a miner who breaks his back each year to pull the stuff out of the earth!"

"But that's the problem," I say. "He was too good at his job. We bled the land dry, and now it's dying."

"Are you *sure* that's the cause of these ground shakes?"

This question comes from the grieving man, who has tear streaks through the gray stone residue coating his face. His question sounds like a plea.

I look over at Raimo, who is leaning heavily on his walking stick as he stands next to the rim of stone slabs that bounds the giant, deep fissure in the plaza. The old man looks somber and pale. Weak. We spent a few hours trying to heal Sig and Oskar, but finally Raimo's strength gave out, and now our Suurin are walking around wounded, still trying to control the vast unbalanced power contained within their increasingly fragile bodies. I think Oskar knew it was scaring me to look at them, because he took Sig down the path to the shore with some muttered excuse about wanting to be close to the water.

Raimo stayed, of course. He is faithful and steady even when he's horribly unsteady, as he is now. He hears the grieving stone worker's question, and he sees my hopeful expression, and he looks toward the gash in the earth. "Our magic comes from that copper, so who knows what else grows from those roots? It seems the land itself depended on it. We ignored that possibility in our greed—and we assumed the supply was endless." He chuckles. "We have made the same assumptions about the magic of the Valtia, that it will always remain here with us, that Kupari will always be its home. What if we were wrong?"

The stone workers gape at him, a new fear written on their faces. "You think the magic will abandon us now?" Livius asks in a choked voice. "Where would it go?"

"If we don't find the Saadella safe and alive, losing the magic is a certainty whether it wants to stay with us or not," I say. Lahja is an ache that nothing but her presence can soothe. The longer she is gone, the more I fear someone else has her.

"Even if we do find her, who knows?" Raimo replies. "The power may abandon us and go back to the stars, or to some other land where the people are more deserving."

The men frown and toss guilty glances in my direction. "Shouldn't have doubted you," one of them mumbles. I don't recognize him from the courtyard where I nearly got my head bashed in, but he easily could have been there.

"Apologies won't heal our land," I say. "But if you help me take this action to save it, all will be forgiven."

This promise seems to energize them. They follow Kaisa along a narrow path that will take them directly to the catacombs. "They'll form a human chain and pull the rocks away, and then we'll bring in carts to move the metal to that fissure," Livius says as he watches them go. His brows are so low that I can't see his eyes. "How much will you dump down that hole?"

"As much as it takes."

He's quiet for a while, his eyes on one of the torches that has been placed nearby. "It might be prudent to set some of it aside. We might need allies, Valtia, and the promise of copper will gain them faster than any desperate entreaty."

Especially because the elders refused to respond to desperate entreaties from other city-states. "We should never have been this isolated. We should never have believed we were sufficient unto ourselves just because we had magic. It was arrogant."

He rubs at the back of his neck as a shout from the crew indicates they've started their work. A rhythmic chant begins, men working as one animal, digging toward our salvation. "The old wielder was right. We always believed the Valtia's magic was infinite, even though no Valtia ever was." He grunts. "Like children, we've been."

"We're all growing up very quickly," I tell him, placing my hand on his shoulder. "I love our people, Livius. I will do everything in my power to ensure we go on."

"I believe you. And those who don't?" He waves a thick-fingered hand. "They're more interested in clinging to the past."

I smile. "I can't really blame them. Sometimes I miss it too." I miss feeling all that potential. I miss my serene belief in my destiny. I miss being protected. I even miss being told what to do, and being shielded from knowledge that would have scared me. "But that doesn't mean I want to go back."

"Forward we go, then," he says. "I'd best go get the carts." He strides off toward the crumbled gates of what was once the pristine white plaza of the temple.

Raimo limps over to me. "Livius is right that the copper could buy the help of allies against the Soturi. The Ylpesians are known for their horsemanship, and the Korkeans for their ironworks."

"What good will it do if the land is ashes and rubble when they get here?"

"I know you want this to work, Elli, but there's no guarantee that it will. The land may crave more than its mined copper."

I sigh impatiently. "As you've said to me before. Would you like me to dive into the hole too?"

"No," he murmurs. "I don't think it's *you* the earth wants."

"Are you suggesting it wants the Valtia?" My laugh is shrill. "You must be joking."

He tugs at his scraggly beard. "The texts I found in Kauko's secret library were all about the power of blood. Some of it is his own writing, from centuries ago. When he first experimented with drinking the stuff."

I think back to that night in the cave where Raimo first revealed the brutal history of the temple. "You told me he knew the first Suurin. It was their blood he drank."

Raimo's eyes are on the path to the shore, the one Oskar and Sig took. "Those Suurin were not unlike ours. Two young men, opposites in every way, and yet they understood each other in ways that no one else could."

I don't want to think of the fate of those young men. I don't want to think of how weary and pained my own Suurin looked as they walked away from me tonight. "There was only ever that one pair before Oskar and Sig. He can't have known *that* much about them."

Raimo turns to me, and his eyes carry a sadness so ancient and deep that I can't find the bottom of it. "He knew their blood carried their magic. And that, when fused with copper from the earth, it would create the most powerful tool a magic wielder could possibly possess. The cuff of Astia stabilizes. Balances. Magnifies. It allows a wielder to control and direct her power. It protects her from the strength of that ice and fire within her mortal body."

"And Kauko is out there somewhere, and apparently he has it."

"The cuff is not our concern right now. The way it was *created* is."

I hug myself against a sudden chill. "If you're suggesting what I think you are, the answer is no."

"Elli—"

"No!" I wave my arms and walk away from him. "You are being careless with their lives, old man, and I won't allow it."

"You are being careless with our entire land simply because of your feelings for Oskar!"

I round on him. "How dare you!"

"I warned you," Raimo says, his hands shaking as he grips his staff. "I warned you that you would regret this love you've allowed to grow between you. Did you think I was merely playing with you?"

"You refused to tell me what you knew, so yes!"

"It would have been cruel, Elli. You were facing so much."

"It's cruel now," I yell. "But of late my life has contained plenty of cruelty." I hold up my scarred hand. I gesture at my own magicless body as a sudden wave of disgust rolls through me. "I can't save the people I love," I say with a gasp. "No matter how hard I try." My eyes narrow and I glare at him.

"But I will not surrender yet. Their lives are precious. We need them to fight. You cannot convince me that—"

"We leave you for but a short while, and look what we come back to," Sig calls. He and Oskar lean on each other as they enter the plaza. "You look like you want to toss Raimo into the crevasse!"

I put my hands over my mouth and Oskar frowns. "What's gone wrong now?" he asks, looking from me to Raimo.

Raimo leans forward, whispering, "Do you want to tell them about this possibility, or shall I?"

"Neither of us will," I snap, praying the sound of the men's chanting drowns out our words. "Until it is a certainty, I refuse to even entertain the idea."

"Elli—"

"*I* am the queen," I say. "Magic or not, it falls to me." If I did have magic, though, I think Raimo would have been reduced to ash by the heat of my glare.

He bows his head as if he realizes it. "You're the queen."

We turn back to Sig and Oskar, and I smile, though it doesn't smooth the wrinkle of concern in Oskar's brow. "How are you feeling?"

The two Suurin enter a patch of light near the rim of the fissure. Raimo lets out a humorless laugh. "Hopefully better than you look."

Sig smirks, and it seems to hurt, because then he grimaces. "We're still prettier than you, old man."

It's all bravado. Raimo isn't covered in barely healed blisters like they are.

"Once we get the copper into the ground, you might feel better," I say cheerfully. "More stable."

"How long will it take them to pull it out of there?" Oskar asks.

I tell them about the crew's work and the carts. "Hopefully by morning we'll begin returning it to its rightful place in the earth." I don't look at Raimo. I don't want to see his expression.

"The Saadella," Oskar says. "Any news?"

I shake my head as my eyes sting with tears. "Some of our temple wielders are searching for her."

"What if her parents have succeeded where they failed before?" asks Sig. "They could have smuggled her out of the city."

Oh, stars. "Let's hope they have more sense than that," I say, trying not to choke on my fear for her.

"Enough talk," Raimo says, "Kaisa has marshaled the surviving kitchen staff and should be nearly ready to hand out cups of bone broth to the citizens. Suurin, go have some and rebuild some strength."

The city is a ruin, and all we have to offer the people at the moment is broth and a wild plan. Their Valtia is pitching their wealth into a crack in the ground, and their Saadella, their hope for the future . . .

"Kaisa plans to ask about Lahja as she ladles," Raimo says as he reads the despair on my face. "Warm food is the best way to get people talking."

"Would I know if she were dead?" I murmur.

"The connection between the Valtia and the Saadella

is a mysterious one," says Raimo. "And in the history of this land, the death of a Saadella has never happened. The elders protected her with every scrap of their power and cunning."

But now she's out there, somewhere within the maze of rubble and teetering buildings—or in the wild outlands beyond. "If she dies, our magic is gone, isn't it? It dies with Ansa, wherever she is."

"I'm sorry we couldn't bring Ansa back to you," Oskar says. "The elder set the perfect trap."

Sig shifts uneasily. "If Kauko has manipulated her to his side, I shudder to think of what they can do. Not to mention the thousand warriors who follow behind."

"One catastrophe at a time." I smooth a lock of my hair back and square my shoulders. "If we can stabilize the land, we can prepare the people for what comes next, and the wielders will be better able to help us defend the city if it comes to that."

A clatter of hooves makes me turn toward the gate to the plaza. I expect to see Livius there with his carts, but instead, two cloaked figures trot toward us. The horses' flanks are heaving and they're lathered with sweat. The two figures slide from their mounts. One of them is very small and skinny.

"Freya!" Oskar shouts, and the girl throws her hood back and runs to him, her face so pale it glows in the darkness.

Maarika follows her, but instead of going to Oskar, she comes straight for me and Raimo. "We were in the north wood this afternoon gathering berries," she says, panting. "And . . . she was there."

My heart leaps. "You saw Lahja and her family?"

Maarika frowns. "No. Ansa."

Oskar squints at his mother. "Alone?"

"No—the Soturi are camped south of the city," says Freya.

"Did they see you?" Raimo asks.

Freya shakes her head. "Well. Ansa and the other woman did. But then Ansa killed her."

Sig's brow furrows. "Ansa killed another Soturi?"

"Perhaps she has gone mad in her grief," Oskar says.

"I think she was stopping the woman from killing us," says Maarika. She shakes her head. "We circled back to see what was happening. The other warriors came to see what the commotion was. And they seized Ansa. The elder was there. Many priests, too."

"So they've aligned themselves with the Soturi," says Raimo. "That's one way to regain the temple."

"But what did they do to Ansa?" I ask. "Is she all right?"

Freya shakes her head. "I don't think so," she says in a small voice. "We fled when some of them spread out to scout, but when we rode away, she was still screaming."

My throat constricts. "No. No. We have to save her." My eyes meet Oskar's.

"I won't fail you this time," he says quietly.

"If what they say is true," says Raimo. "You'll be up against a thousand barbarians and a few dozen well-trained enemy wielders, including old Kauko. You might be Suurin, but . . ." He gestures at their weary, hunched forms.

Freya lifts her chin, all defiance. "It's not as if they'll be alone."

As she says that, a small horde of riders gallops into the plaza. Veikko's lean form is easy to spot, and Aira alights next to him. Both look haggard, but neither appears injured like the Suurin. "We saw the signal."

Freya bounces on her heels as she looks up at Oskar. "We have signals."

He snorts. "Your idea?"

She nods. "Flashes of fire at night. Smoke in the daytime."

Veikko rolls his eyes. "She made us all memorize them."

Aira smoothes her hand over Freya's head. "And it's been dead useful."

The other wielders have dismounted and gathered around. Some of them, like Tuuli and Usko, clasp hands with Sig, careful of his blisters. Others, probably nomads from the outlands recruited by Oskar, incline their heads toward my Ice Suurin.

"So what's happening?" asks Aira. She sweeps her hand across the destroyed plaza. "Apart from the obvious, that is."

"We have a mission," Oskar says. "One that may mean the difference between victory and defeat."

They all exchange glances. "We knew it was only a matter of time," Veikko says. "We're at your service."

"Good," says Sig, "because we need all the help we can get."

"We need you to go to the north woods," I say. "Without being seen or detected by the thousand Soturi warriors who squat there, waiting to attack us."

Tuuli whistles out a long breath that fogs cold with the ice magic inside her. "And if we happen to succeed?"

Raimo taps his stick on the ground. "Then you'll creep past the priests and elder who have allied themselves with those warriors."

Veikko grins. "I've got an absolutely fantastic idea about how to do that, if I may say so myself. But . . . why would I actually do something so risky?"

"Because," I say, "I need you to help me kidnap our Valtia and bring her home."

"You?" Oskar shakes his head. "Elli, if the Soturi have you, it's over for us."

"He's right," says Raimo. "This could play right into their hands."

"She needs me."

"We *all* need you," barks Oskar. Maarika lays her hand on her son's arm, and he winces.

"We can get her by ourselves," says Freya, giving her big brother a worried look before turning her gaze to me. "You are needed here."

My hands clench, sending satisfying pain up my left arm. Ansa isn't the only reason I want to venture out—if Lahja's parents took her beyond the city wall and into the north woods. . . . "Very well. But I'll need a signal too. I need to know that all of you are well, and that you have her."

As Freya begins to explain her system to me, the ground begins to shake again.

CHAPTER NINETEEN

Ansa

I awaken as the earth starts to move. I don't feel it in my bones as I have before. Now I have no warning when the branches start to crack and fall onto our camp. All I can do is watch their leaves waving and pray that one falls on me.

I'm chained to a cot once again.

Not that it would matter, because I don't think I'd try to run if I could. I'm floating in a sea of soul-deep exhaustion, and I don't care what happens to me now. I lie here and shake until a bunch of dark-robed priests grab me, shouting to each other in Kupari. They heft me up and run with my cot. We bounce off trees and they drop me twice. Somewhere to my left, I hear Jaspar call out some kind of order. A priest holding onto the foot of my cot cries out as blisters appear on his forehead. He falls away as the others keep stumbling along.

It's almost funny. I wish I could laugh.

After what feels like a lifetime, they set me down. The ground is still churning, but it's not so bad. More like the rolling of waves of the Torden on a spring day. I look up and see the stars bright above me, framed on one side by the black shadows of trees. The priests have carried me to the perimeter of the wood, and there are warriors further out in the meadow that bounds the forest. I can hear them talking to each other as the earth settles and goes back to sleep.

Kauko appears next to me. A young priest holds a torch so they can see me, and their faces look ghastly in its light. There are streaks of red and black along the elder's cheeks, as well as a crust of white blisters on his nose, but he still manages to look vigorous and healthy. The cuff of Astia glints just beneath his sleeve, and I stare at it as if it could save me.

Really, though, nothing can save me now.

Kauko lays a heavy, clammy palm on my forehead. "You need more broth." He asks the priest a question in Kupari, and the young man answers quickly. He looks pained and out of breath but does not bear any blisters or frostbite like the old man, perhaps because it seems like the most powerful wielders suffer the most. The elder was all right—but now he has drunk so much of my blood that I'm surprised he's not sick with it.

He shoos the young priest away after taking the torch from him. "You are weak, my Valtia."

I don't bother replying. It doesn't matter what I say. I'm not going to drink any broth.

"Kauko!" Jaspar's voice is a snarl as he approaches, carrying a torch of his own. Lines of worry bracket his mouth, and his eyes are red. I think he has been crying for Carina. They probably buried her this afternoon, her sword on her chest. I wonder if there are still berries in her pockets. "What did I feel just now?"

"Chieftain, this one was not as bad—"

"You're a dirty liar, old man," Jaspar says. "You promised us that when the Valtia entered the land, it would settle." He gestures grandly at me, trussed to this cot and too weak to move. "And here she is. Maybe we should have poured her blood over the earth instead of into your fat mouth!"

The elder smiles at him blandly. "Perhaps the evil of the impostor runs deeper than I guessed. Once we take over the temple, we will check the temple stores of copper. Those precious bars are the source of the magic in the land. If she's used them for her own wealth, it could perhaps explain the instability."

"One explanation after another, and all serve your ends," Jaspar says. "How convenient."

"If you have a better explanation, my wise young chieftain, perhaps you could offer it to this foolish old man."

I hear but do not see Jaspar slide his dagger from its sheath, and I watch without blinking as he presses it to the elder's throat.

And then drops it with a yelp as it glows red hot. Jaspar

leaps back as the blade lands in the grass next to my cot. I can feel its heat emanating up from the ground. Jaspar shakes his hand and looks down at his palm, where angry blisters have erupted. "You will pay for that," he says in a low voice.

Kauko shakes his head. "I will defend myself if threatened. You would do the same. And remember that Kupari is not like any other land you've tried to subjugate. You may have iron, but we have ice and fire." He blows a glitter of frost from between his thick rosy lips. "You cannot conquer it without my help."

Jaspar's jaw clenches and he looks down at me. Or through me, really. But I've said I was sorry for Carina and I have no energy left to repeat the apology. "What of Ansa? Will she live out the night?"

"I know how much blood to take, and when it is too much."

"So that means yes?" Jaspar has handed off his torch and is wrapping a loose cloth around his injured hand.

"Yes," says the elder. "We will give her bone broth to restore her, and then I will take more."

"She'll run out eventually. Of blood, if not of magic."

Kauko nods. "We will prolong her life as long as possible. Then I will take it all." His voice trembles slightly as he says this, perhaps with eagerness.

Jaspar looks faintly disgusted, but that is all. He seems to feel nothing for me now that I am no longer under his control, no longer a useful ally to help him achieve his goals.

Now I am just a wineskin for an evil old sorcerer. "Will you have all her magic, then?"

Kauko shakes his head. "As you said, magic is infinite even when the vessel is not. When she dies, it flows into the Saadella. And that little girl is in the possession of the impostor. This is why we must keep this Valtia alive until we take the temple."

"You can have some of our broth if you need it to keep her alive."

Kauko inclines his head in apparent gratitude, then looks at Jaspar's hand with a shrewd glint in his eye. "And I will heal that for you if you promise not to behave like a naughty child."

The look Jaspar gives him is pure hatred, simple, hot, and sure. But all he says is, "You would have my gratitude."

The elder grins, and I see blood between his teeth. "We can sit over there to do it."

A shriek splits the relative quiet as the clank of weapons and the stomping of boots reaches me from the woods. "Chieftain, we have something for you!"

Jaspar squints and holds up his torch. "Ho! Did you find some spies?"

One of the warriors laughs. "I doubt she's a spy."

"Mama!" screams a little girl.

The sound sets my heart beating again. Somehow, I find the strength to raise my head. Near the foot of my cot is a group of warriors. One holds a woman, her head a mass of blood that drips from her brown curls. And the other holds a girl.

A little copper-haired girl. I know her eyes are blue like mine even though the darkness hides the color. She is struggling against the big warrior, reaching for the dead woman.

"This one got crushed under a branch," says the warrior holding the woman. "We killed a man who was with them. He'd been trying to pull the girl free."

"She was snagged by the dress but unhurt," says the one holding the girl. "They must have been camping in the woods. Not sure if there are more—we've got a squad looking."

Jaspar tilts his head as I begin to breathe and see in color, everything bright and sharp. "She's a feisty little thing. A fine raid prize."

Kauko is staring at the girl with wide eyes. His hands are trembling. "Saadella."

When she hears his voice, the little girl wheels around, and her mouth becomes a perfect circle of terror. The scream that comes from her vibrates along my bones and draws tears to my eyes. This is her. This is the one who will inherit the magic that hides inside my marrow. She is tiny and exquisite, too pretty to be real.

"Mine," I whisper.

No one heeds me.

"She's mine," I say, louder.

The girl's screams falter as her eyes fall to me on the cot. Her little brow squinches up. And then she starts to cry, too destroyed to even struggle against the warrior who awkwardly holds her. He doesn't look sure whether to shake her or stroke her hair, so he merely lets her sag from his arms, her little body shuddering.

I have never felt this way before. All I want to do is tear off my shackles and hold the small creature, rock her, smell her hair, and kiss her cheek. I am reeling with this need. This love.

"I'm confused," Jaspar says flatly.

"Chieftain, this must have been ordained by the stars," Kauko says in an awed voice. "This is the girl. This is the princess!"

"You said the impostor had her. Why would the princess be in the woods?"

"Perhaps her mother felt the evil of that fraud and tried to escape with her! And the stars have brought her straight to us!"

"Too late for this one, though," says the warrior holding the girl's dead mother.

"Bury her," says Jaspar. "Do it quickly."

The warrior and two companions tromp off to do the deed. The warrior holding my girl grasps her under her armpits and holds her out like a sack of grain. She hangs there, limp and whimpering.

"What do we do with her?" Jaspar asks. "Does she have magic too?"

"No," says Kauko. "But she will." He is grinning again.

"How do we do that?"

"We allow the girl to rest. I can brew a sleeping draught that will give her peaceful sleep and allow her to recover.

I will send my priests to find other herbs to loosen her muscles and steal her fight. I will need to keep her in a very docile and obedient state for the foreseeable future if this is to work."

"If *what* is to work?" Jaspar looks slightly ill at ease. "Will you bleed her as well?"

"No. She must be calm for the passing and containment of the magic." The elder glances down at me. "We will bleed this one again," he says. "Almost to the point of death." He kneels and touches my cheek, and I feel the burn of my power inside him. "And in the morning, we will kill her, and a new Valtia will rise."

I open my eyes and know I have made it. A warm breeze ruffles my hair as I turn my face to the sun. All around me are sounds I recognize and love—the scrape of a blade against a hide, the shuffle of boots in dirt, the grunts as grapplers collide, the clanging of a hammer on an anvil, the laughter and joking that only come with comradery earned through years of training, raiding, swapping stories by a fire under stars.

My heart aches with joy as I see Sander, his dark hair short, his dark eyes alive with intelligence, circling a sparring opponent while Hilma, his mate, holds their child propped on her hip. And nearby are Einar and Jes, the fathers who chose me, who taught me to be what I was at my very best—a true warrior, a loyal wolf. Jes is queuing Einar's shaggy hair while Einar sharpens his favorite dagger.

They are arguing over which of them must check the traps tonight in the way only destined mates can.

In a happy, floaty haze, I drift past my lost brothers and sisters, the ones taken by illness, the ones snatched away by the witch-made storm. My breath catches when I see Aksel training with a group of younger warriors on a patch of torn up earth, but when he sees me he merely waves and goes back to his maneuvers, as if he doesn't care at all that I gave him an utterly agonizing death.

Up ahead is a tent, and within I see the broad shoulders and scarred arms of Lars. He sits at a table, a cup of ale at his elbow, plotting some sort of strategy . . . with his brother. Nisse is here too, and as I near he gives his brother a good-natured punch on the arm, and the two of them laugh as if they are boys once more.

All is forgiven here, I suppose. Wrongs have been erased, mistakes forgiven. I feel as if I am weightless, free of the guilt that has nestled poisonous and oily in my gut—the people I have killed, all the pain I caused. It's behind me now, and all I have is an eternal future.

"Ansa," Thyra calls, and I spin around. She's walking away from Carina, who smiles and lifts her hand to greet me. Thyra is whole and perfect and so lovely that a tear streaks down my cheek. Her skin is smooth and tanned, her eyes that radiant blue, her short hair messy and framing her exquisite face, her lean arms revealing the taut curves of her muscles.

"I have missed you so much," I manage to say.

She stops in front of me and tilts her head. "What are you doing here?"

"I've died," I say.

A tiny line forms between her brows. "You don't belong here."

I laugh. "Yes, I do. I did my best, but my life ended a few hours ago." And I'm relieved. I don't miss that body at all. Now I feel well and free and simple, no need to fight the fire and ice magic that had knitted itself into my skin and bones and soul. I reach out to touch her cheek, but for some reason, I can't quite lift my arm. It's not obeying me.

Thyra draws her dagger. "I'm sorry, Ansa. You don't belong here."

She moves like lightning, like she always did. Her blade is buried to the hilt in my gut before I even feel the pain. But when it comes, it sears me to the core, as does the cold look in her eye. "You didn't keep your promise," she whispers.

She yanks her blade from my body, and I'm falling, boneless and helpless. The heavenly battlefield refuses to catch me—instead, it opens like a monster's mouth and swallows me, and Thyra and Carina and Aksel and Nisse and all the others gather to watch my descent. They recede until I lose sight of them, and then I'm plummeting through darkness until I slam onto rock and agony explodes along my limbs.

Unable to breathe, unable to move, I lie in my new forever-place and know I have endless time to suffer. Thyra, my Thyra, made this her final gift to me. My tribe dwells in their paradise, backs turned to me and hearts closed. They are my heaven, and I . . . am nothing now. Maybe I've always been this way. Maybe I've only been fooling myself. I have never really been a Krigere.

I am the real impostor.

As if this place has been devised to double my pain, I hear the whisper of Kupari, trilling and indecipherable, and the sound reminds me that though I was born to them, I don't belong there either. I belong nowhere, and that is where I am.

Cursed, apparently, to listen to that awful language for eternity.

When I feel the wolves begin to nibble my flesh, I realize the punishment is only just beginning. Pain burns across my wrists and ankles as they tug at my carcass. And then one of them clutches me in its jaws and hefts me up. I'm not strong enough to fight, and my dangling arms swing like bags of sand.

"Better not be dead," Sig says against my ear. His breaths are harsh and rasping.

Sig? Is he here too? He deserves to be, for what he did to Thyra.

"Can you stand, Ansa?"

"What?" I whisper. How can he be asking me that? I'm being eaten by wolves.

He says something in Kupari—and is answered by a deep voice nearby. Fingers prod my cheek. I fight to open my eyes.

"Aren't we dead?" I ask.

"Quiet."

My eyes pop open, and confusion nearly drowns me. I'm surrounded by black-robed priests—including the one who is carrying me . . . and using Sig's voice. "Sig?"

"Quiet!"

Somewhere to our left, another voice calls out in Kupari—and is answered in Krigere when someone shouts, "What's wrong?"

Sig's arms tighten around me and he starts to run. We're in the trees, and the priests are spreading out around us. One of them, the biggest, turns his head.

"It's you," I cry, realizing that I'm in the hands of the two men who murdered my love. I want to wrap my hands around Sig's throat and burn him to ash, but I'm too weak to even lift my arms.

The big, dark ice wielder asks Sig a question, and Sig trills his answer. I try to struggle as his strides become more urgent.

Fire bursts among the branches just over our heads. Sig flings me to the ground, and I roll, landing on my side at the base of an aspen. The ice wielder whirls around, and his eyes are black as pitch as he sends a blast of thundering ice in the direction the fireball came from. All of a sudden the wood is alive with wielders, ice and fire swirling and colliding all around me. Hooded figures sprint back and forth, diving for cover, hurling billowing frost, blades of ice, waves of blistering heat, balls of flame. Everyone shouts in Kupari and I understand none of it.

All I know is that I'm not actually dead, and I'm relieved, because it means I'm not being eaten by wolves in a black pit of forever-despair. That was slightly worse than being alive.

I recognize the faces of some of the wielders hurling fire and ice—these are the priests who serve Kauko. But the ones with Sig and the dark ice wielder are strangers—until one of them sends a little burst of flame at an oncoming priest, and I recognize her as the girl in the clearing, the one with the older woman.

The one I saved by killing Carina.

She looks young and terrified as she throws herself behind a boulder with the big ice wielder. He clutches her skinny shoulders and looks her over while he speaks sternly to her. The other wielders keep fighting, and one of them shouts at the ice wielder. "Oskar," the woman says as she dodges a fireball hurled by a balding priest.

Oskar. The name makes me think of sand, and racing, and joy, and it makes no sense because I'm going to kill that wielder, who helped Sig take Thyra . . . as soon as I can lift my arms again. Oskar the ice wielder flings blades of ice in the direction of the balding priest. He looks grim as he fights. But Sig, halfway across the clearing, is laughing as he makes two other priests run screaming from the wood with their robes and hair aflame. This is sport for him.

Until Kauko strides into the clearing, his hood thrown back.

"Kauko," shouts Sig. The name is echoed in frightened tones among the hooded figures who were running alongside the traitorous fire wielder.

The elder walks forward, his white cheeks and pale brow lit up by the fire that swirls on his upturned left palm. On his right is a blizzard that looks as if it is contained in a bubble. Perfectly round, completely vicious. He appears calm as always. Calm as he comforts, as he cuts, as he kills. Calm as he drinks my blood, calm as he talks of inviting my magic into the body of the tiny girl who is mine, mine, *mine*.

A spark of fire ignites inside my chest.

"Ansa," Kauko calls, his dark eyes searching the trees. He finds me and chuckles. "Naughty Valtia."

Sig lunges from behind his tree, sending a rolling wave of fire at the elder, who repels it with ice.

"Are you working together, Ansa?" Kauko calls as he destroys Oskar's next icy attack with flame. "Have you been waiting for them to rescue you?"

Sig strikes again, this time with a thin, serpentine whip of fire that he tries to coil around the elder, but Kauko merely laughs and waves his hands at the flames, dissipating them with bitterly frigid air. Sig calls out something to the dark one in Kupari, and then his eyes meet mine as he cowers behind a nearby tree. "Did he drink more of your blood?" he asks.

As if in answer, Kauko lights up the forest with flame. The cuff of Astia is revealed when he brings his arm up to lift the fire into the trees and set the leaves alight. He still looks serene, but there is a glint of savagery in his eye, one I know well—he would be happy to kill tonight.

Sig cries out in pain as a burning branch falls onto his

hiding place, and when he runs into the open to escape it, Kauko blasts him with heat. He falls to his knees, but then Oskar and another lean, dark ice wielder step out from their hiding places and pour wickedly cold air into the clearing, blowing out the flames and making the air breathable again.

I still haven't moved. I'm lying sprawled at the edge of this clearing, and I am shivering and sweating and unable to summon the strength to sit up, let alone protect myself. Then the forest is full of screams and cracking as the ground shakes again. The trees are burning and dark figures run hither and thither in the smoke. I am grabbed roughly and yanked up, and then someone flings me over the back of a horse. The hooded figures around me talk to each other in panic-laced Kupari. Someone mounts the horse and places a hand on my back. An unfamiliar male voice says something in that foreign tongue before kicking his horse's flanks and sending us galloping into the woods. The wielder's body is pressed hard over mine, and my arms and legs hang down and slap against the horse's sides as it flees the heat and smoke and flame.

I am not entirely sure, but I think these wielders have just stolen me from the elder. From Jaspar. From my own execution.

But that does not mean they are my friends. They are allied with the impostor queen.

And they killed Thyra. I saw it happen. I held her as she died. No good deed will save them from my wrath.

When my magic returns to me, I am going to make their world burn.

CHAPTER TWENTY

Elli

I stand at the edge of the fissure with a bar of copper in my hands. Livius and his exhausted crew gather around while Raimo hovers at my shoulder. He's been irritable and shaky as the hours have passed, not that I can really blame him. I haven't been able to gather more than a few minutes at a time in which to sit down, let alone sleep.

"The lads are ready to get the first load of bars onto the cart," Livius says to me. "There was more rockfall than we expected, so it's likely to take us the rest of the day and another night to bring it over to you."

I turn to look at all the men on his work crew. Their faces are smeared with grime and sagging with fatigue. Their eyes are bleak as they watch me holding enough copper to buy a month's worth of food for an entire family. "I'm grateful for your tireless work. We must all make sacrifices to save our land."

Raimo mutters something under his breath, and I pretend like I don't hear him at all.

Livius removes his cap and holds it with both hands. "We trust in your wisdom, Valtia."

I pray to the stars that their trust isn't misplaced. I don't see how this could be wrong, though. With that thought, I turn and toss the bar into the fissure, and we listen to it thump against the ragged walls of dirt and stone in its plunge toward the red abyss below.

I don't know when it hits. The earth is silent as it swallows down this tiny tribute. I hold to the marble that bounds the tear in the plaza and squint at the glowing thread of light deep in the pit. "It's a start."

"We'll load up the first cart, then," Livius says somberly. With a heavy sigh, he waves his men back toward the temple.

The sun is lighting the sky in the east even though it hasn't yet shown its face. A faint trace of wood smoke hangs in the air. Kaisa walks into the plaza from the square, picking her way along amid upturned slabs of marble. She frowns as she approaches me and Raimo and pushes her hood away from her face, revealing her short blond hair.

"Have we found the Saadella?" I ask as she nears.

"No one has seen her or her family since the quake struck," she says. "Also, we've ladled out our entire stock of broth. Many are still hungry."

"Have you spoken to Oona, the butcher's wife?" I ask. "She is responsible for buying meat from the farmers in the outlands and may be able to help us get more bones at least, if not meat. We can help prepare and distribute the food."

"I can try," says Kaisa, "but there is much resentment toward the temple in town. Some people were refusing our charity. A few spat on the ground and said they'd rather starve."

My cheeks grow hot, as if I've been slapped. "Just because the Valtia hasn't saved them from all hardship? When will they realize they're not children?"

"That's all they've ever known," says Raimo. "You can't expect them to change overnight."

Frustration seizes me. "Then we're all going to perish!" I say, my voice shrill. "Because the Soturi will not wait for us to grow up before they invade." Weeks ago, we were headed toward a stronger place. Weapons were being forged and bows were being strung. But since the first quake, courage seems to have abandoned the Kupari people.

And I can't protect them. I'm not enough. I can't even protect one little girl. I bow my head and squeeze my eyes shut, trying desperately to push away the despair that threatens to enclose me. I think the only thing keeping my own people from storming the temple to stone me is fear and catastrophe, not love, not loyalty. "They'll see. When we stop the quakes, they'll see," I whisper.

Distant clanging brings my eyes open. "Are those the fire bells?"

"Look," says Raimo. "To the south."

A dark haze blocks out the morning light. That was the smoke I smelled. "Is that in the city?"

Raimo shakes his head. "It's much farther away."

"The north woods," I say, glancing toward the road as my heart begins to match the pace of the clanging alarms. "Shouldn't they be back by now?"

"It depends on what they encountered," he tells me. "And whether they survived."

"That's unnecessarily dreary," I snap.

"Oh, is it my job to cushion you from the reality of our situation? I'm so sorry." He pats my shoulder. "Everything's going to be fine, Elli. I'm sure that if you just take a nap, the world will be perfect and right when you wake up."

I wrench myself away from him. "You know full well that's not what I'm asking from anyone." My throat is so tight that I can barely speak. "But would you prefer I dwell on the possibility of disaster and ruin instead of having at least a little hope to carry me along?"

"I'd prefer you face hard truths instead of turning your back on them."

"And I'd prefer you not treat men's lives as so completely disposable!"

He leans his forehead on the top of his walking stick. "I can't advise you if you won't listen to what I have to say."

"I have *always* listened," I shout. "But that doesn't mean I must always obey blindly. I did that for my entire life until now, and all it did was make me a slave in the hands of evil men."

Raimo raises his head. "Perhaps you're still a slave—but this time, your emotions and desires are your masters."

"Enough." I cast poor Kaisa an apologetic glance. "Please go do whatever you can to assist in feeding our people. If we have any grain, have it ground to meal. If we have any meal, have it made into bread. If we have any bread, hand it out, but for star's sake, help us be of service!"

Without a word, Kaisa jogs for the side of the temple, where the vaulted food stores have, by some miracle, been left largely undamaged.

"Valtia," comes a cry from the broken gate to the plaza. "You are needed!"

"Ah, here we go," says Raimo.

A constable stumbles into the plaza, panting and sweating. "There's a massive fire in the woods just outside the gate, and the wind blows north! You must come!"

People have begun to gather behind him, looking between me in the plaza and the smoke that hangs in the southern sky. I wonder how many of these people watched my fiery escape from the courtyard of the council hall just before the last big quake hit. They must still think I hold the infinite magic inside my body.

"Can you help?" I ask Raimo.

He looks down at his gnarled hands. "I'm not sure. Despite your grand offering to the earth, I'm still feeling awfully shaky." His tone is so peevish that I want to scream.

"I'll go see what I can do without you, then." I whirl around and walk toward the constable. "Fetch me a horse, please."

"Fetch two," Raimo says wearily.

I look over my shoulder at him. He shrugs.

The smoke on the air seems to be getting thicker by the minute. Somehow, I know, this fire is not natural. It is magical. It stinks of wielders clashing and dying. Though I am immune to its effects, it terrifies me far more than a fire that could melt my bones.

What if Lahja is out there, surrounded by flame? What if Oskar doesn't have enough ice to protect himself? What if the fire only burns because he's already been defeated?

Horses whinny as the constable leads a pair of them into the plaza until he can go no farther for fear of injuring the animals' legs on the scramble of unsteady rocks and fractured slabs. I slowly make my way over to him and hear Raimo's shuffling footsteps behind me.

The constable holds the horse's bridle as I mount. "So used to seeing you high on the paarit with all your bearers," he says with a sad smile.

"My bearers have more important work to do than to carry around a queen who is perfectly capable of sitting atop a mare." I put them to work helping Livius's stone crews.

He pats the side of the horse's brown throat. "Well, the road's tough going. Lots of fissures and rocks. But this one's nimble and sure."

I need to be the same. With Raimo weak and tremulous, I have only a few options for staving off a fiery disaster within the city, and none of them are good or sure. I look up at the gloomy sky and wish for rain. "We need water and buckets."

"Won't do any good," the constable says. "Can't you make us a thunderstorm like the old Valtia did when the Soturi came at us over the Motherlake?"

I almost laugh. "Let me see what I'm dealing with first." I cluck my tongue, and my mare moves. Her ears twitch as the bells become louder. I wonder about the men and women ringing them—the bells are positioned along the walls of the city, some sections of which have crumbled in the quakes. For anyone to climb up there just to warn fellow citizens of oncoming danger takes courage and selflessness. I wish I could have a thousand more just like them.

"Do you have a plan?" asks Raimo as he guides his horse along behind mine. The road to the square is scattered with debris, but a narrow path has been cleared, wide enough for a single rider.

I rub at my eyes. "At this point, I'm not sure it matters. Disaster awaits at every single turn." I cannot win. I know that now. But I will never allow myself to give up—especially as I reach the square and find hundreds of forlorn, beaten-down citizens waiting for me.

They hold out their hands to me and cry. "Save us, Valtia!"

Tears start in my eyes, but I hold my head high as we ride past them. I don't have the strength to offer more empty reassurances. All I can offer is my straight back and the proud angle of my chin.

We ride along the Lantinen toward the southern part of the city, where thatched roofs have collapsed inward, some of them smoking as well. Here the buildings are not more than one floor, so I can see the wall up ahead—and the distant glow of flames behind the green trees that overhang this section of city wall, where the north wood caresses our city boundary.

Raimo curses. "It's closer than I thought it would be."

"It's magical," I murmur. "This was caused by a wielder."

He curses again. "I suppose you would know."

Our horses mince along carefully, bearing us closer to the smoke. Raimo coughs. I do not—I can smell the smoke, but it doesn't hurt my throat. Up ahead is a door that leads directly through the wall and into the woods—I know this because Sig used it to drag me out of the city a few months ago after he killed Mim. "You can stay behind if you like," I tell Raimo as he spits on the ground and then continues to hack.

We are a block or two from the wall, and between the constant clangs of the fire bells, there arises an insistent banging.

"Let us in," a woman shouts from the other side.

"That's Aira," Raimo says in a flat voice.

I urge my horse forward, and when it doesn't move fast enough, I hop from its back and lift my skirts, then jog my way along, past silent, frightened faces peeking out of partially collapsed homes, past men on the streets trying to dig possessions out from under timbers and thatch and slate. My heart is several steps ahead of me as we stumble toward the section of buildings that hide the door—that's where Aira's voice is coming from. A few citizens who must live in this area merely stare mutely toward the wall and watch the smoke billow toward us. They make no move to provide the help that's so desperately needed right now.

"Raimo, please," I say in a choked voice as we turn the corner and come face to face with a thick, bolted door. This time I don't have Sig with me to pick the lock. "Can you open it?"

Raimo winces as we listen to a few hoarse cries on the other side. I put my hand to my chest as I feel a strange pull. I have to get to the other side of this wall. "Please," I say again. "I can't make it through on my own."

Raimo hobbles forward, looking sickly and weak. "I'll try." He offers his hand, and I clasp it, feeling the sharp shocks of his magic as it flows from him to me.

I stretch my scarred fingers toward the copper lock on the door, and pray that by the time we make it to the other side, there are still wielders left to save.

CHAPTER TWENTY-ONE

Ansa

The wielder who carried me through the wood on horseback sweats through his clothes and mine by the time we reach a high wall and can go no farther. I assume the Kupari city is on the other side, but the wall is too high to climb, and these idiots who have kidnapped me seem to have brought us to a place that lacks the one thing we need—a gate.

Smoke is curling around us in a deadly, acrid haze and I can hear the crackling of flames a few hundred yards away. The small group of wielders slides off their horses, and some rush over to help the injured dismount. My captor, breathing hard and coughing, jumps off his horse and yanks me off, then sets me down with my back against the base of the wall.

Sig is laid next to me a moment later. He looks awful, but he's awake, eyes open and on me. I glare my hatred at him.

"Kauko blows his fire this way," says Sig, wheezing. "He could destroy the whole city."

Fine with me. I say nothing.

"We didn't kill Thyra, by the way."

Liar.

A dark shape looms over us. It's the big ice wielder, with his wild brown hair and broad shoulders and strange white hand that hangs limp from his side. He's part dead man and about to become a whole one, along with the rest of us. He asks Sig a question, and I swear it includes my name.

Sig answers in Kupari, then turns to me. "Oskar here wants to know if I can open that door over there," he says weakly, nodding toward a door about a dozen yards away, shielded by overhanging vines. "But it's too hot for me to wield my own magic."

"I won't help you," I tell him. I can barely lift my arms and my magic is just a smoldering pit inside me. Even if I could summon an inferno, I still wouldn't raise a finger to save him.

"Save your cousin, then," he says, gesturing at Oskar.

My gaze flicks to the dark ice wielder and our eyes meet. He offers me a hesitant smile, and suddenly memories of summer days and sand and racing a gangly boy up a dune while Mother laughs and laughs and laughs invade my mind, blocking out the burning forest and the smoke. Are those recollections real, or am I inventing this past of mine? I blink quickly and stare at Oskar again.

He's a stranger. I'd never seen him before I watched him hurl ice at Thyra. My lip curls and I bare my teeth at him. Ice stirs inside me, slow but certain, like it knows the enemy.

His smile dies and he steps back quickly, speaking in rapid, urgent tones to Sig, who lies limp and weak beside me. Sig lets out a rattling laugh. "He can feel the ice growing inside you, Ansa."

"Then let him be afraid."

"We're not your enemy. *He's* out there, blowing the fire toward us. He'll use the flames to burn our shadows into this wall."

Oskar takes a few steps beyond us, facing the oncoming flames. The lean wielder who carried me on his horse stands in the same manner a few yards away. Both of them lift their hands—Oskar only lifts one—and the trees rattle with the force of the wind they produce. Oskar shivers and shakes as the magic pours from him. Just ice. No fire at all. The opposite of Sig. Ice is Oskar's weapon—and his nemesis.

Now I know how to kill him.

A female wielder with dark hair and wild eyes runs between the ice wielders and the rest of us huddled against the wall. She ducks under the hanging vines and begins to bang on the door and shout. I assume she's calling for help, but no one comes.

Sig coughs and cries out in pain as fire begins to eat at the trees to our right and left. We're surrounded, and the two ice wielders have only kept the fire in front of us away. Flames find a way, though. There's no escape now.

I never thought I would die like this. I chuckle. I seem to have that thought every time I'm about to die.

Oskar falls to his knees, but his hand is still outstretched as the blizzard billows from his palm. He's far more powerful than the lean one, yet somehow also weaker. I know that feeling so well.

"I wouldn't have thought Kauko would kill the Valtia so readily," Sig comments. His voice is so quiet that I'd believe he was talking to himself, except he's speaking Krigere. "Usually he wants to control the magic, but once it leaves you, it'll still be out of his reach."

My throat goes tight. No, it won't. He has that little girl with the copper hair and the blue eyes and the spirit that calls out to mine. I am nothing to him now. Worse than nothing. "He wants me to die," I murmur.

The female wielder is banging on the door and coughing, and some of the other wielders, including the skinny little girl with fire at her fingertips, run over to add their voices and fists. Despite the ice wielders' efforts, the air is getting hotter. Sig is sweating rivers as his blisters ooze. The air is choking all of us. My ears are ringing and I don't know if the sound is actual bells or my body telling me I don't have enough air.

If I really end up on the heavenly battlefield today, would Thyra send me away as she did in my dream, or would she welcome me with open arms? Would she stab me or kiss me?

Would she forgive me for failing her, for not avenging her?

I look around for a weapon. At the very least, I can die trying. Sig has a small knife sheathed at his belt, and his arms are limp at his sides. If I can't kill the impostor queen, at the very least I can kill her wolf, the one she sent to cut my beating heart from my chest. I pitch myself to the side, and with clammy fingers I grope for Sig's knife.

Sig realizes my plan as I grab the hilt and yank. With a cry, he grasps my wrist—just as I try to jam the blade into his stomach. I am grim and determined. I do not enjoy this. I thought Sig was my friend once. It is hard to hate him. But his betrayal is unforgivable.

"Stop," Sig gasps as the tip of the knife inches closer to his gut.

"She died in pain," I say through gritted teeth. "Burned and frozen and ruined."

"I—I didn't—I didn't—"

I am weak, but Sig is weaker. The blade pierces the fabric of his shirt. I feel his flesh give.

He screams, and Oskar whirls around on his knees. The wielders by the door cry out too, and all tumble away toward the fiery woods. Oskar lunges for me.

The door to the city bursts open in a blast of frigid air.

All of us go still.

Through the door walks a girl, no older than I am but dressed in a gauzy gown, with sparkling pendants in her coppery hair. She turns as soon as her slippers touch the rotting leaves of the forest floor. Her eyes find mine like she hears my heartbeat. As wielders plunge through the doorway she opened to escape the oncoming flames, she comes toward me. That heartbeat of mine bangs louder, faster.

I know who she is. I know exactly who she is. The impostor is steps away from me.

Sig shoves me away and says something to her in Kupari. I am heedless of the man I was trying to murder mere seconds ago. His knife is still in my fist, and its tip is red with his blood. My fingers spasm around it as I lie on my back and watch her float toward me, her gown billowing around her in swirls of searing, bitter-cold wind, the marriage of Oskar's magic with Kauko's.

"Ansa?" she asks, her voice shaking.

She is the enemy. She is the cause of so much of my suffering. She holds my throne. She sent her wolves to kill my love.

"I have been searching everywhere for you," she says.

She is speaking Kupari. But I understand her. Only her. The others trill away nonsensically, but her? Every word is written clearly in my thoughts.

She holds out her hands. "We have so much to talk about." She sniffles and wipes away a tear. "But first we have to get you to safety."

Sig says something to her, and she chuckles and nods. "Yes, you too, Sig."

I have to kill her. If I do, her tyranny is over, and I will rest knowing that our warriors have a home.

Will they? It's Thyra, whispering to me from beyond. *Will they really?*

I shake my head, confused at the cascade of voices around me and inside me. I am sweating now. Wielders race past me and roll Sig onto a blanket, and then they pick him up like a corpse in a sling and lug him toward the doorway to the city. Oskar and the other ice wielder are still fighting to keep the oncoming flames from eating us alive.

"Can you walk?" the impostor asks me.

She is coming closer. Another step or two and I could bury my blade in her chest. I could burn her flesh off her soft, smooth face with my hands. I can feel the magic coiling inside me like a snake. I knew it wouldn't abandon me for long.

I don't know why my fingers are loosening around the hilt of my weapon. I fight the impulse to drop it and take her hand. The impostor looks at Oskar and the other wielder and yells something in Kupari. The lean one lets his arm fall to his side and runs toward the doorway to safety, but Oskar keeps his hand out. He's on his knees, his head hanging. The impostor strides over to him and slides her palm beneath his hair, onto the back of his neck.

He throws his head back and takes a gasping breath as the impostor sinks down next to him, her other hand rising to cup his jaw. That is all I can see through the smoky haze that hangs between us, but I can tell he is more to her than all the others. He is her love. Her wolf and her love.

Like I was, to Thyra.

After a few moments, the impostor rises. Oskar slowly gets to his feet as well. They both come toward me, looking worried but certain. I look down at the knife in my grip.

For some reason, I cannot bring myself to drive this blade into her body. I know this feeling—I felt the same way toward the witch queen in the midst of the storm. I had a weapon in my hand but couldn't strike. Now I am weak with the loss of blood. My magic has only just returned.

But it *has* returned.

As the two of them come near, power spirals from my chest and along my arm, building as it encircles the knife. I lift the blade.

And I aim it at Oskar's chest.

CHAPTER TWENTY-TWO

Elli

Oskar falls backward, landing hard. His head smacks against a tree, a sound I hear even over the crackling roar of the inferno that's slowly moving toward us. I know Ansa is holding a knife, but I have no mind for her now—all I care about is Oskar. I drop to my knees and shove my hands up his tunic, pressing both into his chest.

That was where she aimed. Right for his heart. He's not offering his magic now. He's still and cold. But I don't need him to give me his power, not anymore. I'm strong enough to take it without help. I focus my energy and pull with all my might, summoning the ice inside him, commanding it to come to me, to submit. It comes like an obedient dog, flashing eagerly along my palms and scurrying up my arms.

Oskar's heart beats once, twice, then picks up a hungry

rhythm, and I sag with relief. "Come help us!" I shout over my shoulder. I had told them to leave us, but now I realize something I hadn't really believed could be true.

Ansa is perfectly willing to kill us.

Anger and devotion twist inside me. They are not easy lovers, and I wince at how much it hurts. Then I remind myself how the world might look from where she lies.

I turn to face her.

The deadly magic she just hurled at Oskar seems to have drained her strength for the moment. She's pale as the moon and sweating. Her eyes are wide and full of wariness, but the knife has slipped from her fingers. I take two quick steps and kick it away, and too late her scrabbling hands reach for it. She lets out a cry of frustration as her head falls back. I can feel the heat of magic fire against my skin. I could walk through it without losing anything but my dress, but Oskar and Ansa will lose their lives if I don't act now.

I squat behind Ansa. She's slender and shorter than I am, but as I loop my arms under hers and start to yank her toward the doorway in the wall, I feel the dense muscles in her shoulders and back. She's heavier than I expect, and I grunt as I slide her along the ground. She kicks feebly but seems too weak to do more than that, for which I am thankful. Veikko and a few others have run back into the woods to load Oskar into a blanket and carry him into the city. It takes four of them to do it.

I'm through the doorway with Ansa a moment later, and so relieved to see the door slam shut between us and the flames that I sink to my knees behind her, still holding her tight. She smells of sweat and smoke and the metallic tang of magic, and her coppery hair is soaked and standing on end. I bow my head to her shoulder, so glad to finally have the Valtia that for a moment I forget how dangerous she is.

And a moment is all it takes for her to remind me. Something hard collides with my head, and the inside of my skull flares with sparkling stars. I lose my sense of up and down and fall backward, my arms flopping to my sides and something wet streaming down my face. A hard body lands on top of me and hands clamp around my throat. I look up into Ansa's tearstained, soot-streaked face, black on white, vivid blue eyes that radiate confusion and pain. *But I love you*, I think as my vision clouds with spots.

Her grip loosens, and then she's torn off me and my world is a chaos of shouting and shuffling feet. Someone drags me backward, and when I crane my neck I see it's Kaisa.

"Are you all right?" she asks in a frantic voice, pressing the sleeve of her robe to my head.

I gasp with pain. "Did she hit me?"

"With a rock." Kaisa looks at Raimo, who is leaning against a wooden post that holds up the partially collapsed roof of a cottage here at the edge of the city.

Raimo is frowning as he watches something in the street. I turn slowly and cry out when I see what's happening. Wielders have surrounded Ansa, who is crouched in the dirt, a knife in her hand. Veikko, whose right hand is bleeding—and whose sheath is empty—is holding his arms out and accepting shackles from a constable. Tuuli and Usko have their hands out too, but they're trying to keep Ansa at bay.

"Her magic should dwarf theirs," Kaisa says, sounding puzzled.

"It does. But she's been bled near to death," Raimo says, pointing to a large bloodstain on Ansa's sleeve. "Look how pale she is. How weak."

Kaisa lifts her robe and peers at my scalp. "She didn't look weak when she nearly caved in Elli's head with a rock."

"Well, she's Soturi, isn't she?" he says.

Ansa sweeps the blade of her knife through the air, holding Tuuli and Usko back. But she doesn't see Aira behind her. The fire wielder smacks Ansa in the head with a wooden board. I clutch my stomach as I hear the sound of impact. Nausea overtakes me as I watch Ansa collapse into a boneless sprawl on the ground. I retch into the stony scree at my feet.

When I lift my head, Kaisa offers me her sleeve to wipe my mouth, and with an apologetic look I accept. Ansa is surrounded now, Veikko shackling her, Tuuli with a blanket to wrap around her to further prevent her from moving. "When she comes back to herself, she'll lash out again," I say. "And when she regains her strength, she'll be able to kill everyone."

My fingertips rise to my cheeks, which are wet with tears. Despite Sig's warnings, this is not how I envisioned my first meeting with my Valtia. I've been fantasizing about the moment for so long that my dreams were impervious to reality. And now . . .

I look around, my heart lurching up into my throat. "Where's Oskar?"

Kaisa squeezes my arm. "Some constables volunteered to carry him and Sig back to the temple. They know Oskar and the others were trying to fight the fire and they're grateful."

I try to look up the road toward the temple, but all I see is a wall of somber faces and hunched shoulders. The townsfolk have gathered a few blocks away to watch the flames overtake us. But as Kaisa helps me to my feet, I feel the wind shift. Smoke drifts away from us and into the sky, and the air cools.

Raimo curses under his breath. "That'll be Kauko." He chuckles. "But our people will probably think it's you."

Sure enough, our people are cheering and calling for me, waving and crying out their thanks.

I absently wave back to them as I consider what Raimo's just said. "It can't be Kauko. To draw a fire of that size away from the city would take the power of the Valtia."

"Which he'll have, if he's been drinking as much of Ansa's blood as I suspect."

"If she dies, Lahja . . ." Fear closes like a noose around my throat.

"If she's alive, we'll find her."

"She's alive," I whisper. "Surely I would feel her loss if she weren't."

"As you said, one thing at a time," Raimo replies as he gestures for the horses to be brought near.

A stout constable helps me up onto my mount. "I'll lead her for you, Valtia," he says, giving me a worried look.

As he leads my horse forward, I touch my forehead, which is sticky with blood. "She really tried to kill me."

From behind me, Raimo says, "I think, if she were really set on killing you, you'd probably be dead. She seems skilled in the art of violence."

I thought I might have seen conflict in her eyes, the war of hate and love. It gives me hope that allows me to lift my chin as we ride through our decimated city and back to the temple. The crowds part and gaze with curiosity as our wielders bundle Ansa along, all wrapped in a blanket. It's a good thing too, because if they realized she was Soturi, they might tear her to pieces. "I'll tend to Ansa myself once we're back in the temple."

"You may be the only one who can," Raimo says drily after the constable releases my horse and waves good-bye to us at the gate of our plaza. "She's likely to freeze or burn anyone else."

As we dismount, we wave to Livius's crew, who are wheeling a cart of copper bars toward the deep crevasse that divides the plaza and runs up to the steps. We're on one side and they're on the other. Livius holds up a bar. "We're on the third load," he shouts.

I kiss my palms and turn them to him, showing my gratitude as I approach the steps. "Our first task is to heal Oskar and Sig."

Raimo groans as he slides from his horse. "Elli . . . I'm not sure I can."

"Raimo, get up here," shouts Veikko from the top of the crumbled steps to the domed chamber.

Kaisa jogs over and slides her arm around the old man. "I'll help you."

I march up the steps ahead of them, tripping once or twice over the edge of my gown, my head pounding the whole way. I know I am a mess, but I don't care. I'm tired of pretending I'm the queen. All I care about is taking care of the people I love.

Freya greets me at the top of the steps, her eyes wide and pleading. "Can you do something for them?" she asks. Behind her, our grand domed chamber is in disarray. Most of the debris has been swept or carried to the edges of the room, and the dome still stands, although it is dented and twisted from the contortions of the structure beneath it, but there are cracks across the floor and places where the smooth marble has poked spiky fingers into the air. Injured wielders lie on blankets that have been hastily thrown down. I spy Oskar and Sig next to each other—their bodies cover the infinity symbol of the Valtia. Ansa is nowhere to be seen.

I give Raimo a desperate look as he reaches the top of the steps. He looks like he needs someone to heal *him*. My heart sinks. "Can you help me tend them?" I ask, turning to rush over to Oskar and Sig.

"Kaisa, see if you can fetch my herb bag from the library, assuming it hasn't caved in." Raimo hobbles along next to me. "My magic is feeble and unsteady now, Elli. I suspect all of us are feeling this way." He staggers and I catch him. "I'm afraid of what it means."

"Another quake? Maybe we can stave it off. Livius and his men are working without rest."

"Oh, Elli," he says sadly.

I give his hand a sudden squeeze. He gasps at the crush of it. "If I can't use your magic to heal them, then tell me what to do," I say in a flat voice.

I know I am being a brat, and that Raimo doesn't deserve this harshness. But I can't help it right now. Oskar is lying at my feet, haggard and pale and sick. His left hand is that of a corpse, and the rest of him shivers and shakes. He's rolled on his side, his knees curled to his chest as he tries and fails to warm himself. Veikko rushes over and tosses another blanket on his friend's body. "I used to be jealous of Oskar," he says quietly to me, then moves away quickly.

Sig is no better. He lies on his side too, facing Oskar. I feel the heat of his body from here, and shamefully, I hope Oskar does as well. What parts of Sig aren't covered by blisters are swollen and red. He barely looks like himself. His eyes are closed but I know he can't possibly be sleeping.

I kneel behind Oskar and bow my head over him. His eyes open as he feels my hands on his throat, tugging his icy magic away from his bones. "Don't," he whispers. "I might need it."

"It's hurting you," I say, pressing my lips to his cool, whiskery cheek.

"Doesn't matter," he says wearily. "You know what's coming."

"All I can do is manage what's right in front of me, and that's you."

Oskar turns his head, and when he sees me, his brow furrows. "What in the stars has happened to you?"

I pull away from his trembling right hand, his fingers stretched to touch my face. His hand falls to his chest. "Our Valtia doesn't know friend from enemy." I smile as one of our temple wielders offers me a clean, wet rag, which I use to wipe gingerly at the cut on my forehead.

"I felt that keenly," he says. "She would have killed me."

"I'll get through to her."

"I remember her so well." Oskar closes his eyes. "She was faster than I was even though her legs were half as long. She was tougher than I was even though she was half my size. She would follow me around and do whatever I was doing, but she always wanted it to be a race, or a fight. She was such a pest."

"So you didn't get along?"

"No, not at all. I couldn't stand her. Until the day we were climbing a tree, and a branch snapped under my weight. I fell and landed hard. Hit my head on a rock."

"How old were you?"

"Only six or so. Ansa was only four. It was the summer before she was taken."

"Were you seriously hurt?"

He shrugs, then grimaces. "I came to as Ansa was dragging me back to her parents' cottage. It was a mile away, and she'd gotten me halfway there by the time our mothers saw us and came running."

"Did that change things between you?"

"It seemed to. We stayed by the shore for a week as I recovered. She refused to leave my side. My mother started calling her my guard dog."

"Do you think she felt guilty about what happened to you?"

"I don't know. Maybe? But from then on, she was so protective of me. This baby of a girl, walking ahead of me and shooing the chickens out of my path, pushing me further from the fire in the evenings—which I badly needed, by the way, because I was always so close that sparks would burn holes in my clothes."

"Because you were cold," I say quietly.

He sighs. "Always." His smile is pained, and it makes my chest hurt. "She would bring me blankets when she saw me shivering. Soup and tea as well. She'd grab the bowl from her mother and bring it to me herself. I don't know what exactly happened between us that day I fell, but somehow it changed things for her."

"You went from being a challenger, someone she had to fight, to being someone she needed to protect." I stroke his cheek. "I wish she felt that way now, but it doesn't seem like she remembers you."

"It's funny—for a moment, I thought she did. But it was just a flash, and then it was gone."

And then she tried to kill him.

"I cried when my mother told me she was gone," he whispers. "I never forgot her. I think I've always wished that I could have protected her the way she protected me. But now she thinks I'm her enemy."

"It's what Kauko wanted," Sig mutters. He's obviously been listening the whole time, though his eyes are still closed and he's completely limp as Freya lays bandages soaked in cold water over the burns on his arms. "He needed to poison Ansa against us, and he had the perfect strategy."

My throat tightens. "We'll get her back. She'll come around."

"Yes. All you have to do is fall out of a tree and nearly die." Sig groans as Freya tries to dab a greasy tincture onto some of the blisters on his chest. "It's pointless, Freya. Don't bother."

"Shut up, Sig," she says, intent on her work. "Drink some of that tea." She nods toward a mug she's set next to his head.

Oskar lets out a quiet laugh. "Mother always said Freya reminded her of Ansa."

"She told me that as well." I raise my head and find Maarika staring at me from across the room. She's helping Kaisa cut and tear old priests' robes for use as bandages and slings for our people and the townsfolk. I smile, and she gives me a quick nod. Her somber gray eyes light on her son for an instant, and then she quickly looks away.

"Well, *I* wouldn't try to kill every single person who tried to help me," Freya says, all sass. Her braid hangs down, and the tip of it has become covered in the tincture, so now it decorates Sig's chest with ointment like a dainty paintbrush. "So I don't think we're alike at all."

"When you've been through what she has, we can talk again," says Oskar.

"Oskar, she froze your heart!" Freya wails. "Veikko told me. He was just coming through the doorway and saw it happen. I'm glad Aira hit her over the head!"

Sig lets out a snarl and shoves her hand away from his chest. "Careful!"

Her eyes fill with tears that overflow and stream down her cheeks. "This isn't fair. Why is all of this happening? Do the stars hate us? Does our own land hate us?"

I think it might. I lay my cheek against Oskar's and think of a cottage by the shore, of watching him stride from the woods, whole and happy. I cling to it as long as I can, letting everything else drop away for a few minutes.

Oskar murmurs that he loves me. He sounds like he's lived a thousand years in the space of this day. I whisper my adoration into his ear, and then I stand up. I walk over to Aira, who has a bandaged burn on her arm but otherwise looks whole. "Where's our captive?" I ask. "I need to go see her, assuming she's still alive. You hit her pretty hard."

"Mad dogs need to be put down," Aira snaps.

"That mad dog is the key to our survival," I tell her. "And she has suffered more than any of us."

"What about Oskar?" she asks in a choked voice. "Hasn't he suffered enough?"

I swallow the lump in my throat. "If I could spare Oskar more suffering, I would. But he'll do what he needs to in order to protect Kupari."

"To protect you, you mean." Her pretty face is twisted with bitterness.

I shake my head. "No, Aira. If Oskar only wanted to protect me, we wouldn't even be standing here." He and I would be tucked into that cottage, wrapped in each other, not thinking of anyone else. "Now, please tell me where I can find Ansa."

She points toward the Saadella's wing. "They took her to the catacombs through the kitchen tunnel, because it's one of the few that hasn't collapsed."

"The catacombs?" Stars. She must be terrified.

Veikko hears my desperate tone and stops next to Aira with a few waterskins hanging from his shoulder. "We had to contain her somehow, Elli. You'll see."

With my heart beating hard, I cross the domed chamber. Raimo rises and joins me. "Veikko told me where she is," he says, sounding grim. "And that she's now awake. We can't keep her down there, Elli. It's not safe if there's another quake." The tremor in his voice is like a promise of more disaster to come.

I divert from my path to snag two stale loaves of bread and a waterskin. "I'll take care of her. Stay here."

He puts a hand on my arm. "She could hurt you, Elli. She already has. And if our Valtia kills our Astia . . ."

"Oh, was that also mentioned in one of those prophecies?" I ask airily.

"No," he says, sounding troubled. "But I'm questioning everything these days."

"I thought you were a strong believer in your own brilliance."

"I was. I am." And it looks like it has made him completely miserable.

I don't want to hear another ominous word from his mouth. "I'll check in after I've talked to Ansa."

"She doesn't speak Kupari."

"I'm certain she understood me, Raimo." The comprehension in her eyes was as clear as the rage. "And I know I'll be able to understand her. It's not something I can explain, though."

A bemused smile lifts his sagging features. "Maybe it'll be all right," he murmurs. His eyes meet mine. "You can't speak a word of her language, and she doesn't seem to understand ours. But somehow, you can communicate. You share a bond."

"I could have told you that. Now, if you'll excuse me." I hold up the bread and water. "I have some work to do."

Raimo bows his head and steps aside, and I head down the hall toward the stairs to the kitchens. I have always known I shared a bond with the true Valtia. I felt it with Sofia, and the mere thought of another queen warms my heart. But as I think of Ansa above me, her hands wrapped around my throat, her teeth bared, I have to wonder.

What if our bond isn't enough?

CHAPTER TWENTY-THREE

Ansa

I don't know how long I scream and claw and curse and kick, but in the end it all bleeds together in the darkness. I am buried and suffocating; I can't breathe, I can't move, I can't think. Nothing makes sense.

Then all the air and the life and the world comes back at once—the door to my prison opens from the top and there's the impostor, with a swollen gash on her forehead and a horrified look in her eye lit by the torches that line the dripping walls.

"I can't believe they put you in here!" she shrieks, plunging her arms into my box and scooping me up. She stumbles as she hefts my weight, and we both end up on the floor, at the base of a metal box laid on a stone slab. I am cold and hot and cannot make my body obey me. She clutches me close, her breaths coming harsh from her mouth. “I let them do this to me once. The priests. I thought being enclosed in a copper coffin would draw out the magic.” She laughs, and it sounds like she’s got something caught in her throat. “I had no idea you had all of it this whole time.”

I understand the words, but not what she’s saying. I didn’t know that was possible. “Let me go,” I croak, every part of me hurting.

She loosens her grip on me but doesn’t release my body. I’m still pressed against hers, and she’s soft and she smells good and she’s warm and I hate her and I love her. I push weakly against her stomach, trying to create my own pocket in which to think.

“I shouldn’t have taken my eyes off you,” she continues. “I shouldn’t have let them hurt you. I swear, I had no idea they would do this to you.”

I turn my head and look up at the copper box in which I was imprisoned. It is the size of a weapons trunk. My magic was nothing to it. The power simmers inside me now, though, waiting for release. I’m still weak, but the ice and fire inside me rages. I wonder if I could melt the impostor’s bones.

The fire spirals inside, excited by the thought. Searing heat streaks along my arms, painful and unstoppable. Before I can decide if I want to hurt her or if I don’t, she cries out. The fire is loose, bursting from my palms with terrible force. She slaps at her dress and rolls away from me.

I lie where she dropped me and wait for her to fall like

Aksel did, like Carina did. But she merely stands there, her back to me, looking down at her stomach. I wonder if she's too paralyzed with horror to cry, if she's staring at her own entrails, cooked by the fire I forced on her.

But then she *laughs*. "Ah, well. Another dress ruined."

She turns around. The entire center of her gown is burned away, revealing a stretch of bare skin, pale and smooth. I stare at her belly button.

She lifts her arms, a mischievous look on her irritatingly lovely face. "If you feel particularly vengeful, I suppose you could burn away the rest. Care to try?"

My eyes narrow. "What sort of game is this?"

"Depends. What kind do you like to play?"

The teasing note in her voice makes me dream of murder. I glance around me, looking for any sharp object. She takes a quick step back, her hands outstretched. Now she's scared. "Ansa, I don't mean you any harm."

"The lies are so easy for you, aren't they?" I spit on the ground. Or, I try, but my mouth is so dry that the thin string of drool just hangs from my bottom lip. I quickly wipe it on my shoulder.

She's watching me with concern, or maybe pity. "I don't know what you've been told about me. But if Elder Kauko was the messenger, I imagine it was quite bad. And quite false." She takes a cautious step closer. "He was never your ally, Ansa."

"Stop calling me by my name as if you know me!" I shout.

She drops quickly to one knee and bows her head. "Shall I call you by your title, then?" She raises her gaze to mine. "My Valtia."

For some reason, that dredges up a wave of sick that curls my body in on itself. I shove her away as she reaches for me, even though the feel of her hands on my cheeks was a brush of heaven. I stare at the pitted rock beneath me, watching the flames flicker lazily in their damp recesses. "I didn't know what I was," I tell her. "I didn't know until he told me."

"I thought I knew exactly what I was," she replies. "Until the time came for me to *be* that thing. And then I wasn't."

I look up at her. "You're a pretender. A fraud. You hold this throne with a lie."

"Yes," she says, her blue eyes, so similar to Thyra's, so similar to mine. "But I do it to keep others safe."

"You do it for power, like everyone else."

"You don't know me, my Valtia," she says in a small voice. "You could if you wanted to, though."

The suggestion stirs something inside me that I don't understand. "We are strangers," I say. "You are not like me."

She laughs again. "How true. But if what Oskar says is accurate, I feel very fortunate to know you."

Oskar. "He isn't dead, then?"

Her smile dies. "No," she says softly. "But he's not well, either."

"Good." I clamp my mouth shut around the question of how he is exactly, and whether he's warm enough.

"He didn't kill your love. Neither did Sig. It was Kauko who used his evil to kill her—and to trick you into seeking vengeance against the wrong target."

"I saw them there, in the woods."

"They were trying to protect Thyra—from him."

I hate this woman. What she's saying sounds agonizingly like truth. "Thyra was hit from either side with fire and ice. Fire from Sig's direction, ice from Oskar's."

"Both of which Kauko, having drunk your blood, was perfectly capable. Oskar and Sig were there as your allies. Kauko is the true enemy, and if you search your heart, I think you will realize that has always been true. Don't let him continue to use you now. It would be the ultimate betrayal of your Thyra."

"Stop saying her name as if you knew *her*."

"I would never claim such a privilege, Valtia. But I believe I know the type of soul she had. Oskar has the same kind of soul. The kind that will give its all to protect those he loves."

"Don't compare them!" It comes out of me weak as I think about him on his knees, trying to keep the fire away from all of us, away from the city.

Elli reaches for me and I shrink away. "You still care for him," she says. "Like you used to."

"I don't know him," I say with a snarl.

"You'll remember if you give yourself permission."

I can barely remember my own name. Everything inside me is wrong and upside down. Even my magic. It sparks in my marrow, jittery like sudden raindrops in a puddle. I shudder.

Her brow furrows. "You don't feel good."

There is nothing I can say to that. I feel as I have felt so often in the last many months, unstable and ready to strike like a lightning bolt, hurting and ready to fly apart, raging and ready to burn, needing to run but no legs beneath me. I've lost Thyra, I've lost my fellow warriors, I've lost my tribe, I've lost any hope for fulfilling my promises. I have nothing except revenge left to me, and here I am, alone with the impostor. My trembling fingers flex over the harsh stones beneath me. I can kill her now. The others will try to take me down, and maybe they will succeed, but they can't save her.

She was foolish enough to come down here alone.

With a swift kick, I sweep her legs out from under her, and with a cry she topples to the floor. Before she can roll, I'm on her back, and my arm slides across her throat. She lets out a little helpless yip before I cut off her air. Fire and ice are knives stabbing at me from the inside out as I squeeze the life from her.

She heaves and bucks, but she's weak and soft. Prey. I feel the tremors in her body now as it fights to keep life from escaping.

But then she lays her hand over mine. My mouth drops open as a heavy tingling courses across my skin.

It's not magic.

It's the opposite of magic. It's numbness and nothing

and I can't do a thing to resist it. The power peels itself away from my bones and flows to the place where our skin touches. It is irresistible and unstoppable, and I sink into the feeling as my strength leaves me.

As soon as my grip loosens, she jerks her shoulder up, and I slide off her like a sack of grain. I lie on my back, panting, and say the last thing I want to say.

"Touch me again."

Her face is red as a late summer apple and she is wheezing, but she inches forward to obey. Her hands are soft but sure as they slide across my cheeks, as she sits up and looks down at me, holding my face in her hands. I stare up at her, more captive and chained than I've ever been. She closes her eyes and lets her head fall back as my magic pours from me, usually so destructive and hateful, now tame and devoted and certain. All of me is tingling, and I don't want this feeling to stop.

It's the first real relief I've felt since the cuff of Astia was taken from me. But this is more complete. It's truer and righter. It is everything.

"We are one thing," she whispers, though I'm not sure she's speaking to me.

She might not be speaking to me. She's an impostor who wants to keep her throne. She's another person who wants to use me. Like Nisse. Like Jaspar. Like Kauko. Even like Thyra, in a way.

If I had no magic inside me, I would be nothing.

With a wretched groan, I shove and kick her away. She

doesn't fight it. She merely falls back in a sprawl, maybe still weak from my attack.

"What *are* you," I say. Because I have realized something—she is not a mere impostor. She is something *else*.

She gives me a sad smile. "I'm your shadow."

"What does that mean?"

She pushes herself up, the hole in her fine dress gaping, revealing all her skin, too smooth to believe. Parts of her are scarred, to be sure—her left hand, for example. She has only three fingers, and only stumps and silvery lumps to remind me of what used to be there. But the rest of her, the parts I can see . . . they are too perfect to look at, and so I look away. "Ansa, the power inside you and me—it's the power of one Valtia. But for whatever reason, when Sofia died, this power split apart. You got the magic."

"And you?"

"The balance. That's all I am."

I shake my head. "That's not what I just felt."

"Well. Maybe I'm a little more than that."

I stare at her. There is something so controlled about her. She is dressed grandly but has no pretense at grandeur. She clearly has power but she drops to her knees so readily. She is rueful when she could be petulant. I can't decide if I want to tear her to shreds or dive into her arms, and the thought is such a betrayal of Thyra that I rock back, feeling sick. "Witchcraft," I mutter. "All of this is witchcraft."

"You can call it whatever you want. Do the warriors have magic?"

Warriors. Soturi. Krigere. It all means the same thing. "No."

"What did they make of you?"

My eyes glaze with unexpected tears and I grit my teeth.

"I'm sorry," she says. "I have a sense of how it feels."

"Do you?" I shove up and swipe a hand across my eyes.

"I was willing to do anything to help the elders draw out the magic we all thought was hidden inside me."

"I was willing to do anything to hide the magic that had taken me over."

"You see," she murmurs. "We can understand each other."

"No," I snap. "No." Because I am alone, and she is surrounded by people who love her and do her bidding. She has no idea.

"You are important, Ansa," she says. "You are the one our people have been waiting for. I'm only a placeholder."

"I have people of my own."

"People who tried to kill you, if I understand correctly. They let Kauko drink your blood. He would have pushed that fire right up against the wall and burned you to bits. The only reason you were spared is that he doesn't want to destroy the city. He wants to rule it."

I set my elbows on my knees and cover my eyes. "He may yet succeed. He has everything he needs except my death."

I can't see her, but I am keenly aware that she has stopped breathing. "He has the cuff of Astia, you mean. And he has drunk your blood."

Our eyes meet. "He has the girl," I tell her.

It is as if I *have* melted her bones. She sinks to the ground, her arms wrapping around her middle. "You are saying this to hurt me." She sounds as if I've kicked her in the stomach.

I feel the way she looks. "That's why he was willing to kill me. He has her. He told me that if I die, the power goes to her. Is that true?"

She nods. "We think so."

"Then what are you? Why do you exist?"

Her smile is radiant in its sorrow. "I have no answer to that, except that the stars ordained it." Her eyes go wide and shiny, and they speak of pain and fear too deep to put into the words we share. Then she seems to shake it off. "But as long as I live, I'll do what I believe is right." She reaches out and touches my arm. "We have to get Lahja back. You understand that, don't you?"

"Yes."

"You don't have to love me, Ansa. My Valtia. You don't have to like me."

"Good. I don't." I don't want to, at least. It feels wrong and right at the same time.

She nods. "All right. But we have a common goal."

"For now."

With surprising steadiness, she walks to the doorway to this prison, where she picks up a waterskin and, heaven help me, bread. She offers them to me, and the look on her face is both submissive, like an andener, and fierce, like a warrior. "For now."

CHAPTER TWENTY-FOUR

Elli

When I enter the domed chamber with Ansa, everyone is on guard. She is a compact, wary creature, and her eyes skitter over the scene while her hands roam at her waist and forearms—then she looks down at herself and curses.

"Looking for weapons?" asks Raimo as he hobbles over to us. "You don't need them."

"What's he saying?" she asks, scowling at him.

"He's just asking me how you're faring," I tell her.

"Liar," she mutters, but her suspicion isn't barbed. She's too busy staring at Oskar. "What's wrong with him?"

"Apart from the fact that you froze his heart midbeat a few hours ago?"

Her nostrils flare. "But you fixed him somehow." She

looks back and forth between him and me. "I am envious of your power," she whispers.

I laugh. "Would you switch places with me, if you could? You might be surprised how much you miss your ice and fire."

She closes her eyes. "You might be surprised how much I wouldn't." After a moment, she tilts her head and watches as Freya helps him sip a cup of hot broth. Oskar is pale and his hands are shaking. I've never seen him look so weak, and it makes me feel sick to my stomach with dread. "How did you heal him?"

"You could do it too, if you learned how," I say. "Wielders with ice and fire in abundant amounts can do it. I had to channel Raimo's magic, though."

She raises her palms and stares at them. "I've never been able to control my power. Only the cuff of Astia helped. And Kauko has it now."

"We'll get it back from him." I turn to the plaza as a sweating constable tops the last step.

"Valtia," he shouts. "Soturi have been sighted on the main road to the city! Hundreds of them, marching this way!"

Everyone starts muttering at once, and despite that, I can still hear warning bells clanging throughout the city. I turn to Ansa. "Are they attacking?"

"They'll want to negotiate a surrender," Ansa says.

Sig sits up quickly, then flops down again, looking weak and dizzy. He says something to her in a guttural language—

her language, I realize. Ansa replies, and I hear her true words, not a one of them carrying any meaning for me. But when she turns back to me and speaks, I understand her perfectly. "I've just told him that Kauko has the little girl, and he thinks that is very bad. He says to ask about your militia."

I think of all the men and women of Kupari who volunteered to defend our city, some of whom have been armed with bows and swords. "Nearly all members of our militia fled to tend to their families when the quakes began, and I haven't called them back. I don't even know how many are still alive."

She gives me an incredulous look. "Have they no discipline?"

"No," I tell her. "They don't. They were not raised to fight. They were raised to expect the Valtia to provide and protect, as she always had."

Her lip curls. "If I am Valtia, they will be expected to defend themselves like true men and women should."

I lean forward. "Against whom? Against Soturi?"

Her fists clench. "My people are led by a rogue now. A rogue and a Kupari priest."

"Are they true allies?"

She grunts. "Only for as long as their interests align. After that there will be war, because both are convinced of their superiority and rightness."

"And my people caught between two opposing forces." They're already on their knees. How much more hardship can they withstand before they crumble completely?

Ansa is looking out on the city, her lips pressed together. "You have no defenses, no fighting force."

"Tell her she's wrong." Sig's voice is ragged with fatigue as he pushes himself up from the floor.

Oskar is already standing. "Kauko will want the temple."

"But it's crumbling around us," I say.

Raimo gestures for the other wielders to gather. "It won't stop a greedy old sorcerer from trying to take what he believes is his." He cackles. "He doesn't know you're tossing all his stolen riches into the ground!"

I translate for Ansa, not wanting her to be excluded.

"Jaspar wants those riches too," she says when I'm finished. "Kauko has filled his head with visions of copper and plenty."

"Will they hurt our people on their way into the city?" I ask.

"Not if they don't resist," Ansa replies.

Oskar interprets the shake of her head. "They'll want to save their strength for those who will actually fight them."

I look at Oskar over the top of Ansa's head. His jaw is set, but there are purple circles under his eyes, and the rest of his face is nearly as white as his corpse hand. The truth hits me with the force of yet another quake—I'm losing him. I step around the Valtia and mold myself to his side, wrapping my arms around his body and pressing my face to his chest. "You don't have to fight," I tell him. "Ansa and I can face them."

"Ansa will be their primary target," says Raimo.

"No, he'll want her power," I mumble. "Her blood. They won't hurt her."

"Sig just told me they have the Saadella," Oskar says, even as he kisses the top of my head. "If they kill Ansa, they will have a Valtia they can control."

"What is everybody saying?" Ansa snaps.

"That you will be the focus of any attack," I tell her.

She bites her lip. "They have archers."

I picture an arrow zinging through the plaza. "But we have wind."

"If we can offer a show of force," says Ansa, "we might be able to cause doubt in the ranks. Maybe one in four warriors was loyal to Thyra. They are united with Jaspar not out of loyalty, but because they don't have any other options."

"Maybe we can offer them one." I take her hand. She stiffens, looking startled, but she doesn't pull away. Her magic prickles jaggedly along my skin. It hurts like no other magic I've felt, but I don't have any other option, either.

The alarm bells are clanging frantically throughout the city now, from one end to the other, and as we emerge from the temple and look out across the city, I see a dust cloud to our south. Ansa points. "That's them. Marching."

Below us, in the plaza, Livius and his men have paused in their crucial task and have gathered next to the crevasse with a full cart of copper. I descend the steps with my wielders behind me. "What is your progress?"

Livius tears his eyes from the cloud and looks up at me.

"This is the last of it, my Valtia," he replies with a bow of his head. "No more could be found."

Relief sings through my veins and I give him a bright smile. "Your timing is perfect. Please finish your task, and then get these men away from here—go back to your families." I raise my voice to make sure the workers all hear me. "The temple may yet have need of you in the service of the Kupari people, but the coming fight is not yet yours. Get to safety once you have completed your service to the land."

My words, combined with the ringing of the bells and the billowing brown dust that signals the approach of the horde, seems to fill the exhausted crew with new purpose. Oskar, Sig, Veikko, Aira, Raimo, Kaisa, and a dozen other wielders stand with me on the steps to watch the last of the temple's vast store of copper tumble into the depths of the earth. "This will stabilize your magic," I say to them. "Do you feel it?"

When the last bars fall, the heat and light within the fissure flares wildly, and though it is hundreds of feet deep, we feel the searing air against our skin. Oskar lets out a breath and puts his hand on my shoulder. I place my fingers over his and squeeze. As the air cools once more, I turn and face my tiny army. "We will fight them together," I tell them. "But if you see the Saadella, take the utmost care. She cannot be harmed." I'm praying to the stars that they've had the sense to keep her away from danger.

Ansa walks next to me as I step onto the crooked marble slabs of the white plaza. She is pale, and her hand shakes as

I lace my fingers with hers. "You have such assurance," she murmurs.

"We are destined," I say. "Me, the Suurin, and you. We're going to fight these barbarians and save Kupari."

"I don't want to kill my own people," she barks, yanking her hand from mine. "You think I am something I'm not."

"But—"

"No. I hate Kauko and want to see him stoned. I hate Jaspar and want to plunge a dagger into his heart. But the rest—they are *good*," she says. "They are strong and true, and they have families waiting for them. Partners and children. They are not barbarians." She scowls at the expanse of our once beautiful city. "They are better than Kupari."

Uncertainty trickles down my throat. "The Kupari are your people, Ansa."

"They are not," she growls.

"Elli," says Sig, "you're making a hash of this. She may be our Valtia, but you're asking her to do battle with her tribe. The people who made her what she is."

I put my hands up, showing Ansa I mean no harm. "I'm sorry. I wasn't thinking about what this is like for you. Can we start from common ground?"

Her eyes narrow.

"The priests. Kauko."

She gives me a grim smile. "Now, them I would be happy to kill."

"Then we must focus on holding back the rest without

hurting them. Would Thyra's warriors rally to your side if they see your power?"

She looks down at her hands, which are shaking more than I'd like. I glance at the crevasse. The air above it is still wavy with the heat that rises from within. The earth's veins flow with copper once more, glutted with a few hundred years of hoarded riches. I frown as I survey my wielders. None of them look as renewed as I'd hoped, but perhaps the new steadiness will take a while to sink in, just as the copper is carried to all the starving parts of our land.

I straighten my shoulders. "Our goal is to preserve life on both sides," I shout—leveling Sig with a particularly hard glare. He sways in place and looks back at me mutinously. "But traitor wielders are a different matter. Kauko and his priests will be your targets."

Sig grins and elbows Oskar, who grimaces. "Hardly a fair fight," Sig says. "But I'll take it."

"Don't underestimate them," Oskar says. "Remember Kauko drank from Ansa, and he has the cuff. That fire in the wood was pure evil."

The other wielders look weary but ready. "We've faced priests before," says Veikko.

Aira swipes her sleeve across her sweaty brow. "Do they feel as bad as we do?" she asks softly.

"Elli . . ." Raimo begins, but something in my expression closes his mouth.

"We'll need wind," I say to the wielders, wishing I could offer them more than words to prop them up. I glance at the open, broken gate to the plaza in time to see Livius and his crew jog through. They make their way past the tottering council building, and I wave at Livius just before he disappears around the corner. Now there are only wielders in the plaza. Fewer than twenty of us against a thousand Soturi. "Ansa and I can take on the priests if the rest of you keep their arrows away from us."

"I don't know how to do this," Ansa mutters. Her hands are trembling. All of her is trembling.

I take both her hands in mine, and I look into her blue eyes. "You and me. As long as we are touching, we are one." I stroke my thumb along the back of her hand, and the throb of her power nearly steals my breath. My lips part.

She watches my mouth. "One what, though?" she whispers, looking troubled.

This answer should be simple, but in this moment it suddenly feels complicated.

"There they are," Sig says to us.

I squint through the dust and see shadows moving within. They're in the square, and I watch the shadows grow darker and darker as more bodies gather. "Stars," I murmur.

They're huge, and there are many of them. I can see the weapons dangling at their sides. I swear I feel the ground rumble with their footsteps. Ansa's palm is sweating against mine. "I don't feel good," she breathes, almost to herself.

How could she? She's facing off against her own people. I peer at them, hoping to spot the wielders who could give her a reason to fight, since the army of warriors before us seems to be sapping her of her will.

Instead of black-robed priests, though, a lone figure walks forward, his arms at his sides, his hands empty. "Is that Jaspar?" I ask. He is yet another she said she'd be willing to kill.

"No," she says, leaning forward, obviously trying to make out the form within the swirling, dun-colored cloud. Then she gasps as the person walks to the threshold of our plaza. He has brown skin, like I have heard many of the Vasterutians and Ylpesians do, and white hair that signals his age despite his broad shoulders and muscular physique. "Bertel!"

Bertel looks like the unhappiest man in this world, and that is saying something.

Ansa gives the wielders a fierce glare, then says something to them in her guttural language.

Sig laughs before translating. "She says that if we touch a hair on his head, she'll kill all of us."

Ansa nods at Sig. She tries to pull away, but I hold on tight. "Ansa! Remember that Raimo said their goal is to kill you!"

She grabs my wrist in an iron grip and my fingers go numb, enabling her to break free. "He's waving a white cloth. They won't attack."

Before I can stop her, she's running across the plaza toward the man, who does indeed have a pale cloth dangling from his belt. He is frowning deeply as he pulls it out and waves it. He is looking at the ground, not at Ansa.

Sig curses. "That's not a sign of peace. It's a signal."

Ansa stumbles and falls to the side as all of us run forward. I blink at her in horror—an arrow perhaps three feet long is protruding from her shoulder. Oskar shouts at Sig. The settled dust in the plaza comes to life in a towering twister that barrels toward the square. The barbarian shouts are thin and faint within the roar of the wind. I kneel by Ansa's side, relieved to see the arrow has not pierced her chest. Her teeth are gritted as she reaches up and clasps the shaft.

It turns to ash beneath her touch, but blisters are forming on the back of her hand. They burst as the wielders pass me, forming a line between me and Ansa and the oncoming enemy. With the arrowhead still deeply embedded in the meat of her shoulder, Ansa tries to rise, but she's so shaky that she falls forward. I catch her, pulling her chaotic magic into myself. It feels like swallowing broken shards of pottery.

I am just wrapping my arms around her and bracing to pull her up when we are blown backward by a force that lifts me up off my feet—magic shouldn't affect me, but it does affect Ansa, and I am carried with her. I land on my back with Ansa on top of me, but she rolls off a moment later, her skin red, swollen, scored. Confusion racks me as I realize I am surrounded by wielders, all crumpled against the slabs of the plaza. I shake as I watch my own clothes fall from me, smoldering and floating away in flakes of ash.

And when I raise my head, Kauko is walking along the road to the plaza. He's almost parallel with the council building. The cuff of Astia is copper-red on his wrist. He is smiling. But his hands shake as he raises them. "If I drop a marble slab on you, will you die?" he calls to me. "Something tells me you won't be immune to *that*. What if I pull the temple down on top of you?"

"Elli," Oskar gasps. He is sprawled against the edge of the crevasse, his face white. His fingers twitch as he stretches out his arm to reach for me, offering me the magic he's too weak to wield.

Sig lies next to him, but he is offering his blistered hand as well, his eyes bright with determination. "Kill him, Elli," he says with a wheeze.

Ansa is convulsing next to me, making terrible high-pitched noises. Was the arrow poisoned?

I begin to crawl toward Oskar and Sig, but their eyes go wide as a huge chunk of marble crashes to the ground between us. I fall back with my hair blowing around my face. Kauko is laughing. "You aren't so hard to kill."

He stumbles back as he's hit with a spinning ball of ice. Raimo is leaning against one of the upturned slabs, his finger pointed at the old priest. He ducks behind the slab-shield when Kauko sends a flurry of fire toward him. I wait for him to rise, but he doesn't. "Raimo?"

"Can't," he says. "I can't . . ."

I find my feet again. My Valtia is severely injured. My Suurin lie just feet away but out of reach. And Kauko has risen, and is grinning once more.

"Who are you without your wielders, impostor?" he taunts.

I lunge for Oskar and Sig, but a thunder of wind hits my back. It doesn't do more than buffet me, but Sig and Oskar shout with pain as they're dragged along the edge of the crevasse. They lie in a heap as the gale continues, but both of them have their hands outstretched, still reaching.

Their faith in me, their need of me, constricts inside my heart. Kauko's laugh turns the feeling to iron. I reach for them, stretching my body across the slab, the tips of my fingers just inches from those of my Suurin.

I am not touching them, but like before, in the woods, I feel the kiss of their magic against my skin. I latch on to the feeling. And I pull.

Like a dam breaking, their magic rushes up my arm, crossing the narrow space between us and roaring into me. Still reaching for them, I turn toward Kauko, who has a massive fireball growing over his head, which he looks prepared to hurl into the courtyard.

There is only one thing I can do to save everyone. I turn the massive power spiraling inside my chest toward the symbol of order and wealth of the Kupari. The magic bursts from my palm in a vicious pulse of fire and ice and charged air. Lightning explodes upward.

It strikes the council building, sending rocks hurtling down into the square and onto the road in front of Kauko, forcing him to stagger back—only a moment before the entire building topples to the ground. The earth shakes beneath my feet as I am deafened by a catastrophe of rock and mortar and dust. I fall to my knees, the magic inside me gone, my breaths blasting from my lungs, happiness and pride and relief welling up.

I just pulled down a building with magic, and I wasn't even touching a wielder. The triumph is expanding inside me, forcing out a laugh, and I look around, wanting to share it with Oskar, Sig, and Raimo.

But all three of them are convulsing now, just like Ansa, and the other wielders are writhing, their fingers flexing. I feel the puffs and coughs of their magic in the air as I watch the wounds appearing on their bodies.

"We gave the copper back to the earth," I murmur just before confusion chokes me.

In the second before the earth tears itself open once more, I understand a terrible truth—I haven't healed the land at all.

I have enraged it.

CHAPTER TWENTY-FIVE

Ansa

My muscles try and fail to wring the magic from my bones, and by the time they give out, I am once again helpless and on my back. This time, the sun shines down on me, a warm kiss from the sky. The roaring in my ears fades, and as it does I hear other sounds—sobbing. Groaning.

I open my eyes to find a changed, upside-down world. Where once a pale green dome blocked the light, there is now open sky. Where once a set of marble steps led up to a monster of a temple, there is now only fractured earth.

I turn my head and see Elli on her stomach, coughing and crying. She looks at me with red eyes and begins to crawl toward me. "You're alive," she says hoarsely. "Thank the stars."

"What—" The last thing I remember was turning the

arrow to ash. I gaze toward the gateway where Bertel stood, waving that pale cloth of parley . . . the one that apparently signaled an archer hidden in one of the nearby buildings to let fly. I was so happy to see his face after being surrounded by trilling strangers, and now I know he was sent to be the herald of my death.

Now all that remains is rubble. The buildings on either side of the road have collapsed, leaving a two-story-high wall of debris between this plaza and the square beyond. I have no idea what happened to the Krigere. All I know is that they have completely forsaken me.

I am truly a queen without a people.

Elli has been talking, but I haven't been listening. She's looking at me as if she expects me to react. "What?" I say again. "What happened?"

She offers a curious, worried expression. "The temple is gone." She looks beyond me, to the fractured earth and the crashing waves of the Torden.

"How can it be gone?"

"The earth opened up and swallowed it," she squeaks. "Now all that's left is that." She points.

The crevasse that split this white plaza of marble has widened, and heat gushes up from it. Molten orange earth flows toward the waves that lick the torn shore, sending up billowing clouds of steam. Beneath me, the earth rumbles again, and I feel its vibration deep inside my body, where the magic hides. "It's not over, though," I say, gasping as the ground moves against me.

"Can you rise?" she asks.

I don't bother answering her. She's already yanking me up. I scoot my feet underneath myself and cling to her for balance. I feel weak, and I am shocked at the steadiness in her soft body. She smells warm and salty and I have the strange urge to cling to her for safety. It reminds me of Thyra, and my chest wells with grief.

My arms fall away from her and I brace my hands on my thighs as I look around. The small group of magic wielders who kidnapped me from the Krigere camp lie scattered amid overturned marble slabs and exposed earth. "Did you kill Kauko?" I ask. "Are the priests dead?"

She turns toward the massive mound of rubble that cuts us off from the rest of the city. I can hardly hear what's going on beyond it—the hissing of steam and the pounding waves of the Torden make it impossible. "They are surprisingly adept at surviving," she says, frowning. "What will the warriors do?"

"I don't know. If any of them survived, they might pull back outside the city walls. We are more accustomed to open fields and the cover of forests, not buildings and roads."

"That is fortunate, if so," she replies.

"Either way, you cannot hope to hold them back." Wielders are stirring, some getting up, most looking a lot better than I feel. Except for two—Oskar and Sig. They lie side by side at the edge of the crevasse, neither moving.

Elli is on her way over to them. She falls to her knees between them and bows her head. Her sobs are quiet, but her sorrow echoes inside me. I make my way over there as well, but on considerably less steady legs. "Are they dead?"

She shakes her head. "Not quite."

I grimace when I see their wretched faces and hear their rattling breaths.

"I don't understand," Elli says, looking over her shoulder at me. "We were supposed to stand together and fight whatever threatens Kupari."

Oskar whispers something to her.

"We didn't defeat them, though. All we did was that!" Elli points to the wall of rubble. "And I have no idea what lies on the other side, but I have no hope that it is our former enemies, now prepared to surrender peacefully." Her shoulders shake. "I have no hope left at all."

As if mocking her, the ground shivers, and I retch as it moves inside me, too. Sig, his eyes swollen and streaming tears, moans.

"I don't understand what we did wrong, Ansa," Elli is saying, stroking Oskar's messy hair away from his ravaged face. He tries to give her a smile, but he seems too tired to make it work. He keeps speaking to her, soft and comforting, but she is inconsolable.

The grizzled old man named Raimo crawls on hands and knees toward the three of them. He murmurs something that causes Elli's head to jerk up. She snaps at him in Kupari, but I don't understand her because she is not talking to me. I can translate the rage in her words, though. She doesn't like what he has to say. Not at all.

Oskar reaches up with a trembling hand and strokes her hair, his voice shredded with weakness and hurt. Elli takes his hand and presses it to her cheek. She is arguing with him, with the old man, and maybe even with Sig, who is muttering something from between his horribly cracked lips. Her voice reaches a fever pitch, and I feel her desperation in the knot in my stomach. When her blue eyes meet mine, I feel as if I might be sick.

"What are they saying?" I ask.

Tears stream down Elli's face. "Raimo says the earth is not satisfied with our copper. He says it wants something else." Her face twists. "Something much more precious."

CHAPTER TWENTY-SIX

Elli

Something is very wrong inside my head. I hear Raimo's voice, and Oskar's, and Sig's, and Ansa's, but I can't wrap my mind around what they are saying. "No," I say, and realize I've been chanting it.

Oskar is shushing me, and even that quiet sound appears to be draining his energy. I clamp my lips shut to save him more effort.

"Elli, you have no choice in this," says Raimo. "I'm sure now that this is the only way."

"You can't be sure," I say, my voice hitching.

"I'm sure," says Oskar. "This is our battle to fight. This is what was always meant to be. Nothing else can save Kupari now."

"Sig," I plead, wanting to clasp his hand, his arm, but

finding no part of him unblistered. "Sig, you don't want to do this. You want to fight. You want war!"

"Seems that war has come to me," he mutters between wheezing breaths. "I have nothing left, Elli."

"You are made of fire," I shout. "Has that abandoned you?"

He groans. "How I wish it had."

I sit back like he's kicked me. As long as I've known him, Sig has been only his magic and nothing else. "What will you be without it?" I want him to be defiant. Angry. Himself, in other words.

"Elli," he says gently. "I'd be at peace."

I collapse over Oskar, my fingers digging into his sides. "Oskar, you can't. Please."

I glance around the courtyard and find Maarika and Freya, holding each other tightly. "You can stop this," I call to them.

Maarika's jaw is set as she looks back and forth from her son to me. Freya's face is buried in her mother's chest. Maarika holds her daughter's head there firmly as she shakes her head, tears pouring down her face. "Enough," she mouths.

Oskar slowly places his one good hand on my back, holding me to him. "If I don't do this, we'll all die, Elli—including my mother, Freya, and everyone I love. I couldn't live with that."

"This is *wrong*."

Raimo, who is weak and unsteady, but not blistered or frostbitten like my Suurin, pats my leg as I lie on Oskar's chest. "Right and wrong are human concepts, Elli. To the stars and the earth, those things are meaningless. There is only what was, what is, and what is meant to be."

"But *you*, a *man*, are interpreting what is meant to be."

His watery eyes focus on my face. "The first Suurin gave their lives to forge the cuff of Astia. The power of that artifact is indisputable."

"Yes, but—"

His fingers tighten over my calf. "And it was in their sacrifice that Kauko himself rose. *He* has driven the draining of the earth. He was the one who secretly hoarded the copper in the catacombs, all in the hope of harnessing the power. But he never really understood the give and take of magic and blood and earth. And now, to stop the damage he has done from destroying us all, we must ask another pair of Suurin for the same sacrifice."

"This is barbaric," I say.

"Our magic is in our blood," Oskar says. "Magic fed by copper. Copper that was then stolen from the earth. You might have given it back, but our blood is the only thing that can complete this transaction and heal the wound."

"Elli," a voice says quietly. I turn to see Ansa, looking pale except for the blisters and patches of frostbite dotting her forehead and cheeks. She looks like she's aged a decade in the last hour.

"Look at her, Elli," Raimo says. "She's dying. If the earth moves again, it will likely kill her."

Ansa doesn't look scared, though. Her blue eyes are filled with sadness as she looks from Oskar to me. "It can have my blood," she says.

My mouth drops open. "What?"

She tries to push herself up, but isn't strong enough. "I have ice and fire. The earth can have me."

She almost looks eager.

"What's she saying?" asks Raimo.

Sig sighs. "Ansa is offering herself in our place."

I stare at my Valtia, the most unlikely queen I could ever have imagined. She is small and fierce and her hair is cropped short and her fingernails are nubs crusted with grime. She's uncouth and violent. She tried to kill Oskar just this morning. The only reason she was helping us was to get Lahja back and to get revenge on Kauko and Jaspar. "Why?"

Our eyes meet as Sig reveals his theory: "She probably thinks that if she dies, she can see Thyra again." He says something in Soturi to Ansa.

She shakes her head. "That's not why," she says to me. "I don't even know if Thyra would welcome me now." She swallows and bows her head. "I have lost my love. She is gone forever." She raises her gaze to mine. "But you do not have to lose yours."

I am caught. I don't know what I want.

Raimo clears his throat. "That's a lovely and noble offer, but it won't work anyway," he says. "If we were to let Ansa sacrifice herself, her magic would find the Saadella. It wouldn't flow into the earth."

Under the stones of the plaza, the entire peninsula rumbles. Ansa, Sig, and Oskar all cry out in pain. Oskar's breath bursts from between his lips in a spray of ice shards flecked with blood, while Sig breathes fire and then coughs up a grisly pink foam.

"They're dying anyway," Raimo says, his voice taking on a new urgency. "You can only save one of them, Elli, and that's your Valtia."

"I can't save anyone," I say. Unable to look at my ravaged Suurin another minute, I start to get to my feet. "I am not even a part of this. I won't be a witness to it."

"You must stand with them." He points a tremulous, gnarled finger at me. "And I would be shocked if you were willing to walk away from them now just to spare yourself pain. Is that who you are?"

"Elli," says Ansa. "Let me do this."

"You can't," I say. "It wouldn't work. It's not right." I glare at her, needing a target for my rage. "You're in luck."

Her expression hardens. "How fortunate I am."

I collapse to the ground. "I'm sorry." Despair is threatening to drown me, but I won't allow it. Raimo is right; I cannot walk away, not when my Suurin need me. Not when they are all that stands between us and doom.

The ground shifts and rocks clack and shudder all around the courtyard. Steam hisses from the point where molten rock slides its tongue into the depths of the Motherlake. The wielders around me moan and cry in their agony.

"Elli," says Sig. "It's time to fight this final battle with us."

It had better be final, because after this I will have nothing left. I nod, my tears drying. "Tell me what to do," I say to Raimo, my voice dead.

"Are you two sure you are prepared to do this?" Raimo asks.

Neither of them answers immediately. They are looking at each other, a silent question passing between them. Sig's jaw clenches. I watch him, expecting him to rise and offer to throw Raimo into the crevasse instead, but he doesn't. He simply tenses and starts to push himself up. "I'm going to do this on my terms."

"If he can stand, so can you," Raimo calls out to the other wielders. "Come help our Suurin to their feet!"

Veikko and Aira, Freya and Tuuli, all of the wielders slowly limp over to where Oskar lies. Carefully, they help him up while Maarika trails behind. Oskar stares at the ground as they help him walk over to the lip of the crevasse, a mound of dirt wide enough for him to rest on. I stand back, numb, as they cry over him, as they help him lie on the earth that wants to devour him. Freya hugs her brother fiercely, her body convulsing with sobs. Maarika kisses her son's cheek before Veikko practically carries her away from him.

Sig lies with his head next to Oskar's and his body pointed the opposite way, toward the Motherlake.

While the others attend to Oskar, Sig takes a deep breath. "Ansa!"

She raises her head, and he says something to her in Soturi—except I hear Kauko's name, spat with contempt. She bares her teeth and offers a tight reply, and he nods, seemingly satisfied.

I approach when the small crowd of wielders backs away

from Oskar. Sig looks up at me. "I don't envy the two of you," he says, glancing upward at Oskar. "Of all feelings, love is the most destructive and hurtful."

Oskar slides his hand up and clasps Sig's, and Sig squeezes his eyes shut, tears falling down his cheeks. He doesn't correct Sig, doesn't argue, simply lets Sig quietly grieve the connection he has always had with my ice wielder, deeper than either of them could ever explain. "I think it is right we die together," Oskar says softly.

"I'm scared," Sig whispers.

"Me too," Oskar admits. "But we'll be together. I won't leave you."

Sig sniffles loudly, but he seems to be past words now. He just clings to Oskar's hand.

Oskar turns his head. "Ansa," he says softly.

From her place on the ground, she looks up at him. She looks too weak to move closer.

"You used to protect me," he tells her. "You used to guard me with your life. You might not remember, but I've never forgotten."

I turn to Ansa and repeat what Oskar said. She stares at her cousin, her eyes a little wider. "I do remember," she says to me. "Tell him I remember."

I do as she asks, and Oskar smiles at her. "This is my chance to do the same for you. Understand?"

I translate, even though the terrible lump in my throat makes the task almost impossible.

"I'm doing this so you have a chance to live and be

among your family. Your people," he continues. "I'm doing this so you can save them. Will you save them?" His gray eyes skate over Freya, who has her face buried in Tuuli's robes while the young woman holds her tight. "Please."

Ansa clenches her jaw. She nods.

"Thank you, cousin," Oskar says. He looks at me and nods, and I know it is time.

I kneel near their heads and Raimo stands behind me. He is holding a small knife.

I can't believe this is happening. It doesn't seem real. But as I look over their destroyed bodies and think about all the pain they've endured, I know ending it will be relief for them. Release. Freedom from suffering they've carried nearly all their lives.

I gently touch Sig's shoulder. "I'm glad you came back to us. And I'm grateful you helped us get our Valtia back. You are more than fire."

"No, I'm not. And I've never wanted to be." I can just see his brown eyes through the swollen slits of his eyelids. "Good-bye, Elli."

I nod, holding his gaze until he closes his eyes once more, and then I lean over Oskar. "In my dreams, I wait for you in our cottage by the shore."

He gives me a faint smile. "In my dreams, I see you in the doorway, beckoning me inside."

I stroke his cheek, then lay my head on his chest. "I've stoked the fire. You'll be warm soon."

Raimo leans over the Suurin. "You might not have asked

for these gifts or this burden, but you have both carried all of it well."

"People say such nice things to you when you're about to die," Sig muses. "Just get it over with, old man." A moment later I hear him gasp.

I press my head to Oskar's chest and hear him tell Raimo he's ready. When I feel Oskar's body flinch, I know the end is coming. "I will always be waiting to welcome you home," I whisper.

"And I will always come back," he says, his voice already fainter. "I will always look for you. I will always . . ."

"Love you," I continue, my tears flowing as his skin grows warmer, losing the chill as his magic flows from his body. "I will find you in the stars, my love. We'll be together again."

"Elli, you must focus on directing their magic into the earth," Raimo murmurs. "Their sacrifice won't be in vain."

I lift my head, but I do not look at Sig and Oskar. I look at the earth. I hate it. I love it. I am utterly ashamed of what we have done to it. I will never forgive it for taking so much from me. I beg its forgiveness, and beg it to accept this gift, freely given.

I close my eyes and hold my palm out. Brilliant, raw fire and ice flutters against my skin. Sig and Oskar. Fire and ice. I have to let them go now. With everything I have inside me, I grow that power. I add my own strength. I braid my soul with theirs.

And then I pour all that life and vibrant magic into the earth.

CHAPTER TWENTY-SEVEN

Ansa

I reel as I watch Elli bow over Oskar and Sig. The old man stands back, blood dripping from the small, sharp knife he holds. The other wielders are crying softly and hugging each other, but Elli is alone, her hands outstretched, her palms hovering over the abyss that threatens to swallow us all. She is still and elegant, like Thyra always was before she fought. My chest aches as I watch Oskar's and Sig's chests shudder and fall silent, as I watch their eyes close and their limbs relax into irrevocable slumber.

The air goes very quiet, and even the hissing of the steam and the waves seems to respect the sacrifice. Inside me, too, something is slowing down, losing its constant tremor.

But then the earth moves. I cling to the slab of marble on which I lie and watch the other wielders rock and try to keep their balance. Elli screams once, sudden and sharp, and when I look up, she's teetering on the precipice, and Oskar and Sig and the earth on which they lay is gone. I lunge for her, wrapping my arms around her legs as she starts to go over the edge. I am jerked forward by her weight, and the heat and orange light of the fissure reaches for me before hands grab my legs and pull me backward. Elli is limp in my grasp as the other wielders pull us back from the edge and yank us out of danger.

"What's happening?" I cry. "I thought the blood was supposed to stop the tremors!"

Elli clings to me, but her eyes are closed and her face is white. She looks like a corpse.

With a wrenching crack, the slabs of the plaza crash together, and then the shaking stops. My ears buzz as I look around and realize the crevasse has closed completely, and now all that remains is a scar of dirt. The hissing of molten earth colliding with cold lake water has ended.

I put my hand on my chest, feeling the magic in me steady, if not completely under control. "I haven't felt this way since I first set foot in Kupari," I murmur.

The old man with the bloody knife trills out a few words. He looks haggard and sad.

"He says it worked." Elli's voice is muffled against my chest. I hold her, not knowing what else to do.

"They saved us," I say.

Elli looks up at me. "But they're gone," she says. She sounds like a little girl.

"Yes, they're gone." What good would it do to hide from this pain? "And we must keep our promises to them."

"I don't know if I can."

I think back to how Thyra made *me* promise, just before she left me behind. "I'm not sure I can, either. But I won't forgive myself if I don't try."

"Then you are a true queen," she says.

I look down at her. She has a grace and selflessness that has carried her along despite having no magic. She has a balance inside her that I cannot be without, whatever that means right now. "I am only a half-queen," I reply. "And without the rest, I will definitely fail. Will you let that happen?" I keep my voice light, but it's husky with grief. I miss Thyra. I miss my cousin, though I never even had a chance to know him. I miss my parents and my lost childhood and my lost tribe. I have only my promises to live for.

"I will stay long enough to finish this battle," she says. Her voice is without sorrow. Without hope. "After that I won't make any more promises. They are a cage in which I cannot abide."

I stare at the sky, bright and sunny and merciless with cheer. "Fair enough," I tell her. "Fair enough."

None of the other wielders speak as they begin to clean up the plaza. They use their magic, and Elli helps, magnifying it in ways that allow them to move rocks and clear away dirt. It seems pointless to me, but to them this appears to be a very important task. With great care, they lay unbroken slabs of white stone along the scar in the earth that marks the place where Oskar and Sig offered themselves and were devoured.

Finally, Elli approaches me. "I need your help," she says. Her face is smudged with dirt but otherwise flawless, smooth and bare of emotion. She gestures at the great wall of rubble that cuts us off from the city. "We have to get through there, and with your help we can do it quickly."

I allow her to take my hand and let her do the work. She wields my magic as her own, and with the old man's help, clears a passage between giant rock mounds, revealing the path to the city's square. Without pausing to rest, she lets me go and strides through it. I follow several steps behind, both wary and weary.

It is clear of Krigere and rebel priests, clear of almost everyone, actually, until Elli comes walking into the center. She turns in place. "The earth has been satisfied of its hunger," she says, only the slight waver in her voice hinting at the pain inside her. She looks at me, perhaps knowing that if she directs her words my way, I will be able to understand. "The ground will not move again. Pass this message along to your neighbors and fellow citizens. It is time to look to our safety and defenses."

There is a muttering coming from makeshift lean-tos and unstable-looking doorways, and a few people emerge into the square. One young man, leading a tiny boy by the hand, asks her a question.

Elli gives him a gentle, sad smile, and then her gaze

meets mine. "With magic. The land was healed with magic."

More and more people are creeping out from their hiding places. They look smudged and scared, hunched backs and timid steps, closer to mice than wolves. I stand with the old man and watch them gather around Elli, the impostor who acts more like a queen than I ever could. She offers hugs, speaks earnestly when asked questions, and smiles.

It is the bleakest smile I have ever beheld. But it remains fixed in place as she lets these people approach her, one after another. One woman emerges from a stout stone building that withstood the shaking. She has loaves of brown bread on a large, flat board, and she brings them over with the help of an elderly man. Together they set the board at Elli's feet, and Elli begins to break the bread and hand it out to her people, feeding them what they've already made themselves.

I am worried for these people. Jaspar and his warriors are somewhere near—they couldn't have withdrawn very far from the city, and if Kauko survived the collapse of that building by the white plaza, he will probably never relinquish the idea that the temple could still be his.

Someone should perhaps tell him that it's not there anymore, and that the copper is gone. It won't stop Jaspar from looting whatever meager supplies these people have, but it might keep him from squatting in the city like he did in Vasterut. The Vasterutians might have been temporarily defeated, but they somehow kept their spirits intact. They worked quietly for months to overthrow Nisse, all while pretending to be docile. But these Kupari? Would it occur to them that they had the power to fight at all?

Elli knows this. She's said as much herself. But right now she isn't pushing them to take care of themselves—she's giving them the illusion that she's going to make things all right. I don't know whether to be disgusted or admiring, but either way it's hard to watch. I let myself fade into the background while the trilling of their language washes over me. I can catch a familiar word every once in a while, but I'm too tired to try to understand it or these people. They are foreign to me, and I want to go back to a home that doesn't even exist anymore, in a time that has past, with a woman who has gone to the eternal battlefield without me.

I stare at the Torden, remembering the night we rode a broken hull across the water, under the stars, shoulder to shoulder. I walk toward the shore, heedless of the crowds gathering on this early summer afternoon. My stomach growls, and I realize I should have gotten some bread from Elli. When I turn back toward the square, though, I see it is impossible. She's surrounded by the throng, and I can barely see her. Most people around her are on foot, but a few are on horseback, wading through the crowd to reach the food. I watch two riders slowly advancing, their cloaks fluttering in a cool breeze.

One of the riders' hoods falls away from his face. My heart is jolted in my chest.

It's Jaspar.

Elli's back is to him as he reaches her, as people around

him realize they have a Soturi in their midst. There's only him and a man I recognize as one of Kauko's priests, and there are close to a thousand Kupari in this square. But when they see Jaspar in his leather armor, when his cloak opens to reveal the dagger in his hand, they stampede—not to protect their queen, but to protect themselves.

I am knocked hard into a pile of rubble as I leap forward, shouting a warning that is drowned out by terrified screams. Jaspar leans down as Elli whirls around. I can't see her face, but her body jerks as Jaspar grabs her and wrenches her up onto his saddle. I open my palm and fire bursts to life in my grip, fueled by my rage, singeing the hairs on my arms and burning my skin. I don't care, though. Jaspar is taking Elli. He's already wheeled his horse around and slammed his heels into its flanks. I hurl the fire desperately, but it is met with ice in the air as his priest guard defends his back.

Two of the other temple wielders are throwing elbows as they try to get clear of the panicked citizens—the lean, dark-haired ice wielder, Viekko, and the young woman, Aira. They reach the edge of the road and hold hands, then shove their palms forward. I don't see ice or fire, but the priest, who was awkward on his mount to begin with, falters in the saddle as he's hit by a fierce gust of wind. He falls from his horse.

Aira and Veikko sprint forward toward the priest, and as Veikko hurls ice, Aira grabs a stray hunk of wood and slams it into the back of the priest's head. He falls boneless to the dirt.

Jaspar doesn't stop. He has no care for the priest—he bends over Elli and spurs his horse on, heading for the exit to the city. Frustration sears my lungs as I try and fail to push toward Jaspar and Elli while everyone else flees. The old man has climbed onto a low wall at the edge of the square, and a rope of fire jumps from his hand and coils in the air. It arcs impossibly high, crackling and dripping sparks, and I want to cheer. It could kill Jaspar—but it won't hurt Elli. But the serpent of flame gutters and falls short as a few people shove the old man while climbing over the wall on which he was perched. He falls into the crowd, and I skirt the edge of the square to try to get to him before he's trampled. He's alive but dazed when I reach him. I climb the wall, desperate to reach Elli and stop Jaspar. I know I have the magic inside me to reduce him to ash, but they're so far away that my aim could never be sure, especially without the cuff of Astia or the help of Elli herself.

She *is* the power I need to save her. If I try to hurl fire or ice now, I could kill all the people between me and Jaspar. It is tempting, but somehow I know Elli herself would never want that. My screech of rage and hatred fills the air. Jaspar has the little girl. Lahja. And now he has taken Elli.

They are *mine*.

People are wailing now, realizing the danger has left their midst but taken their queen. The impostor who is real. And here I am, the true queen who is so *un*real that I am a ghost in their square, a foreign presence unable to quell their fears.

I squat down and poke the old man, then slide his little knife from his belt. I can make better use of it than he can anyway. His eyes are still closed, but his knobby fingers curl over my wrist, surprisingly strong and spry. His mouth works for a few moments before he says, "Go."

In Krigere.

I sit back on my haunches and give him a pull to help him sit. He winces and rubs the bump on his head, his scraggly beard waggling beneath his chin. He gestures for me to help him stand, and I do.

"Elli," I say.

He nods and trills something about the Soturi.

"Krigere," I tell him.

His eyes narrow. "Krigere." He says it like Kauko does, a little twisted. He looks down at his knife in my hand and then down the road where Jaspar fled with Elli. Aira, who I think might make an excellent Krigere, and Veikko are carrying the priest up the road. He is stirring weakly, this Kupari who has betrayed his people, who serves the man who drank my blood and killed my love. He also probably speaks a few words of Krigere and knows what Jaspar and Kauko plan to do with Elli.

I clutch the knife in my sweaty palm. This priest has no idea how much pain I am about to visit upon him.

CHAPTER TWENTY-EIGHT

Elli

The Soturi's hand crushes me to his saddle and his knees jab me in the ribs and hip as his horse carries us out of the city. I am reeling with horror and confusion. One minute, I was numbly handing out food to my weary, frightened people and letting their fragile smiles remind me why I still breathe despite the knowledge that Oskar is gone from this life . . . and in the next, I was in the hands of the enemy, one who came into my city and snatched me right in the square.

For a brief moment, I wonder if Ansa is complicit in this scheme. I am fully aware she is ambivalent at best about Kupari, and that her loyalty to the Krigere holds strong. I believed the only reason she wasn't attacking us was that she really does trust that Kauko is the true—or at least the greater—evil here, and the one called Jaspar is just as bad. Could she have known they would come for me?

No. No, I don't think that makes sense. I saw her make her promise to Oskar, that she would save the Kupari. I have to believe she wouldn't betray him so easily.

My captor thunders out of the city and rides past the charred north woods. After interminable, painful minutes, he steers his mount into a maze of boulders near the shore. He dismounts and ties his horse to a sapling, then brings me to the ground, his hands gentle. I look up into his face. It is handsome by any measure. He has bright green eyes and shaggy blond hair, and his body is muscle and tanned skin and nothing more. He smiles at me, and I look away.

He tries to slide his fingers under my chin to lift it again.

I slap him hard across the face.

He laughs and says something in that guttural language. It is ugly, coming from his mouth. But buried in the grunts and growls is Ansa's name, and he tilts his head when he sees me react to the sound. "Ansa," he says again. "Valtia."

I swallow hard. "Yes, she's the Valtia. And I'm nobody, so you can just let me go."

He shakes his head, clearly not understanding but still chuckling, and shoves me down against a rock. He pulls a wineskin from the back of his horse and offers it to me, but I push it away. He takes a long swig himself and then squats in front of me, looking me over. I fold my arms over my chest. His eyebrow arches.

In this moment, the absence of magic inside me hurts

as much as anything ever has. If I had any power at all, I believe I would freeze this barbarian's blood in his veins.

He touches his own chest. "Jaspar."

I blink at him. This is the leader of all the Krigere.

He's shrewd too. He sees that I recognize his name, and it seems to please him.

I decide, for the moment, that petulance won't serve me well. I touch my own chest and say, "Elli."

He says, in a singsong voice, "Valtia." As if it's a joke.

I keep my face serene. Or, perhaps, flat. I am having trouble reaching my fear. My only wish is that I do not die before I've secured the safety of my people, but after that, he may kill me. I could be with Oskar, then. I could leave this life and have a new one, with him, the one that we dreamed about. Surely the stars will allow us that, given how much we sacrificed.

Jaspar seems done playing with me for now. Having caught his breath, he rises and pulls me up, then lifts me onto his horse again. This time, apparently, I will be allowed to sit up instead of being slung across the saddle like a game carcass. He loops his arm around my waist, and I stiffen but don't struggle.

I watch the path carefully as he rides on. The terrain looks foreign in the aftermath of the quakes, but I recognize that we are riding to the eastern shore, through the dunes. The sun is descending as we round one of the hills of sand, and I catch sight of their camp. I have never seen so many weapons or this much armor. They are in the open here, right by the Motherlake, just far enough from her to avoid the lapping waves. My stomach clutches as I understand how easy it would be for them to rule my people. For a few weeks, I thought I was going to teach the Kupari to fight, but supplying a person with a weapon doesn't mean she knows how to use it. And as I watch two of these Soturi play fighting, their blades glinting as they reflect the setting sun, I see the difference. These people wield swords like Raimo wields magic—as an extension of their body.

Magic is the only thing we have to use against them. But they have magic too. Jaspar waves at sentries and rides into the camp. He holds me tightly as the barbarians stop what they're doing to stare at me. I hold my head high and am grateful for my lack of fear as he pushes deeper into the camp. I think they would be pleased if I screamed, judging by the amused smiles they give me.

In the middle of the camp, there is a makeshift tent, and beneath it sits a man I had prayed was dead. Kauko rises and claps his hands when he sees Jaspar and me. Then he plucks something from the back of the tent and pulls it into his arms before walking forward.

"Lahja," I scream, my breath bursting from me as I realize *she* is the squirming bundle in his arms. Jaspar's arm is iron around me. He dismounts and helps me off, but he does not let me go. I struggle against him, my chest filled with desperation to reach my Saadella. Now my fear has returned. If they've hurt her . . .

"You have been very careless, Elli," Kauko says amiably

as he stops several feet away with Lahja pressed to his chest. She is craning her neck, trying to look at me, but he keeps his large hand on her back and his arms wrapped around her tiny body. "Your Saadella was wandering the woods, alone, when we found her. How could you have lost her? You must not care about her very much. Not like a true Valtia would."

"Let me see her," I beg. "I need to touch her."

He chuckles. "Perhaps. I must think of what is in her best interest, though, and I'm not sure you deserve her loyalty. You're not the true queen, after all."

"You were going to kill the true queen," I snap. "After you drained and drank all her blood."

His thick lips flap with his dismissal of my accusation. "She is flawed—no balance." The corner of his mouth quirks up. "Because you have it. *Astia.*" He says it with relish and holds up his wrist, showing me the cuff. When I catch sight of the red runes, my stomach turns. The blood of the Suurin, exploited by evil.

I had thought to stand with my Suurin to face it, but now I am alone.

"Why have you brought me here?"

"You have somehow gained the loyalty of the people," Kauko says.

I want to laugh. Half of them tried to stone me a day or two ago. My own council tricked and betrayed me. They stole my Saadella and apparently let her fall into the hands of the enemy. Only today, when the land fell quiet, were they willing to embrace me again. "You wish to destroy their hope?" I ask.

Kauko shakes his head. "Of course not. I love Kupari and have served it my entire long life."

I glance at Jaspar, who has let me go but is now watching us as he drinks by the fire. "Do these Soturi know exactly how long that life has been?"

"It doesn't matter. It only means I am the one who has long since proven my devotion to the people and the land."

Again, my stomach threatens to rebel. "Land that has been healed now. From wounds *you* inflicted."

"I?" His eyes are wide, innocent. "What a lie."

"I will not argue. I will simply tell you that we have healed it. Would you like to know how?"

He gives me an indulgent smile. "Oh, please tell me."

I do. And I enjoy the way the blood drains from his face as I tell him his riches have been dumped into the earth. I don't tell him the Suurin gave their lives to complete the cure. I can't.

"You are a fool," Kauko spits.

Jaspar sits up and asks Kauko a question, and the older man seems to remember where he is. He bounces Lahja on his hip as he regains his composure and answers the young Soturi leader in his own language before turning to me again. "If these barbarians know the copper is gone, they'll kill us all," he says.

"They'll find out as soon as they ride to the temple and see it is now under the Motherlake," I tell him. "Jaspar didn't seem to pay it heed as he stole me from the square, but when they ride to claim the throne, something tells me it won't escape his notice."

"They'll kill you, too," Kauko says. "*And* her." He gives Lahja a little shake, and she whines and tries to get down.

Then she bites him, right on the cheek.

He cries out and drops her, and she lands at his feet. I kneel and open my arms, and she scrambles into them, her skinny arms wrapping around my neck. For a moment, I lose myself in the miracle of her. I smell her hair and her skin and feel her warmth against me, drawing me from my numbing grief for a few moments.

"You've turned her into a brat," Kauko snaps, rubbing at his reddened cheek. The barbarians all around us laugh and point. Jaspar seems to find it particularly funny.

It doesn't seem like these Soturi like Kauko very much. Only two do not seem amused, and one of them I recognize as the white-bearded fellow who carried the white cloth in the square—the one Ansa called Bertel, and who gave the signal that brought the arrow slicing into her shoulder. He and a pale-skinned, silver-bearded fellow stand near the rocks and watch me with solemn eyes. I wonder if they are warriors who were once loyal to Thyra. If so, though, why would they lure Ansa to her death? My thoughts spin as I try to untangle possible alliances.

Too bad only my worst enemy speaks my language.

"I'm hungry," Lahja says, reminding me that I'm not quite right about that.

I give her a smile. "Is that why you bit Kauko, you little scamp?"

She scowls at him. "No, I bit him because he's not nice, and he squeezes me too hard."

"He deserved it, then," I whisper in her ear. I offer Kauko a different kind of smile, then, one as condescending as his own. "Elder, from the look of you, the barbarians have fed you well. My Saadella says she is hungry now. Perhaps you could help her to acquire some food."

Kauko makes an ugly face. "Noam!" he barks.

I watch Noam, whom I remember as an obsequious apprentice from my years in the temple, scurry forward. He looks like a praying mantis, all folded arms and long legs. "Elder?"

"Fetch some dinner for the Saadella and the impostor."

Noam gives me a sour look. "She looks well-fed enough."

Cold air flickers against my skin as the elder shows off his power. Noam draws his shoulders up to his ears and jogs away without another word. I suppose only the elder is allowed to insult me.

"Come," says Kauko. "Sit by the fire with me. We might be enemies, but I know you well, Elli. We share a love of Kupari. We can find common ground."

Giving Jaspar an unreadable look, Kauko ushers me and Lahja to a fire near where a group of priests are helping a few of the Soturi reforge and repair some of their blades, using their magic to melt metal. The barbarians look wary but grateful for the help.

"You've made quite an alliance," I say to him.

He speaks quietly while gazing about, perhaps checking if anyone might be listening. Jaspar has laid back and covered his eyes with his arm. His lips are parted and he breathes deeply as he naps. Kauko watches him for a few seconds before responding. "I've done what I had to, Elli, after you and your rebels expelled me and mine from the temple. It had been my home for an eternity."

"Where you tortured and bled countless acolytes, including Sig."

He lets out a long breath. "But I saved Sig, after you almost destroyed him. He should be grateful, but instead he wants to destroy me."

I swallow the lump in my throat. "You could have been the father he needed. Instead you betrayed his trust and used him."

"He is not sane, that one," Kauko says.

"He understood more about the nature of humans than most people I know," I say hoarsely.

Kauko stares at the side of my face. "Understood."

I swipe a tear from my cheek. "You will never drink from him again, Elder."

"And the other—the ice wielder—"

"They are beyond your reach."

Kauko curses. "The Suurin bore magic as powerful as the Valtias! They could have been useful in helping us reclaim our land"—he glances at Jaspar and seems relieved when the young man lets out a snore—"from this scourge."

"Is that what you're trying to do? I thought you were using them to put yourself back in power."

He shakes his head. "I never meant to fall in with them!

They captured me and Sig as we fled after *you* nearly killed us both. And if you want to lay blame for the sorry state of our city and our people, look no further than your own reflection, my dear."

"I am no more to blame than Ansa is." I hope she is faring well. Without Sig, without me, she has no one to understand her. She'll be frightened and angry, based on what I know of her. She might lash out.

"Ansa is Krigere, through and through, Elli. And she is not sane. She needs to be put down. If she is, the magic will be safe inside Lahja."

I tuck Lahja against me. "Lahja is too young to bear that burden."

"We have had young Valtias before. They just need . . . care."

"I wonder if that care comes at the point of a knife."

Kauko flaps his lips again. "Do not scare the child unnecessarily."

Lahja is pinned to my side, and I know she's listening, so I don't say what I am thinking: I fear that if I am still alive when Ansa dies, Lahja wouldn't receive the balance that I hold inside myself. She would need both to be whole. Regardless of Kauko's "care," such massive, unbalanced magic might tear her tiny body apart.

I also do not say this aloud because Kauko does not need yet another enticement to end my life.

He lifts a stone with a wave of his finger and uses his magic to toss it into the fire, throwing up orange sparks. "Remember our lessons together?"

"I used to think you were the wisest man who had ever lived. Also, the kindest." I sigh. "But that was when I was a child. A silly little girl."

"You're still a little girl, Elli. You've been brave and headstrong, but to me, you are still a child." His voice is kind now, absent the cold rage of before. "I can see how much all these burdens have weighed on you. I can only imagine how frightened you've been."

I stroke Lahja's hair with my scarred hand and stare into the fire.

"I'm sorry for blaming this on you," he continues. "I know that I bear responsibility for what's happened. I and the rebel who stole the knowledge I needed to understand what was going on."

"Raimo knew you were evil, even hundreds of years ago."

"Ah, if you insist. But who served the temple for all those years, and who hid away like a bandit, biding his time? Who is in power now within our city?"

"Stop, Kauko."

He bows his head. "I loved you, you know."

The only people who ever truly loved me are dead. Mim, who is a constant ache inside me. And Oskar, who is a fresh, deep wound. "You cannot cajole me to your side, even with honey-dipped words."

His large hands rest on his knees, and the edge of the cuff is visible at the end of his sleeve. "I don't have to, Elli. You're already on my side. You want to save Kupari from the barbarian horde, and so do I."

I look out over the camp. The sun has gone now, and I can see fires illuminating faces that laugh and smile and talk as they dine on dried meat and broth that makes my stomach complain with hunger. These are Ansa's people, decimated by Sofia's storm, the monsters who chased us from the north and have raided our shores for decades. But Ansa told me they were good. Is she telling the truth? Should I be working to drive these Soturi from Kupari, or should I be helping Ansa welcome them, and try to forge some kind of peace? Is such a thing possible?

I look toward Jaspar again, but he has vanished.

"Why did he risk his own safety to kidnap me?" I ask.

Kauko laughs. "He didn't see it as much of a risk, which should tell you what he thinks of our people."

"But why would he go to the effort? What did you tell him?"

Kauko shrugs. "Perhaps I'll tell you tomorrow," he says as Noam arrives with a small parcel of food for us. "Tonight you should rest. You've been through so much."

I unwrap the food and give Lahja most of it, and then I keep her close while she eats. Kauko is the most calculating soul I've ever met. He's got some plan that I figure into. He doesn't care whom he uses or hurts, as long as he ends up with power in the end.

I rub my eyes. I would love to rest. I would love to sink into black sleep and never, ever wake up. But I am not my only concern. I have miles to walk before I reach the end of my journey, and people to look after, not least of which is the little girl who is nodding off with her head on my shoulder. I sit with my back against a log, feeling the wind off the Motherlake, and settle in to figure out a plan.

CHAPTER TWENTY-NINE

Ansa

"Ow! Stop," I shout, kicking the short-haired young woman away from me. She yelps and staggers back, the bloody cloth in her hand waving. With quick, impatient fingers, I grope for the arrowhead that's still embedded in my shoulder. In the hours since Bertel tried to lure me to my death, I had almost forgotten about it. First I was in too much pain to notice, and then I was too relieved by the absence of chaos inside me to notice.

Now I notice. Now I cannot not notice.

My shoulder has swollen to a hard red knot, the edges of my skin puffed up around the wound. The fingers of my left hand twitch with phantom sensation. It feels like that iron arrowhead was dipped in hellfire before it was sent my way. I have to get it out of me or I'm going to go crazy.

These trilling Kupari are trying to help. With the assistance of the townsfolk, the wielders, whose temple is under the Torden, are working on me under some makeshift tent, with plenty of townsfolk watching. Through hand gestures and one particularly grisly drawing, the old man, whose name is Raimo, conveyed that I need to keep my magic in check, lest I frighten the fragile citizens.

Ugh. I hate every single one of them, and every single living person on this earth right now.

Raimo comes over with his hands outstretched. He has also shown me, via a drawing once more—this one of me with big eyes and a big mouth and tiny stick limbs—that they have to remove the arrowhead before he can heal me with magic. At least he made himself look comical in the drawing too, with a beard to his feet and a huge hooked nose. He's trilling at me now, motioning at my shoulder as he holds a pair of blacksmith's pliers.

Oh, excellent.

The blond woman, Kaisa, offers me a wineskin, and I take several generous swigs. I've never been wounded in battle, but I've seen other warriors return with gashes that had to be stitched and arrows that had to be removed from rumps and other meaty parts. Usually nonfatal injuries if one can close them and apply medicinal herbs quickly enough. And in every case, the warriors drank heartily before this part. I take another swig for good measure.

Raimo grins. And then he grasps my shoulder, plunges the pliers into my wound, and yanks the arrowhead from my shoulder with a wrenching twist.

That is the last thing I'm aware of for a while, but I awaken soaked to the bone and dripping. The blond woman is standing behind Raimo, looking frightened and holding a bucket. She babbles to the old man, who waves her away while he cackles. I glare at him, but he doesn't seem intimidated. Either he's addled or I shouldn't underestimate him, or both.

I miss Elli. I am not sure why, so I decide it's because she could understand what I was saying. "Now what," I snap at the old man as he hobbles forward.

He waves those knobby fingers at my shoulder. I think he's going to heal me now. I stare at my wound as he holds out his palms. At first it just feels like a tickle, but then there's a deep throb that I feel in the bone. It goes on and on, pulsing with my heartbeat, and with every one of those beats my skin loses its redness and the wound knits itself back together. Raimo's eyes are half closed as he wields this magic, but I can tell by the tension in his body that he's completely alert. Finally, he lowers his hands and gives the scar, all that remains of the injury, a poke.

He cackles again and then jabs his finger at me.

"I have no idea what you're trying to tell me."

He grabs my wrists and holds my palms down, then waves them over my legs. Maybe he's trying to tell me that I can learn to heal too, just like Elli said. I laugh. "No balance, no healing," I tell him.

He tilts his head. "No," he says in Krigere.

"Right," I say.

"No," he says.

"Ugh." I rise from my chair and sway for a moment as the wine sloshes about inside me. "Now I want to see that priest." I draw the knife at my belt.

Raimo eyes it and then nods. He shuffles out of the tent and down an alleyway. I follow him through a debris-strewn passage to some stables, realizing he must have understood at least some of what I said. Inside the first stall is the priest, shackled to the back. He looks soft and terrified, maybe because Veikko and Aira stand just outside the door, looking ready to attack with magic or shovels, whichever is necessary.

I like these two. I give them a grim smile and they look startled but nod in return. Veikko swings the door of the stable stall open for me and Raimo. When the priest sees me, he lets out a little squeal, like a startled pig. "You understand some Krigere, I think," I say to him. "Speak it to me, and I won't cut you." I twirl the knife on my fingers. "Yet."

"Please," he screeches. "I was forced to help." His accent is worse than Kauko's.

"What is your name?"

He tries to smile, but his mouth is wide and his lips are trembling. "Patu," he says, flecks of spittle glistening on his chin. "Please don't hurt."

"You helped Jaspar kidnap the queen of this city."

His brow furrows. "Not queen. Impostor."

"If she is an impostor, why did Jaspar and your master think she was worth kidnapping?"

He squints at me like he's trying to translate my words in his head. Standing next to me, Raimo wears the same expression.

Finally, Patu shakes his head and gives me an apologetic smile. "I don't understand."

I step forward and jab him in the arm with the knife, burying it in his soft flesh. He screams and jerks, and I come away with his blood on my hands. Raimo looks a little shocked but says nothing while the priest yowls.

When his cries subside, I do it again, this time to his other arm.

I stand back. "I am Krigere, Patu. I am not Kupari, not right now. Krigere do not show mercy. Do you understand?"

"Please," he cries. "I don't know."

I stab him again, this time in the thigh. "Stop lying." Then I point to Raimo. "This wielder can heal. Did you know that? So I'll tell you what. I'm going to cut you open and let you bleed for a while, and then I'm going to have him heal you. Then we're going to do that again. And again. Until you tell me why they took her—and where they are."

Raimo frowns, as if he actually understands what I'm saying. Or maybe it's the obvious—my bloody knife. But I'm too angry and gone to care about any of that now. Kauko will not take anyone else from me.

When I step toward the priest again, he leaps to the side, trying to stay out of my reach. "I tell you," he shrieks.

I move back again. On the other side of the door, Veikko and Aira watch, looking nauseated but stalwart. I give Patu a gesture of invitation, swirling the blade of my knife.

"The Krigere chieftain and Elder Kauko want ensure no resistance when we take city."

I laugh. "*What* resistance?"

He blinks at me. "The impostor has loyalty of people."

I chew on my bottom lip. I think she might have mine as well. "And?"

"If she tells people to accept new master, they will listen."

"She will no," says Raimo.

I stare at him.

He grins, showing off crooked yellow teeth. "I quick learn," he says. His accent is better than all the others', even if his words aren't. "Elli . . . loyal."

I believe him. "What will they do to her?"

The priest bows his head. I poke him with the tip of the knife, and he jerks. Raimo speaks to him in Kupari, sounding fatherly. I scowl at him, but he doesn't seem sorry. "I say Kauko bad," he says.

"Putting it mildly," I mutter.

Patu looks back and forth between the two of us and then starts to babble to Raimo. He casts darting glances at me, Veikko, and Aira as he does. Raimo speaks to him firmly, all while looking troubled. Then he gestures at Patu to tell me something.

And, oh, Patu does.

"I am not supposed to tell you," he says, but nods as I hold up my knife once more. "Kauko will kill Elli. At dawn."

I stalk out of the stable, rage stoking the fire inside me, my fingers flexing over a knife that's way too small to inflict the damage I crave. It was so incredibly tempting to kill that priest, to watch his eyes go blank and then carve a kill mark on my arm. It would have been the first kill in ages that I would have claimed. Instead, I told him I'd be back to kill him later, because he deserves to feel like Elli might feel right now. He deserves that terror.

And now I have to find a way to go get her and Lahja back from a dozen magic priests and a thousand Krigere, without freezing myself solid or turning myself to ash. I have infinite magic, they say, but I can't use it when I need it! The frustration takes over for a moment, and I look up at the sky and shout my fury at the heavens.

When I level my gaze again, I am looking into the eyes of a very startled man. He is holding a pitchfork in one hand and has a shovel strapped to his back, and behind him are several more men, all broad in the shoulder and thick through the body. I drop into my fighting stance, but the man starts to babble and shake his head.

"Livius," Raimo says, appearing at my shoulder. Livius begins to babble to him, all while I'm standing here, wondering what in heaven is happening.

Raimo puts his hand on my shoulder but lets go when I flinch away. "They want help."

"I can't help them. I'm going to get Elli and Lahja."

"No." He points at the group of men, who are all crowded into this narrow alley. "*They* help."

I look at him and then at Livius, who puffs out his chest and waves the pitchfork. "They wouldn't last more than a few seconds against even our weakest warrior," I say.

"Elli is they queen," he says, his brows drawn together. He looks conflicted. "We go with you."

Veikko and Aira come jogging out of the stable and say something to Raimo. He gives me a small smile. "Them also." Aira barks out something else and runs by, edging past Livius and his gang of would-be warriors. "She get wielders."

"I can't be responsible for these people," I say. "I need to focus on getting Elli back."

Raimo's watery eyes glint in the torchlight. "Elli knows how"—he pulls his hands toward his body—"help."

She knows how to accept help. Isn't that nice. "You're all going to die. I might even be the one who kills you, seeing as I can't even control my own magic!"

Raimo's lips curls. "Not about *you*," he says, jabbing his finger at Livius and the others. "About them."

I sigh. "If they want to take the risk, fine. But remind them that it's their choice."

Raimo cackles and shakes his head. "With no Elli, no Kupari. With no Elli"—he pokes me in my newly healed shoulder—"no Valtia." He waves his hand around him. "No city. No nothing." His eyes narrow. "Not about *you*."

He motions for me to head down the alley. I obey, and the men part to allow me through. When I emerge into the square, they follow, and so do others who have gathered around. Not a huge number, possibly fifty. Most carrying tools—hammers, scythes, a long wooden cylinder for flattening dough, of all things. A few have swords that look shiny and untested, and some have bows that they carry awkwardly. It will probably take them at least a minute to nock a single arrow.

I don't know what Raimo has told them, but they all seem to be looking to me for orders or something. Even though none of them can understand anything I say. One of them, a black-bearded man, comes forward and holds out a short sword to me, hilt first.

I accept it, and look out across the square, taking in their frightened eyes and set jaws.

They're terrified but still willing to go after their queen.

My eyes sting. This is what warriors are made of in their core. We have fear, but we layer other things on top of it. Ferocity. Loyalty. Blood and victory. I was taught that by Einar and Jes, my Krigere fathers. I saw Thyra do it again and again. And perhaps, if I can remind her tribe of this, even now that she's gone, they will help me fulfill her vision.

I will probably die today, and so will they. So will these people. This will not be a walk to victory, though I will try with everything inside me to turn the tide in my direction. But perhaps I can salvage something else from it, something that will allow me to find Thyra on the eternal battlefield and see her arms open and waiting.

Maybe I can save her people—and mine.

CHAPTER THIRTY

Elli

Lahja nods off in the crook of my arm, and for a long time, I sit and stare at the fire. I would do anything for this little girl. I don't know if it's instinct or ancient bond or simple, unquestionable love. And I don't think it matters. If I must die for her, I will. Ansa would too. I know this with the same certainty that translates the strange language of my own heart.

But I would prefer it's just me. Ansa is the true queen, and I am tired. If I know Lahja is safe, I can go.

Kauko understands the bond between Valtia and Saadella well, and he intends to use it against all of us. He'll use Ansa's magic and my power to chase the Krigere from our land. My first thought was that would be a good thing. But I must wonder—if they were sent away, would we lose our Valtia, too? She is not fully ours, not at all. She never will be. She loves her tribe, as she calls them, and I can read her loyalty to Thyra in the fierce flash of her blue eyes. If I were to help Kauko, it would destroy any hope of harnessing the magic Ansa was chosen to carry—and my people need it to rebuild the city.

It means I must trust her, but it is not easy. If the Krigere stay, will they treat us as conquered, or can we live in peace? Our city is home to over ten thousand, meaning we outnumber the barbarians, but we aren't fighters like they are. Can we work together as one people? We don't even speak the same language! I squeeze my eyes shut, overwhelmed as I consider all the misunderstandings and problems that would come to us if we had to welcome these people into our land, even the outlands.

I don't have a choice, though. If Kauko were to kill Ansa and use her magic to chase away the Krigere, he would control Lahja as well. The Valtia would go back to being a puppet. The people would go back to being sheep. And the wielders would go back to being hunted and used. All to serve one greedy man who has kept himself alive by draining life from others.

I glance toward the canopy beneath which Kauko sleeps, guarded by his priests, who cling to him because they have never known any other true power. I remember how I believed in the elders once, how I danced right up to the edge of my own execution because of that trust.

Then, I would have died for nothing. Or at best for the wrong reasons. Now is different.

Two priests guard me tonight. They sit on the other side of the fire, trying not to nod off. Yves is older, a priest who wields both fire and ice. Now that he hasn't shaved in weeks, his hair and beard are revealed to be white as frost. Fair-haired, with golden eyelashes, Osten was an apprentice before the battle at the temple, but I suppose he and Noam have been promoted, seeing as they're two of only a dozen surviving traitors.

The Krigere are mostly sleeping now, leaving the priests to guard me. I am hardly threatening. At least, not in any way they can understand. The two who were watching me earlier are lying next to a banked fire perhaps twenty feet away. Close enough for their snores to be heard over the whisper of the Motherlake and the hiss and pop of the dying flames. Jaspar disappeared into the darkness at least an hour ago. No one else seems to heed my presence at all.

Perhaps I have a chance, but only if I can get away from Osten and Yves—with Lahja. She's the key to all of this, because as long as they have her, they have the path to victory. I have to try. I am not helpless. I have abilities these priests don't truly understand. And after what I experienced with Oskar and Sig in the white plaza, I have reason to suspect my power is growing.

I was still inches away from them, but I was able to grab their magic all the same. Was that just their willingness to offer it, or was that something I could do to any wielder, if I were strong enough? I turn my palm to the sky, the back of the hand resting on my knee, my fingers stretching toward Osten, who is less experienced than Yves. He's ten feet away, his head bowed beneath his hood. Staring at his chest, I focus on the fire magic inside him.

I don't feel anything.

I grit my teeth and try again. Raimo told me—I'm an Astia with a will, and surely that is worth something. I'm not a hunk of metal, meant to conduct, amplify, absorb. . . . I'm a living, breathing force, and right now, I need the magic that lies in the wielder across from me.

My fingertips tingle with heat as the flames between us grow and dance, giving off thick smoke that billows gray into the night sky. I frown. Was that Osten's magic or the wind?

The fire subsides, and my fingertips are still tingling, hard, hot prickles that ride along my skin. There is magic here—this is not my imagination. But I don't know if I can actually pull it from him. I try, gathering those tingling prickles close, concentrating on drawing them along my fingers, onto my palm, up my arm. A gasp escapes me as I feel it, thin and faint, like a silken thread, stretching slowly to obey me.

Until it snaps. I flinch—and so does Osten. He sits up with a jerk, rubbing at his chest and wincing. I avert my eyes as he raises his head. My heart is hammering and I'm fighting a smile. Even though we're several feet away from each other, I *did* something to him. Then my hope sinks. . . . I did something to him, but something isn't enough, and I have no time to figure it all out. I miss Raimo more than I ever thought I would.

I rub Lahja's arm, needing to wake her. When dawn breaks, darkness will no longer be our ally, and I so badly need one now. As the little girl stirs, I murmur to her, letting her know she's with me. She whimpers. "I had a bad dream."

I kiss her forehead. "I'm sorry. I wish I could tuck you into your soft bed in the temple." I bend low and murmur in her ear. "We have to try to get away, Lahja."

She stiffens, and then she nods. I hold her head to my chest for a long moment before standing up. "Osten," I say. "Lahja and I must relieve ourselves."

Osten, still awake after his magic snapped back on him, looks over at Yves as if he wishes the older man could tell him what to do. But Yves has his head back and his mouth open, and his snores are deep and slow.

I shift my weight and frown. "Can we go, please?"

In the light of the fire, Osten's cheeks are pink as roses. "I have to take you."

I arch an eyebrow. "If you must."

Rubbing his face, Osten hefts himself up to his feet and stretches. As his hands flop back to his sides, he looks around, then grabs a thick stick the length of his own arm. He dips the blackened end of it into our fire and draws it out when the flames take hold.

I tug on Lahja's hand and tread a path between two dunes while Osten walks along behind us. He looks irritable and tired, but not nervous. This is very good.

"Surely we're far enough from camp to protect your modesty," he says peevishly when I march past another dune. The camp is well out of sight and even the fires are concealed. In darkness, the shore is a wonderful place to hide, because the only way to be seen is by boats on the Motherlake.

I come to a halt with Lahja pressed to my side. "How far must we go to protect our modesty from *you*?"

He rolls his eyes. "I have no interest in looking at your bodies."

"Wouldn't a person who was interested say the same?"

He cringes and I almost laugh, but I don't want to goad him. So I stand here, staring, looking righteous and suspicious.

Lahja's little hand slips into mine while she glares at him. "I don't want you to look at my bum!"

And that does it.

"I'll wait here," he grumbles. "Don't be too long."

"It takes us longer than it takes you," I tell him. "We have to be careful with our skirts."

He sighs. "Fine. Just get it done!" He shivers. "It's chilly out here."

"Of course," I say. "Thank you for your consideration. We'll be back shortly." With Lahja's hand in mine, I march around the next dune, my feet slipping in the soft sand. It's slower going than I'd like, but our footsteps are mere whispers.

"I don't really have to go," Lahja says quietly once we're out of sight.

"I'm glad," I whisper. "Because we must run now. Can you?"

The moon is reflected in her wide eyes, the only part of her face I can see clearly. She nods. And then we begin to jog. I have no idea how long Osten will wait, but probably only a few minutes. My head swivels as I try to retrace the route

Jaspar took as he brought me here, but there are no tracks in the cursed sand. I pause, only knowing I need to head away from the shore, because eventually we'll meet the road. But right now I'm just surrounded by dunes on every side.

"Hey!" comes the shout from behind us, and then I know our direction. As far from the sound as we can make it. My heart pumps terror through my blood as I pull Lahja along, our breaths huffing. I glance over my shoulder to see Osten's dark form barreling toward us.

Lahja screams and tenses, and I loop my arm around her belly and scoop her up. But my feet sink in the sand, and we're too slow. As Osten closes the distance between us, I whirl around to see him with his hands up, preparing to hurl his magic. I shove Lahja behind me and face him as the air around me turns cold. It's so easy for wielders to forget that I'm immune to their power.

And even fewer realize I'm dangerous.

"Nice try, impostor," he says, panting, as he stops in front of me. I take a step back, looking over my shoulder to see Lahja standing ten feet away, shivering and petrified. "Did you really think you were going to escape?"

"We *are* going to escape," I tell him.

He laughs. "You're pathetic. I always thought you were a little brat, always asking questions and demanding answers as if you were already queen."

I take another step back and turn, pretending to run. Osten grabs me around the waist—and that is exactly what I want him to do. I clap my hands on his face and pull his magic with everything that's in me. From across the fire, it was a gossamer strand, but here, with my palms clamped to his narrow face, it is a gushing spring, and I am a basin ready to be filled. Osten gasps and tries to pull away, but I wrap my legs around his hips and continue to steal his magic. He doesn't have even a fraction of what Oskar and Sig had, but I can still feel the fire and ice bright and sparking inside me. He begins to punch at my middle.

"Help us," I say to him, clenching my teeth against the pain. "If you do, all is forgiven."

"Kauko is going to get what he wants," he says with a grunt, trying to pry my legs from his waist. But I've crossed my ankles and am holding fast. "He'll bleed the Soturi girl and have her power, and there will be no stopping him."

"You're wrong," I say. "But either way, I take no pleasure in this."

I release him, knowing I have but a moment. As he staggers back, I raise my arms, and from my hands flow a storm of ice. Osten disappears in a cloud of glittering frost, and when it swirls away, he still stands there, his face frozen in a look of horror, his hands clawed and stiff and still.

I whirl around, understanding Oskar's heavy mood after he was forced to freeze one of his former friends. It does not feel good to end a life. "I offered him a choice," I say to Lahja.

"I heard you," she says in a small voice full of doubt. Tears are shining in her eyes.

I drop to my knees in front of her and take her hands in

mine. "I'm going to tell you something that my Valtia once told me, something I will never forget. Are you ready to listen?"

She nods.

As I speak, I can hear Sofia's voice in my ear, a sweet echo of memory. "Sometimes you are chosen, and sometimes you must choose. I just took a life, but I don't regret that choice. I know it was ultimately to protect our people." I take her face in my hands. "You will one day face these choices, Lahja. When that time comes, you'll do what you need to do. Never doubt."

"Never doubt," she whispers.

"Never doubt. We must get back to our Ansa. She needs me to use her power to protect the Kupari and set things right. She can't do it without our help."

"My help too?"

I nod. "You are most important of all."

"I don't know her."

"But you do, in your heart. And she knows you. It's because of that bond that she'll stay with us and help us. It's because of you that she knows who she is, and she needs that. She is hurting inside."

Lahja blinks at me, her huge blue eyes almost luminous in the darkness. "I'll help her, then."

I smile as tears well in my eyes. "You are very brave, Lahja, and I am very proud of you."

Hand in hand, we hike away from Osten's frozen body as the night wind blows our hair. We don't speak, and I am sure Lahja's little head is full of fear and sorrow, but the ancient magic marked her as its future home for a reason. Her steps are light and sure, and she doesn't complain. We make it to the road, and I hate that we're out in the open, but I know it's the only sure way back to the city. I can only hope the people haven't turned on the wielders of the temple, and that they'll be pleased at my return. There's so much confusion about who I am and about Ansa, and they're so frightened, and those two things are like dry tinder near an anvil. One stray spark will grow to a ravenous blaze in an instant.

By the time the sun begins to glow at the horizon, preparing the sky for its ascension, we are well on our way, and my heart soars. I escaped a Soturi camp guarded by traitor priests! I used a rogue's magic against him. I still can't pull it from an unwilling wielder from a distance, but I swear I'm getting stronger. I—

The distant thunder of hooves sets my heart scampering, and I wheel around to see dust in the distance behind us. "Oh, stars," I murmur, pulling Lahja into a sprint. "You see those woods up there?" I say to her, leaving the road to cross the few hundred yards between us and the northern wood that still smells of smoke.

"I don't want to go in there," she says in a high, panicked voice. "Mama died in there."

I want to curse at the top of my lungs. "You must, unless you want to be at the mercy of those barbarians and priests."

The riders have come into view. There are three of them, bodies pressed low to their mounts, and for a sparkling moment, it looks like they might ride past as if they are racing toward the city and not trying to run us down. But then the one in front turns his mount toward the woods. The horse leaps over a ditch and charges toward us.

"Run," I scream, pushing Lahja ahead of me. "Run and hide!"

"But, Elli—"

"Go!" I give her one last boost over a low hill, and then I run as fast as I can away from her.

I'm the bigger target. And sure enough, the lead rider changes his path to intercept me, ignoring Lahja for the moment. I glance over as I flee and am grimly happy to see my Saadella disappear into the darkness of the woods. Happy because she has a chance.

Grim because I don't.

The man leaps from his horse. It's Jaspar, the leader of the Soturi, and his green eyes gleam with the thrill of the hunt as his powerful legs destroy the distance. He hits my back and takes me to the ground, pressing himself on top of me as I struggle, all jabbing elbows and kicking legs. He grabs my wrists and slams my palms to the ground, and his breath puffs against the side of my face. "No run," he says. His weight lifts from me for a moment as he calls to his fellows, and to my horror, I watch them ride into the woods after Lahja.

It's too much, and a sob bursts from my mouth. Jaspar pulls me up, holding my wrists behind my back. "Kupari," he says in that horrible singsong way of his. He spits on the grass.

I fight him with every step as he drags me back to his horse. He pulls a length of rope from a saddle back and binds my wrists, then does the same with my ankles. I stare at the woods, waiting for the riders to emerge with Lahja, ready to put on a brave face for her, but minutes pass without sight or sound of the others.

Muttering to himself in his ugly language, Jaspar lifts me over the saddle, the edge of it digging into my ribs as my arms hang down. I squirm, and he slaps my bottom, hard. Rage and hatred rise inside me, and suddenly I wish I could hold on to magic longer than a few seconds, because if I had any of Osten's left, I'd set this barbarian on fire.

I am struck by the bloodthirstiness of my own thoughts.

"Kauko want you," Jaspar says, his accent guttural and awful.

"Kauko is a snake," I snap. "And when he's got what he wants, he'll kill you and all your people."

Jaspar laughs, and it is in that moment that I realize he understands more than he's been letting on. "I kill Kauko," he says, and then grins. "But not yet."

A smart barbarian, then. The worst kind. "Don't underestimate him."

He just keeps smiling, but the joy drains from his face as his two riders emerge from the forest empty-handed. He shouts at them, and they shrug and babble, sounding like animals, while I lie like a grain sack over the back of Jaspar's horse, my hope growing by the second.

Lahja did it. She's evaded the barbarians.

But then Jaspar jabs his finger at the woods, and the two turn their mounts around and head back in. He swings himself into the saddle behind me and takes the reins. The horse carries us back over the meadow to the road, and Jaspar leans over me and spurs the animal to a gallop. The motion jars me, knocks the breath out of me. I fight despair, and the only weapon I have is Lahja, and the slim chance she could stay free. But she's still a five-year-old alone in the woods that killed her mother, woods that are home to bears and wolves and all manner of animal that would be delighted to come upon a helpless child. I pray to the stars that I didn't send my beautiful, brave girl to her death alone in the dark.

Despair has the upper hand.

The ride back to the camp is depressingly short. We pass the place where I froze Osten with his own magic, but he's no longer there. When we arrive at the shore, the barbarians cheer.

Jaspar dismounts and pulls me off the horse, then holds me up when my legs nearly give out. He doesn't untie me, merely turns me toward Kauko while the priest approaches with a nasty look on his fleshy face. "So willful and naughty, Elli," he says, his voice gentle and amiable as ever. "You turned Osten's ice against him. He was a good apprentice. It was a waste."

He sounds so calm, and only the slight tremble in his hands warns me of his rage. When those hands produce a knife from the folds of his cloak, my stomach drops. "I have no magic," I say, hating the crack in my voice.

He grins. "But you have something else, my dear. And I think it's time to taste it."

CHAPTER THIRTY-ONE

Ansa

By the time we reach the gates of the city, we have drawn a crowd. People gather along the streets between piles of rubble, straddling cracks in the earth, some offering stale bread and eggs and dried meat, some joining our group, hefting pitchforks and improvised shields made of broken planks hastily nailed together, tongs and iron meat skewers and axes.

We have perhaps two hundred as we cross the threshold into the place they call the outlands. Most of my patchwork militia are men, but there are a few women—the stout, red-cheeked one with the large rolling pin, and the stringy older woman who carries a knife with a large rectangular blade. They have kept their determination as we march through the city, and I know the food and faith of their fellow citizens put iron in their spines.

None of them are ready for what they're going to face.

When all of us have passed through the gates, I put a hand on Raimo's shoulder. "I have to warn them," I say to Raimo. "This could be a slaughter."

Raimo watches my mouth move, and his eyes narrow as he translates. "You say," he finally replies, "and I tell."

I nod, and then turn to face these Kupari. My eyes settle on a man with dark hair and a thick beard. Something about him looks so familiar, and as I gather my words, I realize he reminds me of my father in the few hazy memories I still possess. My throat goes tight. If the Krigere had not stolen me, I would have grown up here. I would know them and speak their language. But even though I don't, there is something in them that is mine to protect.

"I know you are here to rescue your Valtia and her Saadella," I tell them, pausing to let Raimo translate. "But facing the Krigere on an open field will mean death for you. We must find another way."

The one called Livius raises his shovel and says something to Raimo, and the dark-haired man who reminds me of my dead father chimes in. Raimo looks toward the woods. A smoky fog hangs over them in the early morning light. He nods before turning to me. "He say we go in woods. We know these woods. Soturi do not."

It may be our only chance. "Let's see what we can do to lure them in, then."

We reach the edge of the woods, and some of the Kupari jog ahead and hack at the brush with long knives, carving a path. They move so quickly that soon they are far ahead, and then they diverge, two small groups heading in opposite directions, calling back and forth to each other as they work. Livius joins us and talks with Raimo as we push deeper. My muscles are tight with grim anticipation and pent-up magic. When I wield it, I will likely be killed, and so I'm going to wait and take down as many enemies as I can as it happens.

After that, it will be up to Elli. She will be the true queen, the final one standing, and she and the others can take care of the little girl. The princess's face is etched onto my brain, so clearly that I can picture her easily. "The princess," I say to Raimo. "Lahja. Will they hurt her?"

Raimo shrugs. "Many ways to hurt."

This does not make me feel better. "We need scouts," I say abruptly. "We need to know exactly where they're camped out. All I know is it's somewhere south of these woods."

"Agree." He leaves my side to go confer with two men, one of whom is holding a metal hook and the other of whom carries a heavy net. Their skin is brown and weathered, and their cheeks wrinkle as their mouths move. After a few minutes, Raimo returns to me. "They know land and lake," he says. "They find."

The pair heads back for the road. They're fishermen, I realize, probably accustomed to steering their boats along the shore. And our people do have a habit of camping along shorelines, a good source of water and fish. I hope the fishermen know a thing or two about staying out of sight.

While the Kupari work to slice trails through the woods, presumably to join them up with existing trails, I let their trilling language wash over me. I've started to recognize a few words, but it's still a mystery. It doesn't matter, either. I won't live long enough to learn to speak it.

My boots are almost silent as I tread over rotted leaves, through the narrow gash cut through the underbrush. To my right, the west, is the burned swath of forest, which appears to be in the center of a large depression in the earth, like a shallow crater. The ground slopes down until it seems to disappear, and then I see only the tops of trees. I slowly make my way toward the blackened branches to find that a massive sinkhole has opened. This must have been caused by one of the final quakes, because I don't recall it being there as I was carried away from the Krigere toward the city.

It simply looks as if someone cut a huge circle in the crust of ground and let it fall perhaps thirty feet into the hollow of the earth. Some of the trees in the depression are still standing amid jumbles of boulders. Across from me, on the far side of this hole, I see several Kupari talking animatedly and gesturing first at the hole, then at its southern edge. One of them imitates a rider plunging over it, and I realize they are trying to set a trap.

It's an intriguing idea, Jaspar at the bottom of this hole, his bones dashed against rocks, his warriors at the mercy of the Kupari. But then I imagine Thyra's warriors falling in as well, and the satisfaction fades. I would be breaking my promise to her if I let any of them die.

I would be breaking my promise to Elli and to my own soul if I left the little princess to her fate, or Elli herself for that matter.

There can be no way for me to save all of them, to make sure only the evil die while the rest are protected. No matter what I do, I'm going to fail. And although it is tempting to end it now by simply allowing *myself* to fall into this hole in the ground, I know that would be a failure too, and one that would bar the way to the heavenly battlefield forever.

I hike along the edge of the hole, mapping its southern edge, until I hear the strangest sound—crying? Is there an animal in this wood that can make such a noise? I search for the source and end up at the base of a tree.

I look up and at first believe I am imagining things. "What are you doing up there?" I ask the princess.

She is crouched in the crook of a branch high above me, her coppery curls tangled and full of bark and pine needles, her face dirty and tearstained. I clutch my short sword and turn in place, knowing the Kupari aren't the only ones who can set a trap.

"I'm stuck," she says. "I ran away and now I'm stuck!"

"And it's really you?" But then I laugh. It must be her; I understand what she's saying as if she were speaking Krigere. "Hang on. I'm going to help you down." I can hear the eagerness and laughter in my own voice as I walk around the tree, trying to figure out how on earth this little girl got herself up that high.

I find a knot in the wood and use it as a foothold, and

after a few tries, during which my admiration for her agility only grows, I make it up to her. She immediately throws her arms around my neck, and for a moment I know what it means to be a mother, to hold something exquisite and fragile to your chest and to know you might not be enough to keep it alive, to know if it dies, then you will die too, even if your heart still beats.

I suppose that means part of my heart is still alive after all, if I can feel these things.

The princess is crying again, and I pull her away from me and look her over. "Are you hurt?"

She shakes her head. "But they chased me. The barbarians."

"Krigere," I say, because I want her to know where I came from for some reason. "They are Krigere, and there are many good things about them. We can make them our allies if we find the right path."

She only sobs harder.

"You got away from the camp? How did you do it?"

"Elli took me. She turned a priest's magic against him and we ran."

I glance at some of the trees around us, hoping to find Elli in a similar predicament, but all I see is moss and birds' nests. "Where is she now?"

"They caught her." She sniffles. "He jumped on her and pushed her down."

"He." I grit my teeth. "Did he kill her?"

"I don't know," Lahja wails. "They took her away and I did what she told me to. I hid."

So Elli sacrificed herself to help Lahja escape, killing a man in the process. She is made of iron wrapped in the softest fleece, I think. Again, it reminds me of Thyra, and the thought of both of them makes me ache, especially as one devastating truth ricochets around in my head:

The same man who murdered my love now has Elli at his mercy.

"Can you show me where the Krigere are camped, Princess?"

Lahja looks up at me with her big blue eyes. I can see the fear in them, but also the courage. "Will you help Elli?"

"I'll die for her if I need to." I'm going to die anyway. I can think of no better reason.

"I don't want you to die, though," she says to me, her skinny little fingers fisting in my tunic. "I want you to save Elli, and for you to come live with us. We can be a family."

Ah, the foolish wishes of a child. "Let's get the first part done and then see where we stand, all right?" I try to make my voice light, but Lahja is frowning now.

"You do love us, though, don't you?" she asks.

"Yes." It comes easily, this truth. But I can't stand the way she's looking at me. It's as if my chest is water, and she can look right through it and see my heart. I take her by the wrists. "I'm lowering you down to that foothold right there, all right?" I point to the one I mean.

She whimpers but nods, and she doesn't struggle as I ease her off the branch and hold her by one wrist to allow her to wrap her other arm around the trunk and shimmy down. When she's reached the ground, I come down and land next to her. "Let's go find the old man. I want him to know what's happened. Then we'll make a plan to save Elli."

We start to retrace my steps along the sinkhole, and when the Kupari see her, they start to shout and cheer. As we near the clearing where I left Raimo, Lahja slips her hand into mine. When I look down at her, she beams up at me with such confidence, such faith, that for a moment I almost believe I can triumph. So I smile back, and pray to the heavens for victory.

CHAPTER THIRTY-TWO

Elli

I am where Kauko wanted me months ago—tied to a plank, beneath his knife. I would be lying if I said I was not scared. And it hurts, so much more than the blade, to think of what Oskar might have felt when he was living his final moments, when he was saying good-bye to this world and all his hopes and dreams. I would give anything to have him by my side right now, and my only comfort as Kauko and Jaspar and other unfamiliar faces stare down at me is knowing that perhaps I'll be with my love soon.

Kauko dashes my hope quickly, though. "This is but a test," he says to his rogue priests, and to Jaspar, who has dropped the pretense that he does not understand. "In all our history, there has never been a human Astia. We must be cautious in the extreme."

I glare at him, but no one is looking in my eyes now. I am like a hunk of meat on a carving table. I am not a person to these men. I turn my head so I can't see his knife, and when the searing pain comes, I don't scream. But as I feel the warm blood slip across my wrist, as I hear the soft-loud *tap-tap-tap* of it hitting the cup pressed beneath my arm, it takes all I have not to cry. This has been the fate of Valtias in all our centuries past, thanks to Kauko and the priests who followed him. Men who ruled these infinitely powerful women with lies, cunning, and blades.

"We will see what this blood can do," says Kauko. A shadow passes over me, and I look up to see him holding a small, roughly hewn cup over my body. My blood is smeared on his fingers and the edge of the knife hanging from his fist.

He has everyone's attention, but now the two warriors who were watching me before have pressed their way into the circle of bodies around me. Bertel's lip curls at the sight of my bleeding arm, and the gray one's jaw is tense. Something about these two is different.

"Will you drink it now, Elder?" asks Yves, who sounds eager to regain favor with Kauko after letting me and Lahja escape from under his nose.

Kauko gives him an amused smile. "No, not this time, my friend."

Bertel says something to Jaspar, who shrugs. "Should we staunch the bleed?" Jaspar asks in Kupari, gesturing at my arm, which is strapped firmly over my head, to the top of the plank. "Seems valuable."

"Or a deadly poison to those of us who have fire and ice inside us," Kauko says.

All the rogue priests cringe in unison, eyeing the cup in Kauko's hand with new fear. "Poison?" Yves asks.

"Yes, friend." Kauko gives him an appraising look. "What does an Astia do?"

"It amplifies power!" says Noam, his long arms swinging at his sides. "And helps the wielder to control it. If her blood has the power of the Astia, then it could make us all more powerful!"

"Perhaps," says Kauko. "But what else does the Astia do?"

There is a moment of silence in our group, but then Yves says, very quietly, "It balances power by conducting some of it away."

"Away, where?" Kauko asks.

"Out of the wielder," says Yves. "We were taught that this is how the Valtia is able to wield such massive amounts of magic while remaining unhurt by the fire and the ice. Her magic is balanced, but in the process of wielding it, it can tip one way or the other, which can be deadly for her because she has so much of both elements."

"All correct," says Kauko. "In fact, the Valtia has so much magic that sometimes the cuff of Astia is not enough to save her."

"Only because you weaken her by draining her blood," I snap.

Kauko ignores me, as do most of the others, save for the two dour older warriors at the edge of the circle of men.

Bertel mutters something in his guttural language, then abruptly tears a strip of cloth from the bottom of his own tunic and winds it around my forearm. He isn't gentle. I hiss as the edges of my wound are mashed together. As he so often does, Kauko looks amused and says something in Krigere to the man, who doesn't meet Kauko's eyes as he rises to his feet and steps back to stand next to his gray friend.

"My blood is different from the Astia," I say as the pain lessens a bit. "It will drain every drop of magic you have, just like I drained Osten before turning his magic back on him."

The rogue priests somehow manage to look both terrified and steeped in hatred. Kauko is the only one who isn't affected by my words. "You have every reason to lie, dear Elli," he says. "It only makes me more eager to see what your blood can do."

"Then drink, by all means." It's a bluff, but right now a bluff is all I have. I truly don't know what my blood will do to him. I hope it eats his insides, but I'm guessing I won't be that fortunate.

Kauko holds up the cup. I swear, none of those priests are even breathing now. Their full attention is riveted on him. "Shall I solve this mystery?" he asks them.

There is a mumbling affirmation, eager and sweaty. Kauko's smile widens. "Then I shall. Yves!"

Yves blinks at him. "Yes? Would you like me to get you something, Elder?"

"You can bring yourself over here—and drink from this." Kauko holds out the cup, wiggling his blood-smeared fingers.

"But I—I—"

"Come, Yves. You want to be an elder someday, do you not?"

Yves glances at his fellow priests and continues to stammer.

Kauko beckons to him. "It is time to demonstrate your worthiness."

The other rogues have backed away from Yves, just a step, but a step is enough to put him inside the circle instead of on its edge. The Krigere warriors watch with interest, and Jaspar wears a smirk. Yves looks around for support, and when he finds none, his shoulders sag. Without a word, he trudges over to Kauko. His hands shake as he accepts the cup. His nose wrinkles just before his lips touch the rim. He tips it upward and brings it down just as quickly. His lips shine with my blood, and my stomach turns.

"There," says Yves. "As you wished it."

Kauko shakes his head. "Drink it all."

"But—"

"All."

Yves lets out a little whimper. He closes his eyes tightly. The sound of his swallows are loud in the silence of the early afternoon. A few times, his body heaves, as if it is trying to reject this gift of Kauko's, but he manages to keep it all down.

Finally, Yves lowers his trembling hand. He wipes his sleeve across his mouth. "It is done," he says bleakly.

"And how do you feel?" Kauko asks.

Yves opens his eyes. "I feel . . . fine?"

"Show us your fire and ice."

Yves holds out his palms, frowning. For a moment, my heart soars, because nothing happens, and all my wishes that my blood will steal their magic seem to be coming true.

Then a ball of fire erupts on Yves's left palm, and a jagged ring of ice bursts into existence on his right. Yves laughs, his relief thick in the air. "It didn't steal my power!" he crows.

The priests sag, stiff shoulders going soft. Kauko is grinning. "Do you feel more powerful than you were?"

Yves stares at the fire and ice in his hands and frowns. "No," he says after a long moment.

Kauko sighs. "That is too bad."

He holds out his hands and blasts Yves with ice, sending frigid vapors swirling around the circle. The other priests and all the warriors shout and stagger away from the catastrophe, their eyes wide with surprise and horror as they take in the white cloud and glittering splinters of ice that dance in the air. Only Jaspar doesn't retreat—the Krigere prince merely squints into the storm, hard curiosity on his face. And perhaps a bit of jealousy.

Kauko's fingers are clawed and his thick sluglike lips are pulled into a sneer as he quells his ice, but as soon as the glinting mist starts to dissipate, he brings his other hand up and hurls fire. A few of the priests scream as the flames engulf Yves. Cinders and ash spiral into the air and I smell burning wood and cloth.

Kauko calls back the fire and lowers his arm. He and Jaspar and I stare at the smoky cloud around a man who had been one of the elder's strongest remaining priests.

As the haze dissipates, a form becomes visible. Pale and unsteady, Yves blinks at his own naked body. My heart is crushed.

Kauko beams as he turns to Jaspar. "You see what has happened here?"

"The fire and ice. They did not touch him."

"Oh, but they did, Jaspar. They took his robe!"

Yves looks shocked as he tries to cover his privates with his shaking hands. All the other priests seem too stunned to offer him a blanket to cover his fleshy bare body.

Kauko looks as if he's been lit from the inside. "This changes everything. No one will be able to stand before me."

"Before us," says Jaspar, his voice newly suspicious.

Kauko offers him what even I can see is a condescending smile. "Yes, us, of course."

Jaspar moves forward with alarming quickness and snatches the seared cup that was hanging from Yves's fingers. "You give us some of this," he says, shaking the cup at Kauko. He draws a dagger and moves toward me. "So we can fight Kupari."

I press my back against the board, bracing for more pain. Kauko lurches between the Krigere prince and the plank where I lie. "Do not be hasty! We have been given a precious gift here, and we must decide how best to use it!"

It. Meaning me. My blood. My life.

All I can see is Kauko's backside as he stands over me, his hands spread to his sides, his palms radiating power.

"Then let us decide," Jaspar says, his tone as sharp as the blade he planned to use to open my veins.

"My priests and I will be on the front lines of this fight," Kauko explains. "We will be facing a group of vicious criminals who wield a good deal of magic."

"And if my warriors are immune to this magic, they can cut them down in an instant."

"Ah, but do we know how long this immunity lasts?" Kauko tosses fire at Yves, who lets out a shriek. Kauko chuckles. "Not that long, it seems. This blood would be wasted on you and your warriors."

"Making us easy targets for you," says Jaspar.

"We could have attacked you at any point," Kauko replies. "And we have not."

"We could have done the same." The swish of sand tells me Jaspar is on the move, and a moment later he comes into view. He looks me over with the same concern one might offer a barrel of mead. "How much do you think we can get from her?"

"A good portion could go to perhaps fifteen men."

"Really? That's it?" Jaspar gives me a disappointed look.

Kauko turns and looks down at me as well. "That's not all, but we need her alive for a time."

"Why?"

"Because she is the reason the Kupari people will surrender. They want their queen back—and we have her. If we eliminate their fighting force and then offer them this gift, her pathetic and useless life, they will kneel before us, and lives will be saved." He nudges my shoulder with his malodorous toe. "Well, not hers, of course."

Jaspar looks thoughtful. "A quiet people is good. Very good."

Kauko nods. "Yes, far better than what you had in Vasterut."

Jaspar smiles. "Very good." He turns his head and shouts to his warriors, and the camp is immediately in motion, clanking weapons and flapping leather. "We attack now."

My heart is jolted in my chest. "Now?" The city isn't ready. No one is ready. And I'm a tool of their destruction.

Kauko gives me a friendly smile as he draws his knife once more. "I'll drink to that."

CHAPTER THIRTY-THREE

Ansa

I am eating some sort of fish stew by a fire when our scouts come racing into camp, their lips moving as fast as their feet. Lahja presses herself to my side as they shout at Raimo and Livius and Aira and Veikko, who all gather around with frowns and tense shoulders. I can't make out any words, save one: Soturi.

Lahja looks up at me. "They're coming," she says in a choked whisper. "On the march. Everyone's arguing about how to lure them into the woods instead of letting them take the city."

I close my eyes. It's almost time. I kiss the little girl on the forehead. "I have to talk to Raimo. You stay here." I rise, and Raimo turns to me as I approach. "I need someone to take Lahja and keep her safe."

He looks past me to where our princess huddles by the fire. "We can, but . . ." He gestures for the two weathered scouts and trills to them in Kupari before meeting my eyes again. "If Krigere kill all fighters . . ."

"I know. Nothing can keep her safe." Because if I am dead, and if Elli is dead, then Lahja will be the Valtia, and Kauko and Jaspar will try to use her. And, if I am to understand this magic correctly, the moment I die, or maybe when both Elli and I are gone, a new Saadella will be created. A new, vulnerable girl with a mark of red flame somewhere on her body, who can be found and kept just as Elli was. If I don't stop Kauko and Jaspar and all the warriors, things will be exactly as they were. No one will be free. "Tell them to try. I don't care how far they have to take her." A sudden thought occurs to me. "Oskar's mother. She was strong. And she'll need comfort now. If they can, they should place Lahja in her care."

Raimo nods sadly. "I'll tell them."

I return to the fire and put my arms around Lahja. "You have to go with those men now. They'll keep you safe."

Her little face crumples just before she buries it in my chest. "I want to stay with you!"

Tears are on me so suddenly, and I don't understand them. This is good, what I'm doing. It's right, and it will lead me back to Thyra. I shouldn't want to stay. "I have something I need to do, and I'll be better able to do it if I know you're safe and well."

"When will I see you again?"

There is nothing to do but lie. "Soon." I start to let her

go, but then pull her close once more. "Listen to me, Lahja. If this magic comes to you, you must use it. You understand? You use it and you don't hold back." I take her by the shoulders and I look down at her. "You will *destroy* anyone who tries to hurt or control you. You will be your own master, and you don't let anyone make you a slave. You will remember that *you* are the queen. If you do that, I will be with you always."

She is crying. Maybe from fear, maybe because she senses this is a forever good-bye.

"Everyone leaves me," she says. "Mama, and Elli, and you."

"You are strong enough to bear it, Lahja. You will never break." These are the plaintive wishes of my heart, made into sound and sent toward the heavens. If only I did not understand this world half so well.

It can break anyone.

I squeeze my girl one more time and then let her go. The leather-faced scouts speak to her in gentle tones, and one puts a floppy hat over her coppery curls, concealing them. The other wraps her in his cloak and picks her up. I turn away as they carry her from camp.

"They're marching on the city now before they have a chance to prepare," I say, because I hear the shuffling gait of the old man behind me. At least, if we lure them into the woods, the city dwellers will have a bit more time, and more warning. For I do not aim to let this be a quiet battle.

"How they attack?" Raimo asks. "Will expect the trap?" He points to the southern edge of the deep crater, where the Kupari have attempted to obscure the rim and make it look like more of the forest floor using branches as a flimsy platform, decorated with brambles and brush.

"You might catch a few riders that way, but not many."

Raimo swishes his fingers through the air and a hard gust of wind shoves my back. "Maybe more than a few."

"You are much stronger now that the earth is still." Thanks to Sig. Thanks to Oskar. Now they sleep inside the earth, and their blood runs through its veins. Surely that will help us.

"So are you."

I look down at my hands. I am not looking forward to the blisters and frostbite that will spread like frost across my skin. Perhaps I can make things happen so fast that I won't feel much of anything. The fire and ice is building inside me, fierce and infinite. When I release it, I will be a storm that cannot be leashed. All I have to do is hold on enough to focus its wrath—and make sure Jaspar and Kauko are within its reach. "I need to be at the very front."

"The scouts will tell us of the warrior path. More coming." He glances toward the far side of the clearing, opposite the direction the older scouts took Lahja. Veikko is in conversation with two cloaked Kupari women. This camp is full now—throughout the afternoon more and more Kupari have been arriving from the city, carrying hammers and pitchforks and lengths of rope and chain, wooden bats and metal brands, nets and clawlike anchors and hooks. Anything that could possibly be wielded as weapons. They are all pale with fright, but their faces are also lined with determination. They have come two-by-two and four-by-four, trickling from the city like winter runoff, more by the hour. I pray we become a river that sweeps Jaspar and his traitors away, but I know it cannot be that easy.

I know my Krigere. I know what we are capable of. And I know that Kauko nestles evil and cunning within their protection. He has had my blood, and he is nearly as strong as I am.

And he has more control.

The only time I have ever felt in control was when Elli touched me, and they have her, too.

"Any word on Elli?" I ask Raimo.

He shakes his head. "She is who our people want to see."

Because they still believe that without their Valtia, they are helpless.

Veikko jogs over with Aira and speaks to Raimo, who translates. "They're entering the woods on main trail. Riders front, then priests, then foot soldiers."

"So they mean to cut as many of us down as they can with the riders, and then they hope Kauko and his priests will finish the job," I say. Jaspar is trying to conserve his warriors, though he will probably have put his fiercest in the vanguard, confident in their prowess.

"Still want to be at the front?" asks Raimo. "We can stop riders." He uses his stick to jab at Veikko and Aira, as well as a few of the others.

"I need to know where Jaspar and Kauko are." When I go off, I need them near. "Maybe I should just go alone, actually."

Raimo laughs. "Those days are past, Valtia."

I let out a frustrated sigh. "You don't understand. I'm not like other Valtias. I can't control this magic, and when I use it, I'm . . ."

The old man clutches my hand. Where our skin meets, I feel his power. "I will be there." He shakes me by the wrist and lets me go. "Until she is."

I'm not even sure what he means, but it seems silly to argue. All the wielders have gathered in the clearing. At the edge of the woods, Livius is shouting to a horde of Kupari, gesturing with big sweeps of his thick arms. I can't tell if he actually has a strategy or is merely trying to fan the spark of courage inside them to full flame. He says the world "Valtia" several times, and that above all seems to inspire them. They want their queen back and are willing to fight to have her.

When a third pair of scouts rushes into camp to tell us that the Krigere have crossed a creek that divides south from north in these woods, we move to take our positions. The Kupari, led by Livius, gather in front of the southern edge of the crater. It takes some negotiating, but I agree to stay on its western rim with the other wielders, out of sight until the signal is given.

We have several long, tense minutes of silence before the hoofbeats shake the ground beneath our feet. Livius signals to be ready, a wave of a scrap of fabric in the increasingly dim woods. The path is wide, and the first Krigere riders come into view only a moment later. There are perhaps two dozen, and I spot Jaspar by his golden hair as he moves through a beam of sunlight. They ride without fear or hesitation, straight at the Kupari who block their path. Jaspar has the smile of battle on his face, the anticipation that he will feed his sword a feast of blood.

Magic pushes against my breastbone as I watch, and I have to look down at my chest to make sure it's not bowing outward, swelling to accommodate the rush of power and need that grows inside me. This magic seems to know it has a purpose. It knows its time is coming.

Or maybe it's simply ready to find another home.

Livius stands at the front of his line of Kupari, clutching a heavy sledgehammer in his bull arms. The sun catches a glint of sweat on his brow, the only sign of his fear. Jaspar doesn't call his warriors to a halt when he sees the man. There will be no discussion or negotiation or boasting or threats, as that is not what we do. Livius shouts something to his people as the riders break through the trees, leaping over low brush and crowding onto the clear path. One of the Kupari women screams, or perhaps it's one of the men.

Jaspar laughs. "Cut them down," he shouts to his warriors. "These will be their bravest. The others will despair when we crush them!"

"We can't win," I say to Raimo, my insides starting to churn as the future unfolds before me. "We can't—"

As Jaspar and a dozen of his best riders draw their swords and bear down, the Kupari turn tail and run. Livius darts surprisingly quickly—straight toward the edge of the crater. As four warriors on the gallop spy the precipice too late, Livius runs right out onto the flimsy platform, and two follow. The air fills with the cracking of wood and the screaming of horses, and then I see Livius swinging out over the crater—he had a rope tied around his waist the whole time! Other Kupari use hooks to yank him back to safety as the crater devours its victims. The other Krigere scatter, shouting to each other as they try to figure out what just happened, some of them chasing shrieking Kupari around the rim of the crater.

"Ansa!" Jaspar roars, and the laughter has left his voice. He reins in his horse at the end of the path and searches the forest, squinting at rocks and trees, thinking to find me there.

Veikko steps out from behind a boulder just as Raimo tries to pull him back. "Soturi," he snarls, then flings his hand out as cold billows across the clearing. Jaspar rides forward, right into the assault. As Veikko stumbles back, his arms up, ice still pouring from his palms, Jaspar raises his sword. Raimo lunges from his hiding place, sending fire roaring through the space between them.

But when the smoke clears, Veikko is on the ground, bloody and writhing, and Jaspar is still in the saddle. Untouched. And smiling. He advances on the old man as more Krigere fill the clearing. I am dimly aware of the dark robes of priests marching through the brush, and another wave of soldiers behind them, carrying a pale column, perhaps a flag? It doesn't matter, because Aira has joined the battle, using her fire to try to ward off the remaining riders, and Jaspar stands before Raimo, immune to the old man's magic.

"Ready to die?" Jaspar asks, grinning.

"Was ages ago," says Raimo, and then he hurls a jagged ball of ice at Jaspar. It shatters before it touches him. Jaspar raises his sword again. Raimo stumbles over his feet and falls to the ground next to Veikko, a plume of fire rising from his hands as he does. The trees in this forest are alight now, ash raining down. Jaspar steers his mount toward Raimo, no doubt hoping to trample the old man.

It is too soon to use my magic. Kauko has not yet cleared the trees.

But I will not watch this happen. Rising from my hiding place, I draw a dagger from the sheath at my wrist. "Are *you* ready to die?" I shout as I fling the blade.

Jaspar howls as the dagger buries itself in his thigh, and he drops his sword. Warriors and wielders engage the battle around us while the priests march forward. I step out from behind the bush where I had crouched, drawing another blade. Clutching at the reins, Jaspar slides from his horse and with a wrenching tug, he pulls my dagger from his flesh and clumsily tosses it away. Blood seeps through his breeches. His lips are pulled back into a sneer. "Thought you'd come at me with magic."

"That is not all I am."

"Strike at me," he shouts.

I don't. Partly because I know I can't waste my one chance to take out Kauko, but also because I know what I just saw. "The magic didn't affect you."

"Elli," Raimo says, trying to claw his way toward Veikko. Blood has pooled around the young man, too much outside his body and not enough in. Out of the corner of my eye, I see Aira dive between two trees to avoid the slash of a sword, but she's in trouble—the branches over her head are burning. "Elli!"

Jaspar's horse screams as falling cinders sting its rump. He grabs for its reins while swiping his sword from the forest floor. I shouldn't take my eyes off it, but I am distracted by the pillar of white that is hovering just behind the priests.

It has coppery hair. It is the reason Jaspar is immune to Raimo's magic.

"Elli," I call out.

"She can't hear you." The voice snaps me back to the battle, but too late. Kauko is at the edge of the clearing, and his priests are fanning out. Surrounding us.

"Raimo!" I shout.

He answers by shooting a series of icy knives straight for the priests. And it affects them the same way it did Jaspar, which is to say not at all.

I shouldn't have forgotten about Jaspar. As Kauko advances, the traitor prince barrels into me, taking me to the ground. We roll in the dirt. The fire bursts from my palms and lights his tunic on fire. He grabs a fistful of my short hair and slams my head into the ground as he heaves himself on top of me. "I've always wanted to be in this position with you," he says while I struggle, while the fire burns me and leaves his skin smooth and tan.

But then it starts to redden. I watch the first blister form on his chest, shiny with liquid and crimson with rage. He curses. For a moment, my heart beats hard with fury and the certainty of triumph.

Until he plunges his dagger into my side. The pain steals my concentration and my strength. To the tune of Kauko's laughter, screams of agony, the crackle of tinder, the terror of horses, my vision blooms with white and silver and Thyra. I want to reach for her, but I can't quite manage it. Jaspar slides the blade out of my body and gets to his feet, then wipes the edge on his already bloodstained breeches. "I pictured a different ending, though," he says, but there is no regret in his tone.

Blood is searing acid in my mouth as he rejoins the battle. The Kupari are fighting with all they have, and Jaspar's traitors are cutting them down, but with effort. Raimo and Kauko are engulfing the entire clearing with deadly fire and ice. Kauko is immune to the magic, but Raimo is skilled at counteracting nearly anything the elder hurls. Aira and the other Kupari wielders are fighting the priests.

We are losing, and I can't summon the strength to fight. I am dying.

I think I was the only one who believed you weren't beaten, Thyra whispers in my memory.

It was her voice that brought me up from the ground in that fight with Sander. Her voice I heard through the roars and cheers. *Get up*, she says. *Keep fighting*. I can hear her now. *Blood and victory*. She says my name over and over again. She gives me my orders.

I pray I have the power to see them through.

CHAPTER THIRTY-FOUR

Elli

The gray warrior's shoulders flex as he and Bertel carry me through the woods. I am trussed tightly to a post, and they have me upright, my feet at the level of their shoulders, the tips of branches pulling at my hair and scraping at the ropes that keep me in place. Everything is hazy. My wounds are bound, but I think it would barely matter. I don't have much left to bleed.

My heart taps out a sick and frantic beat, and my skin is clammy. I can't stop shivering. Around me I hear shouts and the pounding of boots. I can make out the distant screams and whinnies of horses. I feel the tremors of muscles and inhale the smell of sweat and burning wood. The canopy above me is starting to glow, leaves gilded with flame.

I think I'm still alive, but I also know I am dying.

Everything is buzzing, a hum and tingle that makes it hard to focus on the important things I know must be happening around me. Minutes ago, just after our scouts spotted a group of Kupari with swords blundering into these woods, we stopped. I was cut again. Kauko handed out small cups of my blood to Jaspar and a few of his best warriors who would ride at the front, and then to all the priests who will fight the temple wielders. Kauko saved the largest portion for himself, of course. A full cup, precious drops dancing over the brim. Kauko lapped up every one, though, and then gulped down the rest, leaving his teeth and lips red as the flame mark on my leg.

Now all that is left of me is this shell, to be used as a signal and symbol. To be used to bring my people to their knees.

Bertel frowns up at me. He and his gray friend volunteered to carry me, though I'm not sure why. The two have their weapons sheathed but are tense and ready. The warriors around us seem unhappy, full of misgiving. I wonder if these are the ones who were loyal to Thyra. How I wish I could speak to them in a language they could understand. How I wish I could hold my head up, but I don't have the strength.

With a shout, the two warriors in charge of carrying me through the wood come to a halt and lower me to the ground. The gray one takes a strip of cloth and ties it around my forehead, securing my head to the thick birch pole they're using to carry me. Then Bertel moves close, a knife in his hand. His brown eyes are fathomless. I am too weak to struggle as the blade moves toward my side. His gaze is riveted on mine as I feel first one arm and then the other slip free of the rough ropes used to bind my body. I am not unbound—I am still secured to the post. But my arms can move. "Help," Bertel says, fluttering his hands in a very good imitation of Kauko. "Magic?"

If only.

I respond by sighing wearily. I'm tired of disappointing people.

The warriors are hunched over me, waving the others around us. A few of the frowning ones seem to see what Bertel and his friend are doing, but they do not sound an alarm. Perhaps because I'm still tied up and helpless. If I weren't, I'd simply collapse in the dirt and never rise again.

Bertel loops a rope loosely around my arms before helping the gray one to lift me upright again. When my people see me like this, a sacrifice, an offering, the idea is that they will surrender. At this point it might be the best I can hope for.

I have no path to victory, and I am ready to go. I can almost hear Oskar calling to me from the stars, wishing me a good journey, promising me he is waiting in a cottage by the lake. His voice is the only thing that I can hear now. His murmurs coalesce into one word:

Ansa.

Up ahead is a clearing. Fire rains down on it and snow swirls in the air. Kauko is laughing. He has just reached the edge of it, and he is immune to the searing heat, immune to the bitter cold. It will not last much longer, but it might be long enough for him to destroy any opposing force.

In the center of this catastrophe, Raimo staggers to his feet to face the elder. And there is Jaspar, standing over a body.

It is Ansa. I can tell by her coppery hair, her small size. She's not moving. Her right side is soaked with blood. "Ansa," I say, my voice only a whimper. "Ansa."

Bertel looks up at me, his gaze keen. "Ansa," he shouts.

"Ansa," shouts the gray one. They shout something else, and all the warriors around us join in. I have no idea what they're saying, but Ansa moves. She coughs and rolls to her side. The warriors and priests in the clearing pay her little mind—they are busy fighting our Kupari wielders. Raimo and Kauko are locked in grim and destructive battle. Trees have begun to fall, slamming to the ground on horse's backs, taking the riders down with them.

Raimo doesn't have immunity from magic like Kauko does, but he is quick and clever, deft with his magic. He nearly brings down an oak on Kauko, but the elder uses a gust of icy wind to blow it onto a few nearby warriors. He has no care for his allies, only for his own life. His face is bright with triumph as he raises a ring of fire around Raimo.

I hear the old man cry out with pain.

Ansa is on her knees now. At any moment, Kauko will see her. She holds her palms out. She is staring at him as if her gaze is an arrow. Fire and ice snake from her fingers. Her face twists with pain.

"Ansa!" This time my voice is a little louder, and the

warriors around me begin to shout it in earnest. Ansa. Ansa. Ansa.

Ansa.

She turns her head. Our eyes lock. With all my remaining strength, I reach for her.

And then I reach for her magic.

CHAPTER THIRTY-FIVE

Ansa

Elli is at the edge of the clearing. Bertel and Preben are holding her up. Thyra's warriors surround her. They are all chanting my name.

My magic is eating through my chest wall, pushing through my skin. Dying as I am, I can't hold it much longer. It leaks in gold and silver threads from my fingers just as blood pours from my wound. My entire being is made of agony, knives slicing along every inch of my skin, cutting my organs free from their moorings. I know these are my final seconds. I do the only thing that is left to do, that seems worth doing.

I reach for Elli.

A gasp bursts from my mouth as I feel something take hold of me, pulling my hand into the air and streaking down my arm. It is cool relief where there is fire, and warmth where I had turned to ice. It holds me where I am, lifts me from the ground. I can't take my eyes off Elli, and she is looking right back at me, luminously pale, her right arm swathed in a bloody bandage, her eyes sunken but ferocious.

The connection between us is invisible, but the most real thing I have ever felt. Somehow, even though she is at least twenty yards away, she is me and I am her.

We are the Valtia.

To my left, I hear Jaspar's war cry. He sees that I am on my feet again. He is coming for me. I do not take my eyes from Elli's though. I do not move to defend myself. Instead, I think of what Jaspar deserves.

His scream is quick and sure and certain. With my next breath, I smell his flesh cooking.

I can control this magic with my mind, as long as—

I feel the magic leave me even though I didn't command it. Ice rushes across the clearing and then melts just over Raimo, dousing the old man in water. The ring of fire around him dies, leaving him with soot-blackened skin, heaving for breath. But alive.

Elli did that. She used my power and wielded it as her own.

"Ansa," she says. I hear her voice so clearly, as if it is my own. "Let's finish it."

Kauko is between us. "You can't hurt me," he calls out, a note of panic in his words. "I'm immune!"

He hurls fire at me. I flick it away with icy thoughts.

And then I watch Elli do the same, turning ice to steam that sheens her moon-white skin. She looks on the verge of death, but there is a steadiness in her outstretched hand that tells me she is as alive as I am.

Alive enough.

"Blood and victory, sister," I murmur. "Blood and victory."

CHAPTER THIRTY-SIX

Elli

I hear her. Blood and victory. And I know what she wants. Connected like this, I can see her thoughts as readily as I can my own. I read the longing for Thyra, for peace, for rest. I know how much she wants to go, despite also wanting to stay.

I understand what we need to do.

Using the massive well of her magic, I reach inside and draw up ice. I remember the day Oskar and I first realized what we could do, how I amplified his magic and channeled it.

With a resounding crash, ice bursts from the air and forms thick, glossy walls. They slam down around us, closing us in. The two warriors holding me up cry out with fear, but they do not let me fall. The walls crash down on the ashy remains of Jaspar, reducing him to swirling dust. They close out Raimo and Veikko and Aira and all the others.

They close in Ansa and me with Kauko. The elder raises a fire that licks at our icy walls, but it can never burn through them, for the frost knits all the wounds together. The sight makes me feel as if new blood is pumping through my veins, clean and warm like a summer flood.

Kauko wheels his arms through the air as the cold closes in. "It can't touch me. It can't touch me," he shrieks. His palms slide against our fortress of ice.

Ansa's blue gaze is as deep as the Motherlake. "You have caused so much pain," she says. "You have killed so many." Her jaw clenches. "You took Thyra from me. From our people."

"Just as you took Sofia and all the Valtias before her," I say. "You are not worthy of this magic."

"I alone am worthy of this magic," he shouts. "And I alone can wield it as it was always meant to be wielded!"

"You have had hundreds of years to wield it in the service of our people, and you have only served yourself," I say.

"Now it is time for you to give it back," Ansa says. Though there is blood oozing from her side, her voice is strong. Her focus is a blade. I feel it in my heart. "Elli."

"Yes," I say, knowing it is time.

We break gazes but not our connection, which I maintain through our upraised palms. My post starts to shake as the two warriors tremble and cower within our ice castle. They cry out, maybe for mercy, maybe for their lost chieftain. But Ansa and I are riveted on the elder now.

I feel it in her, the hunt, the chase, the cornering of prey. It is foreign and delicious.

Kauko trembles. He tries to wield against us, but he can't. We feel his intentions and his magic because they came from us. They belong to us. I tilt my head and his arms rise to the stars. He screams when he realizes I am the source of the movement.

Ansa smiles. She blinks and his arms drop. "Our blood is loyal to us," she muses.

She wants me to amplify her power inside Kauko. And I can, because my power is inside him too. So I do, first the fire, and he screeches and clutches his heart. Then the ice, which doubles him over. He falls to his knees.

"I can heal you," he says, all plea, all the gentleness I recall from my childhood, when he taught me about the chambers of the heart, the function of the blood, the way of the veins. "Please, we can reclaim Kupari together. For warriors, too, if you wish."

"His heart," Ansa says. "I can see . . ."

Because now I am thinking about it, and she is sharing my thoughts—the reality of tissue in his chest, and the diagram that we gazed upon during what turned out to be our final lesson.

"Thunder or lightning?" I ask her.

She knows what I mean because we are one right now. Do we want noise and breadth, size and tremor . . . or do we want sudden and simple and irresistible?

"Lightning," she says.

"Lightning," I reply. It seems right. We will reward his evil with no ceremony, no clang and clamor, only a complete and resounding silence.

We stare at Kauko's chest. His eyes bulge as the blood in his heart turns to ice. He makes a soft, choked noise and falls to the ground.

Then he catches fire, which burns so hot that it melts the walls of our ice palace in an instant. My warriors sway a little, and the gray one sinks to the ground while Bertel holds my post with all his might, his face tight with horror and fear. Ansa says something to him in a soothing voice as we feel the wind against our skin. The clearing is full of staring people—no one is fighting. They are all facing us, surrounding us.

Ansa's blue eyes meet mine once more. "Will you offer them safe harbor in this land?" she asks, and because we are still connected, I know she means her warriors.

"We will," I tell her. "Will they treat us as equals?"

"We will."

"Then we will be one people," I say.

I end our connection before she sees the rest of my thoughts. I am too tired to go on. I have lost too much. My body is too broken. She will be the one true queen of this new people. I am meant for the stars.

CHAPTER THIRTY-SEVEN

Ansa

She thought she could hide her plan from me, but she is wrong. I see her arm fall to her side. I read the weariness in her eyes. But she can't die. She can't. She needs to stay and lead these people, because *I* can't. I'm too tired. I miss Thyra so much that my bones are soft with it, and I have lost too much blood. Jaspar has killed me. I wish I could thank him.

I sink back to the forest floor where he left me. I stare up at the sky with its burned-leaf edges. And then I close my eyes and embrace darkness, hoping at any moment Thyra will step out of it and lead me to my new forever-home.

CHAPTER THIRTY-EIGHT

Elli

When I wake, I'm clothed in white, and I am on a straw bed that whispers as I shift my weight. I seem to be inside a tent, and I can hear others bustling about outside. Ansa is lying next to me, in a clean tunic and breeches. Her eyes are open.

Neither of us appears to be dead.

I start as Raimo leans over me, the scraggly ends of his beard swishing against my chest. "You can heal each other," he says, looking back and forth between us. "But you must decide. Either both of you stay, or both of you go. It will take the two of you to bring each other back to life."

I close my eyes. In my dream, I was with Oskar again, in our cottage by the lake. His boots were in front of the fire, and our bed was warm.

"How much do you miss him?" Ansa asks.

I turn my head and look at her, and in her eyes I see the question. "As much as you miss Thyra, I expect."

We stare at each other. My throat goes tight. "I know there is much work to do here," I say. "But if you want to—"

She inhales and then winces with pain. Her skin is like frost in the square, a mix of gray and white. "Do you want to?"

Yes. And no. And—"Lahja."

Ansa sighs. "I know."

If we die, she will be the Valtia, long before she is ready.

I can't tell what Ansa really wants. I don't know if I'm strong enough to stay. I reach over and take Ansa's hand. Her fingers thread with mine. Our connection is forged instantly and easily, a path well-worn. Now we are more than shared magic. We are a shared being.

I feel her longing for Thyra, and I am aware of her pain as she feels my craving for Oskar. If we stay, this pain will always be with us.

If we stay, we can bear it together.

Ansa squeezes my hand. I squeeze back. "Are you sure?" I ask.

"Is it all right if I'm not?" she replies.

I chuckle, weak and pained. But then I grow serious. "There is much work to be done. A city to be rebuilt."

"A people to shelter."

I nod. "And feed."

"And keep warm when the cold comes."

"A Saadella to raise."

"That would be the fun part," she says.

I hold her hand tightly, knowing that if I let go, the darkness will come again. "You can't leave me."

"I know," she whispers. "I won't. But you can't leave me, either."

"All right."

The healing is like breathing. It comes over us that naturally. I feel every part of her body as if it were my own, and I know what it needs. The fire and ice are like eager children, desperate to please, happy to cause a smile. The magic does our bidding without demanding our conscious thoughts. We lie there and share memories while we grow stronger with each minute. We share our hopes, too. For lives without fear or servitude. For peace and plenty.

The Suurin made sure that our land was restored. They gave their lives in exchange for the health of the earth, the future of our people.

The understanding hits me hard—if I had left, it would have been a betrayal of Oskar and everything he sacrificed. He is gone, but I can live for him and take care of what he left behind.

"I know," Ansa says again. "We will."

She understands the same thing about Thyra. Her responsibility to the warriors her chieftain left behind extends beyond their mere survival in this battle.

"We'll make sure of it," I say.

Together, we rise from the table. I let go of her hand and I am myself once more, strong as I ever was. Ansa stands straight, her shoulders square. Raimo grins from our bedside. "Well done."

I frown. "Why didn't you just heal us?"

"Oh, I could have."

"But you risked us choosing to die!"

"No need to be dramatic. I knew you'd make the right choice."

"Why, did you find another prophecy?"

He shakes his head and leans on his walking stick. A warm wind blows through the trees. "I had faith in your *will*, Elli." He nods at Ansa. "And in hers."

Ansa smiles. It is not an easy smile. It is hard won, with an edge of sadness.

We leave our tent. We are in the white plaza, the waves of the Motherlake lapping at the shore beyond. A few yards away is the scar that marks the place where Oskar and Sig saved us with their lives. Ansa's hand slips into mine again, offering me the steadiness I need.

"Elli," shrieks a familiar piping voice. From across the plaza, Lahja comes running, with Maarika and Freya jogging after her. Janeka and Helka stand behind them with the surviving temple wielders, looking worn and weary but alive, alive, alive.

Our Saadella jumps into my arms, and I turn to allow Ansa to join in our embrace. She does, and we are a knot of love and relief. Lahja puts an arm around each of our necks and kisses us each on the cheek. "You did it."

All around us, people are dropping to their knees, and

that is when I realize that Kupari are not the only ones here. Bertel, his gray friend, and a host of other warriors have been helping Livius and his stone crews stack building stones in neat rows. But now they are all kneeling before us.

"Rise, please," I call out, because it seems silly for everyone to stop what they're doing simply because we got out of bed.

Ansa chuckles as she listens to my thought, then she shouts something in Krigere. Her warriors rise with an answering call, and in her mind I understand what it is.

Blood and victory.

Will you change that now? I ask her.

No. It is who we are. I just don't know what that means yet.

Fair enough. We all have some things to figure out.

Lahja is wiggling between us, and Raimo is staring as if he knows we are having a conversation inside our own heads. "The town council requests the honor of your attendance at their next meeting," he says.

"Ansa and I will decide later," I tell him as we put Lajha down. Bertel and the gray one—

"His name is Preben," Ansa interjects.

Bertel and Preben are coming over to us. They kneel before Ansa again, and as they speak, I realize I can understand them because I am touching her.

With his head bowed, Bertel hands Ansa a dagger. "You may kill me now. I betrayed you."

"In his defense," Preben says, even though his head is bowed too, "he was told that if he didn't give the signal, twenty of Thyra's warriors would be executed. Me included."

"You redeemed yourself in the wood," Ansa says. "When you protected Elli and made it possible for her to help me."

"We will serve you for the rest of our days," says Bertel.

"Serve me by gathering a group to go fetch your anden-ers and children," says Ansa.

The two men rise, smiling, and nod respectfully at me as they walk toward a group of other warriors.

"She would have been happy to see this day," Ansa says. "She would have been so happy."

My throat is tight with Ansa's grief. "She would have. Oskar would have been too."

"Will we ever be whole without them?" she whispers.

"I don't know. But together we can live every day, striv-ing to honor their memories, and their sacrifices."

Ansa takes a deep breath as Lahja leans her head against her side. "I don't know anything about ruling."

"Good thing there's two of us," I say.

"Three," says Lahja.

Ansa laughs, and it is a welcome sound. Her gaze falls on Maarika and Freya, then on Raimo, then on her warriors, and on Livius and his stone crew, and then on me. Her smile is beyond words and beyond thought—it is something I feel in my marrow, in my soul. We will take this moment, and we will live in it, and every one that follows. We will carry each other through each breath. We understand our path will not always be smooth, but we also understand that the one that brought us here was impossible, and yet here we stand. We are two girls atop two nations; we are one new and unfathomable thing together. We are unstoppable and sovereign. We are willing to die for our people, and for each other, and for the little girl who is our future.

We are the true queen.

ACKNOWLEDGMENTS

Many thanks to the wonderful team at McElderry for helping me bring this final book of the series to readers, especially my editor Ruta Rimas and editorial assistant Natascha Morris. Thank you to book designer Debra Sfetsios-Conover and photographer Michael Frost for creating yet another visually arresting cover. And thanks to the entire team at Simon & Schuster: Justin Chanda, Clare McGlade, and everyone else who had a hand in making this book. More thanks go to my agent, Kathleen Ortiz, for providing all manner of support and advocacy.

Thanks also to my family and friends. Lydia "Gravy is My Opium" Kang, you are my dearest friend, and I am grateful for your green dot every single day. Peter, you and me in a cottage by the lake, please. Mom and Dad, Cathryn and Robin, Asher and Alma, I love you, I love you, I love you.

And finally, thank you to the readers who stayed with Elli and Ansa all the way to the end of their journey. The path wasn't a smooth one, I know, but I hope in the end the tale was worthy.